Praise for Carla Neggers and her novels

"The unforgettable characters make Neggers' story extraordinarily memorable."
—*RT Book Reviews*, Top Pick, on *Keeper's Reach*

"Neggers delivers another spellbinding, chilling, complex page-turner in this latest Sharpe & Donovan novel."
—*RT Book Reviews*, Top Pick, on *Harbor Island*

"Neggers' Sharpe & Donovan series has developed a wide following, and her books maintain a potent combination of suspense and romance."
—*Kirkus Reviews*

"Well-plotted, intriguing and set mostly in the lushly described Irish countryside, the novel is smart and satisfying, and the paths of three couples growing even more devoted to each other are deftly woven into the suspenseful story line."
—*Kirkus Reviews* on *Declan's Cross*

"*Heron's Cove* gives romantic suspense fans what they want... complex mystery with a bit of romance. Neggers skillfully created a compelling puzzle, refusing to reveal all the pieces until the very end."
—*RT Book Reviews*, Top Pick

"*Saint's Gate* is the best book yet from a writer at the absolute top of her craft."
—*Providence Journal*

"With a great plot and excellent character development, Neggers' thriller *Saint's Gate*, the first in a new series, is a fast-paced, action-packed tale of romantic suspense that will appeal to fans of Lisa Jackson and Lisa Gardner."
—*Library Journal*

CARLA NEGGERS

COLD RIDGE

MIRA

MIRA®

ISBN-13: 978-0-7783-1897-2

Cold Ridge

Recycling programs
for this product may
not exist in your area.

CONTENTS

To Fran Garfunkel

COLD RIDGE

Prologue

CAarine Winter loaded her day pack with hiking essentials and her new digital camera and headed into the woods, a rolling tract of land northeast of town that had once been dairy farms. She didn't go up the ridge. It was a bright, clear November day in the valley with little wind and highs in the fifties, but on Cold Ridge, the temperature had dipped below freezing, wind gusts were up to fifty miles an hour and its exposed, knife-edged granite backbone was already covered in snow and ice.

Her parents had hiked Cold Ridge in November and died up there when she was three. Thirty years ago that week, but Carine still remembered.

Gus, her uncle, had been a member of the search party that found his older brother and sister-in-law. He was just twenty himself, not a year home from Vietnam, but he'd taken on the responsibility of raising Carine and her older brother and sister. Antonia was just five at the time, Nate seven.

Yes, Carine thought as she climbed over a stone wall, she remembered so much of those terrible days, although she had been too young to really understand what had happened. Gus had taken her and her brother and sister up the ridge the spring after the tragedy. Cold Ridge loomed over their northern New Hampshire valley and their small hometown of the same name. Gus said they couldn't be afraid of it. His brother had been a firefighter, his sister-in-law a biology teacher, both avid hikers. They weren't reckless or inexperienced. People in the valley still talked about their deaths. Never mind that weather reports were now more accurate, hiking clothes and equipment more high-tech—if Cold Ridge could kill Harry and Jill Winter, it could kill anyone.

Carine waited until she was deep into the woods before she took out her digital camera. She wasn't yet sure she liked it. But she wouldn't be able to concentrate on any serious photography today. Her mind kept drifting back to fleeting memories, half-formed images of her parents, anything she could grasp.

Gus, who'd become one of the most respected outfitters and guides in the White Mountains, would object to her hiking alone. It was the one risk she allowed herself to take, the one safety rule she allowed herself to break.

She'd climbed all forty-eight peaks in the White Mountains over four thousand feet. Seven were over five thousand feet: Washington, Adams, Jefferson, Monroe, Madison, Lafayette and Lincoln. At 6288 feet, Mt. Washington was the highest, and the most famous, notorious for its extreme conditions, some of the worst in the world. At any time of the year, hikers could find themselves facing hurricane-force winds on its bald granite summit—Carine had herself. Because of the conditions the treeline was lower in the White Mountains than out west, generally at around 4500 feet.

It was said the Abenakis considered the tall peaks sacred and never climbed them. Carine didn't know if that was true, but she could believe it.

Most of the main Cold Ridge trail was above four thousand feet, exposing hikers to above-treeline conditions for a longer period than if they just went up and down a single peak.

But today, Carine was content with her mixed hardwood forest of former farmland. Gus had warned her to stay away from Bobby Poulet, a survivalist who had a homestead on a few acres on the northeast edge of the woods. He was a legendary crank who'd threatened to shoot anyone who stepped foot on his property.

She took pictures of rocks and burgundy-colored oak leaves, water trickling over rocks in a narrow stream, a hemlock, a fallen, rotting elm and an abandoned hunting shack with a crooked metal chimney. The land was owned by a lumber company that, fortunately, had a laissez-faire attitude toward hikers.

She almost missed the owl.

It was a huge barred owl, as still as a stone sculpture, its neutral coloring blending in with the mostly gray November landscape as it perched on a branch high in a naked beech tree.

Before Carine could raise her camera, the owl swooped off its branch and flapped up over the low ridge above her, out of sight.

She sighed. She'd won awards for her photography of raptors—she'd have loved to have had a good shot of the owl. On the other hand, she wasn't sure her digital camera was up to the task.

A loud boom shattered the silence of the isolated ravine.

Carine dropped flat to the ground, facedown, before she could absorb what the sound was.

A gunshot.

Her camera had flown out of her hand and landed in

the dried leaves two feet above her outstretched arm. Her day pack ground into her back. And her heart was pounding, her throat tight.

Damn, she thought. How close was that?

It had to be hunters. Not responsible hunters. *Insane* hunters—yahoos who didn't know what they were doing. Shooting that close to her. What were they thinking? Didn't they see her? She'd slipped a bright-orange vest over her fleece jacket. She knew it was deer-hunting season, but this was the first time a hunter had fired anywhere *near* her.

"Hey!" She lifted her head to yell but otherwise remained prone on the damp ground, in the decaying fallen leaves. "Knock it off! There's someone up here!"

As if in answer, three quick, earsplitting shots cracked over her head, whirring, almost whistling. One hit the oak tree a few yards to her right.

Were these guys total idiots?

She should have hiked in the White Mountain National Forest or one of the state parks where hunting was prohibited.

Just two yards to her left was a six-foot freestanding boulder. If these guys weren't going to stop shooting, she needed to take cover. Staying low, she picked up her camera then scrambled behind the boulder, ducking down, her back against the jagged granite. The ground was wetter here, and her knees and seat were already damp. Cold, wet conditions killed. More hikers in the White Mountains died of hypothermia than any other cause. It was what had killed her parents thirty years ago. They were caught in unexpected freezing rain and poor visibility. They fell. Injured, unable to move, unable to stay warm— they didn't stand a chance.

Carine reminded herself she had a change of clothes in

her pack. Food. Water. A first-aid kit. A jackknife, flash-light, map, compass, waterproof matches. Her clothes were made of a water-wicking material that would help insulate her even when wet.

Her boulder would protect her from gunshots.

The woods settled into silence. Maybe the shooters had realized their mistake. For all she knew, they—or he, since there might only be one—were on their way up her side of the ravine to apologize and make sure she was all right. More likely, they were clearing out and hoping she hadn't seen them.

Three more shots in rapid succession ricocheted off her boulder, ripping off chunks and shards of granite. Carine screamed, startled, frustrated, angry. And scared now.

A rock shard from her boulder struck her in the fore-head, and her mouth snapped shut.

Good God, were they *aiming* at her?

Were they trying to kill her?

She curled up in a ball, knees tucked, arms wrapped around her ankles. Blood dripped from her forehead onto her wrist. She felt no pain from her injury, but her heart raced and her ears hurt from the blasts. She couldn't think.

Once again, silence followed the rapid burst of shots.

Were they reloading? Coming after her? *What?*

She tried to control her breathing, hoping the shoot-ers wouldn't hear her. But what was the point? They had to know now, after she'd screamed, that she was behind the boulder.

They'd known it before they'd shot at it.

She couldn't stay where she was.

The low ridge crested fifteen feet above her. If she could get up the hill, she could slip down the other side and hide among the trees and boulders, make her way back to her car, call the police.

If the shooters tried to follow her, she'd at least see them up on the ridge.

See them and do what?

She pushed back the thought. She'd figure that out later. Should she stand up and run? Crouch? Or should she crawl? Scoot up the hill on her stomach? No scooting. She'd be like a giant fluorescent worm in her orange vest. Take it off? No—no time.

She'd take her day pack. It might stop or impede a bullet.

Or should she stay put? Hope they hadn't seen her after all?

Every fiber in her body—every survival instinct she had—told her that she'd be killed if she stayed where she was.

She picked out the largest trees, a mix of evergreens and hardwoods, their leaves shed for the season, between her boulder and the ridgeline. The hillside was strewn with glacial boulders. It was New Hampshire. The Granite State.

Inhaling, visualizing her exact route, she crouched down racer-style, and, on an exhale, bolted up the hill. She ducked behind a hemlock straight up from her boulder, then ran diagonally to a maple, zigzagged to another hemlock, then hurled herself over the ridge crest. She scrambled downhill through a patch of switchlike bare saplings as three more quick shots boomed in the ravine on the other side of the ridge.

A whir, a cracking sound over her head.

Jesus!

They *were* shooting at her.

A crouched figure jumped out from behind a gnarled pine tree to her left, catching her around the middle with a thick arm, covering her mouth with a bare hand, then lunging with her back behind the tree.

"Carine—babe, it's me. Tyler North. Don't scream."

He removed his hand, settling in next to her on the ground, and she jerked herself away, although not entirely out of his grasp. "Was that you shooting at me? You *jackass*."

"Shh. It wasn't me."

She blinked, as if he might not be real, but she was sprawled against him, his body warm, solid. Tyler... Tyler North. He was at his most intense and focused. Combat ready, she thought, feeling a fresh jolt of fear. He was a PJ, an air force pararescueman. PJs were search-and-rescue specialists, the ones who went after pilots downed behind enemy lines. Carine had known Ty since they were tots. She'd heard he was home in Cold Ridge on leave—maybe the shooters were firing at *him*.

She tried to push back her fear and confusion. She'd been taking pictures, minding her own business. Then someone started shooting at her. Now she was here, behind a tree with Ty North. "Where—where did you come from?"

"I'm hiking with a couple of buddies. We saw your car and thought we'd join you for lunch. Figured you'd have better food." He frowned at her, peeling hair off her forehead to reveal her cut, and she remembered his search-and-rescue skills included medical training above the level of a paramedic. "Piece of flying rock hit you?"

"I think so. Ty, I don't know if they were aiming at you—"

"Let's not worry about that right now. The cut doesn't look too bad. Want to get out of here?"

She nodded, thinking she had to look like a maniac.

Bloodied, twigs in her hair. Pant legs soaked and muddy. She was cold, but a long way from hypothermia.

Ty eased her day pack off and slung it over his shoulder. "We're going to zigzag down the hill, just like you came up. That was good work. Hank Callahan and Manny Carrera are out here, so don't panic if you see them."

Hank Callahan was a retired air force pilot, and Manny Carrera was another pararescueman, a master sergeant like North. Carine knew them from their previous visits to Cold Ridge. "Okay."

"All right. You got everything? If you're woozy, I can carry you—"

"I'll keep up."

North grinned at her suddenly. "You've got the prettiest eyes. Why haven't we ever dated?"

"What?"

As much as his question surprised her, he'd managed to penetrate the fear that seemed to saturate her, and when he took her hand, she ran with him without hesitation, using trees and boulders as cover, zigzagging down the hill, up another small, rounded hill. They ducked behind a stone wall above the leaf-covered stream she'd photographed earlier. Carine was breathing hard, her head pounding from fear and pain, the cut on her forehead bothering her now. They were getting closer to the main road. Her car. A place where she could call the police. She had a cell phone in her pack, but there was no service out here.

Leaves crunched nearby, and Hank Callahan joined them, exchanging a quick smile with Carine. He was square-jawed and blue-eyed, distinguished-looking, his dark hair streaked with gray. He had none of the compact, pitbull scrappiness of tawny-haired Tyler North.

"Christ, Ty," Hank said in a low voice, "she's hurt—"

"She's fine."

"I'm scared shitless! Those bastards were *shooting* at me!" Carine didn't raise her voice, but she wasn't calm. "Yahoos. Hunters—"

Hank shook his head, and Ty said, "Not hunters. A hunter doesn't take a three-shot burst into a boulder, even if he's using a semiautomatic rifle. These assholes knew you were there, Carine."

"Me? But I didn't do anything—"

"Did you see anyone?" Hank asked. "Any idea how many are out there?"

"No, no idea." Her teeth were chattering, but she blamed the cold, not what Ty had said. "There's an old hunting shack not far from where the bullets started flying. It looked abandoned to me. I took pictures of it. Maybe somebody didn't like that."

"I thought you took pictures of birds," North said with a wry smile.

"I'm just most known for birds." As a child, she'd believed she could see her parents as angels, soaring above Cold Ridge with a lone hawk or eagle. Ty used to tease her for it. "I was just trying out my digital camera."

But she was breathing rapidly—too rapidly—and Ty put his hand over her mouth briefly. "Stop. Hold your breath a second before you hyperventilate."

Already feeling a little light-headed, she did as he suggested. She noticed the green color of his eyes. That wasn't a good sign. She'd never noticed anything about him before. She couldn't remember when she'd seen him last. Fourth of July fireworks? They were neighbors, but seldom saw each other. His mother had moved to the valley just before Ty was born and bought the 1817 brick house that Abraham Winter, the first of the Cold Ridge Winters, had built as a tavern. She'd called herself Saskia, but no one believed that was her real name. If she had a husband, she'd never said. She was a weaver and a painter, but not the most attentive of mothers. Ty had pretty much grown up on his own. Even as a little boy, he'd wander up on the ridge trail for hours before his mother would even realize he was gone. She died four years ago, leaving him the house and fifty acres of woods and meadow. Everyone expected him to sell it, but he didn't, although, given the demands of his military career, he wasn't around much.

Hank Callahan shifted. "I don't know about you, but I'd like to put some serious mileage between me and the guys with guns."

Carine steadied her breathing. "What about your other friend Manny—"

"Don't worry about Carrera," Ty said. "He can take care of himself. What's the best route out of here?"

"We could follow the stone wall. There's an old logging road not far from the shack—"

He shook his head. "If the shooters are using the shack, that's the road they'd take. They'll have vehicles."

She thought a moment. "Then we should follow the stream. It's not as direct, but it'll take us to where we parked."

"How exposed will we be?"

"From a shooter's perspective? I can't make that judgment. I just know it's the fastest route out of here."

"Fast is good," Callahan said.

Ty nodded, then winked at Carine. "Okay, babe, we'll go your way."

She didn't remember him ever having called her "babe" before today.

Thirty minutes later, as they came to the gravel parking area, they heard an explosion back in the woods, from the direction of the shack and the shooters. Black smoke rose up over the trees.

Hank whistled. "I wonder who the hell these guys are."

Manny Carrera emerged from behind a half-dead white pine. He couldn't have been that far behind them, but Carine hadn't heard a thing. He was another PJ, a dark-haired, dark-eyed bull of a Texan.

"Good," Ty said. "That wasn't you blowing up. The shack?"

"That's my guess." Manny spoke calmly, explosions and shots fired in the woods apparently not enough to ruffle him—or North and Callahan. "There are two shooters, at least one back at the shack. I couldn't get close enough to any of them for a good description."

"I have binoculars you could have borrowed," Carine said.

He grinned at her. "But they were shooting at you, kiddo."

"Not necessarily *at* me—"

"Yes. At you. They just didn't want you dead. Scared, paralyzed, maybe. Otherwise, they wouldn't have missed, not that many times. They were using scoped, semiautomatic rifles." His tone was objective, just stating the facts, but his eyes settled on her, his gaze softening slightly. "Sorry. It wasn't an accident. It wasn't target practice gone awry. They didn't mistake you for a deer."

"I get it." She tried to be as clinical about her near-death experience as the three men were, but she kept seeing herself crouched behind the boulder, hearing the shots, feeling the rock shard hit her head. The bullets had been flying at her, not them. "Maybe they saw me taking pictures, but—" she took a breath "—to me it was just a hunting shack."

"That's enough for now," Ty said. "We can speculate later. You have a cell phone on you?"

Carine nodded. "I doubt there's any coverage out here."

She took her day pack from him and dug out her phone, but she was totally spent from dodging bullets, diving behind trees and boulders, charging through the woods with two military types, all after tramping around on her own with her camera. She hit the wrong button and almost threw the phone onto the ground.

North quietly took it and shook his head. "No service. Hank and Manny, you take my truck. I'll go with Carine." He turned to her, eyeing her pragmatically. "Can you drive, or do you want me to?"

"I can do it."

There was no cell coverage—there were no houses—until they came to a small lake on the notch road north of the village of Cold Ridge. Even then, Ty barely got the words out to the dispatcher before service dropped out on him.

He clicked off the phone and looked over at Carine. "I'm serious," he said. "Why haven't we ever dated?"

She managed a smile. "Because I've always hated you."

He grinned at her. "No, you haven't."

And she was lost. Then and there.

By the time state and local police arrived on scene, the shack was burned to the ground and the shooters were gone. According to various law enforcement officers, Carine had likely stumbled on to a smuggling operation they'd had their eye on but couldn't pinpoint. They smuggled drugs, weapons and people into and out of Canada and were, without a doubt, very dangerous.

Everyone agreed she was lucky indeed she hadn't been killed.

Even if the pictures she took of the shack were the reason the shooters came after her, they didn't tell her anything. She'd printed them out in her tiny log cabin while she and her military trio had waited for the police to get there. They'd been and gone, taking the memory disk with them. She still had the prints. A shack in the woods with a crooked metal chimney. It looked innocent enough to her.

Ty cleaned and treated the cut on her forehead. She kept avoiding his eye, aware of her reaction to him, aware that, somehow, everything had changed between them. She'd known him forever. He'd always been a thorn in her side. He'd pushed her out of trees. He'd cut the rope on her tire swing. Now, he was making her tingle. It had to be adrenaline—a post-traumatic reaction of some sort, she decided.

Hank and Manny built a fire in her woodstove. Hank, she learned, was a newly announced, dark horse candidate to become the junior U.S. senator from Massachusetts. He was a former air force rescue helicopter pilot, a retired major who'd received national attention on his last mission a year ago to recover fishermen whose boat had capsized.

As unflappable as he'd been in the woods, Hank Callahan was rendered virtually speechless when Antonia Winter walked into her sister's cabin. It made Carine smile. Her sister was a trauma physician in Boston, but she'd been drawn to Cold Ridge for the thirtieth anniversary of the deaths of their parents. She was a couple of inches shorter than Carine, her auburn hair a tone lighter, but Gus said both his nieces had their mother's blue eyes.

Antonia inspected Ty's medical handiwork, pronouncing it satisfactory. Ty just rolled his eyes. She was focused, hardworking and brilliant, but if she noticed Hank's reaction to her, she gave no indication of it.

Gus arrived a few minutes later and shooed out all the air force guys, glowering when North winked at Carine and promised he'd see her later. Gus let Antonia stay.

Their uncle was fifty, his dark hair mostly gray now, but he was as rangy and fit as ever. In addition to outfitting and leading hiking trips into the White Mountains, he conducted workshops in mountaineering, winter camping and mountain rescue. His goal, Carine knew, was to reduce the chances that anyone would ever again die the way his brother and sister-in-law had. But they did. People died in the mountains almost every year.

He brought in more wood for the woodstove and insisted Carine sit in front of the fire and tell him and her sister everything.

She did, except for the part about Ty saying she had pretty eyes.

Gus wanted her to head back to town with him, but Antonia offered to stay with Carine in her small cabin. Their brother, a U.S. marshal in New York, called and agreed with the general assessment that the shooters hadn't "missed" her. If they'd wanted her dead, she'd be dead. "Lay low for a few days, will you?"

Out of Antonia's earshot, Carine asked Nate what he'd think if she dated Tyler North.

"Has he asked you out?"

"No."

"Thank God for small favors."

The next day, Ty and his friends ended up rescuing a Massachusetts couple who got trapped on Cold Ridge. Sterling and Jodie Rancourt had recently bought a house off the notch road and set out on their first hike on the ridge, for what they'd intended to be a simple afternoon excursion. Instead, they encountered higher winds, colder temperatures and rougher terrain than they'd anticipated. Ty, Hank and Manny, prepared for the conditions, helped transport them below the treeline, where they were met by a local volunteer rescue team.

Jodie Rancourt had sprained her ankle, and both she and her husband were in the early stages of hypothermia, in danger of spending the night on the ridge. Given their lack of experience and the harsh conditions, they could easily have died if the three air force guys hadn't come along when they had.

An eventful weekend in the White Mountains.

After Manny went back to his air force base and Hank to his senate campaign, Ty and Carine were alone on their quiet road in the shadows of Cold Ridge.

Gus sensed what was happening and stopped by to tell Carine she'd be out of her damn mind to get involved with Tyler North.

She didn't listen.

Her uncle's warning was too late. Way too late. She was in love.

She and Ty set their wedding date for Valentine's Day.

A week before she was to walk down the aisle, he showed up at her cabin and called it off.

He couldn't go through with it.

Enter Tyler North into her life.

Exit Tyler North.

As quick as that.

One

For the first time in weeks, Carine didn't spend her lunch hour thinking about photographing wild turkeys in the meadow outside her log cabin in Cold Ridge. She wandered through Boston Public Garden, eating the tuna sandwich she'd made and packed that morning. Every dime was critical to her ability to afford both her cabin in New Hampshire and her apartment in the city. Not that it was much of an apartment. Not that she could ever live in her cabin again.

The last of the leaves, even in Boston, had changed color, and many had fallen to the ground, a temptation on a sunny, mild November afternoon. Carine remembered raking huge piles of leaves as a kid with her brother and sister—and Tyler North—and diving into them, hiding, wrestling.

Ty almost suffocated her once. Unfortunately, she hadn't thought of it as a premonition. It was just Ty being Ty, pushing the limits.

But the nine months since their canceled wedding had taught her not to dwell on thoughts of her one-time fiancé and what might have been. She dashed across busy Arlington Street to a French café, splurging on a latte that she took back outside with her. Of course, it was true that she *could* be photographing wild turkeys in Cold Ridge— or red-tailed hawks, mountain sunsets, waterfalls, rock formations, alpine grasses. She was still a nature photographer, never mind that she'd been in Boston for six months and had just accepted a long-term assignment photographing house renovations.

Not just *any* house renovations, she thought. Sterling and Jodie Rancourt had hired her to photograph the painstaking restoration and renovation of their historic Victorian mansion on Commonwealth Avenue.

Carine sighed, sipping her latte as she peered in the display windows of the upscale shops and salons on trendy Newbury Street. But Ty kept creeping into her thoughts. Even when she'd chased him with a rake at six, spitting bits of leaves out of her mouth, she'd known not to get involved with him, ever. The six-year-old inside her, who knew better than to trust anything he said, must have been screaming bloody murder when she'd fallen in love with him last winter.

The man could jump out of a helicopter to rescue a downed aircrew—it didn't matter where. Behind enemy lines, on a mountaintop, in a desert or a jungle or an ocean, in snow or heat or rain. In combat or peacetime. He had a job to do. Getting cold feet wasn't an option.

Not so when it'd come to marrying her.

Carine hadn't spoken to him since he'd knocked on her cabin door and said he couldn't go through with their wedding. He'd disappeared into the mountains for a few days of solo winter camping, lived through it, then returned to his base. She'd heard he'd been deployed overseas and participated in dangerous combat search and rescues. CSARs. He'd also performed humanitarian missions, one to treat injured women and children in an isolated area. Carine appreciated the work he did, and gradually, her anger at him had worn off, along with her shock. They were easy emotions to deal with in comparison to the hurt and embarrassment that had followed him walking out on her, the palpable grief of losing a man she'd come to regard in those few short months, maybe over her lifetime, as her soul mate.

Even when he was away, there were reminders of him everywhere in Cold Ridge. And, of course, when he was on leave, when he could get away for a couple of days, *he* was there.

By early summer, Carine knew she had to pick up the pieces of her life and make some changes, explore new options, expand her horizons—not that it always felt that way. Sometimes, even now, it felt as if she were still licking her wounds, still running from herself and the life she wanted to lead.

But not today—today was a gorgeous late autumn day, perfect for *not* thinking about Cold Ridge and Tyler North. As far as she was concerned, he was back to being the thorn in her side he'd always been. She'd trust him with her life—who wouldn't? But she'd never again make the mistake of trusting him with her heart.

That was what Gus had tried to tell her after the shooting incident in the woods last November. "You can trust him with your life, Carine, but—damn it, he'll break your heart in the end."

She'd thought her uncle was just worrying about her. People tended to worry about her. She wasn't a tough U.S. marshal like her brother or a physician who'd seen everything like her sister—people saw her as the sensitive soul of her family, a nature photographer who'd never really left home.

Well, now she had.

She finished her latte and decided to head back to Commonwealth Avenue and the Rancourt house, although she wasn't under any time constraints. The Rancourts hadn't just hired her out of the blue. They weren't part of her horizon-expanding. They'd hired her, Carine knew, because she was from Cold Ridge, friends with the three men who rescued them the year before. Hank Callahan and Antonia had started dating in Boston after that first meeting in Carine's cabin. He was now her brother-in-law. As of a week ago, the voters of the Commonwealth of Massachusetts had made him their junior senator-elect. Since he was friends with Ty and Antonia was a fiercely loyal sister, their relationship had suffered after Carine's aborted wedding. Then Antonia found herself trapped on an island off Cape Cod with a violent stalker and with a hurricane about to blow on shore; Hank had come after her, ending any doubts either of them had. The media—and voters—lapped up the story. But it was clear to everyone that Hank hadn't been thinking about their opinion when he'd headed to the Shelter Island.

No, Carine thought, she had no illusions. As much as she liked them, Sterling and Jodie Rancourt had their own reasons for asking her to do the job.

She walked slowly, in no hurry. Her hair was pulled back neatly, and she wore jeans, a black turtleneck, her barn coat and waterproof ankle boots, comfortable clothes that permitted her to go up and down ladders, trek over drop cloths and stacks of building supplies and tools, do whatever she had to do to get the particular picture she wanted. She was used to climbing mountains and edging across rock ledges to get the right light, the right color, the right composition. Negotiating house renovations didn't seem that daunting to her. It had been a quiet morning—she hadn't even taken her camera out of its bag and had left it at the Rancourt house while she was at lunch. She was using her digital camera today, at Jodie Rancourt's request—Jodie wanted to get a better idea of the technical differences between digital and film.

A shiny black sports car pulled alongside her, and Louis Sanborn, also newly employed by the Rancourts, rolled down his window and flashed his killer smile at her. "Hey, Ms. Photographer, need a ride over to the big house?"

Carine laughed. "Thanks for the offer, Mr. Security Man." Louis was tall and, despite his prematurely gray, scrub-brush hair, younger than he looked, probably just a year or two older than she was. The Rancourts had hired him two weeks ago as the assistant to their chief of security. "I don't mind walking. We won't get many more days like today. It's beautiful out."

"Only according to you granite-head types."

"It's in the fifties!"

"That's what I'm saying. Having a good lunch hour?"

"An excellent lunch hour."

"Me, too. See you over on Comm. Ave."

His car merged back into the Newbury Street traffic. Carine continued on up to Exeter Street, then cut down it to Commonwealth Avenue. With its center mall and stately Victorian buildings, it was the quintessential street of Boston's Back Bay, all of which was on reclaimed land that used to be under water—hence its name.

Still in no hurry, she sat on a bench on the mall, famous for its early springtime pink magnolias, now long gone. A toddler ran after a flutter of pigeons, and Carine tried not to think about the babies she'd meant to have with Ty, but, nonetheless, felt a momentary pang of regret. The toddler's mother scooped him up and swung him in the brisk November air, then set him back in his stroller. He was ticked off and started to kick and scream. He wanted to chase more pigeons. Two months ago—a month ago—the scene would have made Carine cry, but now she smiled. Progress, she thought.

She walked across the westbound lane to the historic brick-front mansion the Rancourts had snapped up when it came onto the market eighteen months ago. It was a rare find. Its longtime owner, now dead, had never carved it up into apartments, in fact, had done few renovations—many of the house's original features were still intact. Hardwood floors, ornate moldings, marble fireplaces, chandeliers, wainscoting, fixtures. It had taken most of the past eighteen months for the team of architects, preservationists, designers and contractors just to come up with the right plans for what to do.

Carine's job photographing the renovations could easily take her through the winter, while still leaving room for her to pursue other projects. She'd been at it for six weeks. Work would happen in a frenzy for a few days, the place crawling with people. Then everyone would vanish, and nothing would happen for a morning, an afternoon, even a week. That left her with spurts of time she could put to use doing something more productive than drinking lattes and window shopping.

She noticed Louis Sanborn's car parked out front and smiled, shaking her head. Leave Louis to find a convenient parking space—she never could, and almost always walked or took public transportation in the city.

Since she'd left for lunch, someone had set out a pot of yellow mums on the front stoop; the wrought-iron rail was cool to the touch as she mounted the steps to the massive dark wood door. It was open a crack, and she pushed it with her shoulder and went in, immediately tossing her latte cup into an ugly green plastic trash bin just inside the door. Sweeping, graceful stairs rose up to the second floor of the five-story house. She'd never been in any place like it. Not one inch of it reminded her of her little log cabin with its rustic ladder up to the loft.

"Hello?" she called. "Anyone here?"

Her footsteps echoed on the age-darkened cherry floor of the center hall. To her left was a formal drawing room with a marble fireplace and a crystal chandelier, then a smaller room and the library. There was even an elegant ballroom on the second floor. The Rancourts had promised to invite Carine the first time they used it, teasing her that they wanted to see her in sequins.

She retrieved her camera from a cold, old-fashioned radiator in the hall. There had to be someone around. Nobody would leave the door open with the place empty.

"Louis? Are you here? It's me, Carine."

He could be upstairs, she thought, slinging her camera bag over her shoulder. She'd assumed workers would be in this afternoon, but she didn't keep close track of their comings and goings. As she turned to head back to the front entry, something caught her eye in the library. She wasn't sure what—something out of place. Wrong.

She took a shallow breath, and it was as if a force stronger than she was compelled her to take a step forward and peer through the double doorway. Restoration work hadn't started yet in the library. Intense discussions were still under way over whether it was worth the expense to have its yellowed wallpaper, possibly original to the house, copied.

Carine touched the wood molding, telling herself she must have simply seen a shadow or a stray drop cloth. Then she jumped back, inhaling sharply, even as her mind struggled to take in what she was seeing—a man face-down on the wood floor. Louis. She recognized his dark suit, his scrub-brush hair. She lunged forward, but stopped abruptly, almost instinctively.

A pool of something dark, a liquid, oozed toward her. She stood motionless, refusing to absorb what she was seeing.

Blood.

It seeped into the cracks in the narrow-board floor. It covered Louis's outstretched hand.

Help...

She couldn't speak. Her mouth opened, but no sound came out.

His hair...his hand...in the blood...

"Oh, God, oh, God—Louis!" Carine leaped forward, yelling back over her shoulder. "Help! Help, someone's hurt!"

She avoided stepping in the blood. It wasn't easy— there was so much of it. *Louis...he can't be dead. I just saw him!*

She had only rudimentary first aid skills. She wasn't an ER doctor like her sister or a highly trained combat paramedic like North and Manny Carrera. But they weren't here, and she forced herself to kneel beside Louis Sanborn and control her horror and fear as she touched two fingers to his carotid artery. That was it, wasn't it? Arteries beat with the heart. Veins didn't. To see if he had a pulse, she had to find an artery.

There was no pulse, not with that much blood.

"Louis. Oh, God."

She looked around the empty room, her voice echoing as she yelled again for help. Had he fallen and landed on a sharp object—a stray chisel or a saw, or something? The back of his suit was unmarred. No blood, no torn fabric. Whatever injury he had must have been in front. But she didn't dare turn him over, touch him further.

She rose shakily. No one had come in answer to her yells for help. Louis Sanborn was dead. She was alone. She absorbed the reality of her situation in short bursts of awareness, as if she couldn't take it all in at once.

Hey, Ms. Photographer, need a ride over to the big house?

What if she'd said yes? Could she have saved his life? Or would she be dead, too?

How had he died?

What if it wasn't an accident?

It wasn't. She knew it wasn't.

She ran into the hall, her camera bag bouncing on her hip. Where was her cell phone? She needed to call the police, an ambulance. She dug in the pocket of her barn coat, finding her phone, but she couldn't hang on to it and dropped it on the hardwood floor, startling herself. She scooped it up, hardly pausing as she came to the front hall.

The front door stood wide open. She thought she'd shut it when she got back from lunch. Was someone else here?

She could feel the cool November air.

"Help!"

She looked down at her cell phone, realized it wasn't on. She hit the Power button and ran onto the front stoop, knocking over the pot of mums, hoping someone on the street would hear her. She charged down the steps to the wide sidewalk. She'd call the police, stop a passing car.

Suddenly Manny Carrera was there, as if she'd conjured him up herself. He'd danced with her at Hank and Antonia's wedding a month ago and cheerfully offered to cut off Ty's balls the next time he saw him.

"It's Louis…he…" She couldn't get out the words. "He's—oh, God—"

Manny swept her into his embrace. "I know," he said. "I know."

Two

Tyler North pulled two beers out of his refrigerator and brought them to the long pine table where his mother used to sit in front of the fire with her paints. Gus Winter was in her spot now, lean, scarred and irritable—and tired, although he'd never admit to it. He took one of the beers and shook his head in disgust. "You always have to allow for the moron factor."

"People make mistakes."

Gus drank some of his beer. It had been a brutal day, but one with a happy ending. "Forgetting your sunscreen's a mistake. These assholes didn't bother to check the weather conditions. They didn't take enough food or water. You saw how they were dressed—jeans and sneakers. It's November. Any goddamn thing can happen on the ridge in November. They're lucky to be alive."

No one knew better than Gus Winter that what he said was true. Ty didn't argue with him. He sat with his beer and stared at the fire in the old center-chimney stone fireplace. Three seventeen-year-old boys from the local prep school decided to skip classes and hike the ridge trail. If they'd stayed on it, they might have been okay, but they didn't. By early afternoon, they were cold, lost, battered by high winds and terrified of spending the night above the treeline.

"If Fish and Game determines these guys were reckless, they'll have to cough up the bucks for the rescue," Ty said.

"They're complaining because we didn't send a helicopter! Can you imagine? They figured they'd dial 911 on their cell phones if they got into trouble—"

"That's what they did."

Gus snorted. "Yeah. And we came. What's with this picture? We should have waited, let them get good and scared." He drank more of his beer. "I'm telling you, North. The moron factor."

Ty expected the three boys they'd just rescued were the sort of hikers the New Hampshire Department of Fish and Game had in mind when they came up with their protocol for charging expenses for search and rescues in cases of out-and-out recklessness. Rescues could be difficult and dangerous—and expensive. Lucky for the boys, they hadn't encountered moisture. Even a light rain would have soaked their cotton clothing, a poor insulator when wet. As it was, they'd suffered mild hypothermia. And intense, warranted fear for their lives.

"I did dumb-ass things at that age," Ty said.

"You do dumb-ass things now. But do you expect people to come to your rescue?" Gus shook his head, not waiting for an answer. "Not you, North. You've never expected anyone to come to your rescue in your entire life, not with your mother, may she rest in peace. Lovely woman, but in her own world. It's the arrogance of these jackasses—"

"Let it go, Gus. We did our job. The rest isn't up to us."

Reckless or not, the boys today weren't the first people he or Gus had pulled off Cold Ridge. It was unlikely they'd be the last.

But Gus wasn't willing to let it go. "Cell phones give people a false sense of security. They should be banned."

Without a cell phone, the kids undoubtedly wouldn't have been missed before nightfall. They'd have ended up spending the night on the ridge—a dangerous situation that might not have had a happy ending. On the other hand, without a cell phone, they might have taken fewer risks or even gone to their classes instead of sneaking off on an illicit hike. Other hikers had made the mistake of thinking their cell phones worked anywhere and didn't discover there were gaps in coverage until they were ass-deep in trouble and had no way to call for help. Even if they did get through, help wasn't necessarily around the damn corner.

Either way, it was North's job to rescue people. He did it for a living in the military, and he did it as a volunteer when he was home on leave.

Gus set his beer bottle down hard on the table. "People think because the White Mountains aren't as high as the Rockies or the Himalayas, they're not dangerous. The reason the treeline's lower in the northeast than it is out west is because we've got such shitty weather here. Three major storm tracks meet right over us—ah, hell." He gave a grunt of disgust. "I'm preaching to the converted. You know these mountains as well as I do."

"I've been away a lot."

That was an understatement. His career as a pararescueman had taken him on search-and-rescue missions all over the world. The pararescue motto—These Things We Do That Others May Live—underscored everything he did as a PJ in both combat and peacetime. A pararescueman's primary mission was to go after downed aircrews. Anytime, anywhere. In any kind of terrain, under permissive or hostile conditions. If there were injuries, they treated them. If they came under fire, they took up security positions and fired back.

The job required a wide range of skills. When he enlisted and decided to become a pararescueman, Ty had only a limited understanding of what it entailed. For starters, two years of training and instruction—the "pipeline." It began with ten weeks of PJ indoctrination at Lackland Air Force Base in San Antonio. Running, swimming, calisthenics, drownproofing. Serious sleep deprivation, or at least so it seemed at the time. Of the hundred guys who showed up for indoc with him, twenty-four were still there after four weeks. He was one of them.

Then it was on to a series of specialized schools. He went through the Army Special Forces Underwater Operations Course and Navy Underwater Egress Training—navigation swims, ditching and donning of equipment underwater, underwater search patterns, getting out of a sinking aircraft. He made it through the Army Airborne School, where he had to make five static-line jumps before he could move on to freefall school, which took him through jumps at high altitude, with oxygen, at night, during the day, with and without equipment.

Fun stuff, he thought, remembering how he'd steel himself into not quitting, just sticking with it, one day—sometimes one minute—at a time.

At Air Force Survival School he learned basic survival skills, evasion-and-escape techniques, what to do if he was captured by the enemy. Then it was on to the Special Operations Combat Medic Course and, finally, to the Pararescue Recovery Specialist Course, where, over a year or more, all the previous training got put together and more was added—advance EMT-paramedic training, advance parachute skills, tactical maneuvers, weapons handling, mountain climbing and aircrew recovery procedures. They worked through various scenarios that tied in all the different skills they'd learned, seeing their practical application for the job that lay ahead.

Then came graduation, the PJ's distinctive maroon beret, assignment to a team—then Ty thought, the real training began.

PJs had been called SEALs with stethoscopes, ninja brain surgeons, superman paramedics—if people knew what they did at all, since so many of their missions had to be done quietly. It wasn't a job for someone looking for money and glory. Ty cringed at all the nicknames. He thought of himself as an average guy who did a job he was trained to do to the best of his ability. He'd become a PJ because he wanted an action-oriented career where he could save lives, a chance to "search and rescue" instead of "search and destroy."

But he could "destroy" if he had to. PJs were direct combatants, and, as such, pararescue was a career field that remained closed to women.

Ty was currently assigned to the 16th Special Operations Wing out of Hurlburt Field in the Florida panhandle. As the leader of a special tactics team, he had performed a full range of combat search-and-rescue missions in recent years, but it was seeing Carine Winter under fire last fall that had all but done him in.

The "incident" was still under investigation.

The only positive outcome of the whole mess was that Hank Callahan and Antonia Winter had met and fallen in love. Ty had missed their wedding a month ago. Antonia was too damn polite not to invite him. His behavior toward her younger sister had put a crimp in the budding romance between his friend the ER doctor and his friend the helicopter-pilot-turned-senate-candidate—fortunately, they'd worked it out.

Senator Hank Callahan.

Ty shook his head, grinning to himself. He and Hank had damn near become brothers-in-law. They would have, if Ty had gone ahead and married Carine in February. Instead, he'd cut and run.

It was the only time in his life he'd ever cut and run.

"Have you decided whether or not you're selling the house?" Gus asked him.

Ty pulled himself from his darkening thoughts. "No. I haven't decided, I mean."

He'd been on assignment overseas when his mother took a walk in the meadow and died of a massive stroke. Carine had found her and tracked him down to make sure he got the news, to tell him his mother had painted that morning and died in the lupine she'd so loved. But Saskia North had never really fit in with the locals, and few in Cold Ridge knew much about her, beyond her skills as a painter and a weaver—and her failings as a mother.

"You should sell it," Gus said. "There's nothing for you here, not anymore. What do you want with this place? You're never here long enough to fix it up. Basic maintenance isn't enough. It'll fall down around your ears before too long."

Now that Ty had broken Carine's heart, Gus wanted him to clear out of Cold Ridge altogether. The man made no secret of it. It hadn't always been that way, but Ty knew that was before and this was now. To Gus, Carine was still the little girl he'd loved and protected since she was three years old—the little girl whose parents he'd helped carry off Cold Ridge.

People make mistakes.

It was the way life was. You make mistakes, you try to correct them.

North frowned at a strange ringing sound, then watched

Gus grimace and pull a cell phone out of his back pocket. He pointed the cell phone at North. "Just shut the hell up. I've never used it to call for someone to come rescue me." Then he clicked the receive button and said, "Yeah, Gus here." His face lost color, and he got to his feet. "Slow down, honey. Slow down. What—" He listened some more, pacing, obviously trying to stay calm. "Do you want me to come down there? Are you okay? Carine—" He all but threw the phone into the fire. *"Goddamn it!"*

Ty fell back on his training and experience to stay calm. "Service kick out on you?" He kept his voice neutral, careful not to say anything that would further provoke Gus, further upset him. "It does that. The mountains."

Gus raked a hand through his gray, brittle hair. "That was Carine."

Ty felt a tightening in his throat. "I thought so."

"She—" He sucked in a sharp, angry breath. "Damn it, North, I hate it that she's in Boston. With Antonia and Hank married, she's alone there now for the most part. And, goddamn it, she doesn't belong there."

North didn't argue. "You're right, Gus. What happened?"

Tears rose in the older man's eyes, a reminder of the years he'd invested in his brother's three children. His own parents couldn't take them on—they were shattered by the untimely deaths of their older son and daughter-in-law and had chronic health problems. It was Gus who'd made the emotional commitment at age twenty to raise his nieces and nephew. Ty thought of the sacrifices, the physical toll, it all had taken. For thirty years, Gus Winter had put the needs of Nate, Antonia and Carine ahead of his own. He was the only one who didn't know it.

"Gus?"

"There was a shooting. A murder. She found the body. Christ, after last fall—"

"Where was she?"

"At work. She's photographing the renovations on that old house the Rancourts bought on Commonwealth Avenue. She went out for a latte—Christ. That's what she just said. *Gus, I went out for a latte.* When she got back, she found a man dead on the library floor." Gus snatched up his beer bottle and dumped the balance out in the sink. "She didn't want me to hear about it on the news."

"Did she say who the victim was?"

He shook his head. "She didn't have a chance. I'll go home and call her." He grabbed his coat off the back of the chair, and when North started to his feet, Gus, refusing to look at him, added abruptly, "It's not your problem."

"All right. Sure, Gus. If you need me for anything—"

"I won't."

Ty didn't follow him out, but he was tempted. He pulled his chair over to the fire and let the hot flames warm his feet. He still had on his hiking socks. It felt good to get out of his boots. One of the prep-school boys needed to be carried off the ridge in a litter. The other two responded to on-site treatment, warm duds and warm liquids, and were able to walk down on their own. Gus didn't think they were contrite enough. But Gus had been in a bad mood for months. For good reason. Antonia's wedding had temporarily lifted his spirits, but North's return to Cold Ridge had plunged him back into a black mood.

The old house seemed huge and empty around him, the late afternoon wind rattling the windows. It got dark early now. November. No more daylight savings. North put a log on the fire. The fireplace supposedly was made from stone that Abraham Winter had pulled off the ridge when he carved the main ridge trail, still almost intact, almost two hundred years ago.

Ty felt the flames hot on his face. His mother had never minded living out here, even after he'd gone into the air force and she lived in the big house all alone. She said she was proud of him, but he doubted she really knew what the hell a PJ did.

"I understand you," she used to say. "I understand you completely."

Whether she did or didn't, Ty had no idea, but he had never come close to understanding her. When she died, she'd left him the house and fifty acres, which he'd expected.

A trust fund. He used to make fun of people with trust funds.

For five years, he hadn't touched a dime of it except what he needed to hang on to the house.

He lifted his gaze to the oil painting his mother had done in those solitary years here. It depicted the house and the meadow on an early summer day, daises in bloom. She hadn't put Cold Ridge in it. She'd never said why. As far as he knew, she'd never climbed any of the hundreds of trails in the White Mountains.

He wanted to call Carine. He wanted to be in Boston. Now.

His telephone rang. His hard line. He thought it might be Gus, changing his mind about wanting to shut him out. He got up from the fire and picked up the extension on the wall next to the refrigerator.

"North? It's Carrera." Manny Carrera's normally steady, unflappable voice sounded stressed, tightly controlled. "I've got a problem. I need you here."

"D.C.?"

"Boston."

North didn't let himself react. "Why Boston?"

"I flew up here last night to talk to Sterling Rancourt about Louis Sanborn, his new security hire. By the time I got to Sanborn, he was dead."

"Manny—"

He took a breath. "You've heard."

"Carine just called Gus. I don't have the details. She found this guy shot to death? What happened? Where the hell were you?"

"There. I don't want to get into it now. We both gave statements to the police. They want me to stick around in case they have more questions. Which they will. I figure I don't have long before they slap on the cuffs."

"Cuffs? Manny, you didn't kill this guy—"

"It's not that simple."

North stared out the kitchen window into the darkness. The fire crackled behind him. Manny Carrera had surprised everyone when he retired from active duty in August, but North didn't fault him. Manny had done his bit, and he had different priorities nowadays: a son who'd almost died and a wife who was on edge.

But North wasn't going to coddle him. Manny would hate that. "What's not simple? You either killed him or you didn't kill him."

"I'm not going there with you."

"Then what about Carine?"

"She doesn't know the police have their eye on me. When she finds out—"

"She'll want to spring you."

Carine had always liked Manny Carrera. Everyone did. He'd show up in Cold Ridge from time to time for a little hiking, fishing and snowshoeing. Even Gus liked Manny. The air force tried to tap him as a PJ instructor, but he was determined to retire and go into business for himself. He was in the process of getting a Washington-based outfit off the ground, which trained individuals and companies in a broad range of emergency skills and procedures—not just self-defense and how to treat the injured, but how to think, how to respond in a crisis, *before* a crisis. He wanted his clients trained, prepared, able to help themselves and others if something happened. Ty didn't know how it was going or what kind of businessman Manny would make. Manny Carrera was a hard-ass, but he was fair, scrupulous and, at heart, a natural optimist.

He also had the skills and worldwide connections to disappear before the police got to him—just melt away. If he put his mind to it, he could probably even gnaw his way out of a jail cell.

Except he had a fourteen-year-old son with severe asthma and allergies at the prep school just outside the picturesque village of Cold Ridge.

"What do you want me to do?" Ty asked.

"Make sure Carine doesn't pursue this thing. She knew Louis Sanborn. She liked him. She found him dead. Plus," Manny added pointedly, "she had her life pulled out from under her not that long ago. She's ripe for trouble."

"She's a Winter, Manny. She's always ripe for trouble." What Manny didn't say—what he didn't need to say—was that Ty was the one who'd pulled her life out from under her. "Is she in danger?"

"Five minutes sooner, she'd have walked in on a murder. Anything could have happened. For all I know, it still could. Just keep an eye on her, North. That's all I'm asking."

Ty was silent a moment. "You're not telling me everything."

Manny almost laughed. "Hell, North, I'm not telling

you anything." But any humor faded, and he asked seriously, "You'll do it?"

As if there was a question. "If Gus doesn't let all the air out of my tires before I can get there. If Carine doesn't kill me when I do. I haven't seen her since I left her at the altar." North sighed heavily, feeling the fatigue from his long day. He hadn't quite left her at the altar. At least he'd come to his senses and called off their wedding a full week in advance. It could have been worse, not that anyone else saw it that way. "Manny, Jesus. Murder—what the hell's going on?"

"Looks like Carine and I are shit magnets these days. Jesus. Look, Ty. She found a dead man this afternoon. I should have made sure that didn't happen. I didn't, so now I'm asking you to do what you can to make it right." He groaned to himself. "Ah, screw it. You're on a need-to-know basis. It's the best I can do. Just get down here."

"I'll be there tonight."

Manny hesitated. "I saw the story about the rescue you did today on the news. My son—"

"Eric wasn't involved. He's only a freshman. These guys are seniors."

"Geniuses, from the sounds of it."

"Ivy League material. They've got their applications in. Watch. They'll all be running the show when we're in the home."

"Scary thought. Ty—"

"Forget it. It's okay."

But Manny Carrera said it, anyway. "I know I'm asking a lot. Thanks."

Three

After throwing up for a third time, Carine staggered into her kitchen. She hoped that was the last of it. Nerves, she thought. Fear, disgust, grief, horror. Poor Louis. Dead. Murdered. *Why?*

She found the little bag of oyster crackers the Boston Police Department detective had given her when she'd almost passed out on him. He'd said she looked green. At least she hadn't thrown up then. She'd given her statement, read it, signed it and, when told she could leave, got a cab and came straight back to her apartment. She didn't know what else to do. The Rancourts were with the police. Manny was with the police. And Louis Sanborn was dead, his body transported to wherever the medical examiners performed autopsies.

Her hands trembled, and she couldn't get a good hold on the package of crackers to pull it open. Finally, she grabbed a fork from the strainer and stabbed the cellophane, and little round crackers popped out all over her counter and floor.

"Damn it!"

She picked one up off the floor and nibbled on it,

making herself fill her kettle with water and set it on the stove for tea. It wasn't much of a stove—it wasn't much of an apartment. It was a one-bedroom unit on a narrow, crooked street off Inman Square in Cambridge, an eclectic neighborhood of working-class families, students and professionals. She'd painted the walls and her flea-market furnishings with a mix of mango, lime green, raspberry, various shades of blue and violet, whatever she thought would be cheerful and not remind her of the rich, woodsy colors of her log cabin in Cold Ridge.

The tiny cracker didn't sit well in her stomach. Her mouth was dry. She was wrung out. She'd cried, she'd screamed, she'd barfed. Yep. What a rock she was. But she didn't care. She wasn't embarrassed by her reaction— she didn't ever want to get used to coming upon a murder.

Manny Carrera had called the police by the time she got out to the street. He wouldn't tell her a thing—why he was there, what he saw, nothing. Just that he was consulting for the Rancourts, whatever that meant. Then the police arrived, as well as Sterling and Jodie, their security chief, the media, onlookers. Carine and Manny were separated. He was as self-contained as ever. Definitely a rock.

"Think of it," he'd said in the minutes before the police got there, "if you'd married North, you could be in flea-infested military housing right now."

"Manny… I knew Louis. He—he was shot, wasn't he? Murdered?"

"Carine, something you need to keep in mind."

He hesitated, but she prodded him. "What?"

"Louis Sanborn wasn't a nice man."

He didn't have a chance to elaborate, and she'd repeated his words to the detective when he asked her what she and Manny had talked about.

Louis Sanborn wasn't a nice man.

Manny could have meant anything. It didn't have to be ominous.

She switched off her kettle. Even tea wasn't going to stay down. She wished she hadn't called Gus. Talking to him was comforting on one level, because he was unconditionally on her side, but, on another level, it added to her tension—because he'd wanted to head to Boston. It'd been a near thing to keep him up north. She'd called him for moral support. She needed time to pull herself together. Gus would hover. He'd scowl at her living accommodations. He'd tell her she didn't belong in the city.

He'd make her soup. He'd listen to her for as long as she wanted to talk.

Her doorbell rang, the noise sprouting an instant headache. Carine knew she was dehydrated, her reserves exhausted, but her first-floor apartment didn't have an intercom or buzzer, which meant she had to stagger out to the front hall. Her old tenement building had three floors, with two apartments on each floor and a main door that creaked and stuck half the time, making it easy for people to just walk in.

Her sister gave her an encouraging smile and wave through the smudged glass panel. When Carine pulled open the heavy door, Antonia grimaced and shook her head. "Good God, you look awful."

"Is that what you say to all your ER patients? I've been throwing up."

Antonia felt her sister's forehead, then grabbed her wrist. "No fever. Your pulse is a bit fast. Are you keeping anything down?"

"I just ate an oyster cracker."

"Try a little flat Coke."

"I don't have any."

Carine led her sister back to her apartment, but Antonia's tight frown only worsened when she looked around at the kitchen and the spilled crackers. "Half the rats in Boston live better than you do."

"What? It's a great apartment."

Antonia sighed. She was dressed elegantly in a black top and pants and a pumpkin-colored coat that brought out the softer tones of her auburn hair. It was shorter than Carine's, not as dark. "You can only do so much with paint," she said. "Why don't you go home? Let Gus fuss over you."

"I live here now. Don't you remember your hand-to-mouth years in medical school?"

"That's the point. I was in medical school. You're just—I don't know what you're doing. Marking time." She squatted down and scooped up a handful of the crackers, dumping them in the trash. "You weren't going to eat them off the floor, were you?"

"Antonia—"

Tears welled in her sister's eyes. "I'm sorry. I'm not being very sensitive or helpful. Oh, Carine, I'm so sorry about what happened. I'm supposed to take the shuttle down to Washington tonight. There's some function tomorrow for freshman senators—Hank left this afternoon, before he heard about the murder."

Carine nodded without comment.

"He's tried several times to reach Manny. No luck." Antonia tore open the refrigerator with more force than was required. "Do you have any ginger ale? Carine, what on earth is *that?* It's blue!"

"Oh, that's my Gatorade. I've been trying to do more exercise. It's good for restoring electrolytes, isn't it?"

"I wonder how they get it that shade of blue. Well, drink it if you can keep it down. It'll help with any dehydration. Is there someone who can spend the night here with you? I hate the idea of leaving you alone—"

"I'll be fine." Carine manufactured a weak smile. "Go on and catch your plane, Antonia. I just want to crawl into bed. It wasn't a great day for me, but I'm not the one who was killed. Poor Louis."

"Did you know him well?"

She shook her head. "Just to say hi to."

"What a nightmare. What *is* it about you and the month of November? Well, at least last year no one was killed. Look, if you need me to stay—"

"No! Go be the smart doctor wife to your handsome senator-elect husband. Wow Washington. Thanks for stopping by."

Antonia smiled, but she didn't look reassured. "You really won't eat any crackers off the floor, right?"

"Promise."

"Call my cell phone anytime, day or night. Okay? I can be on the next shuttle back here. Just say the word."

Five minutes after Antonia left, Nate called from New York. He didn't want to hear about crackers and blue Gatorade—he wanted to make sure Carine had told the police absolutely everything and wasn't going to get involved any more than she had to be. She assured him she was being the good soldier.

"Good," he said. "Keep it that way."

Her brother, too, wanted her to go back to Cold Ridge. He'd left their hometown, and Antonia had left, but they both still considered it home, their refuge. Carine, who'd never left, wasn't as nostalgic about it, and she didn't like the idea that she might run into Tyler North.

She promised Nate she'd take care of herself and hung up, pouring herself a glass of Gatorade. She hoped she kept it down, because damned if she wanted to throw up anything blue.

* * *

Ty made the three-hour trip to Boston in under two-and-a-half hours, but lost time in Inman Square and the tangle of five million streets that radiated out from it. He went past a fancy bakery, a hardware store, a lesbian bookstore, several churches, a mosque, service stations, a Portuguese restaurant, a Mexican restaurant, a Moroccan restaurant, a Jewish deli, a Tibetan rug shop and an Irish bar with a shamrock on its sign. He went down the same one-way street twice. Maybe three times. Where the hell was his GPS when he needed it? Never mind satellite navigation—he could have used a damn map.

Finally, he found his way to a crowded street of multifamily homes with pumpkins and mums on their front steps and foldout paper turkeys and Pilgrim hats in their windows. There were a few fake cobwebs strung to fences, left over from Halloween. A couple of strings of orange lights in the shape of little plastic pumpkins. Hank Callahan and Manny Carrera, who'd both been inside Carine's apartment, reported that it was a solid, working-class neighborhood, but her building needed a little work.

Her building was a dump. The porch roof sagged. The steps had holes in them. The whole place needed paint. Outdoor lighting was nonexistent. Tall, frostbitten hollyhocks bent over the walkway—Carine's doing, no doubt. She'd always loved hollyhocks. The neighborhood dogs probably loved them, too.

A pack of boys careered down the dark street on scooters and skateboards. One kid, who couldn't have been more than thirteen, had a cigarette dangling from his mouth. It was just shy of ten o'clock on a school night. North mentally picked out which ones he'd liked to see go through PJ indoc. Pass or fail, they'd get in shape, learn a little something about themselves.

"Live free or die," the boy with the cigarette yelled as he sailed past North's truck with its New Hampshire plates and their Live Free or Die logo. "Yeah, go for it, woodchuck."

That one, he thought. That one he'd liked to see tossed in a pool with his hands and feet tied.

On the other hand, maybe the kid would make a good pararescueman. Stick with it, don't give up, don't drown— it wasn't always easy to tell who'd make it and who'd wash out.

Antonia Winter Callahan, wife of senator-elect Hank Callahan, lifted a swooning hollyhock out of her path, stood on the main sidewalk a moment, then frowned and marched up to Ty's truck. He kept a truck in Florida, too. This was his at-home truck. Rusted, nicely broken in. Recognizable to someone who'd known him most of his life.

He rolled down his window. "Nice night. Warmer down here in the big city."

"I don't believe you, Ty. Gus didn't send you, did he? No, of course he didn't. What was I thinking?" She groaned, her hands clenched at her sides. "God, Ty, you're not what Carine needs right now. She's been sick to her stomach."

"She's never come upon a murder before."

Antonia nodded reluctantly, calmer. "It's awful. She knew the victim, Louis Sanborn. He worked for the Rancourts. Did you know him?"

"No."

Her eyes narrowed. "You heard Manny Carrera was on the scene? He's had a rough year. He—" She broke off, giving a little hiss between clenched teeth. "Ty, don't tell me—did Manny send you? Is that why you're here?"

"Sorry, Dr. Callahan, I'm in the dark as much as you are." He thought that was a diplomatic way to stonewall her. "You looked like you were in a hurry a minute ago."

"I am. I have a plane to catch—damn, I hate this. She says she's fine. You know Carine. She's resilient, but she's also proud and stubborn, sensitive about being sensitive. Ty, I swear to you, if you do anything, and I mean *anything,* to make matters worse for her, I will find you and inject you with something that'll sting parts that you don't want stinging. Do I make myself clear?"

He leaned back in his seat. "You bet, Doc."

She hissed again, disgusted with him. "The jackass fairy must have visited you every night when you were a kid," she snapped. "Some days I don't know how you stand yourself."

"I'm a disciplined military man."

She straightened, glancing back at her sister's apartment. No foldout turkeys. No Pilgrim hats. Carine's life here seemed temporary, something she was trying on for size. An escape. When Antonia turned back to him, Ty thought she looked strained and worried. "Promise me," she said seriously, in an exhausted near whisper. "You'll be good?"

"Relax, Antonia." He smiled at her. "I'll be very good."

"You're not going in there tonight, are you?"

He shook his head. "I'll give her some time. Besides, I hate barf."

"Yeah, right, with all you've seen in your career?" She started to say something, then just heaved a long sigh. "I'm trusting you."

It was progress, Ty thought. A Winter hadn't trusted him in months.

Antonia climbed into a taxi that had been idling farther down the street, and Ty watched it negotiate the crooked street, the oversize cars parked in too-small spaces, the potholes, the kids on skateboards.

He'd never had a thing for Antonia. It was always Carine.

Always and forever.

Four

Val Carrera learned about Louis Sanborn's murder when she flipped through the *Washington Post* over her morning coffee, and it pissed her off. A man was dead, and her husband hadn't bothered to tell her he was involved. He was in Boston. It wasn't like he was on a secret military mission. He could have called her.

But here she was, once again, on a need-to-know basis, with Manny Carrera deciding what she needed to know and her having to live with it.

Bastard.

The details in the article were sketchy. It said photographer Carine Winter found the body when she got back from her lunch break. It said the Rancourts had hired Manny to analyze their personal security needs and make recommendations, and, most important, to train them and their employees—of which Louis Sanborn was one—in the basics of emergency medicine and survival in various types of environments and conditions. After their scare in the White Mountains last fall, the Rancourts said, they wanted to be more self-reliant.

"What a crock," Val muttered over her paper. "Damn phonies."

She hadn't liked the Rancourts since Manny had pulled them off Cold Ridge on a weekend he was supposed to be resting, having a good time. Sterling—who'd name a kid Sterling?—and Jodie Rancourt had donned expensive parkas and boots and trekked up the ridge, never mind that they didn't know what in hell they were doing. They got a dose of high winds, cold temperatures and slippery rocks and damn near died up there.

"They should be Popsicles," Val grumbled.

Instead it was Hank Callahan and the PJs to the rescue, although Val was of the opinion that someone else could have done the job. But that wasn't the way it was with Manny, North or Callahan, not when they were right there and could do something.

Now the Rancourts were returning the favor, helping Manny establish his credentials in their world. And the big dope fell for it. He didn't see that they were ingratiating themselves—he didn't see that he should have stayed in the air force, teaching a new generation of young men how to be pararescuemen.

But Manny hadn't listened to her in months, and, depending on her mood, Val didn't blame him.

She sank back in her chair at her small, round table in what passed for an eating area. The kitchen wasn't much bigger than a closet, and the bedroom was just big enough for a double bed and a bureau. She hadn't slept *that* close to Manny in years. Fortunately, she was a petite woman herself—black-haired, brown-eyed and, at thirty-eight, still with a good future ahead of her. If she stopped screwing up her life.

The living room was kind of cute—it had a large paned window shaded by a gorgeous oak tree, its leaves a rich burgundy color now that it was November. A one-bedroom apartment on a noisy street in Arlington was the best she and Manny could find—and afford—on short notice. At least it was clean and bug-free. If he made a go of his business and they decided to stay in the Washington area, they'd start looking for a house.

Their son was doing well, and she was off antidepressants.

Remember your priorities, she told herself.

She folded up the paper and called Manny on his cell phone, getting his voice mail. "Hi, it's me. I heard about what happened. Sounds hideous. Call me when you can and let me know you're all right."

There. That was nice. She hadn't yelled anything about being his wife and having a goddamned *right* to know. For all she knew, he could be in jail.

She doubted he'd call back. He'd given her six months to get her shit together. He'd stick it out with her until then. If she stayed on her current track, he was gone. That was five months ago, and she was doing better. Manny was the same. He was a bossy, stubborn SOB and refused to recognize his own stress reaction to the utterly crappy time they'd had of it lately, but Val couldn't control what he did—she'd finally figured that one out after months in psychotherapy. Twenty years of sleeping with him hadn't quite done it.

But Manny wasn't responsible for the allergies and asthma that had come so close—so very close—to taking their son's life. Neither was she, but that had taken more months of therapy to sort out, because she'd wanted someone to blame. Otherwise—why? What was the point of a thirteen-year-old boy almost dying from eating a damn peanut? Coughing and choking just trying to breathe?

She didn't want her son having to struggle for the rest of his life with a chronic illness. She wanted her son to have a chance to be a PJ like his dad if that was what he chose.

She wanted the Manny Carrera she'd married back—smart, funny, sexy, self-aware.

And she wanted herself back, the tough Val, the Val who didn't take shit from anyone.

But Manny was struggling, although he wouldn't admit it, and she was struggling, and Eric would never be a PJ, his choices limited by asthma and allergies so severe he had to wear a Medic Alert bracelet and carry an inhaler and a dose of epinephrine wherever he went. He was on daily doses of four different medications. Even with the promise of new treatments and desensitization shots, he'd never be accepted into PJ indoc—it just wasn't going to happen.

None of it was anyone's fault. It just was.

And Eric was doing fine, with a long, good life ahead of him. He would say to her—"Mom, Dad could never be a ballet dancer or a calculus teacher. That's okay, right? Then it's okay that I can't be a PJ."

Val debated calling him at his prep school in Cold Ridge, but decided Manny should be the one to talk to their son about whatever had gone on in Boston. Whatever was still going on. It wasn't easy having Eric away at school, but it was what he wanted—and, after weeks fighting it, she could see it was what he needed at least right now. Between a scholarship and scraping together what they had, she and Manny were managing the tuition. *Just* managing.

She'd been such a trouper through those early days of diagnosis and treatment. Supermom. She'd done it all. Manny's work was demanding, his paycheck not optional. When Eric went into anaphylactic shock the first time, last spring, Manny's paramedic skills had saved his life. But he wasn't around for all the late-night asthma attacks, the trips to the emergency room, the ups and downs as Eric's illness got sorted out and brought under control. Val quit her job as a bookstore manager and devoted herself one-hundred percent to restoring her son's health.

But even when Eric was on his feet, she didn't back off and return to her job at the bookstore near the base where Manny was stationed. She became a total nutcase, a control freak, suffocating Eric—suffocating herself. And Manny. He was caught in the cross fire.

Not that he'd done anything to help the situation. He was oblivious, content to let her handle all the details, the doctors, Eric's volatile emotions—do it all, until it started affecting him.

Last fall in Cold Ridge hadn't helped matters. Manny had put everything on the line to sneak around in the woods after Carine Winter was shot at, then traipsed after a couple of rich people in trouble—Val knew he was just doing what he did, but what about her? Why the hell couldn't he be there for her?

That was when she'd started on antidepressants. Manny dug in, finally threatening to kick her butt out the door if she didn't get her act together.

She smiled ruefully to herself and folded up the newspaper. Well, that was her version of events, anyway.

Manny would say he'd been at his wit's end with her inability to rebound and had enough to cope with himself. He'd say he understood perfectly well that depression was an illness—that wasn't what bugged him. He'd say he'd done the best he could. She supposed it was true—they'd all done their best. Anger, blame, fear and exhaustion weren't a good mix. On a good day, sparks tended to fly between the two of them. They liked it that way—it worked for them. But they hadn't had very many good days since their son had nearly died.

Now the *ass* had retired and moved her to Washington, D.C., so he could play around with rich guys like Sterling Rancourt, and what did he get for his trouble? A dead guy at his feet, the police on his case.

Val groaned to herself, heading to the bedroom to get dressed. "No wonder Eric wanted to go to school in New Hampshire. Get away from his parents."

Ten minutes later, she was standing on the sidewalk in front of her building as Hank Callahan pulled up. She jumped into his pricey rented car and grinned at him. "What, no police escort? I expected something a little fancier now that you're a senator."

"Senator-elect," he corrected. He was in a subdued gray suit with a pale blue tie, as handsome as ever. "Thanks for getting up early to join us. Antonia'll meet us at the restaurant."

"Are you *sure* you want to hire me, Major Callahan?"

He smiled. "Just Hank is fine, Val. When did you ever stand on ceremony?"

"Senators scare me even more than majors do. All that pomp and circumstance."

"You've never been intimidated by anyone or anything."

She tried to smile but couldn't. "I should have been an astronaut like my mother wanted." Both her parents had worked for NASA; they were retired now in Houston. "I got to pick what I wanted to be. I'm lucky that way. Hank—I don't know. I've worked in bookstores for the last ten years. For most of the past year, I've been a nutcase."

"I haven't changed my mind. Neither has Antonia. The job's still yours, if you want it."

Joining the staff of a United States senator—Val loved

the idea, although maybe not as much as having her own bookstore. "I didn't vote for you. I'm not a Massachusetts resident. I didn't even know the Callahans were a hot-shit Massachusetts family until your wedding last month."

Hank pulled out onto the street, and two stoplights later, Val realized he wasn't going to mention Manny's situation. He was too polite. She'd have to do it. "Hank, you know about Carine and Manny, don't you? What happened yesterday at the Rancourts' house in Boston? And Antonia? She knows, right?"

He nodded but kept his gaze pinned on the road. "Antonia almost stayed in Boston last night. She stopped by to see Carine. I gather she's in rough shape."

Val winced. "I can imagine."

"Have you talked to Manny?"

"Are you kidding? I had to read about his goings-on in the morning paper. Do you know anything about this Louis Sanborn, the man who was killed?"

"Just what you know from the paper."

"I don't understand why the Rancourts hired Manny if they already had this guy Sanborn and the other guy, the one who hired him—"

"Gary Turner," Hank supplied.

"Right. So, what, are the Rancourts paranoid? Are they afraid of something? I don't get it. Why do they need Manny to teach them how to tie off a bleeder? Jesus, call 911 like the rest of us." Val tried to stifle a sudden pang of fear, recognized it as her habitual anxiety reaction to everything these days—fear, foreboding, a palpable sense of gloom. "Hank, do you think something's going on with the Rancourts that Manny doesn't know about? What if they're holding something back?"

Hank shrugged, no sign he was experiencing the same kind of apprehension she was. "I haven't heard of anything. I think they just like hanging around people who do this kind of work."

"Manny's not hired muscle. He—"

"I know, Val. Manny's one of the best at what he does."

"He's demeaning himself, working for those phonies. He should be training new PJs," she said half under her breath, then sighed. "Just what Manny needed, a couple of wannabe types sucking him in. What the hell's the matter with him?"

"Val."

She glanced over at the pilot-turned-senator, the man whose skill and quick thinking as a Pave Hawk pilot had saved more than one life in his air force career. He said he wanted to work toward the common good as a senator. Hank Callahan had steel nerves and a kind heart, but right now, Val could sense his uneasiness. "What is it, Hank?"

"Manny should call you—"

"Manny's not going to call me. He won't want me to worry."

Hank sighed. "Val, the police think he's their man. You need to prepare yourself if he's arrested."

She couldn't take in his words. "What?"

Hank said nothing.

She absorbed what he'd said, then made herself stop, breathe and think, not let her first physical reaction get out of control, suck her in to the point where she couldn't function. It was as if all her nerve endings had been rubbed raw by the months of stress over Eric, how close she'd come to losing her son—and now that he was okay, she could let her emotions run wild. She had to work to keep them in bounds.

There was no way Manny had committed murder. He was a lot of things, but not a murderer. If the police thought they had their man, they were wrong.

It was that simple.

She glanced over at Hank. "Are you reading the tea leaves, or do you know?"

"I know."

He was a senator, and he was a Callahan. He knew everyone, had contacts everywhere. If he said he knew, he knew. "Carine Winter?"

"Innocent bystander."

"Manny—should he get a lawyer?"

"He has one."

Val sank back in her seat, her coffee crawling up her throat. Manny Carrera was her husband. He was in Boston facing a possible murder charge. So much had happened, and all she knew, she'd learned from the newspaper and her friend the senator-elect from Massachusetts.

That *bastard*.

She cleared her throat, summoning her last shreds of dignity. "Thank you for telling me."

"Val—"

"Manny's a big boy. He can take care of himself. If he needs me, he'll be in touch." She stared out her window and saw that they were on one of the prettier streets of Arlington now, the last of the autumn leaves glowing yellow in the morning sun. "Let's go see your beautiful bride and have breakfast. I'm starving."

Five

❧❧❧

Carine tried sleeping late, but that didn't work, and she finally got up and made herself a bowl of instant oatmeal that tasted more like instant slime. She downed a few spoonfuls, then drank a mug of heavily sugared tea while she pulled on her running clothes. When she didn't pass out doing her warm-up routine, she decided she might be good for her run.

She did a quarter mile of her one-and-a-half-mile route before she collapsed against a lamppost, kicking it with her heel in disgust. A quarter mile? Pathetic. She was determined to do one-and-a-half miles in under ten minutes and thirty seconds. It wasn't the distance that got to her— she could run ten miles—it was the time, the speed. But running a mile and a half in ten-and-a-half minutes or less was one of the fitness requirements for the PJ Physical Abilities and Stamina Test, which, if passed, led to a shot at indoctrination. She'd pulled the PAST off the Internet.

Of course, she was a woman, and women didn't get to be pararescuemen. But she didn't want to be a PJ—she just wanted to pass the initial fitness test. It was the challenge that drove her. The test included the run, plus swimming twenty-five meters underwater on one breath—she'd damn near drowned the first time she tried that one. Then there was swimming one thousand meters in twenty-six minutes…doing eight chin-ups in a minute…fifty sit-ups in two minutes…fifty push-ups in two minutes…fifty flutter kicks in two minutes. Technically, she was supposed to do the exercises one after another, all within three hours, but she had to cut herself some slack. She was thirty-three, not twenty.

Normally, it was the swimming that killed her. And she hated flutter kicks. Who'd invented flutter kicks? They were torture. But this morning, after yesterday's shock, she suspected everything on the list would do her in.

She decided to be satisfied she'd been able to keep down her oatmeal.

She trudged back to her apartment, pausing to do a few calf stretches on her porch before heading inside to shower and change clothes. She made short work of it—jeans, sweater, barn coat, ankle boots, camera bag. She doubted she'd be taking any pictures today, but she wanted to go back to the Rancourt house. Provided the police no longer had it marked off as a crime scene, she thought it might help her to see the library again, although it wouldn't, she knew, erase the memory of Louis. After the incident last fall, she'd returned to the boulder on the hillside and touched the places where the bullets had hit. *Real* bullets. No wonder she'd been scared. Going back had helped her incorporate what had happened into her experience, accept the reality of it and find a place for it in her memories so it didn't float around, popping up unexpectedly, inappropriately.

But she'd had Ty with her that day.

She'd parked her car, an ancient Subaru Outback sedan, down the street. She'd gone to the trouble of changing her plates from New Hampshire to Massachusetts and getting a new license, just so she could get a Cambridge resident's sticker—otherwise, parking was a nightmare. But she didn't like driving into Boston and took public transportation whenever she could, picking up the Red Line in Central Square, which was a fifteen-minute walk from her apartment. It could be her exercise for the day.

She stopped at a bakery for a cranberry scone and more tea. Her mind was racing with questions and images, but she pushed them back and tried to focus on her scone, her tea, the brisk morning and the other people on the streets. Kids, workers, bag ladies, students. She passed a nursery school class of three- and four-year-olds hanging on to a rope to keep them together, their young teacher skipping along in front of them like the Pied Piper. The kids were laughing, making Carine smile.

She got a seat on a subway car and shut her eyes briefly, letting the rhythms of the rapid-transit line soothe her as the train sped over the Charles River, then back underground. She got off at the Charles Street stop and walked, peeking in the shop windows on the pretty street at the base of Beacon Hill, giving a wistful glance at the corn stalks and pumpkins in front of an upscale flower shop. They reminded her of home.

When she turned down Beacon Street and her cell phone rang, she almost didn't answer it, then decided if it was Gus and she ignored him, she risked having him send in the National Guard. She hit the receive button and made herself smile, hoping that'd take any lingering strain out of her voice when she said hello.

Gus grunted. "Where are you?"

"Just past the corner of Beacon and Charles."

"Boston?"

"That's right," she said. "What's up, Gus? How's the weather in Cold Ridge?"

"Gray. Why aren't you home with your feet up?"

"I'm on my way to the Rancourt house. I want to see—"

"Carine, for chrissake, they can't possibly need you today. Why don't you drive up here for the weekend? Or jump on the train and go visit your brother or your sister for a couple days. They'd love to have you."

"I'm fine, Gus. I've been thinking about it, and I just need to go back there."

"For what, closure? Give me a break." But he sighed, and Carine could almost see him in his rustic village shop, amid his canoes and kayaks, his snowshoes and cross-country skis, his trail maps and compasses and high-end hiking clothes and equipment. "The police haven't arrested anyone for this guy's murder. You know what that means, don't you? It means whoever did it is still on the streets."

"I'll be careful. Besides, the police and reporters are still bound to be there—and if not them, the Rancourts, their security chief—it'll be okay."

"You thought it'd be okay yesterday before you walked into the library, didn't you?"

"Gus—"

"Yeah. Yeah, I know. Nothing I can do. But I don't have to like it."

She heard something in his voice and slowed her pace. "Gus? What?"

"Nothing. Take care of yourself. You even *think* something's wrong, you call the police, okay?"

"Believe me, I will."

She clicked off, feeling vaguely uneasy. Gus was holding back on her. It wasn't like him. Normally he was a straight shooter. He had warned her about getting mixed up with Tyler North, when it was obvious their long tolerance for each other had sparked into something else. Her uncle said his piece, then shut up about it. When Ty dumped her a week before the wedding, Gus'd had the moderate grace not to actually say the words "I told you so." But he didn't need to—he *had* told her so, in no uncertain terms.

What wasn't he telling her now?

When she reached the stately mansion on Commonwealth Avenue, Carine could feel her scone and tea churning in her stomach. The police cars and yellow crime-scene tape were gone, and she didn't see any obvious sign of reporters. She mounted the steps and noticed the yellow mums were gone, too.

Sterling Rancourt opened the front door before she knocked. He was a tall, silver-haired man in his early fifties, and even the day after a man was murdered on his property, he radiated wealth and confidence. He was raised on the South Shore, where he and his wife owned their main home, and had gone to Dartmouth and Wharton, taking over his family's holdings in business and real estate twenty years ago. He was dressed casually and looked only slightly tired, perhaps a little pale—and awkward at seeing her. Carine thought she understood. He'd tried to do her a good deed by hiring her to photograph his house renovations, and she'd ended up discovering a dead body.

She mumbled a good morning, feeling somewhat awkward herself.

"How are you doing, Carine?" he asked. "Yesterday was a nightmare for all of us, but for you, especially."

"I'm doing okay, thanks." Suddenly she wondered if she should have come at all. "I guess I didn't know what to do with myself this morning."

He acknowledged her words with a small nod. "I expect we all feel that way. We won't get back to work here until next week at the earliest. Why don't you take a few days off? Go for walks, visit museums, take pictures of pumpkins—anything to get your mind off what happened yesterday."

Carine leaned against the wrought-iron rail. He hadn't invited her in, but she thought it would seem ghoulish and intrusive to ask outright if she could see the library, even if it was the reason she was here. "That's probably a good idea. I thought—look at me. I brought my digital camera. I don't know what I was thinking."

"It's all right. We're all struggling today. I'm not quite sure what I'm doing here myself. You're a photographer. Having your camera must help you feel like it's a normal day."

"Louis—his family—"

"Everything's being handled, Carine."

She suddenly felt nosy, as if she'd overstepped her bounds. "Have you talked to Manny Carrera? Do you know where he is?"

"Carine—perhaps it's best if you go home." Sterling's voice was gentle, concerned, but there was no mistaking that he wanted to be rid of her. "The police know how to get in touch with you if they want to speak with you again, don't they?"

"Of course—"

Gary Turner, Sterling's security chief, appeared in the doorway next to his boss. He nodded at her. "Good morning, Carine," he said politely. "It's nice to see you, as always. The two lead detectives will be back later this morning. I'll tell them you stopped by."

Dismissed, Carine thought, but without rancor. Sterling was just as on edge as she was, neither of them accustomed to dealing with this sort of emergency. But Gary

Turner radiated calm and competence, a steady efficiency, that she found reassuring. He was a strange guy. The Rancourts hired him in the spring, and she'd met him in Cold Ridge a few times before she went to work for them herself. She didn't understand exactly what he did, or what Manny Carrera was supposed to be doing, for that matter.

She was aware of Turner studying her, an unsettling experience, not just because he was so focused—he looked as if he'd lived most of his life underwater, or maybe in an attic. He had close-cropped, very thin white hair. He might have been in his eighties instead of, at most, his forties. His skin was an odd-looking pinkish-white, its paleness exaggerated by his habitual all-black attire. He had no eyebrows to speak of, and his eyes were a watery, almost colorless gray. He was missing his middle and ring fingers on his left hand. Carine knew he carried a concealed nine-millimeter pistol and assumed he could fire it, but she'd never asked.

"How are you doing?" Turner asked softly. "I'm sorry I didn't get a chance to talk to you yesterday."

"You were busy, and I'm doing fine. Thanks for asking. Look, I'm sure you both have a lot to do. I won't keep you—"

Turner stepped out onto the stoop with her. "You've experienced a trauma. Finding Louis yesterday was a physical and mental shock, a blow on multiple levels to your well-being. Perhaps you'd like for me to arrange for you to talk to someone?"

She shook her head politely. "There's no need to go to any trouble. I can always ask my sister for a recommendation, if it comes to it."

"Give yourself some time. It'll be hard for a while, but if after a few weeks you experience flashbacks, nightmares, sleeplessness, feelings of panic or emotional numbness—then don't wait, okay? Go see someone."

"I will. Manny Carrera—I'm worried about him—"

"That's understandable," Turner said mildly, then glanced back at Rancourt, who seemed paralyzed in the doorway. "I'll walk with Carine a minute."

"Of course. I'll see you back here later." Rancourt rallied, taking a breath. "Carine? If there's anything Jodie and I can do, please don't hesitate to let us know. I mean that. I'm so very sorry it had to be you yesterday."

"Thanks," she said. "I'm just sorry about Louis."

"The media—" Sterling paused and leaned forward to glance down the street, as if he expected someone to pop up out of nowhere. "I'd like you not to speak to any reporters. It's quiet at the moment, but they'll be back. Be polite, but be firm."

"Not a problem. The last thing I want to do is talk to a reporter."

He withdrew without further comment, the heavy door shutting with a loud thud behind him.

Gary Turner walked down to the sidewalk without a word, and Carine followed him, her knees steadier, her stomach still rebelling. "I shouldn't have come," she blurted. "I have no business being here. There's nothing for me to do, and you and the Rancourts must have your plates full."

"You thought it would help you to revisit the scene," Turner said.

"I suppose I did." They crossed Commonwealth to the mall, where a half-dozen pigeons had gathered on dried, fallen leaves. There was no toddler today. Carine felt none of yesterday's sense of peace with her life in Boston. "I'm not sure I really know what I was thinking."

"You're fighting for some sense of normalcy." Turner

spoke with assurance, as if he knew, then fastened his colorless eyes on her. "Did you drive?"

"I took the T to Charles Street and walked."

"Walking's good. Keep it up. And eat right. Don't overdo anything. It's good to try to follow your normal routines as much as possible, even if you're not working." He smiled at her, seeming to want to help her relax. "Fortunately, your work lends itself to an erratic schedule—you're used to switching from one job to another. It's not like you've been getting up every day for the seven-to-three shift at the factory and suddenly there's no factory."

"That's true. I appreciate the advice, but please don't worry about me."

He paused, folding his hands behind his back as he walked smoothly, steadily. "But people do worry about you, Carine," he said finally. "I expect they can't help it, and you might benefit from their attention. Don't try to control what other people are feeling. Right now, just focus on what you need. The rest of us will manage."

"Mr. Turner—"

"Gary." He laughed, shaking his head. "You call Sterling Rancourt by his first name, but me—"

She tried to return his laugh. "I think it's because you carry a gun."

"Ah. Well, for you, Carine, I'd take it off, if it would make you feel more at ease."

"That's not necessary." She picked up her pace, feeling a fresh surge of awkwardness. She never knew what to say to him. She changed the subject. "I've known Manny Carrera for a long time. Do the police suspect him of being involved in Louis's death? Because it's not possible—"

"The police don't tell me what they think. One step at a time, Carine. Keep your focus on the here and now. Don't think back, don't think ahead. It's the best advice I can

give you. Mr. Carrera is perfectly capable of taking care
of himself." Turner stood back a moment, then frowned
at her in a way she found faintly patronizing. "You aren't
thinking of playing amateur detective, are you?"

"No! It's just that Manny's a friend. Do you know
where he's staying?"

"If I did, I wouldn't tell you." There was no hint of con-
demnation in Turner's tone. "Take yourself out to lunch,
Carine. Treat yourself to dessert. Browse the galleries on
Newbury Street. Do you have a friend who can join you?"

"Most of my friends are working, but—"

"Your sister?"

"She's in Washington. She'd come if I called her."

He looked at her. "But you won't. You're a strong
woman, Carine. Stronger, I think, than people often realize at first."

Hey, Ms. Photographer.

Poor Louis. Dead. She still could see the blood on his
fingers.

Louis Sanborn was not a nice man.

Manny, clear-eyed and uncompromising. What did he
know about Louis?

Carine swallowed hard, pushing back the memories of
yesterday. Turner was right—she needed to stay focused
on the present. "To be honest, I don't worry about whether
or not people think I'm strong. Louis stopped me on my
way back from lunch and asked if I wanted a ride. If—"

"Don't. No ifs. They'll drive you crazy." Turner
squeezed her upper arm. "Take it easy on yourself, okay?
Go take some pretty pictures. You didn't do anything
wrong yesterday. Remember that."

She blinked back sudden tears, feeling light-headed,
her stomach not so much nauseated as hurting. "Thanks."

Her voice faltered, and she cleared her throat, annoyed with herself. "I just need some time, I guess."

"Newbury Street. Art galleries." He started across Commonwealth, pausing halfway into the lane of oncoming traffic and shaking his head at her. "You might want to hold off on the dessert. You're looking a little green."

She managed a smile. "It wouldn't be a good idea to get sick on Newbury Street, would it?"

He chuckled. "You'd be banned for life."

Sterling Rancourt stared into the library, its wood floor still marred by crime-scene chalk and dried blood. The police forensics team had done its work, and a cleaning crew that specialized in ridding all trace of this sort of mess was due in that afternoon. Gary Turner had arranged for it. He'd been incredibly helpful—steady, knowledgeable, even kind.

Gary was in his office in the Rancourt building in Copley Square at the time of the shooting, while Sterling was enduring an interminable business lunch a few blocks over at the Ritz-Carlton Hotel. Afterward, he'd planned to meet his wife at a designer showroom on Newbury Street, so she could model an evening gown she wanted to wear to a charity ball over the holidays. She liked having his approval. Ten years ago, she'd bought a dress he didn't like, and he'd been stupid enough to say so—now she insisted on these modeling sessions for anything that cost more than a thousand dollars.

But he'd received the news about Louis at lunch and excused himself, heading straight over to Commonwealth Avenue, calling first Jodie, who was on Newbury Street, then Turner. They all met at the house, where police and reporters were already swarming. Detectives quickly pulled aside Carine Winter, white-faced but functioning, and Manny Carrera, as stalwart as ever. Sterling was unable to speak to either of them alone.

Jodie had remained at their South Shore home this morning. She said she didn't want to see or speak to anyone unless she had to—as far as she was concerned, if the police wanted to interview her again, they could drive down to Hingham and find her.

She knew nothing, Sterling thought. None of them did. Louis Sanborn had been in their lives for two weeks. That was it.

Manny Carrera couldn't have killed him. Manny saved lives. He only took a life when he came under enemy fire and had no other choice. Sterling had read up on PJs and their heroic work, although Manny and Tyler North would be the last to call what they did heroic. It wasn't false humility—Sterling would have recognized it if it were.

He and Jodie owed Manny Carrera *their* lives. But if the police wanted to waste their time pursuing him, that was their choice. There was nothing Sterling or anyone else could do.

"Mr. Rancourt?"

Gary Turner walked down the hall, his nearly colorless eyes and extremely pale skin disconcerting, off-putting even before anyone had gotten to the point of noticing the missing fingers. But he was quiet and supremely competent, and Sterling knew better than to underestimate him because of his strange appearance. Jodie said she found him fascinating, even sexy in a weird way. He wasn't ex-military or ex-law enforcement—Sterling suspected he was ex-CIA. Whatever the case, his credentials in private and corporate security had checked out. He hadn't said a word when Sterling hired Manny Carrera as a consultant. Either he was too self-disciplined to criticize his employer's decision, or he approved. Sterling hadn't asked him his opinion.

"Carine's on her way?"

Turner nodded. "She doesn't know what to do with herself."

"A shock reaction. She'll rally. It just might take a little more time than she wants it to. I've met her brother and sister—and her uncle—and they're all strong, resilient people."

But he could tell concern over Carine Winter wasn't why Turner was here. The man shifted slightly, lowering his voice although there was no one within earshot. "There's been a new development. Tyler North is in town. I just saw his truck on Comm. Ave."

"Tyler? Interesting." Sterling didn't share Turner's sense of drama over this news. Of course Tyler would be here if was able to. He'd known Carine since childhood and had almost married her in February, and Manny was a friend. They'd gone on missions together. "He must be on leave—he'll have heard about Manny's predicament. Word like that travels like wildfire."

"I don't think he's here because of Mr. Carrera. Not directly."

Sterling nodded, sighing. "Of course. Carine." He pictured Tyler North, a compact, rugged man, incredibly loyal despite being something of a loner himself. "Well, she won't like it, but I suppose having him here will be a distraction for her."

"What do you want me to do?" Turner asked.

"About Tyler?"

Sterling thought a moment. He hated the situation he was in, how out of control it felt. Boston's best homicide detectives were on the case, but he wasn't involved— they didn't answer to him. A man, an employee, had been found murdered in a house he owned. Everything about him and his life was fair game. Yet the murderer was probably a drifter, a petty thief or a drug addict, who'd wandered in after Louis stupidly left the door open and, for reasons that might never be known, decided to shoot him.

The police had no motive, no murder weapon, no suspect in custody. Until they did, Sterling thought, he and Jodie, Gary Turner, Carine Winter, Manny Carrera—none of them would have much room to maneuver.

"Tyler's a friend," he told Turner. "Do nothing."

Six

Boston Public Garden, which dated back to 1859, was one of Carine's favorite places in the city. Its curving Victorian paths, lawns, gardens, statues, benches and more than six hundred trees were enclosed within arched, wrought-iron fences, making it feel like a retreat, as if she'd stepped back in time.

If only she could step back to yesterday morning, she thought. She could warn Louis not to go back to the Rancourt house alone—delay him, get in the car with him, talk him into watching the pigeons with her.

She crossed the small bridge over the shallow pond where the famed Swan Boats, a century-plus tradition, would cruise during warmer months. They were put away for the season, and now just fallen leaves floated on the water. But she didn't linger, instead took a walkway over to Tremont Street and the Four Seasons Hotel. When the Rancourts had people in town on business, they tended to put them up at the Four Seasons. Manny Carrera couldn't afford it on his own. Neither could she, but if she wasn't paying the tab, she'd stay there. Maybe Manny would, too.

She entered the elegant lobby and wandered over to a seating area that looked across Tremont to the Public

Garden, its soft sofas and high-backed chairs occupied by a handful of well-dressed men and women in business attire. Carine felt out of place in her barn coat but didn't worry about it—she didn't plan to stay.

She spotted Manny on a love seat in front of a window as he drank coffee from a delicate china cup. He wore a dark suit with a blue tie and motioned for her to join him, shaking his head as she sat on a chair opposite him. "I saw you beating a path across the park. Got a brainstorm I was here?"

"It's not a park. You're not supposed to walk on the grass."

"Then what is it?"

"A public botanical garden. It was designed by Frederick Olmsted. He did Central Park, too, which *is* a park."

"Ah."

She leaned forward. "Manny—"

"I'm stuck here, Carine. You're not. Why don't you go home?"

"I am home. I live in Boston now."

"*For* now, you mean."

"Why are you stuck here? Did the police say you can't leave? You're not under arrest or you wouldn't be here."

He shrugged, not answering. He had broad shoulders, a thick neck—his suit was tight around his upper arms and thighs. He was six feet tall and strongly built. Carine doubted the PJ Physical Abilities and Stamina Test had given him any trouble. He and Ty both insisted a pararescueman didn't have to be big, but Manny was one who was.

"Manny, I'm not trying to interfere in your business. I just—" She sighed, uncertain how she could explain why she was here. "We both were there yesterday. I guess I just wanted to see you. I'm not having an easy time of it, and I thought—I don't know what I thought."

His dark eyes warmed slightly. "The police want to talk to me again today. I'm cooperating. If I don't, they'll probably find a reason to throw me in jail sooner rather than later."

"Why at all?"

"They have to do their thing." He leaned over to refill his coffee cup from a silver service set on the low table in front of him. "You know what's good about staying at a fancy place? You can pick out the cops. They fit in about as well as I do."

"There's a police officer here?"

"I'm under surveillance. I think it's supposed to be covert."

"Manny!" Carine found herself glancing around at the occupied seats, noticing an older couple, a middle-aged man reading a *Wall Street Journal,* a young woman tapping at a PalmPilot. "The woman?"

"Uh-huh."

"Manny, doesn't this bother you? Having the police waste their time on you, when you know you had nothing to do with Louis's death?"

He sipped his coffee. "Getting bothered isn't going to change anything."

"So, what're you going to do, sit here and do *nothing?*"

"Sure, why not? Enjoy the fancy digs while I can. Rancourt hasn't told me to clear out yet. So long as he's footing the bill, I can—"

"You can what, drink coffee out of a silver pot?"

His eyes didn't leave her. "I have to tell you, drinking coffee out of a silver pot suits me just fine."

She immediately regretted her words. Manny wouldn't bring it up, but he and North had been in Afghanistan and

Iraq. Manny's last mission before he retired was to recover an aircrew killed in a training accident. "I'm sorry. I didn't mean—"

"Actually," he added with a hint of a smile, lifting his pinkie finger from the too-small handle of his cup, "I'm drinking out of a china cup, not a silver pot."

Carine didn't know what to say. She could feel tension and frustration eating away at any calm she'd found during her walk in the Public Garden. "What can I do to help?"

"Nothing. Go back to Cold Ridge." He looked at her over the rim of his cup, his dark eyes unrelenting. "For all you know, I could be guilty. I could have killed Louis Sanborn."

"You had no motive."

He was motionless for a split second. "I had motive."

"What?" She lowered her voice, aware of the cop and her PalmPilot. "Manny, what are you talking about?"

"Why do you suppose the police have me under surveillance but not you? Come on, Carine. You don't know what I was doing at the Rancourt house yesterday."

She sat back, irritated with him for playing games with her. "I don't care. I don't care if you didn't think Louis was a nice guy or what you're doing in Boston, it's impossible—Manny, I'm your friend. I know you didn't kill him."

"You're my friend's ex-fiancée. That's a little different."

Carine's mouth snapped shut, and she stared at him. He'd obviously meant to sting her, and he'd succeeded. "All right. Why tell me Louis wasn't a nice man?"

"Because he wasn't."

"That's not an answer."

"I thought it'd be enough to scare you into going home. A minute ago I thought telling you I'm under police surveillance would scare you into going home. Now I'm telling you I had a motive—"

"Stop saying that!"

"Listen to me, Carine." He set down his cup again. "I don't need your help."

"You're being an ass just to get rid of me."

He smiled faintly. "It's not working very well, is it?"

"What about Ty? Have you talked to him? He'd help you. You know he would."

"Ty's on a mission, not that I'd ask him for his help. He's still on active duty. He doesn't need to get mixed up in a murder investigation." Manny sat back, studying her for a moment. "That's what this is, Carine. A murder investigation. A man was killed yesterday. You need to back off."

"Yes," she said, "I'm well aware a man was killed."

His expression softened. "I'm sorry. I haven't forgotten you were the one who found him. How're you doing?"

"Okay."

"Sleep last night?"

"Not much."

He winked at her. "Now you're looking for trouble to distract yourself, aren't you? I know it's hard to figure what to do after something like yesterday."

"It was hard enough getting shot at last year. This—"

"Give yourself some time. And don't worry about me, will you? I'll be fine. If I need help…" He shrugged, deliberately not finishing.

"If you need help, you won't turn to a nature photographer, not with all the tough types you know." She gave him a quick smile and got to her feet. "Just stating the facts, not putting myself down. You're not going to tell me anything, are you?"

"The police asked me not to talk to anyone."

"Right. Like you needed their say-so to keep your mouth shut."

He rose, and she could see the lines at the corners of his eyes, the strain. He'd just gotten his son back on his feet, and now he was in the wrong place at the wrong time when a murder was committed—but he didn't let any of that show. He kissed her lightly on the cheek and admonished her one more time. "You don't have a dog in this fight, Carine. Stay out of it."

When she got back out onto the street, she made herself take three deep cleansing breaths before she decided what to do next. Her hands were shaking. Her stomach muscles were tight to the point of soreness, but at least she didn't feel as if she'd throw up—minor progress, but progress nonetheless.

She fished out her cell phone and dialed Gus's number. "Gus? It's me. The police have Manny under surveillance. Can you believe it? They think he killed Louis. Why don't they think *I* killed him?"

"What the hell were you doing talking to Manny Carrera?"

"Relax. He's at the Four Seasons having coffee." She sighed, starting down Tremont Street toward the intersection of Arlington Street, the Public Garden across from her, people passing her on their normal routines. "Manny's in trouble, Gus. He won't admit it, of course. He's going to have ulcers and heart disease in a few years from keeping it all under such tight control."

"Carine—"

"I'm thinking about calling Ty. Do you know where he is?"

"Why do you want to call him? Manny can take care of himself."

"Manny's *not* taking care of himself. You should see

him. Maybe Ty can talk to him. He must have heard about what happened."

Gus hesitated. "He heard."

Carine stopped abruptly, a man in a suit nearly crashing into her as he rushed past. Gus was being evasive, and that wasn't his nature. He'd been evasive earlier, and she'd let it go. Normally he was the most straightforward person she'd ever encountered. "Gus?"

"What, honey? You sound stressed out—"

"Gus, where is Tyler? Is he on leave? Manny said he was on a mission."

"You haven't seen the news, have you? Well, you'll find out sooner or later—North and I pulled three prep school seniors off the ridge yesterday."

"So, he's there. I'll call him at home."

"Try his cell phone."

She frowned. "Gus? Gus, what is it you're not telling me?"

"Ah, shit, honey, I'm losing the connection. I can't hear you. Can you hear me?"

"I can hear you fine."

"What? Carine? Are you there? These goddamn cell phones."

"Gus—"

He disconnected.

And she knew. Ty was en route to Boston or already there. The fact that Gus didn't want to tell her meant North had come because of her. Gus wouldn't like it either way—Ty in Boston, her there on her own.

"Mission, my ass."

Manny had to know. He must have contacted Ty and put him up to keeping an eye on her—probably to take her back to Cold Ridge, since that seemed to be the general consensus of what she should do with herself. Go home. Stay out of trouble. Don't *cause* any trouble.

She didn't feel warm and safe and less isolated, less vulnerable, as if her family and friends were trying to do right by her after she'd had a shock.

"Ha," she muttered. "I know better."

She'd been conspired against by her own uncle, by Manny Carrera—and North. They'd obviously believed she couldn't resist meddling.

She could see herself standing in the library door yesterday and relived the jolt of awareness that had warned her something was wrong. She saw the blood. Louis's hand. She felt herself running in panic out of the house, into Manny Carrera's arms.

If she hadn't been there, would Manny have slipped away before the police arrived?

Was it her fault he was under suspicion?

Louis Sanborn was not a nice man.

Maybe not. But Manny hadn't shot him in cold blood.

She dialed Gus's number. "When did Ty leave for Boston?" she asked him.

"Can't hear you," her uncle said, and hung up.

Seven

Antonia had already tracked Ty down on his cell phone and given him an earful about leaving her sister on the loose in Boston, and now he was getting it from Manny Carrera. Ty just listened. They didn't realize what it was like to watch Carine do calf stretches on her porch—watch her as she sipped tea and tried to eat a scone on her way to a murder scene.

He'd lost her on the subway, picked her up again on Beacon Street. It wasn't as if he didn't know where she was going. He'd reminded Antonia of the promise she'd extracted from him last night not to make things worse for her sister. Hell, he was trying.

But as a practical matter, Antonia wanted Carine back in Cold Ridge, out of harm's way. Everyone did. It was the only reason Gus had let him out of town alive—because he figured Ty would come back with Carine, one way or another. She didn't like it that people worried about her, but they did. And not without cause. A year ago, she unwittingly disturbed a smuggling operation and came under fire while she was off taking pictures. Then she'd gone and fallen in love with him. Now it was out-and-out murder that had her life in an uproar, her family wanting to keep her safe.

She'd surprised him, sneaking into the Four Seasons and tracking down Manny. As usual, Manny's instincts were right on target—she wasn't going to back off. But that was Carine. She never backed off. Ty had seen her lie in wait for the perfect shot of a spruce grouse. She had focus, commitment, inner reserves. He remembered her making a break for it from behind her boulder last fall, zigzagging from tree to tree, launching herself down the hill, out of the line of fire. She might have made it out of there just fine if he hadn't been around.

Manny exhaled, looking out at the busy street. "I hope I put the fear of God in her. She was all set to jump in headfirst and prove my innocence."

"She likes you."

"Big deal. And that's not it. She has this strong moral compass. You know, this acute sense of right and wrong— as in, it was wrong for you to skip out on her a week before your wedding."

Ty didn't squirm. Nobody had liked what he'd done. "It was wrong for someone to murder this man, Louis Sanborn. If she wants to do the right thing, she should back off and let the police do their job."

"Not if she's not convinced they're going after the real killer. She'll feel it's her duty not to walk away."

"Because she found Louis," North said.

"Because she thinks she could have saved his life. He offered her a ride, and she refused. If she hadn't—"

"Then we'd have two dead bodies instead of one."

"Carine doesn't see it that way. And," Manny added, with obvious reluctance, "she thinks it's her fault the police are sniffing my trail."

"Is it?"

"Not really. She went screaming out of the house, and I was there. That put me on the scene, but—" He shrugged. "The police have more than that to go on."

North didn't ask what that was. If Manny intended to tell him, he'd already have done it. "Carine sees things the way she wants them to be, not necessarily the way they are. She has a rosy-eyed view of the world. You don't ever see her taking a picture of an osprey ripping apart a baby duck, do you?"

"Christ, North. I just had breakfast."

"You're making too much of her reasoning. She's just bored."

"Maybe. I don't know." Manny leaned back against the soft cushions of the couch and frowned at his longtime friend. "Why haven't you gotten her out of here by now?"

"Timing. She had to go back to the scene. Maybe she had to see you, too, but I should have prevented that. By the time I realized what was going on, she was sitting across from you."

"I should have told you where I was staying."

Ty didn't comment. "If I grabbed her too soon, she'd be impossible to keep still. She'd be back down here in a flash. Now—" He sighed, picturing her as she'd left the hotel. He knew her so well, her body language, the way she thought. "There's a chance."

"You're not giving yourself enough credit. Toss her butt in the back of your truck and beat a path to New Hampshire. You know how to hold a prisoner if you have to."

It had been a long night in his truck, Ty thought. He'd had to move it several times, and he was stiff. "I'm still an outsider in Cold Ridge."

"You've lived there your whole life—"

"Doesn't matter. The Winters have been there since 1800. Figure it out, Manny. I live in their old house."

"Your mother bought the place from a Winter?"

"No. A Winter built it. Last one moved out in 1878. Doesn't matter. I'd be holding a prisoner in enemy territory."

"You mean the bad-ass uncle wants you to go easy on her."

Ty shrugged. "I'm on death row with Gus as it is."

Manny leaned over and poured the last drops of coffee into his cup, not because he wanted more, North thought, but because he needed something to do. "You're sure you're not dragging your heels because you're afraid to face her?"

"I'd be afraid to face her if I'd done something I shouldn't have done. I didn't."

"Right," Manny said with open sarcasm. "Bet Carine looks at it that way, too."

North got to his feet. "I should head out before she gets too big a lead on me. You know what you're doing, Carrera?"

His friend relaxed his guard, his dark eyes showing his tension—his fear. "I came up here to recommend the Rancourts fire Louis Sanborn."

"That's reason for him to kill you, not the other way around."

"Suppose I got to him first, before he could kill me?"

"I'm not speculating, Manny. You want to tell me the whole story, fine. Tell it. Otherwise—"

"I've told you what I can. I don't have the whole story. There are gaps I need to fill in."

"Can you do it from here?" But Manny wasn't going to answer, and Ty didn't push him. "You know how to get in touch with me. Stay safe, okay?"

"If something happens to me and I can't—" He paused,

searching for the right words, then went on, "If I can't function, remember I love Val. All right?"

"Yeah, Manny. Sure. She knows—"

"Just remember. I've got computer files—" He broke off. "That's all I'm saying. You'll remember."

North turned to cross the plush carpet, noting a woman with a PalmPilot, making no bones about watching him. A cop. She must have realized she'd been made. It wouldn't be easy to conduct covert surveillance on a man with Manny Carrera's training and experience. Maybe she was the reason for Manny's cryptic comment about loving his wife and computer files.

"One more favor," he said quietly.

Ty glanced back at him, not knowing what to expect.

"Eric—could you look in on my kid if you get the chance? I don't know if Val's talked to him. I haven't talked to either one of them. I don't like the idea of having to explain to the police why I called my family."

"What do you want me to tell him?"

"Not to worry."

Ty nodded without argument, because there was no way to tell Manny Carrera that a fourteen-year-old boy was going to think what he wanted to think, worry if he wanted to worry.

When North got back out to Tremont Street, he noticed the smell of exhaust fumes and the noise of the traffic speeding past him. He was used to making quick switches in his environment, but he'd never liked cities. Carine had been out of his sight for less than fifteen minutes, but he didn't think it'd be difficult to pick up her trail. She was on foot, and she was aimless, restless, ripe for doing something she shouldn't. The Winters were all risk-takers at heart. Even Carine, except none of them saw it.

She was a nature photographer. She had a camera with

her. Maybe she'd slipped back into Boston Public Garden to take pictures of the trees.

Ty waited at a red light at the corner of Arlington and Tremont, debating his next move. Head to Copley Square? Turn onto Arlington and check Newbury Street? Or go back to the Rancourt house, or to Inman Square and her apartment—or chuck it and head back to New Hampshire without her. Mind his own damn business.

He hadn't made up his mind when she swooped up from the steps of the subway station on the corner, diving at him as if he'd just tried to mug her. She damn near knocked him on his ass.

He caught her around the middle. "Hey—babe, there are cops all over the place."

"You've been following me. For how long?"

He kept a tight hold on her, taking due note of her strong abdominal muscles and overall increased level of fitness. He'd followed her on her halfhearted run this morning—from the shape she was in, he'd guess she'd had better mornings.

"Not that long," he said. "Take it easy."

"Why should I?"

Good point. He held her arms down, but she kicked him. He had on khakis and his brown leather jacket, too warm for the city temperatures. He'd be working up a sweat with too much more of this. He grabbed her camera bag in self-defense. "Want me to throw this under a car? Come on. Get a grip. I have tender shins."

"You don't have tender anything. When did you get here?"

"Last night."

"You've been following me since *last night?*"

He dodged her next kick. People passed by, eyeing them nervously, and one guy pulled out his cell phone.

North smiled, trying to look nonthreatening, and Carine, apparently realizing the scene she was making, backed off. Strands of hair had pulled out of her loose ponytail. She grabbed her camera bag back and adjusted it on her shoulder, breathing hard, a little wild-eyed.

"Manny sicced you on me, didn't he?" she demanded.

"I had a feeling you wouldn't thank me. Does it feel better to go on the offensive?"

She sighed, shaking her head. "I wish it did. At least I didn't push you out into traffic." She seemed calmer, but Ty could see the effects of the past twenty-four hours in the puffy, dark circles under her eyes, the paleness of her skin, the rigid hold she had on her camera bag. Her eyes, so damn blue, narrowed on him. "Are you on leave? I don't want you wasting any more of it on me. You can turn around and drive back to New Hampshire. There's a deli on Arlington. I'll buy you a sandwich for the road."

"Carine...hell, babe, you look like you're in tough shape. Let me—"

"Good. I'd hate to look great the day after I discovered a dead body." She looked up at the traffic light, apparently waiting for a walk sign. "And don't call me babe."

"Why'd you attack me?"

"I thought about throwing a rock through your windshield, but I couldn't find your truck. Or a rock."

North shrugged. "Makes sense, I guess."

"It *was* Manny who sent you, right? Gus wouldn't. He'd stonewall me if he knew you were on your way, but he would never ask you to keep an eye on me." She still didn't look around at North. "Does Manny think I'm in danger from the real murderer, or does he just not trust me to mind my own business?"

"Nobody trusts a Winter to mind their own business."

He resisted touching her. "Damn it, I'm not going to stand out here talking murder with you. Let's go."

"The deli's just up Arlington—"

"You're not buying me a sandwich and sending me on my way."

A bit of color rose in her cheeks, and she refused to look at him, her shoulders hunched as she continued to wait for the walk signal. It came, but she didn't move. Ty remembered why he'd fallen in love with her—why, ultimately, he'd walked away from her. She was sensitive, loyal, artistic, a fighter and a dreamer. He was loyal and a fighter, but sensitive? Artistic? A dreamer? No way. Although she was the youngest of the Winter siblings and remembered their parents the least, she was also the one who seemed most affected by their deaths. She deserved a man who led a safer life than he did.

"This was a bad idea," Ty said, half under his breath. "All right, suit yourself. You're on your own."

She stood up straight and whipped around at him. "I am?"

"You bet. Go on. Scoot. I won't strong-arm you."

"You'll follow me," she said. "You're an expert in evading pursuit."

"I'd be doing the pursuing. That's a different skill."

"You'd manage."

"Not around here. I like the desert. Caves. Bugs to eat. A jungle's good, too. I could manage in a jungle."

She almost smiled. "You're totally impossible, Tyler. I don't know why I ever wanted to marry you." She thought a moment, then sighed. "But, seeing how you're listening to reason, I suppose I could let you drive me back to my apartment. I don't have the oomph to walk, and I don't think I could handle the subway again right now."

"Better me than the subway?" He grinned at her. "It's a start."

"You won't try to take me to New Hampshire against my will?"

"No, ma'am."

She looked faintly skeptical, but she was, at her core, the most trusting person he'd ever known. She wasn't naïve—she knew more than most about what life could throw at people, without rhyme nor reason. But she was an optimist, a glass-is-half-full type, a believer in truth and justice, all of which, in Ty's view, guaranteed she'd be a pain in the ass with Manny and this murder investigation. No wonder Manny had enlisted him to get rid of her.

Carine spotted his truck on Boylston and shot ahead of him, leaning against the passenger door until he got there to unlock it. She had her arms crossed, and more hairs had pulled out of her ponytail. "I know you're trained to resist the enemy," she said. "I probably could shove burning bamboo sticks under your fingernails, and you wouldn't talk."

"You're not the enemy." He unlocked her door and pulled it open. "And you wouldn't have the heart to torture me."

"I'd have the heart. There's just no point if it's not going to work."

She climbed into the truck, and when North got behind the wheel, he saw the tears in her eyes. But she turned away quickly and gazed out the passenger window. He started the engine. "Carine...ah, hell..."

"Feel like a heel, do you? Good." She sniffled, not looking at him. "Just don't get the idea that I'm not over you, because I am. I just need protein, that's all. I'm having a sugar low."

"You might be over me, but you're not neutral—"

"I've never been neutral about you. I wasn't neutral when I was six years old and you cut the tire-swing rope on me. It doesn't mean anything."

He let the engine idle a moment. "I'm sorry I hurt you."

"You didn't hurt me, Ty. You did me a favor." She glanced at him sideways, her tears gone. "Isn't that what all the men who get cold feet say?"

"It wasn't cold feet."

"No, not you. You're way too tough for cold feet."

She wasn't going to give him an inch. He didn't blame her—she'd given him her heart, and he'd broken it.

He shifted his truck into gear. "Just for the record," he said, "I've never been neutral about you, either."

Eight

When they reached her apartment, Carine climbed out of the truck, thanked Ty for the ride and told him to have a safe trip home. She gave him a parting smile, shut the door and mounted her porch steps at a half run, not so much, he thought, because she wanted to get there fast but because she wanted to prove to him she could do it. Maybe to herself, too. She'd had a shock, and she was back on her feet, up and running.

He wondered how long before she figured out he wasn't going anywhere.

Hauling her back to Cold Ridge against her will was out, but Manny had his reasons—however close-mouthed he was being about them—for asking Ty to keep an eye on her. She'd found Louis Sanborn dead. She'd worked with him. A murderer was on the loose. Something was up.

And Ty couldn't abandon her again. Gus would pitch him off the ridge for sure. When he wasn't looking, just when he let his guard down—off a ledge he'd go.

But it was more than Gus, more than Manny, more than murder that was keeping him in Boston—it was Carine, seeing her again after all these months. He had to do right by her, somehow make up for what he'd done.

She seemed to be having trouble with the front door.

That wasn't it. Her keys were in her hand. She hadn't touched the door. She glanced back at him, her eyes wide, her mouth partly open, and Ty was out of his truck in an instant. "What's wrong?"

"I don't know. Nothing, probably." She took a breath, pushed back more hair that had escaped from her pony-tail. "The door sticks. I'm sure that's all it is. People leave it open all the time."

"Let's take a look."

Ty took the sagging steps onto the porch. The door to her building had dirty glass and peeling white paint that had grayed with neglect and the onslaught of city soot and grime. It was open slightly, about six inches.

"I don't want to overreact," Carine said.

"It's okay, Carine. Anyone would be on edge after what happened to you yesterday. Why don't I check your apart-ment, make sure everything's okay?"

She hesitated, long enough for him to push the door open the rest of the way and enter the outer hall. It was poorly lit and smelled like cat litter. Dirty steps led up to the second floor. Carine fell in behind him, then gasped and lunged forward, but Ty grabbed her wrist, keeping her from shooting past him. He saw what she obviously had already seen—the door to her apartment was also open.

There was no sign of forced entry—no ripped wood, no broken locks.

"I locked up this morning," she whispered. "I know I did."

Ty released her. "It was a rough morning for you. You were off your routines. Anything's possible."

"Anything's *not* possible. I locked my door. It's not something I even think about anymore. It's routine—"

"All right. You locked your door. Do you want to call 911 and let the police check it out?"

She grimaced, then sighed heavily. "Not yet. I'd feel ridiculous if they're just going to tell me I forgot to lock up. I'll have a look first." She glanced at him. "It's my apartment, so it's my responsibility."

"Suppose someone's in there?"

"I'll yell."

Ty rolled his eyes. "Right."

"Don't argue with me. It's not like you came down here with an M16 strapped to your back." She lowered her camera bag. "Hang on. I'll get out my cell phone—"

"If someone hits me over the head, you'll call 911?"

"I might," she said, but her smile didn't quite make it.

While she dug out her cell phone, North slipped inside her apartment, moving quickly down a short hallway into the kitchen. The other rooms all connected to it. Bathroom, living room, bedroom. The doors were open, the apartment was quiet, still and, he thought, very bright. Yellow, citrus green, lavender blue, dashes of raspberry. Some white, but not much. Not enough.

He snatched a paring knife out of the dish drainer, Carine behind him, her cell phone in hand. She got her own knife and followed him as he entered each room and looked around, seeing no sign of a rigorous search or any obvious missing valuables. Television, laptop and stereo were all intact. What else there was to take, he didn't know. Carine had never been into jewelry. He remembered she'd wanted a simple engagement ring. When he pulled the plug on their wedding, she'd offered to feed it to him.

She led the way back into the kitchen and sank against the sink and its citrus-green cabinets, her arms crossed, the last of her ponytail gone. She chewed on the inside corner of her mouth. "Maybe you had a point and I did forget to lock up."

"Is that what you think?"

"I don't know that I *can* think. I'm a damn wreck. I keep expecting any minute I'll just put it all out of my head and be fine—" She broke off with another sigh. "It doesn't look as if anyone got at the door with a crowbar—I suppose it could have popped open on its own. This place is old, and the landlord doesn't fix anything until it's absolutely necessary. But why would it pop open *today?*"

"Who else has a key?"

"Antonia. When she started spending more time in D.C. I gave one to the Rancourts in case I ever lose mine. And Gus. He has one."

Ty returned the knife to the dish drainer and stood back from her, taking in her pale skin, her tensed muscles, her shallow breathing. A thick covered rubber band clung to the ends of a small clump of hair. He pulled it out and handed it to her. She'd had enough. She'd reached her saturation point. Time for him to break through. "Ten minutes," he said.

"What do you mean, ten minutes?"

"You've got ten minutes to pack up. We're leaving."

She straightened. "Says who? What about the police?"

"You're not even sure there's been a break-in."

"You don't want to explain why you're here to them, do you? You'd have to tell them about Manny—"

"You're under nine minutes. Keep talking." He settled back against the sink next to her, noticed the photograph of a red-tailed hawk above her table. It was one she'd taken—he remembered she'd had to lie on her stomach and hang off a ledge to get the angle she wanted. "If you don't have time to pack, I can always run into Wal-Mart with you for new undies."

She didn't budge. "What if I tell you to go to hell?"

He smiled, leaning in close to her. "Eight minutes."

Her arms dropped down to her sides, and she scowled at him. "You're serious, aren't you?"

"Yes, ma'am. You need to get out of here and clear your head. Anyone in your position would, so don't take it as a knock on you. You just can't see it. I can." He glanced at his sports watch. "I'm counting."

She disappeared into her bedroom without further argument. His head was pounding. Maybe it was all the cheerful, bright colors, so different from the warm, dark colors of her log cabin in Cold Ridge. It wasn't the same, not having her across the meadow, waking up to the smell of smoke from her woodstove on cold mornings. She was down here, finding dead people and painting things lavender.

A wave of nostalgia and regret washed over him, and he wondered if they could ever go back to the easy friendship they'd had before he'd decided he was in love with her, or recognized that he was, had been for a long time. Whatever it was.

He walked over to her bedroom doorway and watched her load things into a soft, worn tapestry bag opened on her bed. "Need some help?"

"No, thanks."

Cool. A hint of irritation. She womped a pair of jeans into her bag. North smiled. "Give it up, Carine. If you didn't want to go with me, you'd make me hit you over the head and carry you out of here."

She fixed her blue eyes on him. "Being an experienced combat medic, you'd know just where to hit me so it wouldn't inflict permanent damage, wouldn't you?"

"Actually, I would. But you want to go home. Admit it. You don't want to stay here by yourself—"

"Fine. You're right. So let's do it. Let's go home."

She zipped up her bag, slung it over her shoulder and marched across the shaggy blue rug to him, but when she started past him, he caught one arm around her waist. "Are you going to be mad the whole trip?"

"I knew I'd have to face you again one of these days," she said. "I just didn't think it'd be under these circumstances. No. I won't be mad the whole trip. I can't stay here. I know that."

She let her bag fall to the floor, didn't move away from him. He didn't know why, unless she was remembering, as he was, what it was like when they'd made love. "Ty—" She broke off, a warmth in her tone that hadn't been there before. "I don't know anyone else who'd do what you've done, come down here, follow me around, let me come close to shoving you into oncoming traffic."

"It wasn't that close."

But she was serious, sincere, and didn't respond to his stab at humor. "Here you are, trying to look after me, whether I want you or need you to or not, even when you know—well, never mind what you know. Thank you."

"You were going to say even when I know what I did to you."

"I guess what I should say is even when we know what we did to each other."

"Damn it, Carine." He could hear the pain in his own voice, wished it had stayed buried. "I can't undo what I did. If I could…"

"It's okay."

She touched her fingertips to the side of his face and, without any other warning than that, kissed him, lightly, gently, but not, he thought, chastely. It was like being mule-kicked, like setting a match to superdry kindling. All the clichés. There'd been no other woman since her.

He kept thinking there should be, that he ought to get on with his life, but the weeks had ticked by, now the months.

He fought an urge to carry her to bed, but she pulled away from him, smiled at him, her skin less pale, less cool to the touch. "A lot's changed in a year, hasn't it?"

He smiled back at her. "Not some things."

She gave him a pointed look. "Sex isn't everything, Sergeant North. You said so yourself when you gave me my marching papers."

"Did I say that?"

"Not in as many words—"

"Yeah, no kidding." He held her more closely, suddenly not wanting to let go. "The reason I didn't marry you was because of me, not because of you."

"Semantics. You ready?"

"Not quite."

And he kissed her this time, felt her arms tighten around his middle, her shirt riding up—he touched the bare skin of her midriff, and when she inhaled, he deepened the kiss. She responded, sliding her hands around to his belt buckle, her fingertips drifting lower, outlining his obvious arousal. She took his hand and eased it over her breasts.

"Carine—"

"Just this once." Her eyes were wide, alert, nothing about her anywhere but here, right now. "It's been such an awful twenty-four hours. Ty—please, I know what I'm doing."

She touched him again, erotically, and he was lost. He swept her up and carried her to the bed, laying her on top of her down comforter. He paused, looking at her for any indication she'd changed her mind, giving her the chance to send him back to the kitchen. Ty told himself he should put a stop to this insanity, but he didn't. Neither did she.

She scooted out of her clothes, and in five seconds, he was out of his, on top of her, stroking her smooth hips, her breasts—but she was in a hurry.

"Make love to me," she whispered. "Now."

She pulled him into her, shutting her eyes, no hesitation now. He kept his eyes open, watching her as he made love to her, the flush on her face, the way she bit her lower lip when she came, seconds before he did. It was then he shut his eyes, savoring his release, the feel of her body all around him.

Making love to her was natural. Perfect. And it couldn't happen again.

He kissed her forehead and rolled off the bed, grabbing his clothes. "No regrets?"

She shook her head. "Not this soon. Later, maybe."

"Carine—"

"Just turn your head when I get my clothes back on."

He did as she asked.

He had regrets. About a thousand of them. He couldn't seem to keep his head glued on straight when he was around her. He'd almost sent her an old-fashioned telegram to call off their engagement, just to make sure he got the message delivered, that she understood it—he couldn't marry her. Not that next week, not ever.

As if to prove his point, here he was. One minute, he was checking for intruders with a sharp knife, the next minute, making love to a woman who'd pretty much had him by the short hairs all her life. She deserved someone more like her, someone more attuned to her sensibilities. He wasn't as creative or perceptive or optimistic as she was. He was restless, an adrenaline junkie for as long as he could remember. He needed the kind of physical and mental challenges his work as a PJ provided. Even his mother would have had less trouble with a quieter kind of kid—he'd see her eyes glaze over many times as she became so absorbed in her work she was unaware of what was going on around her, and he'd clear out, head up the ridge. It wasn't like he'd sat there and played quietly by the fire.

Carine cleared her throat. "I'm ready. You can turn your head now."

North didn't feel self-conscious about his own absence of clothing. He supposed he should, but this wasn't the first time he and Carine had made love—the first time was almost a year ago, a few days after the shooting in the woods, less than twenty-four hours after he got rid of Hank and Manny. It was in the loft in her log cabin, with the fire crackling in her woodstove, and it hadn't seemed sudden at all. It had seemed natural, as if they should have been making love for years.

He pulled on his pants, noting that she didn't turn her head away, but when he grinned at her, she made a face, blushing slightly. "Regrets?" he asked.

She shook her head.

But that was now, he thought. Give her a couple of hours in his truck and see what she thought.

She swore under her breath and grabbed her tapestry bag and her cameras, not asking him to carry a thing as she pushed past him into the kitchen.

He had a feeling it was going to be a long drive back to New Hampshire.

Nine

```
⟬∾⟭⟬∾⟭
```

The lead homicide detective had Sterling take him through the entire house after lunch, describe each room and explain its status in terms of renovation. Sterling tried not to let his impatience show, but he could see no relevance in having the detective inspect the fifth-floor maid's quarters. But the man insisted, and Sterling cooperated. Afterward, the detective thanked him, and Sterling returned to his office in a deceptively plain building that his company owned in Copley Square.

He was exhausted and uneasy, and try as he did, he couldn't summon much sympathy for Louis Sanborn. Why the hell hadn't he taken more care not to get himself killed? Or at least, if it had to happen, why not somewhere else? Why on Rancourt property?

Sterling stood in front of the tall, spotless windows in his office and looked across Boylston at Trinity Church and the mirrored tower of the Hancock building. He could see a corner of the original wing of the Boston Public Library, the oldest public library in the country. So much history all around him. It was something he loved about Boston. He thought of it as his city. He and Jodie had such great plans for the house on Commonwealth Avenue. They wanted to entertain there, open it up to charitable events, allow for people outside their immediate circle of family and friends to enjoy it.

Now it was tainted by murder.

If not Louis, why hadn't Gary Turner done something to prevent this nightmare? Sterling would give anything for yesterday never to have happened. At this point, the best he could hope for was a quick arrest, preferably of someone who had no connection to him. A drug dealer or a drifter who'd followed Louis into the house and shot him in an attempted robbery, or just for the hell of it.

But that didn't look likely. The detectives had refused to tip their hand, but Sterling knew Manny Carrera was in their sites. A consultant *he'd* hired. A man he'd trusted.

He had to be patient and let the investigation play itself out.

His wife, however, didn't have a drop of patience in her character. She didn't last long at their home on the South Shore and stormed into his office, dropping onto a butter-soft leather couch she'd picked out herself. She was his partner, always at his side. Whenever he felt his energy and drive flag, Jodie would be there, reinvigorating him, urging him on. She was forty-eight, trim, independent—and a little remote. Even after fifteen years of marriage, Sterling couldn't help but feel an important part of her lay beyond his reach. He wondered if it would have been different if they'd had children, but that had never been in their stars.

She was ash-blond, elegant in every way, yet buying their place in Cold Ridge had been her idea. Venturing onto the ridge last November—again, her idea. She continued to insist they'd have survived, even if they'd had to spend the night on the ridge. Sterling knew better. They'd have been lucky if they'd managed to set up their tent in the high wind, and if they'd succeeded, there was a real possibility they'd have suffocated inside it with the amount of snow that fell by first light. Simply put, they were out of their element. But the situation was made less galling, at least to her, because it was Tyler North, Manny Carrera and Hank Callahan who got to them first. If Jodie had to be rescued, better by a hero-pilot-turned-senate candidate and a pair of air force pararescuemen.

It came as a surprise to people that she enjoyed their home in Cold Ridge as much as her husband did. Sterling liked that. He liked having people not quite able to figure them out.

"I can't stand the tension, Sterling." She jumped back to her feet, her restlessness palpable. "I really can't."

He went around his desk and sat in his tall-backed leather chair, giving her room to pace. "I know. It's getting to all of us. I think today will be the worst day. Once we know what we're dealing with, we can adjust. It'll get better, Jodie. You know that."

She didn't seem to hear him. "I thought Louis was this smart security type. How did he manage to get himself killed? He should have been able to save himself—" She stopped, waving a hand at him as if to forestall the criticism she knew was coming. "I'm sorry. That's a terrible thing to say."

Sterling made no comment. Sometimes his wife's lack of compassion, her inability—or her unwillingness—to connect with other people, startled him. But usually it was momentary, and he never gave up hope that there wasn't a window into her soul.

She seemed slightly calmer. "Gary wants me to go up to Cold Ridge at least until the police make an arrest. I don't know what I'd do up there all alone. Go crazy, probably. And I don't want to leave you down here—"

"Gary's already told me he thinks I should go with you. I don't feel I can right now, but perhaps it's a good idea for you—"

"Why can't you? The police haven't said you can't leave town. If they need anything, they can call you in New Hampshire." She flounced onto the couch once more, stubborn more than upset. "We've done nothing wrong. I can't believe our lives are so turned upside down just because a murder was committed on our property."

"Jodie," Sterling said quietly, hearing the admonishment in his tone, "a man who worked for us is dead."

"I know. Oh, God, I *know!*" She groaned, shaking her head in frustration, fighting tears. "My reactions are all over the place. I can't believe—" She swallowed, looking down at her feet, her voice lowering to almost a whisper. "Who'd have thought something as small as a bullet could kill Louis Sanborn? He was so alive, wasn't he?"

Sterling felt a sudden sense of loss, although he hadn't known Louis that well. But he was so young, and now he was gone. "I know what you mean."

"I feel sorry for Carine." Jodie shook her head, displaying one of her rare tugs of real compassion. "Of all the people to find him. I hope she's gone back to Cold Ridge. She should just sit in front of the fire in that little log cabin of hers and relax for a few days."

"Manny Carrera is a friend."

"I know he is. There's just nothing good to be found in this situation, is there? I thought we were doing Carine a favor when we hired her. Now look. It's hard to believe Manny could murder someone, but I suppose we have to keep an open mind."

Sterling shook his head. "I can't do it, can you? Manny's no murderer. I refuse even to consider that he might be guilty."

"That's because you're fascinated by him," Jodie said. "Speaking of doing people favors—"

"Don't, Jodie. I won't take responsibility for Manny's situation. I didn't ask him to show up at the house when he did."

"Why was he there?"

"I have no idea. He's a good man, and I'm sorry he's under even the slightest cloud of suspicion. That doesn't make it my fault."

"No, of course not." She smiled abruptly, unfolding her legs and sliding to her feet. "But who are you trying to convince, hmm? Keep in mind that normal people don't jump out of helicopters to rescue people."

"Manny helped save our lives, Jodie."

"And how many times have he and Hank Callahan and Tyler North said we don't owe them a thing? They *like* what they do. They didn't rescue us because it was us— they rescued us because we were in a tight spot and they were in a position to help."

"Still—"

"Don't let your gratitude and respect affect your judgment."

He watched her walk across his office, her impatience less visible as she came behind his desk and kissed him on the top of the head. He grabbed her hand and squeezed it gently. "We'll get through this," he said.

"We just need to remember to take care of ourselves."

In a business situation, Sterling would know what to do to take care of himself. But this was different. He felt a spurt of pain in his temples. "I'm so damn tired. I keep picturing Louis—"

"Don't," his wife said. "It won't get you anywhere. I know, I've been doing the same thing."

She eased in front of him, then lowered herself to his

lap, sinking against his chest. He could feel her exhaustion. "We'll get through this, my love," she whispered, but it seemed almost as if she was addressing someone else. "I'll make sure we do."

He leaned back with her, rocking gently, but he was aware that he had no physical response to her. Not that many years ago, he'd have cleared his desk and made love to her then and there. A tense, difficult situation wouldn't have stopped him. He'd have welcomed the distraction, the release. So would she.

But Jodie was different these days, or he was different, and certainly he'd never dealt with a murder before, the deliberate taking of a human life. A man he knew, a man he'd hired. It changed everything, and he was afraid, terrified to his very core, that his nonreaction to his wife was only the beginning, and ultimately the least of his worries.

Ten

The Mount Chester School for Boys occupied three hundred acres on the outskirts of the village of Cold Ridge, its picturesque campus dotted with huge oak trees still hanging onto their burgundy-and-burnt-orange leaves under the darkening November sky. Carine was almost relieved when Ty said he needed to stop at the school to check on Eric Carrera, Manny's son. It gave her a chance to get her bearings now that she was back in her hometown for the first time in months.

She'd said little during the three-hour trip north. There was no taking back what she'd initiated at her apartment. She'd wanted it to happen. Emotionally, she was over Tyler North. Physically—physically, she thought, he was a hard man to resist.

"Did you notice my abs?" she'd asked him during the drive.

He'd almost driven off the road. "What?"

"My abdominal muscles. I've been running and swimming, doing all sorts of calisthenics." She didn't mention she was trying to pass the PJ preliminary fitness test. "Chin-ups. Flutter kicks."

"Sure, Carine. That's what I was thinking. *Gee, she's been doing flutter kicks.*"

"Flutter kicks are the worst, don't you think?"

He hadn't said a word. Now, apparently as tense as she was, he used more force than was necessary to engage the emergency brake. "I'll be right back."

She watched him head up the stone walk to the late-nineteenth-century brick administration building, whose design was classic New England prep school, with its tall, black-shuttered windows and ivy vines, that died back in the autumn cold. If she'd lived, Carine thought, her mother could still be here, teaching biology to another generation of boys. Mount Chester was a solid private high school with a good reputation, but it didn't have the prestige of an Andover or Choate. Carine, her sister and her brother—and Ty—had all attended the local public school.

She knew sending Eric to Mount Chester had to be a financial stretch for the Carreras, but they believed it would be good for him to be on his own, although Carine suspected there was more to it than that.

She climbed out of the truck, immediately noticing that the air was colder, a nasty bite in the wind, but she could smell the leaves and the damp ground, not yet frozen for the winter. Fallen leaves covered most of the lawn, most already dry and brown, some still soft, in shades of yellow, orange, maroon, even red—although the reds tended to drop first.

"Eric'll meet us out here," Ty said, returning to the small parking lot.

Carine nodded, sticking her hands into her pockets, trying to acclimatize herself to being back in New Hampshire.

Eric Carrera shambled down the blacktop walk from the main campus and waved, grinning as he picked up his pace. He was dark-haired and dark-eyed like his parents, and small for his age, but the way he walked reminded Carine of his father, although he didn't possess Manny's economy of movement.

"Hey, Uncle Ty, Miss Winter," Eric said cheerfully, "what's up?"

"Your dad asked me to put eyes on you," Ty said.

"Because of what happened? Mom told me. She called a little while ago. She said she wasn't sure if Dad would have a chance to call. You know, because of the police and everything. She wanted me to know what was going on in case I heard it on the news."

"You okay?"

"Yes, sir."

He wore a hooded Dartmouth zip-up sweatshirt and cargo pants, but he looked cold and too thin. He'd joined Manny and Val Carrera at Antonia and Hank's wedding a month ago. Antonia had told Carine that Eric was doing well, managing his asthma and allergies with medication and experience, knowing what triggered attacks, taking action once he felt one coming on—calming himself, using his inhaler. He wore a Medic Alert bracelet and, in addition to his rescue inhaler, carried an EpiPen—a dose of epinephrine—everywhere he went. He could treat himself in an emergency, save his own life. At least now he knew what his deadly allergy triggers were: bee stings, shellfish, peanuts. His allergies to tree pollen and dust mites, although troublesome, were less likely to produce an anaphylactic reaction that could kill him.

But it had been a long road to this point, and it had taken its toll, not only on Eric, but on his parents. Carine had seen that at Hank and Antonia's wedding.

"How's school?" Ty asked.

"It's okay." Eric shrugged with a fourteen-year-old's

nonchalance. "I'm playing soccer. I'm not on the varsity team or anything, I just play for fun."

"That's great. This thing with your dad—it'll get figured out."

The boy nodded. "I know. He called you?"

"No. I was in Boston today and talked to him."

"Oh. Well, I have to go. I have a French test tomorrow."

"Sure." Ty cuffed him gently on the shoulder. "You'll call me if you need anything, right? Anytime. I'm in town for a few days at least."

Eric cheered up, looking more energetic. "Yes, sir. Thanks. I heard about the seniors yesterday. What dopes. They don't think they did anything wrong."

"They did a million things wrong, but they were very, very lucky."

"The school warns us. They have a film. It talks about some of the people who died on the ridge. One of them used to teach biology here—"

"That was my mother," Carine said. "She and my father both died on the ridge when I was three. They weren't lucky."

Eric gave her a solemn look. "I'm sorry."

"It was a long time ago, but the ridge is just as dangerous now as it was then. Weather reports are more accurate, and good equipment is readily available, but still."

"You have to be take proper precautions," Eric said. "I'd like to climb the ridge sometime."

Ty seemed to like that idea. "Your dad and I can take you up there."

Eric shook his head. "Dad doesn't think I can do anything."

"You think so? Then you'll have to educate him."

"And Mom—Mom worries about me all the time." He sighed heavily, as if he had the weight of the world on his shoulders, most of it in the form of his parents. "She keeps encouraging me to do things, but I know it scares her when I do."

"Does it scare you?" Ty asked.

The boy shrugged. "A little. Sometimes. I do it anyway. The seniors, those guys you rescued—one of them picks on me. He says I'm skinny, and he calls me Wheezer Weasel. Not to my face, behind my back. I think that's worse. His friends laugh. They don't think I hear them, but I do."

"I guess there'll always be a certain percentage of seniors who pick on underclassmen. They see it as their job." Ty winked at the high school freshman. "Wait'll they get the bill for their rescue."

Eric's face lit up. "No kidding, they'll be so pissed! I can't wait!"

He coughed in his excitement, but there was a spring to his step when he headed back to his dorm. Ty watched him, his jaw tightening in disgust. "Wheezer Weasel. Assholes. I wish I'd known before I rescued them. I could have hung them off a ledge by their heels."

Except he wouldn't have, Carine knew. "The Carreras haven't had an easy time of it this past year. I hope the police come to their senses soon and realize Manny's not their murderer."

"He should call his kid."

Ty tore open his truck door and climbed in. Carine followed, shivering, the temperature falling with the approach of dusk. Once he got the engine started, she turned on the heat, but her shivering had as much to do with fraught nerves as it did with being cold.

"Manny told me he had a motive to kill Louis," she said. "Or at least what could be considered a motive. Do you know what he meant?"

"He's not giving anyone the whole story."

Which didn't answer her question, but Carine didn't push it. If Manny had told Ty more than he'd told her, there wasn't a thing she could do about it except respect their bond of friendship—because she wasn't getting it out of Master Sergeant North.

"I figure he meant that people could perceive that he had a motive to kill him," she said, "not that he actually had one."

Ty made no comment, his hands clenched tightly on the wheel.

Yep, she thought. Manny had told him. She leaned back against the cracked, comfortable seat. How many times had they driven along this road? Countless, even before she'd fallen in love with him. She'd known him all her life, but their romance had been a total whirlwind, catching them both by surprise. She'd tried to chalk it up to the adrenaline of her experience in the woods with the smugglers, the shooters, but that wasn't it. If he hadn't called off their wedding, she'd have married him.

"Just drop me off at my cabin," she said quietly. "Then you can go back to Boston and figure out what's going on with Manny. You know it's driving you crazy."

"We're going to Gus's, not your cabin. He said he'd have a pot of beef stew waiting." Ty shifted gears and made the turn into the village. It was just a few streets tucked into a bowl-shaped valley surrounded by the White Mountains, its Main Street dominated by a white-clapboard, early-nineteenth-century church and a smattering of storefronts, although it wasn't a big tourist town. "It was the only way I was going to get out of town. I had to promise to bring you by."

"For what, inspection?"

"Pretty much."

Carine groaned, although this development was not unexpected. She and her sister and brother might all be in their thirties, but their uncle, just fifty himself, liked to see them after a crisis, make sure they were intact. They indulged him, not just because they loved him and life was easier if they complied, but because they understood—he'd survived combat in Vietnam only to come home and lose his only brother and sister-in-law on Cold Ridge. If he sometimes was overprotective, he was allowed. But he'd never let his anxiety spill over into irrationally stopping his nieces and nephew from pursuing their interests, taking risks.

"All right," Carine said. "I'm not going to argue. Drop me off at Gus's. Then you can head back to Boston."

"Not tonight. I need some sleep. Rescuing three kids off a mountain, driving hither and yon, sleeping in my truck—" He glanced at her. "Making love to you. I'm beat."

"You don't get tired, North, and I wouldn't call what we did making love. We—" She grimaced, remembering. "Well, you know what we did."

"Sure do."

"North, I swear—"

"Relax. Gus'll never be able to tell."

Gus lived in the 1919 village house in which his brother and sister-in-law had planned to raise their three children. It was cream stucco with white trim and had a front porch, a small, screened back porch, dormers, bay windows, leaded glass, hardwood floors and a fireplace. Carine used to think he'd sell it once she and her siblings were off on their own, but he didn't. He hung on to it, redoing the kitchen and bathroom, updating the wiring. At the moment, he was wallpapering the downstairs half bath.

But he had the worst taste, and when Carine scooted into the half bath, she wasn't that surprised to be greeted by a tropical oasis of parrots, frogs and palm trees. The design was garish and out of place, but neither would bother Gus—or Stump, his big part-black Lab, part-everything-else dog, who'd tried to follow her in.

When she returned to the kitchen, her uncle was stirring a bubbling pot of stew on the stove. He grinned over his shoulder at her. "Bathroom makes you think you're in the rain forest, doesn't it? I thought it'd be good during March and April, when you're sure you'll slit your throat if you see another snowflake."

"I wouldn't mind being in the rain forest right now," Carine said, smiling as she hugged him. "I've missed you, Uncle Gus."

He'd driven down to Boston a few times to visit her and Antonia, but it wasn't his favorite trip, especially if it didn't involve Celtics, Bruins or Red Sox tickets. Antonia barely knew which team played what sport. Now she was married to a senator—Hank Callahan was Manny's friend, too, a tidbit the media hadn't sunk their teeth into since Louis's murder but no doubt would. Carine expected it was only a matter of time.

Ty had retreated to add wood to the fire, obviously giving uncle and niece a chance to reconnect. Gus nodded in the direction of the front room. "How're you doing with him?"

"Okay. I thought about shoving him into traffic and being done with him, but—Gus, yesterday was so awful—"

"I know, honey. I'm sorry you had to go through that." He set his wooden spoon on the counter. "Being back up here'll help you get your bearings, even with North around."

"I hope you're right." She leaned over his bubbling pot. "Gus, what's that in the stew? The green stuff?"

"Christ, you sound like you did when you were six, always sticking your nose in my cooking." He picked up his spoon again, stirring gently. "It's okra. You know, that stuff they eat down south. I thought I'd toss some in, see if I liked it."

"I'm not sure okra's supposed to be in beef stew."

"It is now. Set the table, okay?"

They ate in the kitchen. The okra wasn't a big hit with Ty, who left it on the side of his plate and said it looked like something out of a swamp. They'd pulled through a fast-food place on their way to New Hampshire, but Carine hadn't eaten much. She ate two plates of Gus's stew, and after dinner, she brought a stack of Oreos out by the fire. She sat on the floor, her knees up, and when Gus and Ty joined her, she told them everything that had happened to her over the past day and a half, start to finish. About her lunch and how she hadn't thought about photographing wild turkeys, about Louis Sanborn asking her if she wanted a ride and the toddler chasing the pigeons on the Commonwealth Avenue mall—and finding Louis dead, what she saw and heard, how she'd run out of the house and straight into Manny Carrera.

She left nothing out, except for launching into bed with Tyler North. He knew, she knew and Gus didn't need to know.

When she finished, her uncle got up and put another log on the fire. "I want you to hear me out on one thing, Carine." He stared into the fire, not at her, and its flames reflected on his lined, lean face. "Don't try to pretend you didn't see a man you know dead in a pool of his own blood."

"Gus, please—"

"Don't fight it. Don't hide from it." He shifted his gaze, glancing down at her. "Give it time. You'll learn to live with the memory."

"I don't have any other choice."

"That's just it. You do have a choice."

He brought in more wood while she and Ty did the dishes. Carine washed, dipping her hands into the hot, sudsy water, trying to stay focused on the simple chore, the routines that reminded her of normalcy. She and her sister and brother used to take turns doing the dishes. In his various home improvements, Gus had never seen the need to buy a dishwasher.

She rinsed a handful of silverware under hot water and set it in the dish strainer. "You've seen dead men," she said. "Men you knew."

"Yes," Ty said.

"What do you do?"

He lifted out the silverware into a threadbare towel. "Focus on the job I'm there to do."

"That must be when all the years of training pay off. Do you think Manny misses the work?"

Ty opened a drawer and sorted the dry silverware into their appropriate slots. "I think Manny's eaten up inside."

After they finished the dishes, Carine put on her barn coat, noticing her reflection in the window. She didn't look as raw-nerved and traumatized as she had earlier, but she was exhausted. "It'll be good to sleep in my own bed tonight."

"Sorry, toots." Ty shook his head, shrugging on his brown leather jacket. "You don't have a guest room, and I'm not sleeping on your couch. Been there, done that. I don't fit, even without you."

"Ty—you can't be serious." Once she got to Cold Ridge, she thought she'd be on her own, at most with only Gus's hovering to deal with. "I'm home. I'm safe. It's okay—"

He wasn't listening. "I have three guest rooms, and there's a pullout sofa in the den. You can have your pick."

"I'm not in any danger!"

"Someone broke into your apartment today."

"We don't know that."

"You were first on the scene after a murder yesterday. We do know that. And we know the police haven't made an arrest and are, in fact, barking up the wrong tree for their man. So—" he zipped up his jacket "—it's my house or here with the parrots and the okra."

"Let's not make this Gus's problem."

"Suits me."

She was left to choose between bad and worse—staying with Gus and Stump was clearly worse. At least at North's place, if it came to actually staying there, which she hoped it wouldn't, she'd be within short walking distance of her cabin, and there wouldn't be dog hair on her blankets. "All right. Have it your way."

"I know you're not giving in, Carine," he said cockily. "You're buying time. You think you can talk me out of it before we get to my place. Put yourself in my position. What would you do?"

"Give me a nine-millimeter to put under my pillow."

"You might be good at flutter kicks, but a gun's a different story."

"Gus gave us basic firearms instruction when we were kids. I can shoot." But she didn't want a nine-millimeter— she wanted her life back, and she thought North knew it. "You're in your Three Musketeers mood, Ty. I'm not going to fight you."

"Because you don't know what happened yesterday."

"No, because I *do* know what happened." Her barn

coat, she realized, wasn't warm enough for the dropping nighttime mountain temperatures. "I hope the police don't focus on Manny for too long. Whoever killed Louis—" She swallowed, feeling a fresh wave of uneasiness, even fear. "I don't want anyone else to end up dead. That's all I care about. Just catch whoever killed Louis, and make sure no one else gets hurt."

Ty nodded. "Fair enough."

Gus appeared in the kitchen doorway. "You two leaving? Carine, I'm here if you need me. Got that?"

"I know, Gus. Thanks. I love you."

"Love you, too, kid." His tone hardened. "North? You'll be wanting Carine looking better tomorrow morning, not worse."

A neat trick that'd be, Carine thought, but said nothing as she followed her ex-fiancé outside, the night clear, cold and very dark. But without the ambient light of the city, she could see the stars.

By the time they reached his house, Ty noticed that Carine was ashen, sunken-eyed, drained and distant. He'd watched the energy ooze out of her during their ride out from the village, along the dark, winding road to his place, the ridge outlined against the starlit sky, a full moon creating eerie shadows in the open meadow that surrounded the old brick house her ancestor had built.

He suddenly felt out of his element. What the hell was he doing? Even with the dangers and uncertainties of a combat mission, he would know exactly what was expected of him, exactly what he was supposed to do. Right now, nothing made sense.

Carine was used to his house—she'd been coming there since they were kids. His mother had given her painting lessons, helped to train her artistic eye and en-

couraged her to pursue her dream of becoming a photographer. As much as odd-duck Saskia North had been
a mother to anyone, Ty supposed she'd been one to orphaned Carine Winter.

Carine insisted on carrying her tapestry bag to the end
room upstairs and said she could make up the bed herself,
but North followed her up, anyway. Her room was next to
his mother's old weaving room, which he'd cleared out a
couple of years after her death. The different-size looms,
the bags and shelves of yarns, the spinning wheel—he had
no use for any of it and donated the whole lot to a wom-
en's shelter. His mother would sit up there for hours at a
time. Her room had a view of the back meadow and the
mountains, but she seldom looked out the window. She
had a kind of tunnel vision when it came to her work, a
concentration so deep, Ty could sneak off as a kid and
she wouldn't notice for hours.

He didn't know why the hell he hadn't died up on the
ridge. Luck, he supposed. But he'd started to wonder when
his luck would run out—how much luck did a person
have a right to?

"It's so quiet," Carine said as she set her bag down on
the braided rug. "I never really noticed before I moved to
the city. One of those things you take for granted, I guess."

"It's supposed to be good weather tomorrow. On the
cool side, but maybe we can take a hike."

"That'd be good."

Ty got sheets out of the closet, white ones that had been
around forever, and they made the bed together, but Carine looked like she wouldn't last another ten seconds.
"Sit," he told her. "Now, before you pass out."

"I've never passed out."

"Don't make tonight the first time."

"You've got your own medical kit downstairs. What

do you call it?" She smiled weakly. "Operating room in a rucksack."

"Yeah, sure. If you start pitching your cookies, I can run an IV."

"Is that a medical term? 'Pitching your cookies'?"

"Universally understood."

"I'm fine."

But she sank onto a chair and started shivering, and he tossed her a wool blanket, then threw another one over the bed. He added a down comforter, thinking, for no reason he could fathom, of her and her ab muscles. Flutter kicks. Hell.

"Tomorrow will be better," he told her.

She gazed out the window at the moonlit sky. "I didn't win any battles today."

"No one was fighting with you, Carine."

"It felt that way. Or maybe I'm just fighting myself—or I just wish I had someone to fight with, as a distraction. I don't know. It's weird to be this unfocused. Last fall, at least we had the police out combing the woods for clues. I heard the bullets. Manny saw the guys, even if he couldn't get a description. This thing—it's like chasing a ghost." She paused, tightening the blanket around her. "What about you? Are you okay? Manny's your friend."

"Manny can take care of himself."

"You PJs. Hard-asses. Trained to handle yourselves in any situation, any environment."

"Carine—"

She didn't let him argue with her. "I know, just average guys doing their job. Thanks for coming after me." She got to her feet and looked for a moment as if she might keel over, but she steadied herself, grabbing the bedpost. "I think I'll just brush my teeth and fall into bed."

He wanted to stay with her, but he'd done enough damage for one day. "You know where to find me if you need anything."

He went back downstairs, hearing her shut the door softly behind her. They'd planned to fix up the place after they were married, turn her cabin into a studio. She was so excited about the possibilities of the house, he'd teased her about falling for him because of it.

Never. It could burn down tonight and I'd still love you.

Ty poured himself a glass of Scotch and sat in front of the fireplace, the wind stirring up the acidic smell of the cold ashes. He felt the isolation of the place. Three hours to the south, a man was dead. Murdered. Shot. The police thought Manny had pulled the trigger.

And he was on Carine duty. Manny was the one in Boston under police surveillance. Whatever he was dealing with, he was doing it on his own. His choice.

When he finally headed upstairs, Ty walked down the hall and stood in front of Carine's door, listening in case she was throwing up or crying or cursing him to the rafters, although he didn't know what he'd do if it was crying. The other two he could handle. He'd never been able to take her tears, as rare as they were, as much as he told himself she was stronger because she could cry. He remembered coming upon her in the meadow, sobbing for his mother soon after her death, and even then, when he never thought he'd let himself really fall in love with auburn-haired, sweet-souled Carine Winter, it had undone him.

But he didn't hear anything coming from her room, not even the wind, and he went back down the hall to his own bed.

Eleven

❧⤸⟳⟳⤸❧

Val collapsed into bed early, but she didn't sleep for more than an hour at a time. She finally got so frustrated at her racing thoughts, she threw off her blankets and turned on a light, her gaze landing on her wedding picture. Manny was in uniform, so handsome and full of himself. Clean-cut in his maroon beret. Lately, he didn't even shave every day.

She grabbed the picture and hurled it across the room.

He hadn't called. *Bastard, bastard, bastard.*

But she was so worried about him, it was making her sick. At least Eric was okay. She'd talked to him, and he sounded saner than she did. And her breakfast with Hank and Antonia had gone well—they'd formally offered her the job. An assistant in the Washington, D.C., offices of a United States senator. It sounded exciting.

"Okay, so you won't stick your head in the oven to-night," she said. "You'll get through this."

Manny. Damn him. Why wouldn't he talk to her?

Because he wanted to protect her. Because she couldn't be trusted not to go off the deep end when faced with the truth, even an artful lie.

Except neither was true. He hadn't called her because

he was in trouble, and he was a proud man, independent to a fault. Even if she hadn't turned into a nutcase, he wouldn't have called. He was Manny Carrera being Manny Carrera.

Her shrink had suggested she stop referring to herself as a nutcase and playing fast and loose with phrases like "sticking her head in the oven."

She'd promised she would.

She stepped on a book she'd tossed on the floor after three pages. Tolkien. Bookworm that she was, she'd never gotten hobbits. But Eric had read the *Lord of the Rings* trilogy twice, and she'd promised she'd try again.

So many promises.

Her laundry was still stacked on the bureau. She'd meant to put it away after she got back from her meeting with the Callahans, but she hadn't gotten around to it. No energy. No focus. She'd heated up leftover Thai food and checked the Internet for Boston newspapers and television stations, trying to get an update on Manny's situation. Not much new. No arrests yet—that was something. At least it meant he wasn't in jail.

She wandered into the living room and opened the blinds. Damn. Still. Dark. She glanced at the clock—4:18. Too early to make coffee.

With a husband in the military, she was accustomed to being on her own—she didn't get spooked. She lay down on the couch and pulled a throw over her, but knew she was too fidgety to sleep. She turned on the television and watched CNN. Nothing much going on in the world. That was probably good. She flipped over to the Weather Channel and got the weather for Europe. She wanted to go to Spain one day. Paris and London didn't interest her as much. Rome might be fun.

At six o'clock, with a mug of hot coffee in her and a

sketchy plan of action in mind, she flipped through Manny's address book on the computer and found Nate Winter's number in New York.

He answered on the first ring. She almost hung up, but he was a U.S. marshal and probably the naturally suspicious type. "Nate? It's Valerie Carrera, Manny Carrera's wife. We met at your sister's wedding. Actually, we've met a couple of times—"

"Of course, Val, I remember you." He was polite, almost formal, no doubt because he knew he was talking to the wife of a possible murder suspect. Or maybe because she'd never called him before. "What can I do for you?"

God, she was an idiot. A card-carrying idiot. "Nothing," she whispered. "Nothing. I'm sorry to bother you."

She hung up.

She couldn't ask a U.S. marshal to do a background check on Louis Sanborn on the sly. That just wasn't the way to go. Manny would have her head. Her ass'd be out the door for sure.

She'd have to do it herself.

Twelve

Carine woke up in the wrong bed. Wrong bed, wrong house.

But she knew where she was. She wasn't disoriented for even half a second as she sat up in the snug, four-poster bed and tried to guess what time it was. Seven? Sunlight angled in through the windowpanes. At least seven.

She imagined her life pre-Tyler North, pre-Boston, pre-Louis Sanborn's murder, when she'd get up in her cabin across the meadow on just such a sun-filled, pleasant morning and make herself a pot of tea and build a fire in her woodstove to take any lingering chill out of the air before she got to work. She loved every aspect of what she did. Assignments from various magazines and journals were her mainstay, but she was selling more and more prints, earning a name for herself at shows, and she had her own Web site and taught nature photography workshops. Before moving to Boston, she'd been putting together plans for a set of New England guidebooks, new specialty cards and her annual nature calendar for a local mountain club.

She viewed her life in the city as a kind of sabbatical, not a permanent move. But she'd felt that way about her log cabin, too, when she moved in five years ago. She hadn't meant to spend the rest of her life there.

After his mother died and Ty decided not to sell the house, he'd asked Carine to check on it when he was away, make sure the yard guys were mowing the lawn, let the cleaning people in, pick up packages. He'd offered to pay her, but she considered herself just being a good neighbor. She had no idea how he could afford to keep up the place—a big house with a shed, a long driveway, fifty acres. The property taxes alone had to be astronomical. Even after they became engaged, she hadn't asked for specifics, which, in a way, summed up their relationship. She hadn't taken care of business. But, she hadn't exactly been thinking straight.

Like yesterday in her apartment, she reminded herself with a groan.

She debated going for a run, then remembered collapsing against the lamppost yesterday morning. Ty would have been on her trail then and must have seen her. She didn't like it that he'd caught her at her most vulnerable, in shock, shattered by what she'd seen. But she didn't have to be professional, distance herself. It wasn't her job to catch the killer.

But a run could wait until she was more secure on her feet.

When she got out of bed, she felt steadier, less stripped raw by her experience. She headed down the hall to the shower, taking her time, washing her hair twice, scrubbing her skin with lavender-scented bath salts left over from her last stay there. She took the time to blow-dry her hair and dressed in her most comfortable pair of jeans and her softest shirt, determined to go easy on herself today in every way she could.

She brought her digital camera downstairs with her and

set it on the table then she poured herself a cup of grayish coffee. Jodie Rancourt liked the instant gratification of the digital camera, but Carine had explained her preference for film. It'd be a while before she replaced her 35 mm Nikon and 300 mm zoom lens with a digital camera. But she wasn't resistant to change—she would do whatever worked, whatever got her the right picture.

The coffee was undrinkable. Ty must have made it hours ago. Carine spotted him outside at the woodpile, splitting maul in hand as he whacked a thick chunk of wood into two pieces. He looked relaxed, at home. He deserved this time off, she thought, dumping her coffee in the sink. She knew his military career had been intense during the past nine months—he didn't need to spend his leave making sure she didn't meddle in a murder investigation.

She returned to the table and decided she'd take pictures today. That would reassure everyone she was back in her right mind. She popped out the memory disk she'd used at the Rancourt house and popped in another disk with less memory. Whoever broke in to her apartment yesterday had ignored her less sexy Nikon, but her digital camera might have been too great a temptation if she hadn't brought it into Boston with her that morning.

She slipped the Rancourt disk into an inner coat pocket and headed outside with the camera. The morning was brisk and clear, the frost just beginning to melt on the grass. "You need a dog," she said, joining Ty at the woodpile. "Maybe Stump could father puppies."

He paused, eyeing her as he caught his breath, his eyes greener somehow in the morning light. "I'm never here long enough for a dog, and if I were, I wouldn't get one with any blood relation to Stump. He digs."

"All dogs dig."

"All dogs *don't* dig. All *Gus's* dogs dig."

She smiled. "Gus has never been much of a disciplinarian."

Ty lifted another log into place. He was wearing heavy work gloves, with wood chips and sawdust on his jeans and canvas shirt. She noticed the play of muscles in his forearms. "Your brother called," he said.

"Nate? What did he want?"

"He said Val Carrera called him at the crack of dawn and hung up." He glanced up at her, everything about him intense, single-minded. "What do you suppose that was all about?"

"I have no idea. Did Nate?"

"Nope. He and Antonia talked last night—apparently they decided you were in good hands. Or at least you could be in worse hands. He says Hank and Antonia are hiring Val as an assistant."

"With all her bookstore experience, I think she'd be great at just about anything." Carine didn't know Val Carrera all that well but liked her. "It must be weird for her with Eric away at school. She was so devoted to him when he was sick."

"Still is. She knew she had to pull back." Ty swung the heavy maul idly in one hand. "Nate told me to tell you hi."

"He's not happy about this situation, is he?"

"Hates it. But we all do."

Ty raised the maul, then heaved it down onto the log, splitting it in two, both pieces managing to fly in her direction. She jumped aside, and he grinned at her, shrugged without apology. If she didn't know how to get out of the way when someone was splitting wood by now, she deserved her fate. She felt an urge to grab a maul and have at a chunk of wood herself.

"Nate thinks Louis's murder had something to do with

Hank, doesn't he? Newly elected senator, and the Rancourts supported him in the campaign—"

"A lot of people supported him."

"But I'm right?"

"Hank didn't know Louis Sanborn. I told Nate that."

"There, you see? That's my brother, ever one for a conspiracy theory." She moved a few steps out of the sun, which was higher in the sky than she'd expected. She hadn't looked at a clock yet, but it was more like nine, not seven. "I'd like to walk over to my cabin. Gus has supposedly been checking on it, but I think he's been preoccupied with his tropical paradise half bath. Do you want to come with me?"

"Want has nothing to do with it. I'm coming." He leaned the splitter against the shed, a mix of weathered wood and black tarpaper that, like the rest of the place, needed work. "I'll scramble you up some eggs first. Gus brought them by the other night. Apparently there's some new egg lady in town. I think he's sweet on her."

"Gus?"

Ty laughed. "Don't look so shocked."

She jumped up on the counter and watched him while he brewed fresh coffee and made eggs and toast, but he finally said she was in the way and shooed her over to the table. He brought her a steaming plate, then sat down with a mug of black coffee. "Gus has already called this morning, too. The Rancourts rolled in last night. They stopped by his shop this morning to congratulate him on the rescue of the boys from Mount Chester. He thinks they were fishing for what he knew about what happened in Boston."

The Rancourts' twenty-acre property was a rare chunk of private land in that part of the surrounding White Mountain National Forest, up an isolated hill with incredible views and just yards from a seldom-used trail, a spoke off the main Cold Ridge trail.

"Did Gary Turner come with them?" Carine asked. "He's their chief of security—"

"The one with the skin and the missing fingers?"

She nodded. "You were paying attention yesterday."

"Always. Gus didn't mention him."

Carine hid her relief. She didn't want to have to deal with the Rancourts, much less Gary Turner. "Turner encouraged me to come up here. So did Sterling. He and Jodie must have decided they liked the idea themselves. Well, I suppose it's their house. They can come and go as they please."

"You don't much care for them, do you? Why'd you take the job if you don't like them?"

She shrugged. "I don't *dislike* them. I'm neutral."

Ty laughed, getting to his feet. "Yeah, right. Define *neutral*. I'm ready to go whenever you are." He dumped out the rest of his coffee in the sink, then stared out the window a moment. "Carine—I never meant to run you out of town."

She took her dishes to the sink. "You didn't."

He shifted, eyeing her. "You know that's not true."

"It's true enough." She rinsed off her plate and put it in the dishwasher, drank the last of her coffee, aware of his gaze still on her, as if even the small things she did might betray her. "I've always lived in Cold Ridge. It's been good to expand my horizons."

"You've traveled all over the Northeast, taken assignments in the Caribbean, Mexico, Costa Rica—don't give me 'I needed to expand my horizons.'"

"I didn't say I needed to. I said it's been good—"

"Hairsplitting. You should have been a lawyer."

She smiled. "This has always been home. I've never lived anywhere else."

"It still is your home."

She sighed at him, slipping her coat back on. "Do you want to listen to me or argue with me?"

He leaned back against the counter, his arms crossed on his chest as he studied her. "Then no bullshit."

"You cut-to-the-chase military types. Think creatively—"

"Carine."

"All right, all right." But she didn't have the emotional resources to dig deep and could only try to explain in a superficial way what the past nine months had been like for her. "After you dumped me—"

"Jesus," he breathed.

"Well? You're the one who doesn't want any BS. Call a spade a spade. After you dumped me, I started to look at my life here in a new way and realized I had taken everything I have for granted."

"You've never taken anything for granted."

He'd always argued with her, pushed her, prodded her. For most of her life, it'd been irritating. But last winter, she'd loved him for it. She'd thought she could talk to him about anything and hoped he could do the same with her. Only that wasn't the way it was. He'd never opened up his soul to her the way she had hers. Maybe that was why it'd been easy—at least possible—for him to walk away.

But she pushed back such thoughts. He wasn't asking about him and their relationship, but about her. "I was too rooted," she said. "I didn't want this to be the only place I'd ever lived, ever *could* live."

"What about men?" He tilted his head back, but if he was trying to be lighthearted, he was failing. There wasn't a hint of amusement in his expression. "Expanding your horizons where men are concerned?"

Carine groaned as she buttoned up her coat. "I give up. I lived a good life before you, and I've been living a good life since you. So don't feel sorry for me because of what you did. Let's just leave it at that. Whatever else that might or might not be going on with me is none of your business. Not anymore."

"Fair enough." He pulled away from the sink and grabbed his leather jacket off the counter, shrugging it on. "People wouldn't blame you if you'd set my house on fire before leaving town."

"I think they're breathing a sigh of relief that we didn't get married, after all. Imagine the kids we'd have had." Her voice caught, but he didn't seem to notice. She quickly headed for the back door. "I'm not still in love with you, if that's what you're worried about. 'Lust' might still be an issue, but, trust me, I can resist."

"Like you did yesterday afternoon?"

"Like I am right now," she said lightly, pushing open the door, smiling back at him. "There's something about a sweaty man covered in wood chips."

"If that's all it takes—"

But she was out the door, walking quickly down the driveway before she could do anything stupid. So far she'd had a good start to her day. She didn't want to blow it by ending up upstairs with him, or, even worse, having him decide her easy manner with him was an act and she wasn't over him, after all.

Keep practicing, she thought, and maybe the act would become reality.

Thirteen

***

Her cabin was cold and empty and had an odd nasty smell that she noticed the minute she walked through the back door. Ty located the cause before she did—a recently dead bat in her woodstove.

Lovely, Carine thought, and tried not to view it as an omen.

Ty carried the bat carcass out on a cast-iron poker, and she turned on the heat and stood in her kitchen as if she were a stranger. She touched the scarred, inexpensive countertop, ran her fingers over the small table, which barely fit in front of a window that looked out on the back meadow. The kitchen, bathroom and the small room that served as her studio were all on the back of the cabin. The great room stretched across the front, with its woodstove and hooked rugs, its comfortable furnishings. A ladder led up to a loft under one half of the slanted ceiling. Her bedroom. At night, she could peer through the balcony railing and watch the dying embers of the fire through the tempered-glass door of her woodstove.

It was, at most, a two-person house, all wood and dark greens, rusts, warm browns, intimate and cozy. Carine had done a lot of the work on it herself. Gus would help,

Antonia and Nate—and Ty—when they were in Cold Ridge, even Manny Carrera a couple of times.

No one in town had believed Saskia North would sell Carine the one-acre lot. Saskia likes her isolation, they'd said. Her privacy. She's strange, weird. Indeed, she had been a solitary, intensely creative woman, in her late seventies when she surprised her doubters and sold Carine the lot. Even as a neighbor, Saskia was unreliable in many ways, not showing up when she said she would, making and breaking countless promises as if they were nothing. It was as if her brain was so cluttered up with ideas and whims, sparks of imagination, that little else could get in, never mind stick. Anything she thought of would be worth pursuing, at least for a while.

But only her best ideas grabbed her and held on, and when they did, she pursued them with a vengeance—a painting, a tapestry, a collage, whatever it was. That was something to see. Her folk art was sought by collectors, and had become even more popular since her death, although Ty seemed only vaguely aware of either the financial or the artistic value of what his mother did.

After she died, Gus had often said he didn't know which he liked less, having Carine out there alone, or having her out there alone with Tyler North.

Ty came in through the back door. "Bat's where it won't stink up the joint."

"Did you bury it?"

"No, Carine, I did not bury it or hold a memorial service for it. I threw it in the woods." He zipped up his jacket. "I'll leave you here and go back and finish up the wood. Take you to lunch in town?"

His words caught her off guard. Leave her on her own? Suddenly she didn't want him to leave, or perhaps she just didn't want to be here alone, raking up memories, trying to feel at home. But she didn't want him to notice her ambivalence. "That'd be good."

He winked. "It'll be okay. See you soon."

The door shut softly behind him, and Carine felt the heat come on, clanging in the cold pipes. She checked the refrigerator. Empty, no scum to clean out. She ran the water in the kitchen sink and walked down the short hall to her studio, her desktop computer, her easel, her worktable, her shelves tidy but dusty, as if she'd died and no one had gotten around to cleaning out her house.

"Damn," she breathed, darting outside into the cold air.

Nothing was the same. Nothing would ever be the same again.

She went into her one-car garage, her much-diminished woodpile just as she'd left it months ago. She loaded cordwood into her arms, one chunk of ash, birch and oak after another, until she was leaning backward against the weight of it. Gus had brought her two cords last fall, before the shooting, and dumped it in her driveway, figuring that'd spur her to get it stacked before winter. What was left was super-dry and would burn easily. But she'd need another two cords at least if she planned to spend any part of the winter here.

She dumped her sixteen-inch logs into the woodbox she'd made herself from old barnboards, then went back for another load.

A midnight-blue car with Massachusetts plates pulled into her dirt driveway, and Gary Turner waved from behind the wheel, smiling, as if he thought she might be on edge and wanted to reassure her. He climbed out, wearing a black pea coat with no hat, the slight breeze catching the ends of his white hair. "I was going to call, but I don't have your cell phone number—"

"That's okay. I don't have it on, anyway, and coverage

out here is iffy at best." She brushed sawdust off her barn coat. "I heard the Rancourts were in town. I wasn't sure if you'd come up with them."

"I drove up this morning. I was going to drive up with Mrs. Rancourt last night, but Mr. Rancourt decided to join her, so they came on their own." He squinted at her, his eyes washed out, virtually colorless in the sunlight. "You look better, Carine. Being back here must agree with you."

She smiled. "I suppose it does."

"To be honest, I don't know why you left, man problems or not."

"It's complicated."

He laughed, surprising her. "Probably not as complicated as you think. You've just got a knack for complicating things, and that's not an insult. It's why you can do what you do with a picture of a bird. To most people—you know, it's a bird. With you, it's part of a bigger deal." He looked at her a moment, shaking his head. "You can see why I ended up in security work, not in the arts. How're you doing?"

"All right. I was just stacking wood."

He glanced around, sizing up the place. "I've driven past here a number of times. It's nice. Cute. Kind of like Little Red Riding Hood living out here all by yourself, though, isn't it?"

"It was her grandmother who lived in the woods."

"Yeah, she's the one who got eaten by the wolf. I read my fairy tales as a kid. My favorite was Rapunzel. What a little bastard that guy was, stomping his foot when he didn't get his way—" He grinned at Carine, pointing at her with a victorious laugh. "There! I knew I'd get you. A real smile."

"It feels good." She returned to the garage and squatted down, lifting a chunk of wood, its bark mostly peeled off. "But you didn't come out here to talk fairy tales and make me laugh," she said as she rose, grabbing another log on her way up. "Is there something I can do for you?"

"You're right. I have news." He sighed from the open garage doorway, his manner changing, suggesting there was nothing casual about this visit. "I thought you'd want to know. It's being reported in the media, and I have it confirmed by a source, that Manny Carrera was in Boston to recommend that Mr. Rancourt fire Louis Sanborn."

"Fire Louis? Why?"

"I don't have those details. Mr. Carrera arrived Tuesday night, and he went to see Louis on Wednesday around noontime—"

"Had Manny talked to Sterling already?"

"No. Mr. Rancourt knew Mr. Carrera was in Boston and expected to meet with him later Wednesday afternoon. The Rancourts had an appointment after lunch, that, obviously was canceled due to Louis's death. Mr. Carrera—"

Carine smiled at him. "You can't just use their first names?"

He seemed slightly self-conscious. "It's not my habit. I don't know for certain why he—Manny—went over to the house, but apparently it was to see if he could find Louis and talk to him ahead of his meeting with Mr. Rancourt. It's possible he wanted to give Louis a chance to explain whatever it was Manny had on him."

"I'm sure Manny's cooperating with the police." Carine picked up another log, another bald one, but she couldn't get a good grip on it and dropped it, narrowly missing her toes. She was grateful when Turner didn't jump to help her. "Do you have any idea why he thought Louis should be fired? He must have found out something."

"I don't know. I'm sorry."

"And the police and the media—this story's out there? It's solid?"

"Just that Mr. Carrera was in Boston to recommend Louis be fired. The facts are what they are, Carine. None of us can help that."

She squatted partway down and retrieved her dropped log. "Sterling—what's his role? I still don't understand why he hired Manny in the first place."

"Mr. Rancourt didn't ask Manny to investigate or make recommendations regarding personnel. He was to provide analysis and training. I admit," Turner added coolly, his eyes never leaving Carine as she loaded up her wood, "that I don't know anything about fast-roping out of a helicopter or treating combat injuries. Those aren't typically the skills one needs to do my job."

She peered at him over her armload of logs. "You think Sterling was wasting his time hiring Manny."

"His money, my time. But it wasn't my call. He and Mrs. Rancourt felt they owed Manny for saving their lives last November and wanted to help him get a start." Turner stepped forward, apparently just now noticing she was weighed down. "Can I help you?"

"I've got it, thanks." The load of wood was up to her chin, and she had to maneuver carefully out of the garage to avoid tripping and having it all go flying. "It feels good to get back to my old routines, actually. Did the Rancourts ask you to tell me about Manny and Louis? Is that why you stopped by?"

"It's one reason. They want to keep you up to date. So do I," he added, his voice lowering uncertainly as he followed her out of the garage. "Something's going on here, Carine, beneath the radar, so to speak. I think you should be extra cautious until the police make an arrest."

She paused, glancing back at him. "What do you mean?"

"I wish I could be more specific. Just be alert, more aware of what you say and do than you might normally be—and who you choose to be around." He hesitated, then said quietly, "It's easy for any of us to miss things when it involves our friends."

"Do you mean Manny? Or Ty North, too? You know he's in Cold Ridge, don't you? Gary—I don't get it. You're creeping me out."

He laughed. "Carine—you amaze me. For an artistic type, you're very direct, aren't you? Then again, I mustn't forget you're from New Hampshire."

"Louis called me a granite-head."

"He was a charmer, wasn't he?"

"I liked him. Look, Gary—" She dumped her logs on her small back deck, caught one before it rolled off into the grass. "If you're holding back because you have no choice, I can understand, but if it's to spare me, then please don't."

"I'm not holding back," he said. "I've told you as much as I know. The rest—instinct, experience, speculation. Nothing more. It's easy for me to see the people around you in a different light than you do, because I don't know them as well."

"That can work the other way around, too."

"Of course. Just be vigilant."

"I will. Thanks for the advice."

She thought he'd leave, but he didn't. She sat on her deck, reluctant to invite him in. The air was cool, with a periodic breeze stirring, and she could feel the mountains all around her, Cold Ridge rising up from the wide, flat meadow. A friend of hers from the Midwest, another photographer, had found the mountains oppressive, the valley beautiful but claustrophobic. Not enough flat space.

Not enough sky. At least, not until she was atop a high peak gasping at the stunning, panoramic views. Hikers on Mount Washington on a crystal-clear day could see the ocean to the east and as far as Mount Marcy in the Adirondacks, a hundred and thirty miles to the west.

Before she'd moved to Boston, Carine wouldn't have even noticed the ridge on a day like today.

"I didn't come here to upset you." Gary placed one foot on the deck next to her. He wore good hiking boots, but she saw they weren't new. "But I'm not just here about Manny Carrera wanting to recommend Louis be fired. Carine—you took pictures the other morning."

His words caught her off guard, but she was immediately aware of the disk in her inner pocket. She'd almost forgotten about it. "A few, yes. Why?"

He glanced down at her. "Mr. Rancourt would like them."

"I haven't uploaded them—"

"You can give me the disk."

"Actually, I can't. I don't have it with me." She didn't know why she lied, but she had no intention of giving him the disk. "Anyway, now that I think about it, shouldn't I give it to the police?"

"I don't see why. You took the pictures hours before you found Louis."

"Ninety minutes." She could feel herself digging in. "I took the last one ninety minutes before I found him."

"I can't imagine they'd have any significance to the investigation." Turner's manner was calm, almost as if he himself didn't understand why he'd been sent on this errand. He straightened, putting his foot back on the ground. "If you're uncomfortable turning the disk over to me, you can take it up with Mr. Rancourt. I certainly didn't come here to argue with you or force you to do anything that makes you uncomfortable."

Carine stretched out her legs, the grass damp and soft, the icy morning frost long melted. She felt chastised, as if she was being petty and stubborn. "I can provide them with prints and a separate disk of just their pictures, as I have right along."

Turner considered her words, then nodded. "I'll tell them."

Ty's truck pulled into the driveway and bounced over a rut before it came to a stop alongside Turner's car. Ty climbed out, his manner casual, easy-going—deceptively so, Carine thought. "I brought you a load of wood," he told her. "Enough for a few days."

She got to her feet, feeling a self-conscious rush. He'd think Turner showing up proved Manny's point that she needed to have Ty stick to her, keep an eye on her. If she didn't ask for trouble, it'd find her.

The two men introduced themselves and shook hands briefly. "I thought you and I'd get the chance to meet each other before now," Gary said. "I guess we've just missed each other."

"Guess so." Ty walked back to his truck and opened up the tailgate, playing the good neighbor, but Carine could feel his intensity. "Don't let me keep you two."

"I was just leaving," Gary said.

"Glad I didn't block you in."

But, of course, he deliberately *hadn't* parked behind Turner—he meant to run him off, if not to be rude about it. He wasn't even being that subtle. Carine didn't know if she should be relieved, because he wasn't a bad guy to have on her side and Turner had just been ratcheting up the pressure over the pictures, or annoyed, because she'd had the situation under control and Turner was, in fact, taking no for an answer.

Turner shifted back to her, his pale eyes almost transparent in the late morning light. "Now that I've mentioned the memory disk, I know you won't be able to resist looking at it. I warned Mr. Rancourt this could happen if I asked you for it, but it's the risk he decided to take." He smiled faintly. "He knew I wasn't going to wrestle you for it."

"Gary, I honestly don't know what you're talking about—"

"I know you don't. Think back to this conversation when you view the pictures." He seemed more tired, even ill at ease, than irritated. "Remember that I tried to be discreet."

He nodded politely at North, who'd obviously taken in every word as he dumped wood out of the back of his truck. Then, without another word, Turner got into his car, started the engine and backed out.

Carine exhaled, almost choking on tension. "Damn. Ty, listen, I don't know what the hell's going on, but I need—I need to go back to your house and get my camera."

He tossed another couple of hunks of cordwood onto her driveway. He wasn't wearing his work gloves, and she noticed he'd scraped a knuckle, not badly. "Uh-huh. You want to give me a hint what this is all about?"

"First you tell me if you knew Manny planned to recommend Sterling Rancourt fire Louis Sanborn."

"It came up. Why, is it out there?"

"Apparently."

"Pissed I didn't mention it?"

"Does it matter?"

He shrugged, unapologetic. "It doesn't explain anything."

"Then why not tell me? You don't need a security clearance, Ty. Keeping your mouth shut comes naturally to you."

"That's what my third-grade teacher told the security guys when they came up here and checked me out."

"You're making that up."

He jumped out of his truck, landing lightly on the dirt driveway. "Is Gary Turner going to break into my house and steal your camera if we don't get over there?"

"He might, but I think he credits himself with playing by the rules."

North examined his skinned knuckle, then shrugged it off. "Depends on whose rules we're talking about, doesn't it?"

"Anyway, it won't do him any good if he does steal the camera," Carine said. "I have the disk he's after in my coat pocket."

"Well, well, aren't you lucky he didn't frisk you?"

"I thought about taking pictures today—I didn't want to use the same memory disk. I had my camera with me yesterday when my apartment was searched. If it *was* searched."

"Rancourt and Turner both saw you yesterday with the camera." Ty frowned at her, thinking. "I take it you didn't have it with you during lunch on Wednesday?"

She shook her head. "I left it in the hall of the Rancourt house." She swallowed, not relishing what she had to do. "I hope Gary's wrong and there's nothing on the disk but pictures of the drawing room mantel."

Ty stood very close to her, smelling of wood, reminding her of their intimacy yesterday in her apartment. She'd known he wouldn't refuse her. Somehow, she'd known that.

Had someone slipped into her apartment to find her digital camera?

What was on the damn disk?

Ty smiled at her. "You look like someone's asked you to eat a dead bug."

"That's one way to put it."

"I've done it, babe. It's not so bad."

Her shoulders sagged, and she almost managed a laugh. "Ty, damn it—"

"Come on. Hop in my truck." He slung an arm over her shoulders, still playing the good neighbor, the buddy who'd been at her side for as long as she could remember, even if it was sometimes so he could push her out of a tree. "Let's go see if someone borrowed your camera at lunch and took incriminating pictures before, during or after poor Louis Sanborn got shot with a .38 in the library."

Carine angled a look at him. "You don't know it was a .38."

"It's an educated guess."

"Whose? Yours or Manny's?"

"Colonel Mustard's. Come on, Carine. Give me a break."

"What else did Manny tell you that you haven't told me?"

"That you'd be a meddling pain in the ass if I didn't keep you occupied." He dropped his arm, opening the truck door. "He fed some line about you having a strong moral compass."

She climbed into the passenger seat, fighting an urge to let him take the disk and see what was on it while she stayed here and stacked wood. "I have a feeling if my strong moral compass was working, I'd have given Gary Turner the disk."

Carine could have popped the memory disk back into her camera and looked at the pictures on its tiny LCD screen, but she waited to boot up the computer in Ty's den, attaching a USB cable to the corresponding port on her camera. A screen came up on the monitor, with a contact-like sheet of all the photos on the disk. It was a fresh disk. The only photos on it, at least as far as she knew, were those she'd taken Wednesday morning on Commonwealth Avenue, before lunch, before she found Louis.

She was supposed to click on what she wanted to do with the pictures—copy them to the hard drive, view a slide show, print them—but she was so stunned, all she could do was gape at the monitor.

The few pictures she'd taken were there, idle shots of the drawing room mantel and chandelier—she hadn't expected to keep any of them. But it was the four pictures she *didn't* take that had her attention.

All four depicted a mostly naked Jodie Rancourt up against the library wall, her legs wrapped around the waist of an apparently fully clothed Louis Sanborn. His back was to the camera, but there was no question of his identity—or what he and Jodie were up to.

Ty whistled, peering over Carine's shoulder. "I wonder who took these last four shots."

Carine shook her head, stunned. "It wasn't me. Someone must have used my camera while I was at lunch. The pictures—the angle—" She paused, making herself breathe, and tried again. "Whoever took the pictures must have stood in the doorway to the hall. My camera was right there on the radiator."

"Talk about nature photography."

She elbowed him. "That's lame, North."

"Just trying to ease the tension in the room. Damn. You didn't have any idea—"

"No. None. Jodie Rancourt and Louis Sanborn? He'd only worked for the Rancourts for *two weeks*."

"Doesn't looked forced on her part, does it?"

"No," Carine said. "No, it doesn't."

Ty squinted, eyeing the pictures more closely, then gave another low whistle. "Agreed. I guess you never know what goes on between two people."

But Carine's throat was tight, her heart racing. "My blood pressure must be a thousand over a thousand. Ty, I swear, I never had an inkling they were having an affair."

"Maybe it was a moment," he said, "not an affair."

"Well, it was a 'moment' not long before one of the two people involved in it was killed. Louis asked me if I wanted a ride while I was on my way back from lunch—he and Jodie must have—" Carine hesitated, trying to steady her breathing, calm herself. "They must have had their liaison before he went out."

"Liaison?"

"Ty, *please.*"

"Babe, they were screwing each other blind. Facts are facts. How long were you gone? About ninety minutes?"

She nodded, transfixed by the pictures on the screen, embarrassed for the participants. But if they'd wanted privacy, they could have skipped the library and gone somewhere else. Had there been any clues, any hints she'd missed? Did Sterling know? Turner? "I wasn't in a hurry. There wasn't much going on at the house…that I knew about, anyway."

"Ninety minutes is plenty of time for a quickie in the library." Ty shook his head tightly, obviously as uncomfortable with what they were seeing as she was. "Jesus. What a nasty business. They took a hell of a risk if they didn't want to be caught. Anyone could have walked in on them—"

"Obviously someone did and took pictures."

Carine sank back in the chair, an ergonomic design

that she'd helped choose when Ty purchased his computer. The den was tucked in the southwest corner of the house, a sun-filled room with original 1817 twelve-over-twelve paned windows that looked onto the front yard. It was prosaically furnished with a pullout couch, a beat-up leather club chair, a rolltop desk and the computer table. One of Saskia's collages hung on the back wall, depicting images of the White Mountains.

"Do you think Manny knew?" Carine asked quietly.

Ty shook his head. "I don't know."

"What if—" She cleared her throat, her hands shaking as she turned back to the computer screen. "What if he walked in on Jodie and Louis?"

"Manny didn't take those pictures."

"No, but maybe he came in after someone else had. I wonder if he said something to the police, if Turner found out—Gary obviously knew, or at least guessed, these pictures existed. He said he was asking me for the disk on Sterling's behalf, but I'm not sure now."

"Maybe Turner took the pictures."

Carine sighed. "Lots of questions, no answers."

"It's not our job to come up with answers," Ty said.

She stared at the screen. "I didn't take these pictures."

"I didn't ask."

"Someone will. I don't think there's a way I can prove it, but—I didn't take them. Why would anyone do such a thing?"

"Blackmail. Titillation. To humiliate and embarrass one or both of the two lovers, or the jilted husband."

"The possibilities are endless, aren't they?" Carine quickly completed the process of uploading the pictures to Ty's hard drive, as a backup to the disk in case something happened before she could get it to the police. "We should notify the detectives on the case. If Jodie Rancourt told the police she was out shopping, and instead she was with Louis—"

"She could have told the police the truth," Ty said. "They might just have kept it to themselves. For all we know, this is old news to them."

"I hope so. I hate the idea of being the rat." Carine popped out the memory disk and disconnected the USB cable. "Gary Turner said to remember he tried to be discreet."

"Right," Ty said skeptically. "Maybe that's why he took the trouble of using a key instead of a crowbar when he broke into your apartment yesterday."

She tucked the disk into her coat pocket. "We don't know that was him."

"A lot happened on your lunch hour, that's for damn sure."

"And I didn't have a clue."

Ty straightened. "We can call the Boston cops on the way to lunch and ask them what they want us to do with the disk."

"Us? Ty, there's no reason for you to get involved."

"Too late. The minute you found Louis Sanborn, I was involved." He headed for the door, glancing back at her, his eyes a soft green, a real green, but as unreadable as if they'd been green rocks. "But you knew that, didn't you?"

"Maybe I did," she said, and slipped past him into the hall.

Fourteen

His lungs were bursting from sucking in the cold air, rushing up the path too fast. His legs ached. But Sterling pushed himself harder, determined to make it up the last thirty-foot, near-vertical stretch of the path. He'd started from his house, thinking he'd only go for a short walk to blow off some steam, and now he was almost onto the main ridge trail, the same one Abraham Winter had carved almost two hundred years ago.

How had his life gotten so miserably, abominably out of control?

What the hell had happened?

He groaned, lunging upward, crab-walking on the rocks and exposed tree roots. The path was still below the treeline, winding through lichen-covered rocks and fir trees. He had no business being out here alone, but he didn't care.

"Fuck," he muttered, "I don't care about anything."

With a final spurt of energy, he made it to the top of the hill, onto a rounded rock with a blue-splashed cairn marker that indicated he had come, at last, to the Cold Ridge Trail. If he kept going, soon he would be above the treeline, walking along the narrowest section of the ridge, then up to a summit and back down to the cliffs and the famous, awe-inspiring view of valley and ravines, a mountain lake, a river. He'd never gotten that far. Last year, he and Jodie had barely made it above the treeline before they got into trouble.

He paused, sweating, gazing out at the cascade of mountains, some of the highest ones snowcapped, others bald rock against a cloudless sky—which wouldn't last. November was a gray month in northern New England, and the weather forecasters promised that new clouds would move in before sunset.

The days were shorter, the sun lower in the sky. With no city lights, the nights were long and dark, and he could feel the claustrophobia eating at him, just knowing there were only a few more hours of sunlight left. He didn't know how people lived up here all winter.

He wondered if God had intended for him and Jodie to die on the ridge last November and that was why, ever since, their lives had come apart bit by bit, piece by piece.

Exhausted and frightened, shivering uncontrollably, Sterling remembered, with a wince of regret, how he'd grabbed hold of Manny Carrera after their rescue and sobbed. "I was so scared, so damn scared. I thought I could survive up here on my own."

"Nobody survives on their own, pal," Manny had said in his matter-of-fact, unwavering way. "We all need a helping hand."

"You don't—you survive on your own."

"No, I don't. I'm part of a team, they're part of a squadron, and on up the ladder it goes—get it? We each have a job to do. We look out for one another. Right now, I'm looking out for you. So, just rest easy, okay?"

"But if you were stuck behind enemy lines, or attacked

or captured, you'd know how to handle yourself. You'd know what to do."

"Yes, sir, but I'd also know I had people who'd never rest until I got back to safety. They'd come for me, the way I am here for you right now. You want to keep talking about this shit, or do you want to get off this goddamn mountain?"

Manny Carrera...*ah, Manny.*

Had Manny taken those pictures of Jodie and Louis Sanborn? Had he known about their affair and that was why he wanted Sanborn fired? Had he tried to take advantage of the situation?

Sterling liked to believe if he'd signed up to become a PJ as a young man, he'd have made it through the rough training. The washout rate was high—often more than eighty percent. But over celebratory drinks at his house in the mountains, after they'd all warmed up last year after the rescue, Manny had told him he hated the word *washout,* because it implied guys didn't cut it, that they were lesser, somehow, failures. "They just weren't where they were supposed to be. Not everyone figures that out the easy way."

Manny had stared into his beer as if he had bigger worries. It was only later that Sterling learned that Eric Carrera had almost died of an asthma attack.

It was inconceivable Manny Carrera would take pictures like the ones the local police now had in their custody, awaiting two Boston detectives who would arrive later that evening.

Sterling had no doubt that Gary Turner had done his best to get his hands on the disk. He'd been caught between a rock and a hard place. Jodie had told Turner about the pictures and pressed him to get them before anyone found out—including Sterling. Gary had hinted that he needed Carine's pictures from Wednesday morning to prevent a scandal, but he hadn't gone into detail, instead asking Sterling to trust his sense of discretion. When he'd returned empty-handed, Jodie had been forced to come clean about her lunch-hour rendezvous in the library.

Lies and deception—Sterling had no idea what to believe anymore. She said it was her first and only time with Sanborn, and she didn't have a clue anyone had taken the pictures, never mind who. It was a chance encounter, she said. No one could have predicted it. Had Sanborn planned to seduce her, arranged for a cohort to take the pictures? Had someone merely stumbled onto the illicit goings-on and taken advantage of the situation?

Had Manny Carrera seized the moment and snapped four quick shots himself?

But why leave the damn camera behind?

A strong gust of wind blew up the side of the ridge and went right through Sterling's thin jacket. It wasn't a long hike back down the trail, but he knew he needed to get moving soon, before the temperature started dropping with the waning sun. He could feel darkness closing in on him, as if it could suffocate him. His head ached. He hadn't paced himself well.

Although he hadn't seen the pictures himself, he kept imagining them over and over and over. His wife and Louis Sanborn in the library. Dear God.

Jodie herself could have arranged to have the pictures taken.

It would be retaliation. Revenge. Evening the score. Payback. *My turn, Sterling. See? Here's the proof.*

He'd had a short-lived affair with a woman in the office, after their rescue last November. It had lasted six weeks. She was gone now—Jodie had made him fire her. He said he'd drifted because of their near-death experience, and it was nothing as ordinary as a midlife crisis, nothing as tawdry as sex on the side. She claimed to believe him, to have forgiven him. More lies? More deception?

He spotted her down on the trail, circling toward him, moving fast, not hurrying but determined. She was hatless, and the wind caught the ends of her hair. He wondered what she would do if he jumped. He could time it just right and smash onto the rocks at her feet, let her screams of horror be what he heard last as he died.

She could cry buckets at his funeral and get herself a boy toy, play the rich widow, spend all her poor dead husband's money. But she had plenty of her own—she came from a well-heeled family, far better off than his own had been. He'd been so proud when he married her.

He wondered if he'd ever come close to understanding her.

She joined him on his rounded section of rock. "May I?"

"There you go, Jodie. You do what you want, then ask if it's all right."

"I'm sorry," she whispered, although her tone and expression didn't change. She had it all under control, he thought. She stood next to him, squinting out at the mountains, panting slightly from exertion. "Gorgeous, isn't it?"

"I can't focus on the scenery. I keep seeing you—"

"Don't. Don't do it to yourself, Sterling. That's what I did when it was you and your bimbo, and it does no good."

He wondered if he could get away with pushing her. Probably not. Learn your wife screwed a man minutes before he was murdered, that there are pictures—then, oops, she dies in an accident on Cold Ridge. Nobody'd believe it.

"It was like it was happening to someone else." She spoke quietly, staring out at the mountains. She had on her parka and carried water in a hip pack, marginally better prepared than he was for the conditions. "I felt as if I was floating on the ceiling, looking down at myself, at this woman I knew but didn't know. I was horrified, a little fascinated. And frightened because I knew what a risk she—what a risk I was taking."

"Jodie, I don't want to hear about it."

She angled her head up at him. "Was it that way for you when you had your affair?"

"I try not to think about it. I've put it behind me."

"Of course," she added, as if he hadn't spoken, "I was with Louis only that one time."

Sterling turned away from the view, taking the first, precipitous steps back down the steep section of the path. He'd just wanted to make it onto the ridge trail. That was all. He glanced back at his wife. "I suppose I deserved that."

"Neither of us deserves what we're doing to each other. I felt—I feel tainted. Dirty. Then, to have Louis killed."

"Did you do it?"

"What!" She almost fell backward, and automatically—he couldn't help himself—Sterling reached out for her, but she was too far away and had to regain her balance on her own. The near-fall upset her, all that elegant reserve gone now. "No, goddamn it, *no*. I didn't kill him. Where the hell would I have gotten a gun? Why would I—"

"It was a stupid thing to say."

"An affair is one thing, Sterling, if that's even what it was—but murder—" She choked back her outrage. "I'd hoped you wouldn't find out. I had no idea about the pictures. I never saw, never heard—"

"You were too busy with other things."

"Goddamn it! I'm trying here, Sterling. I'm trying to

make up for lost ground and be honest with you. I realized, even before—I realized then and there, while I was in the library, that I didn't want to hurt you. All my desire for revenge fell away, and that was what was left. That I loved you."

He breathed through his clenched teeth, not knowing what the hell he felt. Anger? Pity? Humiliation? Not love, not at that moment. "I should have had Gary take the damn disk from Carine, steal it if he had to."

"I tried to steal it yesterday. I went to her apartment— I have a key—"

"Jodie, for God's sake!"

She blinked through her tears. "I had no choice. I told the police I was with Louis, but I never mentioned what we were doing. I didn't lie to them. I just didn't tell them everything."

"You lied to me."

She nodded. "I know, and I'm sorry."

But Sterling frowned, her words sinking in, the holes they presented. "Jodie, if you didn't hear anyone while you were with Louis, how did you know there were pictures?"

She didn't speak for a moment. "I had a call."

"What?" This time he really did almost lose his footing.

"It just said, 'There are pictures.'" She licked her lips, not meeting his eye. "That was all. Like it was a friendly warning, and I should take action."

"Christ." Sterling raked a hand over his head, whipped around on the path, stones flying up under his hiking boots. *"Christ Almighty!"*

"I told Gary this morning. I didn't know what else to do. He decided you had to know about the disk, but I begged him not to tell you how I knew, to let me tell you first—"

"For God's sake, Jodie. For *God's sake!* How could you not have told me?"

She ignored his question. "I think it was Manny who called." Her voice was hoarse from the dry wind, the tension. "I think he took the pictures. He must have planned to use them as further leverage against Louis, maybe to get him to quit so he didn't have to tell you what he knew. He probably didn't take the camera because Louis was about to catch him—or he figured he could get it from Carine since they're friends."

Sterling's head was spinning. "The police will look at the pictures as more evidence against him."

"We can't help that," Jodie said quietly.

He bit off a sigh, but his rage had subsided. He was tired and cold, past the point of feeling anything. He took another step down the path, hardly paying attention to the tricky footing. "I'm heading back to the house. You can do what you want to do."

"Can I walk with you?"

He nodded without enthusiasm. "Suit yourself."

"Sterling—we'll get through this together."

"I'll get through it," he said stiffly. "I don't care if you do or not."

Fifteen

❧⟞⟐⟐⟐⟞❧

Val Carrera waited until midafternoon for Manny to call her. When he didn't, she started calling him and leaving him messages on his voice mail. One every fifteen minutes. After the tenth, he called her back. "Damn it, Val, can't you take a hint? I don't want to talk to you."

"Tough. Where are you? Not in jail, I presume, or you wouldn't have your cell phone."

"My hotel. A different one. I'm on my own dime now. I'm climbing the fucking walls. There, you happy?"

"Police watching you?"

"Yes."

Her heart jumped. It was real. Her husband was under suspicion for murder. "Jesus, Manny. How the hell did this happen? Is there anything I can do?"

"I don't know how the hell this happened. There's nothing you can do. Well, there is." He paused, and she could feel his smile—she swore she could. "You could get a job. You drive people crazy when you're not working."

"Ass. I've got a job. Hank and Antonia hired me this morning. Manny—" She choked back a sob, hating herself for displaying any weakness. "Do you want me to come to Boston?"

"No."

"Have you talked to Eric?"

"No. You?"

"Yesterday. I'll call him again tonight. He's—well, you know how tight-lipped he is. Gee, I wonder where he gets it. But I can tell he's worried about you. I am, too. Sorry, bub, but you can't control how we feel."

"Val, listen to me. Worry all you want. Tear your hair out, curse me to the rafters. I don't care. Just stay out of this mess. Understood?"

"Manny, you're my husband. What happens to you—"

"What happens to me doesn't happen to you. When I jump out of a helo, I don't see you strapped on my back."

He clicked off.

She hated him. She really did.

She hit Redial on her phone, since his number was the only one she'd called all day. She got his voice mail again. He'd probably shut off his cell phone, knowing she'd call back.

Her apartment reeked of cheap pizza, half of it still in the open box on the coffee table. She'd had it delivered, and next time, she thought, she was going to make them wait until she got it out and give them the damn box back, let them get rid of it.

"Someone ought to come up with a self-destructing pizza box," she grumbled, carrying it into the kitchen.

She stuck the leftover pizza in the refrigerator, no plate, no aluminum foil—she just laid the two cold slices on the rack by themselves. If she was still here, she'd heat it up for supper. If not, it could rot. The pizza box she dropped onto the floor and jumped on, flattening it, then used her feet to fold it as small as she could, but even that didn't fit into her trash can.

When he was home, Manny did the trash. He never

complained about it. They shared the cooking, but she didn't think he'd ever touched a toilet brush in his life. Maybe in PJ indoc somebody made him swab out a toilet. If so, it was the last damn time.

She scooped a stray piece of pepperoni off the floor, dumped it in the trash and wiped up the spot with the toe of her running shoe. Okay, so she wasn't a great housekeeper. She liked books. She could read one a day. She *loved* talking books with her customers back when she was a store manager. She'd read anything—mystery, romance, thrillers, the women's book club books, biographies. She'd gotten into self-help for a while, but it always made her feel inadequate, sitting there answering the questions about dreams and goals, writing her own eulogy. That was pretty sick. *Here lies Val Carrera, who read a lot of books and tried to do right by her family, even if she screwed it up most of the time.*

She hoped there were readers on Hank's staff. If they were all policy wonks and just wanted to talk about reforming the health-care system, she'd slit her own throat.

She grabbed her lukewarm Diet Coke off the coffee table and took it with her to the computer, set up in a corner of the living room. Pepperoni pizza and a Diet Coke. Made a lot of sense. But she was wired as it was, and sugar in addition to the caffeine would put her over the top. Then she would get in her car and drive up to Boston. Manny was acting as if he was on a combat mission and she was out of line for wanting to show up. No wives on search-and-rescue missions. Except he wasn't in the air force anymore.

Two years in uniform had done it for her. She had no interest in being career military. She knew women who could be generals and wanted the job a whole lot more than she ever did.

She'd wanted what she'd had. A sexy, irreverent husband who rescued people. A smart, healthy son. A job she loved.

But she didn't have any of those things anymore.

"Negative thinking, negative thinking."

The monitor had gone into sleep mode. She got it up and running again, but she was having the same problem she'd had since she got back yesterday from breakfast with Hank and Antonia—she couldn't access Manny's files without his password. Why did the bastard need a password? Had he decided she was nuts and couldn't be trusted with access to his files?

She'd tried every possible password combination she could think of. Eric's middle name, his birthday, the name they'd picked out if he'd been a girl. *Her* middle name. Her maiden name. Their wedding date. Manny was a sentimentalist at heart, and he wasn't particularly creative or intricate in his thinking. It *had* to be something obvious.

Irritated, she typed *bullheaded,* but that didn't work, either.

Tyler North? Nope, not in any combination she tried.

If she called Manny and asked him for his password, he wouldn't tell her. He'd just say "butt out" and hang up. Or not bother to call her back at all.

Stubborn.

Irritating.

Nothing was working. She flopped back against her chair and sipped her Diet Coke. She had to stay busy. If she didn't, she'd think. She'd relive the scary, early days of Eric's illness. She'd relive charging off to the emergency room while Manny was out of the country, facing dangers of his own—he couldn't talk about most of his missions, but she was well aware of what he did.

She didn't think, not then, that she could lose them

both, her husband to combat, her son to illness. Only afterward, only when they were safe. It was sick, but there it was.

She suddenly realized she was shaking, crying. Her gaze settled on the number of her therapist, which she'd written on an orange Post-it note and stuck to the side of the computer. She grabbed it and reached for the phone, but she didn't dial, instead doing her relaxation and visualization exercises until she felt the incipient panic pass.

It'd be okay. She was getting better.

For grins, she typed *crazywoman,* but nothing happened.

"Maybe I should just shoot the damn thing."

If she couldn't get into Manny's files and he didn't want to talk to her, what *could* she do?

She dug her date book out of her handbag and looked up Tyler North's number in New Hampshire. If he wasn't on duty, he'd be there. She used to be critical of his weird, crazy mother. Not anymore. For the most part, she'd done the best she could. She made mistakes. But she'd been lucky.

If Manny had confided in anyone, it'd be his best friend and fellow PJ. Obviously, Val thought, it wasn't his wife.

Sixteen

❧❧❧

Ty tried to concentrate on the scenery as he drove Carine up the notch road, a pass in the mountains with a small lake, a waterfall, a rock-strewn brook, ledges, cliffs and breathtaking views. But it wasn't easy to focus on anything but the tense and distracted woman beside him. She wanted to see the Rancourts. He told her he didn't think it was a good idea. She said, fine, she'd rent a car. She'd take a bus back to Boston and get her own damn car. She'd hike up the ridge to the connecting trail that led down to the Rancourt house.

She wouldn't get Gus to take her, that was for damn sure. Gus didn't like the idea of her going up to the Rancourts, either. She and Ty had dropped off the embarrassing pictures of Jodie Rancourt with the Cold Ridge police and met Gus for lunch at a village café. Gus didn't get it. Why would Carine want to see the Rancourts? Why would they want to see her?

But Gus couldn't talk her out of it, and Ty sure as hell couldn't. They tried all through lunch. The café was owned by a couple of ex-hippies who scrawled their daily menu on a chalkboard. Carine had turned over her digital camera and camera bag as well as the memory disk. The police had warned her to expect a visit from the Boston detectives now on their way to New Hampshire to pick up the evidence—they'd want to talk to her, as well as the Rancourts.

Carine had hardly touched her sweet potato chowder. Gus had a bowl, too, but Ty didn't go near it—he had a bacon-lettuce-and-tomato sandwich. He didn't like Carine's lack of appetite. "Flutter kicks'll really kill you if you don't keep up your strength," he told her.

"They kill me, anyway."

"Why are you doing flutter kicks? Why not just take an exercise class in Cambridge? Pilates. Kickboxing. Something like that."

She'd given him a smile that he couldn't quite read. "Maybe I'm training for a triathlon."

"Okay. You've always been fit. You need to do flutter kicks to train for a triathalon?"

"Can't hurt." She seemed evasive. "I have endurance. I don't have a lot of power and speed. I'm working on it, though. You can swim twenty-five meters under water on one breath, right?"

He suspected she was trying to distract herself—or distract him. "It's not something I do every day—"

"How did you do it at all?"

"Willpower."

"I have willpower."

"When it comes to a picture you want. You'll wait around for the wind to blow the right way a lot longer than I ever would. But swimming underwater—nothing's at stake for you if you pop up for another breath. For me, it was a requirement. I had to do it."

"You're saying if you want to be a PJ bad enough, you'll stay under."

"It helps."

"That's a crock. I think it has more to do with lung capacity and efficient strokes."

He grinned. "There's that, too."

But she hadn't smiled back, and he knew the illicit pictures bothered her. She'd liked and trusted Jodie Rancourt and Louis Sanborn, but they'd committed adultery in such a way that she'd become involved. She felt used, tainted.

Gus had shaken his head over his soup. "I thought you'd be out of the fray up here, but now they're all up here with you. The Rancourts, this Gary Turner. Next it'll be Manny Carrera."

Gus was all for outfitting his niece for a three-day hike in the mountains. He even said Ty could go with her, seeing how he was more like a brother to her these days. That was designed, Ty had no doubt, to draw a response from Carine, and it did, just not the one Gus expected. He'd wanted, clearly, a hint about what was going on with the two of them. Instead, she shoved her bowl across the table at him and stormed out of the café.

"I guess 'brother' was a bad choice of word," Gus said, not particularly remorseful. "North?"

"I'm doing the best I can, Gus."

"No, you're not. You're just as scared as she is."

"Doesn't matter. I'll do what I have to do."

"To keep her safe—or to keep Manny Carrera safe? Whose side are you on? His or Carine's?"

Ty had attempted a joke. "I'm on the side of truth and justice," he'd said, but Gus didn't laugh, instead sticking him with the bill.

The access road to the Rancourt property snaked up a fifteen-hundred-foot rise of pitted pavement with one bona fide hairpin turn. It wasn't the sort of location people who lived in the region full-time generally chose for their homes, even if they could afford it. Ty glanced at

Carine as he negotiated a relatively straight incline, the hill falling away on her side, the bare-limbed trees offering vistas that seemed almost endless. "We still have time to give this up and take Gus's advice and disappear in the mountains for a few days."

She smiled briefly. "Do you still have a taste for beef jerky? I remember as a kid you'd grab a piece of beef jerky and head up the ridge. You weren't even eight years old. I don't know how you lived."

"I don't know, either, but I've got MREs these days. Good stuff."

"Purloined 'meals ready to eat.' Well, I understand they're better than they used to be. The prepackaged camping foods certainly are." She looked out her window, the road twisting again now, evergreens hanging over rock outcroppings. "Once I pass the PJ Physical Abilities and Stamina Test, I'm going to take one of the Appalachian Mountain Club winter camping courses. I think that'd be a challenge."

"Once you pass the what?"

She glanced over at him, a welcome spark in her blue eyes. "The test aspiring PJs take to be accepted into the program."

"Ah. I forgot that's what it's called. Ominous. I just remember running my ass off, nearly drowning a few times, and sweating a lot. Indoc was more of the same, just worse. This explains all the running, swimming and flutter kicks?"

"I'm having fun. I've read up on what you do. All these years with you in and out of my life, and I never really knew much about what a PJ does. Is it true that instructors strap you into a helicopter, blindfold you and throw you in the water to see if you can get out?"

"It's a simulated helicopter."

"Real water."

"I remember," he said.

"You got out?"

He smiled. "I'm a PJ, right? I got out."

She sighed, staring back out her window, the distraction of PJ talk not lasting. "I shouldn't have gotten mad at Gus. He's just trying to help. He doesn't want to see me making the same mistakes all over again with you."

"Maybe, but he was also trying to make you mad. Get your blood up. Put some color in your cheeks."

"Well, it worked."

"You're lucky Gus hasn't locked you in your room by now."

Her vivid eyes stood out against her pale skin. "You taught me how to go out a window on a bedsheet."

"As if you needed teaching."

"It's the age difference. It was more telling when we were six and ten. Now—" She turned back to her window as they passed a steep, eroded embankment. "Never mind."

Ty could see she was preoccupied, dreading her visit with the Rancourts. "I can turn back."

She shook her head. "I need to do this."

He downshifted, taking the last section of hill before the road dead-ended at the Rancourt driveway and the start of the trail that merged with the main Cold Ridge trail. A wild turkey wandered into the road in front of them, and he stopped while it stood sentry for a dozen other turkeys that meandered out from the woods. Carine sat forward with a gasp of excitement, as if she'd never seen a wild turkey before. "Look at them! I wish I had my camera." She bit down on her lower lip, then added, reality intruding, "My Nikon."

Ty couldn't stand another second of seeing her so shattered by her experience in Boston, finding Louis Sanborn dead, running into Manny and now finding the four pictures that had appeared on her camera disk. "Ah, hell." He gripped the wheel, damn near stalling out. "Carine, I'm sorry. I don't know what else to say. If I'd just married you—"

"Don't, Ty." Her voice was surprisingly gentle, more so than he deserved. "It doesn't help. Something worse might have happened if we'd gone through with the wedding. We don't know. We could have been robbed and killed on our honeymoon."

"We postponed a honeymoon. I only had a few days. I had to get back to Hurlburt—"

"You know what I mean."

Actually, he did. It was a rationalization, a way to make herself feel better about what he'd put her through. But he said nothing.

"Anyway, you *didn't* marry me," she went on. "And I didn't accept Louis's offer of a ride, and I didn't call the police from inside the Rancourt house and not run into Manny."

"That's not the same."

"You're not responsible for what's happened to me this week. Or last week. Or ever. I'm responsible for my own actions. Don't you think I understood the risks when I let myself fall for you? Ty—I've known you all my life."

He let the truck idle a moment. "When did you first want to sleep with me?"

She groaned. "You can be such a jackass, you know."

"Your sister says the jackass fairy must have visited me every night when I was a kid. You two work that one out together?"

"No, but I like it." This time her smile reached her eyes. "I wonder what a jackass fairy looks like."

"I'm really a nice guy. Everyone says so."

She went very still, her hands on her thighs. "You're the best, Ty. I've known that for a long, long time. But you're not—" She sighed, grinning suddenly, unexpectedly. "You're not normal."

"Normal?"

She nodded.

"Right. Like you are, she who can outstare an owl."

"Did you see my barred owl in the woods last fall? I think he knew I was going to be shot at. He flew away. I sometimes think if he hadn't, I might have been killed."

Ty shook his head. "Not to burst your bubble, babe, but it wasn't the owl that saved you. Those guys were using a scoped rifle. They missed you on purpose."

"You're probably right."

Carine settled back in her seat, and he continued up the road and turned onto the Rancourt driveway. Its blacktop was in better shape than the road, the sprawling house visible farther up on the hill.

"I think my digital camera's cursed," she said quietly. "When the police return it, I'm getting rid of it."

Ty stopped the truck at the bottom of the driveway and pulled on the emergency brake. When he reached over and touched her cheek, she didn't tell him to go to hell. "Your camera's not cursed. You're not cursed. And I loved you last winter. I loved you as much as I've ever loved anyone."

"I know."

He kissed her cheek, then her mouth, her lips parting. He threaded his fingers into her hair as their kiss deepened, memories flooding over him, regrets, longings—for her, for himself—but nothing that he could put to words.

She was the one who pulled away, brushing her fingertips across his jaw before she sat back in her seat. "You're a complicated man, Sergeant North."

"Not that damn complicated. I could pull over somewhere more private—"

"I think you've made your point."

Not very well, he thought. He knew Carine, and she'd
be thinking he was just interested in sex and that was why
he'd kissed her. And he was—he was very interested in
sex. Hell, so was she. But his feelings toward her were
more involved than that, only he didn't know how to get
at them, crystallize them in a few words that made any
sense. That was how he'd ended up waiting until the last
minute to pull out of their wedding, just trying to think
of how to say what he had to say, so that she'd understand
and not blame herself. He got the blaming part right—
she blamed him instead. But he'd mucked up getting her
to understand.

He continued up the Rancourt driveway, which swept
them into a parking area in front of an attached three-car
garage. They were at a fairly high elevation, the expansive
views of the surrounding mountains impressive, majes-
tic more than intimate. The landscaping was natural and
minimalist, designed to blend in with the environment,
with a sloping lawn, stone walls and plantings limited to
those that occurred in the area—flowers only in pots, no
ornamental trees and shrubs. The glass-and-wood house
was built into the hillside, two levels in front, one in back,
with a screened porch and several decks. A separate dirt
track curved up from the parking area to a rustic-look-
ing outbuilding that Ty remembered served as a garden
shed in summer and a kind of a warming hut in winter.
It had its own potbellied woodstove and a ground-level
porch where the Rancourts and their guests could leave
their skates and skis.

If they wanted to, Ty thought, Sterling and Jodie Rancourt could convert their place into a bed-and-breakfast

or a ski club. It was big enough and had all the right amenities.

"I should go in there alone," Carine said, unbuckling her seat belt.

"I don't think so."

She let the seat belt snap back into place and looked over at him as if he hadn't kissed her at all, never mind that she regretted it. "Back off, okay? I'm not in any danger from the Rancourts."

Ty had no intention of backing off. "What if Louis Sanborn's murder is the result of a garden-variety domestic dispute? Sterling comes in, finds his wife and their new employee in the library and renders his own personal justice."

"And takes pictures before he starts shooting?"

"To keep the wife in line in the future."

"But he leaves the camera."

"Because Manny shows up."

Carine still was skeptical. "Sterling has an alibi."

"So did Jodie Rancourt. Hers didn't hold up, did it?" Ty unfastened his own seat belt—she wasn't going in there alone. "I'm playing devil's advocate, babe. All I'm saying is that anything's possible. And I'm with you all the way. That's not so bad, is it?"

She pushed open her door, one leg hanging out as she turned back to him and gave him a quick once-over. "You're not armed. If Sterling or Jodie or whoever decides to shoot me, they'll shoot you, too."

"Consider me a deterrent to violence." He gave her his best cocky smile. "And who says I need to be armed?"

That drew a small laugh. She looked steady enough when she got out of the truck. Ty followed her up a short walkway to a flat stone landing at the front door. He leaned into Carine and whispered, "Don't you feel like you've just climbed the beanstalk to the ogre's castle?"

She bit back a smile, but she had her hands twisted together, obviously trying to keep them from shaking. It wasn't a pleasant errand she was conducting, but Ty knew she wouldn't give up now. That was Carine—in for a penny, in for a pound. Maybe it was her "strong moral compass" at work, but Ty suspected it was also plain stubbornness.

"We can still go camping," Ty said. "I'd keep you warm—"

"So would a good sleeping bag. Will you stop?"

But when Sterling Rancourt pulled open the door a moment later, Carine somehow managed to look less tentative and guilty. It wasn't her fault the police had the pictures of Jodie Rancourt and Louis Sanborn, but that only just now seemed to sink in. Sterling looked like a wealthy country gentleman in his wide-wale corduroys and Patagonia sweater, but it was clear he was prepared for this encounter with his photographer. He must have seen them coming up the driveway, Ty thought.

"Carine, Sergeant North," Rancourt said coolly. "What can I do for you?"

Ty checked out the guy's stiff manner. No tea by the fire today. But Carine, stuffing her hands in her pockets, not intimidated, plunged ahead. "I'm sorry about the disk, and I'm sorry things have turned out the way they have." She paused, but Rancourt didn't say a word, and she went on. "I didn't feel I could give the disk to Gary Turner. I had no idea what was on it—Sterling, I hope you believe me when I say that I had nothing to do with those pictures."

He shifted in the doorway, not meeting her eye. "I'm sure you did what you felt was right. It's not a pleasant situation for any of us, but I haven't seen the pictures. I'm not in a position to discuss them."

"I understand. Given what's happened, I think it's best I quit my job. Jodie has all the pictures I've taken so far. I really appreciate the opportunity you and Jodie gave me—"

"As you wish, Carine. Anything else?"

She took a breath. "No."

Rancourt tipped his head back slightly, studying her, but Ty wasn't fooled by his outward calm or superior manner. The other shoe about to drop—the guy was debating how big a jerk he was going to be to her. Payback. Carine had gone off the reservation. She hadn't turned over the disk to him when asked or consulted him about what to do once she realized what was on it. He'd had no control over what she did. He'd been powerless over her and the entire situation, and he didn't like it. To Ty, it was real simple.

"A bit of friendly advice before you leave." Rancourt's tone was anything but friendly. "If you want to make it in the real world in a big way and not limit yourself to taking pretty pictures of birds and flowers, you'll need to learn to get along with people. You're too independent."

Carine didn't go after him, but Ty saw her hands tighten into fists and knew she wanted to. *He* wanted to. But it was her show, so he kept still and let her handle the bastard. "You're upset," she said calmly, "and you've had a shock, so I'm not going to argue with you."

"I'm not trying to be harsh, but we live in a harsh world." Rancourt wasn't going to back off. "You've been lucky, Carine. You've lived up here in Cold Ridge most of your life. Sheltered, protected."

Right, Ty thought. That was how she'd ended up an orphan at three. Every fiber of his body focused on not interfering, not pounding this prick into the dirt for taking his humiliation and anger out on Carine. But she didn't say a word, just went pale again, as if she'd taken a body blow.

It didn't stop Rancourt. "If you want to achieve the kind of success I think you do. You'll have to change your ways."

She stiffened, but took the hit. She'd always been something of a hothead when it came to him, Ty thought, but she wasn't letting this guy get to her. Maybe she was cutting Rancourt some slack because she'd just given police pictures of his wife with another man. Maybe she didn't have the strength to fight him at the moment. Ty did—he could cheerfully knock Sterling Rancourt on his rich pompous ass.

"Ty," Carine said quietly, "we should leave."

But Rancourt wasn't ready to give up. "I'll take it on faith that you didn't take those pictures on Wednesday, Carine, but there's no proof, either way."

Ignoring him, she started back down the stone walk to the truck.

"It's never easy when you know what someone needs to do." Rancourt had shifted to Ty and spoke in a patronizing man-to-man tone. "I can see the mistakes she's making, not because I'm more brilliant or talented, but because of my circumstances, my experience—"

"You don't know anything about her work or her life."

"Perhaps you're right. But I'm in a position to help her, if she chooses to break from the course she's on—well, that's her call. Not everyone wants to play in the big leagues."

Carine reached the truck and sank against the driver-side door, facing the house. "Ty—whenever you're ready."

Rancourt smiled nastily, his attention still on Ty. "It's not easy to tell her what she needs to hear, is it? You've been there."

Ty felt every muscle in his body coil, but Rancourt suddenly slumped against the doorjamb and put up his hand, as if to ward off a blow he knew he deserved. "I'm sorry. I—Christ, I'm so sorry. It's been a terrible day. I don't know what I'm saying."

"Yeah. Okay." Ty didn't know what the hell to do. "Carine's right, we should leave."

Jodie Rancourt eased beside her husband. She looked tired and drawn, self-conscious, but also, Ty thought, curiously elegant, as if she was trying to maintain some level of dignity. "Please accept my apology, too. You and Carine. It's been a very difficult few days for all of us. I'm sorry I put you all in such an untenable position."

"Mrs. Rancourt—"

She smiled politely. "Jodie, please. I knew I was taking a risk, just as I knew we were taking a risk last November when we tried to hike Cold Ridge. As then, the consequences have been far worse than I ever imagined." She averted her eyes, her voice lowering, almost as if she were talking to herself. "That's something I'll have to learn to live with."

Her husband positioned himself in such a way that she had to step back into the entry or take an elbow in the cheek. She withdrew, and Rancourt shut the heavy door without another word.

Ty gave a low whistle as he walked back to his truck. "Yep. That went well."

Carine took her hands out of her pockets and breathed out in a long, cathartic sigh, then managed a halfhearted smile. "Some deterrent you were."

"Think of how much worse it would have been if I hadn't been there. He might have slugged you."

"I don't know, a black eye might have been easier to take."

Ty stood close to her, aware of her hurt, her lingering anger. It was cold on the exposed hill, the wind blowing up from the valley in gusts, penetrating his flannel shirt. He thought about zipping up his jacket, but Carine still had her barn coat unbuttoned. He had to keep up his image of strength. But his attempt at private humor didn't catch hold, and he knew all he wanted to do was get her out of there. "A few days in the mountains," he said. "It's still an option."

"Maybe I'll go take pictures of stupid birds and flowers."

"You're not going to let him get to you, are you?"

Her mouth twitched, her eyes sparking with sudden irreverence. "If I did, would you fly through the door and kick his teeth in?"

Ty shrugged. "Sure."

"Probably get in trouble with some general, wouldn't you?"

"Nah. I'd get a medal."

She sighed, releasing some of her tension. "He was rude and obnoxious, but he's hurting."

"He's not hurting, Carine, at least not in the way you mean. He's pissed that someone else played with his toy without his permission."

"Shoot-the-messenger time."

"Yep. And he doesn't like not being able to control you."

She gazed out at the beautiful view, the seemingly endless cascade of mountains—blue, white and gray against the November clouds. "Maybe it was selfish of me to come. I didn't make anything better."

"Not your job."

One of the garage doors hummed open, and Gary Turner walked out onto the parking area. "I failed in my mission, so now I'm on clean-the-SUV duty," he said with a self-deprecating smile, gesturing back to an expensive white SUV parked in the garage. But his smile didn't last, and he shook his head regretfully. "I overheard you all. Obviously I should have handled this situation differently."

"It's okay," Carine said. "At this point, what's done is done."

Ty opened his truck door, hoping Carine would take the hint and realize it was time to go, but she didn't. "Did Jodie Rancourt use my key yesterday and search my apartment for the disk?" she asked casually, as if it was only of passing interest to her. "The locks are tricky. She must have gotten frustrated or nervous, because she left the door open."

Turner gave an almost imperceptible nod. "She didn't take anything? No one took advantage of the situation?"

Carine shook her head.

"Then I hope we can leave what she did as an act of poor judgment on her part, nothing more. Since you did give her a key—"

"How did she know there were pictures?"

"I can't say. I'm sorry. There's nothing more I can tell you. The police asked us not to discuss our statements with anyone else."

"I understand."

She probably did, Ty thought, but it wouldn't stop her from listening if anyone wanted to talk. But he kept his mouth shut and climbed in behind the wheel. Turner led Carine around to the other side of the truck and opened the door for her. Ty noticed the missing fingers, mentally ticked off various possibilities of how people lose fingers. But mostly he noticed Turner's attentiveness toward Carine. He knew it shouldn't make a damn bit of difference to him, but it did.

"Coming up here was a mistake," Turner said, still very focused on Carine, edging in close to her as she climbed in the truck. "I'll encourage the Rancourts to head back to Boston as soon as possible. We all need to be patient and let the police conclude their investigation. Then we'll know what went on the other day."

"The Rancourts have as much right to be here as I do," Carine said.

"You could use the peace and quiet. I'll see you sometime. Take care of yourself."

"You, too. Thanks."

He shut her door, and Ty started back down the mountain way too fast. He almost two-wheeled it on a curve and slowed down, aware of Carine getting quieter and paler beside him. "You're not going to be sick, are you?"

"I'm fine."

"Good, because I just cleaned my truck."

She lifted her eyes to him, but it was obviously an effort to pull herself out of her thoughts. "You did not. It's filthy."

"It's not filthy. I got out all the wrappers and crud—"

"Look at the dashboard. Dust, grime. And you didn't vacuum."

"Vacuum? Babe, if I vacuumed, I might suck out something this thing needs to keep running. There's a certain balance of nature at work here. It's my New Hampshire truck. My truck on base is spotless."

She let a small smile escape. "Isn't there some general who can call and send you somewhere?"

He grinned. "Am I getting under your skin?"

"Underfoot," she said, "not under my skin. Maybe I miss Boston."

"The cockroaches or the kitty litter in the front hall?"

"There are no roaches in my building."

"I saw one the size of an alligator."

"Watch it, North. Once I've mastered the PAST, I'm going to become a marksman. Try my hand at tactical maneuvers."

"Soon the generals'll be calling you."

She shook her head. "You didn't hear me say I was planning to take up parachuting, did you? That's an unnatural act, jumping out of a perfectly good aircraft." She settled back in her seat, watching the passing scenery—rocks, evergreens, birches. No wild turkeys. Wherever they went on late November afternoons, presumably they were there. "At least I don't mind helicopters. Antonia hates them."

"And here she is married to a helicopter pilot."

"Life can be funny that way, can't it? She still says she's never going to be the doctor in the helicopter with the patient, not if she can help it. She'll be the doctor waiting at the hospital for the patient."

"Have you been on a helicopter?"

"A number of times, on various photography assignments." She sighed, adding dryly, "But I guess that wasn't in the 'real world.'"

"You don't have anything to prove," Ty said, slowing down for a series of ruts and potholes, "you or your sister."

She glanced over at him. "Neither do you."

Seventeen

In the village of Cold Ridge, November was a time between seasons. The leaf-peepers had gone, and the winter
sports crowd hadn't yet arrived, leaving the shops and restaurants more or less to the locals for a few short weeks.
When Ty parked his beat-up truck in front of Gus's outfitting shop, Carine jumped out first, although by now
she knew she wouldn't go far without him. He was definitely in Musketeer mode, her own personal d'Artagnan
shadowing her wherever she went—because she'd found
a dead man, because his friend had asked him to.

But it didn't seem fair. He was on leave after months
leading his pararescue team in combat and training missions that were the subject of speculation and rumor
around town but seldom got fleshed out with specifics.
Special operations, unconventional warfare. It was all
something that happened far away, removed from their
northern New England village.

Except Tyler North was one of their own—even if,
Carine thought, he didn't see himself that way, but as the
outsider, the boy with the weird mother.

Regardless, he should be hiking and fishing, sitting by

the fire with a book, puttering in his rambling house, not traipsing around after her.

But they'd had that discussion on the way into town. "Relax, babe," he'd said. "I haven't fared too badly hanging out with you."

Meaning the sex and the kisses.

That'd teach her to open her damn mouth.

The alternative to having him on her tail—running around on her own—had its appeal, but Carine thought if she could just make the leap to Tyler North as a Musketeer, she wouldn't feel so hemmed in. But it wasn't just his presence, it was that every time she looked at him, a part of her remembered that he was the man she'd loved so much last winter and almost married.

She eyed him as he joined her on the sidewalk and wondered what they'd think of each other if they were meeting for the first time now. He was thirty-seven, she was thirty-three. They weren't kids. She tried to look at him objectively, pretend she hadn't known him forever—hadn't gone to bed with him just yesterday. She took note of his superfit physique, his military-cropped tawny hair, his green eyes and bad-road face. The jeans, the battered brown leather jacket.

She'd be attracted to him, no doubt about it.

Just as well she knew better, experience ever the hard teacher.

He seemed to guess what she was thinking and grinned at her. "Just think. Manny could have asked Gus to keep you out of trouble instead of me."

"Do you see now why I've always hated you?"

"If I'd known what you meant by 'hate,' I could have started sleeping with you when you were sixteen."

"Gus would have killed you."

"Hang on. He might yet."

It was in the fifties in the valley, warm by Gus's standards. He had the wooden front door of his store propped open with a statue of a river otter, the afternoon breeze blowing in through the screen door. Carine went in first, the old, oiled floorboards soft under her feet. Her uncle had started the business, now one of the most respected outfitters in the valley, when she was in the second grade, and he called it Gus & Smitty's. There was no Smitty and never had been, but he insisted that just Gus's was too prosaic. It was located in a former Main Street hardware store. Customers liked the old-fashioned atmosphere, but they came for the state-of-the-art equipment and unparalleled services.

Carine wove through the racks of winter hiking and camping gear to the back wall, where Gus, in a wool shirt and heavyweight chinos, had a map of the Pemigewasset Wilderness opened on the scarred oak counter. They'd hiked in the Pemigewasset countless times. It was a sprawling federally designated wilderness area resurrected from shortsighted logging-and-burning operations that had nearly destroyed it between the mid-nineteenth and the mid-twentieth century. Now it was protected by an act of Congress, and human activity there was strictly regulated.

"Planning a hike?" Carine asked.

He peeled off his bifocals and looked up from his map. "Nah. Just dreaming."

Stump wagged his tail but didn't stir from his bed at Gus's feet.

Ty whistled at a price tag on an expensive ski jacket.

"Only the best," Gus said.

"At that price it should come with its own search-and-rescue team." Ty emerged from the racks, joining them at the counter. "Just add water."

"You come in here to make fun of the merchandise?"

"No, sir. We're here to invite ourselves to dinner."

Gus folded up his map and tucked it back in a drawer. He sold a wide selection of maps, guidebooks, how-to books and outdoor magazines. "I'm cooking a chicken in the clay pot. You two can go over to the house and put it in the oven if you want. I'll close up here in a bit."

"I never can remember what to do with a clay pot," Carine said. "What part you soak in cold water, for how long, if you're supposed to preheat the oven—"

"Instruction book's right in the pot. How'd it go at the Rancourts?"

Ty leaned over a glass cabinet of sunglasses, sports watches and jackknives. "Sterling was frosty, Jodie was hangdog and Gary Turner drooled over Carine."

She groaned. "Gus, that's *not* how it went."

"It's the short version." North pointed to a pair of Oakleys. "Let me see those."

Gus shook his head. "I'm not wasting my time. You've never paid more than twenty dollars for sunglasses in your life."

"Twenty bucks? When have I ever paid that much for sunglasses?"

"Go to hell."

Ty put a hand to his heart in mock despair. "Is that how you treat a paying customer?"

"The key word is *paying*." Gus dismissed him and turned to Carine, his tone softening. "You don't ever have to see the Rancourts again, you know. You quit, right?"

She nodded. "If I'd just taken my camera with me during lunch—"

"If Jodie Rancourt and Louis Sanborn had just behaved themselves."

"I promised Sterling we'd be discreet."

"Too bad his wife wasn't."

"It's water over the dam at this point," Carine said. "I hope the Boston police will be here soon. I just want to get it over with."

"Go put the chicken on. Cooking'll help keep things in perspective."

The screen door creaked open, and Eric Carrera wandered unexpectedly into the store, making his way back to the counter. Flushed and out of breath, he spoke first to Gus. "My friend and I are in town collecting leaves for earth science class," he said. "How's it going, Mr. Winter?"

"Not bad, Mr. Carrera," Gus replied.

Ty, eyes narrowed as he took in the boy's appearance, stood up from the glass cabinet. "No trees on campus?"

Eric shifted, deliberately avoiding contact with his father's friend. "Yes, sir, there are, but not any ginkgoes and larch trees. There's a ginkgo in front of the Cold Ridge library…." But the boy's voice trailed off, and he sniffled, coughing as he adjusted his backpack and pretended to look at a rack of lip balms. He had on his habitual cargo pants, today's too-big hooded sweatshirt from Amherst College. "I saw your truck out front, and I—I was wondering if you'd heard anything from my dad."

"Not today." He stepped toward Eric, forcing the boy to face him. "You have your meds with you?"

Eric nodded. "I'm okay. I'm just—" He coughed, a sloppy sound in his chest, but he waved off any help, although Ty hadn't made a move in his direction. "My dad… the dead guy…that's not his real name. Louis Sanborn. You know about that, right? It was on the news."

Ty slung an arm over the boy's thin shoulders and maneuvered him to a wall of cross-country skis, sitting down with him on a wooden bench. Carine edged behind a rack of socks to eavesdrop, ignoring Gus's disapproving frown, but she suspected he was as shocked by Eric's news as she was—and wanted the details.

"We haven't heard anything," Ty said gently. "You want to fill me in? Relax, buddy, okay? Take your time."

Eric, who seemed to be making an effort to stay calm, coughed again, but with more control. "The police said the dead guy's identity doesn't check out. They don't know who he is. My dad told the police he doesn't know, either."

"That's what they said on the news?"

"Yeah. Yes, sir."

"Eric, is your dad under arrest?"

He shook his head, sniffling. "The reporter said the police are still not calling him a suspect. I don't know what that means. He's innocent, right, Uncle Ty? He didn't kill anyone?"

"Your dad's not a murderer, Eric."

Carine noticed Ty's careful choice of words and felt her abdominal muscles clamp down, a wave of nausea coming out of nowhere as the news sunk in. Louis Sanborn used a phony name? *Why?* Then who the hell was he? But she didn't move, didn't say anything.

"My mom called," Eric said. "She tried not to sound upset, but I can tell. She said if I need her, just say so and she'll come up here. I told her no."

"You haven't talked to your dad?"

He shook his head. "Not yet."

Ty glanced around the dark, quiet shop. Canoes and kayaks hung from the ceiling, but Gus & Smitty's was in winter mode. "Where's your friend who's collecting leaves with you?" But he'd obviously seen through the boy's lie immediately, and when Eric squirmed, Ty cuffed him on the shoulder and got to his feet. "Come on. I'll give you a ride back to school. If you want to come stay with me, we can work something out with the powers-that-be. Okay?"

"I still have to collect some stupid leaves."

"We can grab some on our way." He glanced back at Carine, pointing at her as if he'd known all along she was there. "Pick me out a pair of socks while you're at it." There was just the slightest hint of sarcasm in his tone. "I'll meet you at Gus's."

"North's good with the kid, I'll give him that," Gus said after they'd left. "I like Eric. He's got a lot of guts, coming up here to school. But, Christ, what next? It doesn't look good for Carrera."

"Something must not add up for the police not to have arrested him yet." Carine grabbed a pair of hiking socks, uneasy, restless. "I should have gone for my run this morning. Ty found a dead bat in my woodstove. I wonder what that means."

"It means you have bats."

"Can I take these socks?"

"Take?"

"I'm unemployed."

"You're self-employed. There's a difference."

She dug in her coat pockets, looking for money. "The police must be putting the thumbscrews to Manny. It's got to be killing Ty not to know what's going on. He doesn't say anything—"

"He won't. It's not his style. And it'd take more than thumbscrews to get Carrera to talk if he doesn't want to."

"Why wouldn't he want to?"

"I didn't say he doesn't. Just don't you worry about it. He can take care of himself. I know, I know—so can you." He rubbed his booted toe over Stump's hind end, the dog wagging his tail in appreciation. "Something like this happens, it's like you're a little kid again. I can't help it."

Carine pulled a few quarters out of one pocket. "It's comforting to know there's someone in my life who cares as much as you do."

"Honey—"

"Don't go there, Gus. Ty's been a perfect gentleman. It's okay."

"Gentleman? Sure. I believe that."

"I'm handling being around him." She set the quarters on the counter. "I don't have my wallet with me."

"You can owe me."

"Do I at least get a discount?"

He offered ten percent. She argued for thirty and settled for twenty. When she tried to throw in new cross-country skis and socks for Ty, he shooed her out the door.

It was dusk, the sun dipping behind the mountains in a pink glow as Carine made the familiar three-quarter mile walk up the hill to her uncle's house. She smelled smoke from a fireplace in the neighborhood. She kicked through dry, fallen leaves on the sidewalk, and when she got to the house, she sat on the top step of the front porch. She could see herself and Ty as kids up in the maple tree in the side yard, still sweating and panting from raking up the huge pile of leaves under their thick branch. He threatened to push her if she didn't jump on her own.

Saskia North had never come up to Gus's house. Not once, not even to pick up her son. Ty had been on his own for a long time. It was what he knew, and Carine wondered if she'd been crazy to think he'd ever really let anyone in.

North dropped Manny's son off at school with his bag of leaves and a full head of worries. But there wasn't much Ty or anyone could do to ease the mind of a fourteen-year-old boy who knew his father was in a mess—who knew his father hadn't called to reassure him and probably wouldn't.

For which Ty could cheerfully strangle his friend. But on one level, he understood. Manny, in his own particular, annoying way, was doing his best to protect his son. He'd put everyone on a need-to-know basis. They could worry, they could get mad, but if he didn't think they needed to know something, he wasn't going to tell them.

Carine could try her burning bamboo shoots on Manny Carrera, too, but they wouldn't work.

Carine. Hell, she'd had no idea Louis Sanborn wasn't Louis Sanborn. It'd been obvious from her reaction. The guy she'd found dead—the guy she'd *liked*—wasn't who he said he was. If Manny had found out, it would explain why he'd headed to Boston to recommend Sterling Rancourt fire him. Rancourt couldn't employ someone who'd lied to him—especially for security.

"Not to mention screwing the poor bastard's wife," Ty muttered to himself.

But had Manny known *that?*

North turned onto Gus's village street, and although it wasn't even six o'clock, Cold Ridge was already engulfed in darkness. Gus's house was all lit up because Carine was there—otherwise, her uncle would have just the kitchen light on. Ty pulled into the short driveway, his cell phone ringing, and he just barely made out Val Carrera's voice through the static. "You must have some kind of mother radar, Val. I just saw Eric. He's worried about Manny, but he's okay."

"Is he eating?"

"Not much from the looks of him, but he had his meds with him. He was coughing, but lungs sounded pretty clear. The house parents at his dorm were waiting for him when we got back—"

"Got back from where?"

"Town. We were leaf-collecting."

"I should—never mind."

"I know it's hard, Val, but he'll make it through this thing. We all will."

"What other choice is there?" She was grumbling, worried and out of sorts, but she didn't sound as fragile as she'd been six months ago. "Manny's not talking to you, either, is he?"

Instinctively, despite his own frustration with his friend, North found himself offering a defense. "Manny doesn't have a lot of room to maneuver."

But Val wasn't one to cut anyone, herself included, much slack. "How much maneuvering does it take to dial a goddamn phone? Okay, never mind. That's not why I called. Look—I'm driving myself crazy here with the computer. You don't happen to know his password?"

"Why would I know his password?"

"I don't know. He tells you things he doesn't tell me. I thought if he knew he might be in deep trouble, he'd maybe clue you in on how you could help him if he really got in over his head."

"I don't know how to help him, Val. I wish I did."

"He's hámstrung. He can't do a damn thing except smile at the cops."

If I can't function... I've got computer files...you'll remember.

Hell, North thought. Only Manny. "Try *I love Val.*"

"What?"

"For the password. Manny said something to me yesterday at the hotel. It didn't make sense at the time—"

"What, that he loves me?" she asked in that wry Val tone.

"No, that he felt the need to mention it. Christ, Val, you can be irritating."

He heard her tapping her keyboard. "It didn't work, so there. Wait, let me try—" She gulped in a breath. "Bingo! I'll be damned, North, that's it! I used a *u* for love and one *v*. I'm in. *I-l-u-v-a-l.*"

"Val—"

"I knew you'd know. I wish I'd thought of you ten million failed passwords ago. I'm surprised this thing didn't self-destruct like in *Mission Impossible,* just start smoking."

"Val, what's on the screen—"

But it was as if her mind was inside the computer. "I'll call you back if I find anything interesting. Watch, it'll just be a spreadsheet of how much he's won in the football pool. He loves those damn spreadsheets."

She clicked off, and Ty could have thrown his phone out the window. He adored Val—everyone did, just like everyone adored Manny. They were straightforward, high energy, fighters. But both of them could drive Ty straight up the wall if he let them.

I love Val.

Why hadn't the big oaf just said it was his goddamn password?

The cop with the PalmPilot, probably. Manny wouldn't want to tip her off. But if he had anything on Louis Sanborn, anything that could help his situation, he needed to be spilling it to the damn police, not making cryptic remarks to a PJ buddy.

Maybe whatever was in the files *didn't* help his situation.

Or maybe there was nothing in his files, North thought, and he and Val were just grasping at straws, trying to help a friend and husband who may have lost it two days ago and blown a man away. It'd been a rough year for Manny. He shouldn't have retired. He needed a couple more years to get Eric out of school, Val back on her feet and in a new job. Starting his own business—it was a different world for Manny Carrera, unfamiliar territory.

But he hadn't lost it. He hadn't blown Louis Sanborn—or whoever he was—away in Boston on Wednesday.

Ty rousted Stump out of a hole he was digging in the backyard and joined the Winters in the kitchen, the uncle and the auburn-haired, blue-eyed niece arguing over butternut squash. Bake or boil. Nutmeg or cinnamon. Real butter or the soft stuff made with olive oil. Boiling won out, because there wasn't enough room in the oven with the clay pot.

Carine retreated with Stump to the front room to sit by the fire, and Ty wondered if he looked as agitated and frustrated as he was, as ready to get into his truck and charge down to Boston.

"You were afraid you'd die on her this year." Gus's quiet words caught him off guard. "You knew what kind of missions you had coming up. She'd just had that business with those assholes shooting at her. What happened to her parents up on the ridge is a part of her—you see that. You let it spook you."

Ty sat at the table; the small kitchen was steamed up, smelling of chicken and baking onions. "Gus, you're off base. I can't do my job if I'm worried about dying. But I'm not going there with you."

"You're not getting my point. You can't do your job if you know she's back home worried about you dying." Gus glanced up from his cutting board. "That's the devil, isn't it?"

Ty watched him dump the deep orange squash into a pan of water on the stove. The man had done combat in the Central Highlands of Vietnam. An infantryman. A kid plucked out of the mountains of northern New England and sent off to fight a war he didn't understand. He'd probably thought about his family back home worrying about him.

But it didn't matter—Ty's relationship with Carine was for them to sort out. "You know you could make soup out of that squash?"

Gus returned to his cutting board for another chunk of squash. "Butternut squash soup is a favorite at the local inns. They put a little apple in it, sometimes a little curry."

"I'd rather have apple than curry, wouldn't you?"

"North... I was out of line." Gus sighed, his paring knife in his hand as he brushed his wrist across his brittle gray hair. "You and Carine—what's between you two is your business."

Ty grinned. "What have I been saying, huh?"

Gus pointed his knife at him. "You're going to live to be an old man, North, just to torment the rest of us."

"And you're going to kill yourself with your own cooking." Ty was on his feet, frowning at the stove. "What the hell's that in the frying pan?"

"Braised Brussels sprouts with olive oil and a little parmesan."

"Jesus. I think I've got an extra MRE out in the truck."

Gus threw him out of the kitchen, and Ty joined Carine in front of the fire. He sat on the couch, and she sat on the floor with her back against his knees, comfortable with him, he thought—and for a moment, it was almost as if he'd never knocked on her cabin door and canceled their wedding.

Eighteen

~~~⚜️~~~

Carine climbed onto her favorite rock on the lower ridge trail and looked out at the valley and mountains, the view that had captivated her since she was a little girl. It was midmorning, the trees, even the evergreens, almost navy blue against the bleak gray sky. If only she could stand here and let her worries and questions float out on a breeze, dissipate into the wilderness.

She remembered Gus taking her and her brother and sister onto the ridge after their parents died. She'd dreamed about that day for years. She spotted an eagle and swore she saw her mum and dad flying with it in the clear summer sky. The image had been so vivid, so absolutely real to her.

But, so had her dreams, her images, of her life with Ty. So vivid, so real.

She half walked, half slid down the curving granite, rejoining him on the narrow, difficult trail. They'd gone far enough. Neither had the attention span for a long hike. They'd loaded up a day pack after breakfast and set out, crossing the meadow, climbing over a stone wall, then walking up a well-worn path to the trailhead. The dirt access road was quiet, the parking lot empty, not atypical of November. It was Saturday, but still early.

There was a threat of light snow and high winds above the treeline. They weren't going that far, but Carine had gone back to her cabin and dug out her lighter winter layers for the hike. Thermal shirt, windproof fleece jacket, windproof pants, hat, gloves. Her hat and gloves were still in the day pack. She wore her new hiking socks. No cotton—she'd even banned it from her summer hikes.

Ty had approved of her wilderness medical kit, but he'd raised his eyebrows when she tucked the manual into the pack. "Look at it this way," she told him. "If I fall and hit my head, you won't need the manual. If you fall and hit your head, I'll need the manual."

"Only if I'm unconscious."

"Of course, because if you can talk, you'll just tell me what to do."

"If I'm conscious," he said, leaning toward her in that sexy way he had, "I'll treat myself."

She told him she had treating blisters down pat. She knew CPR and basic first aid. She'd have done her best if Louis Sanborn had still been alive when she found him. But Antonia was the doctor in the family—Carine didn't like blood and broken bones, people in pain. Not that Antonia, or Ty, did, but they had a calling when it came to medicine that she simply didn't have.

Of course, Ty's calling also involved guns, diving, fast-roping and the insanity of HALO—High Altitude Low Opening jumping, where he would depart a plane at very high altitudes, with oxygen, a reserve chute, a medical kit and an M16, the bare necessities to survive the jump and get to a crew downed in hostile conditions.

Not that *he* thought HALO was insane. Just another tool in his PJ tool bag of skills, he'd say.

Carine respected his skills and abilities, his nonchalance about them, but she wasn't intimidated, perhaps because they seemed so natural to him, integral to who he was.

She'd spent an hour last night in his kitchen answering questions from the two Boston Police Department detectives, who had been sent to take possession of the memory disk, camera and camera bag. It hadn't occurred to her to have an attorney present. After they left, her brother called on Ty's hard line, which meant Ty could listen in on the extension as Nate told her in no uncertain terms to go mountain climbing today. He wouldn't go into detail about anything he'd found out, but Nate wasn't one to overreact. Although he never said so directly, Carine received the strong implication that her brother had talked to his law enforcement sources and had good reason to make sure his friend and his sister stayed out of what was apparently not a simple case of murder.

After she hung up with Nate, Ty tried to call Manny, got his voice mail and almost threw his phone into the fire. He tried Val Carrera, also without success.

Carine had her Nikon with her on the hike and took several pictures, anything that struck her eye. Ty had said little all morning. Inaction, she thought, was getting to him. She knew he wanted to be in Boston, pulling information out of Manny Carrera, a syllable at a time if he had to.

She slipped the camera into an outer pocket of the day pack, strapped to his back. "Hiking can be a substitute for my run," she said.

"Nope. You hike, then you go back and do your run."

"Says who?"

He grinned over his shoulder at her. "That's something we hear a lot in the military. 'Says who?'"

He was teasing her, a good sign his mood had improved. "Fortunately, I'm not in the military. I'm just a simple photographer who wants to run a mile and a half in ten minutes and thirty seconds or less."

"You can do it. How close are you?"

"Twelve minutes. Well, once, anyway. I'll get there. I told you, it's the swimming that kills me. I always get water up my nose." She zipped up the compartment and patted him on the hip. "Tell you what, Sergeant, if you run with me, I'll do my mile and a half after we get back."

"Think I can't?"

"I think you need to burn off more excess energy than this little hike of ours will accomplish. You're not sleeping, Ty. You were up at dawn again this morning."

"Dawn's not that early in November."

"You're preoccupied, worried about Manny—and Val—"

"Having you down the hall isn't the greatest sleep-inducer, either."

She sighed. "Ty, it's not always about sex."

"It's not?"

"I am trying—"

He winked at her. "I know you are, babe. Don't worry about me. I'm doing just fine." He started down the trail, moving easily over the roots and jutting rocks. "One thing, though. You're not a simple anything, but you're sure as hell not a simple photographer. You're a brilliant photographer."

"You don't have to say that."

"Yes, I do." He held out his arm for her to grab as she

jumped off a two-foot rock in the middle of the trail. "You have the talent, the skills, the drive. I look at your pictures—I can't explain it. There's something going on there. I know it's nothing I or most people could do with one of those little throwaway things."

She was taken aback. "I appreciate that. Really. Thank you."

He continued down the trail, not taking any time to enjoy the scenery. "When we get back, I'll try Val again. Then I'm heading down to Boston to see Manny. You can hang out with Gus and Stump. It's the slow season. You two can wax skis. Argue about squash recipes."

"I'd rather go to Boston with you."

"I know you would."

"I could get my car, water my plants—"

He glanced back at her. "You don't have any plants."

She kept up with his killing pace, no more pauses to check out the view or pick up the perfect fallen leaf. The steep pitch of the trail eased into a long, gentle downward slope, the trail widening as it took them over a stream and back out to the parking area. When they reached the meadow, the wind gusted and howled down the mountains from the north, blowing an icy snow in their faces.

But the snow ended abrupty as they crossed into Ty's backyard and didn't even cover the ground. The sun beamed white through a thin cloud. Dark, lumpy clouds shifted over the valley, and the long, looming ridge with its high summits. Carine, more aware of the sky than she'd ever been in the city, tried to remember various cloud formations—stratocumulus, lenticular, cirrostratus. Each was associated with its own particular weather, but she was rusty on which was which.

Ty left the back door open for her, and she didn't linger outside. The wind blew into the kitchen, where the fire was almost out. He set the day pack on the table. When the phone rang, Carine, who was closer, picked it up. She didn't even get a chance to say hello. "Tyler? It's Val Carrera. The police are at my damn door with a search warrant."

"Val, it's Carine. Ty—"

Val didn't seem to hear her. "I'm sorry I didn't call back last night. At first I was too stunned, and then I fell asleep at the computer. I tried this morning but didn't get through—Jesus, Ty, he's got all kinds of garbage in these files. PJ stuff. Football scores. I *told* you I'd find football scores. At least I didn't find any porn."

"Slow down, okay? Let me get—"

She was talking rapidly, breathless. Ty made a move for the phone, but Carine was afraid they'd miss something important if she tried to transfer it to him with Val so oblivious to who was on the other end.

"He's got your e-mail address here. I'm sending you the file I think we're interested in. Jesus, will they break down the door if I don't answer?" She yelled, away from the phone, "I'm coming! Hang on a sec!" Then she returned, adding in a lower voice, "They'll haul off his hard drive. You know damn well they will."

In spite of her tough language, Val sounded panicked and fragile. Carine held up a hand, stopping Ty from ripping the phone from her. "I'll tell Ty—"

"It looks like Manny suspected Louis Sanborn was using an alias and having an affair with Jodie Rancourt, maybe extorting money from her. Something. I haven't gone through it all. I hope it doesn't get Manny into hotter water with the police."

Carine went still. "Manny suspected Louis and Jodie were having an affair *before* he got to Boston?"

"Yeah. I think so. Carine? Is that you?"

Ty snatched the phone. "Val, what the hell's going on?" He listened a moment, then said, "Open the damn door for the police. Do what they tell you. For Christ's sake, don't argue with them. Do you have a gun in the house? Val—" He glared at the phone then sighed at Carine. "She's gone."

"Did you get anything more out of her?"

"I need to check my e-mail. Jesus, those two." He looked ready to kick something. "We don't know what Manny's told the police. Goddamn it, we don't know anything."

Carine knelt down to see if she could revive the coals in the fireplace. She blew on them, and a few glowed red. She lifted a skinny log out of the woodbox and laid it on the coals, trying not to suffocate them, the familiar work only a partial counter to her tension.

She'd found Louis dead, but the Carreras were Ty's friends more than they were hers. He and Manny had been in combat together.

"Go on," she said. "Check your e-mail for what Val sent. I'll join you in a minute."

But Ty came behind her and hooked an arm around her waist, lifting her to her feet and kissing her softly, unexpectedly. He threaded his fingers gently through her hair. "This'll all work out. You know that, don't you?"

She wondered if he was trying to convince her or himself, but she nodded. "Manny's a rock. Val, too, in her own way."

He headed to the den, and Carine returned to the fire, the log catching with no additional effort on her part. Nate could have called last night and encouraged her to go mountain climbing because he'd found out Louis's murder involved blackmail, extortion, an adulterous affair—people with connections to her and Cold Ridge.

She set another log on her reborn fire, then made her way down the hall to the den. With the gray sky, it seemed more like late afternoon than midday. Ty didn't look up from the monitor. "I downloaded Val's file. It looks like some kind of personal log Manny kept."

Carine resisted the temptation to read over his shoulder. "I'll leave you to it."

She returned to the kitchen and put another larger log on the fire, then stood in front of it, her fingers splayed out over the flames. She remembered those crazy few days last November with the shooting and the Rancourts' rescue, Ty grinning at her and calling her babe, telling her she had pretty eyes, as if he'd never noticed her in all the years they'd known each other. He and Manny Carrera sneaking around after the shooters and pulling Jodie and Sterling Rancourt off the ridge like it was no big deal—and Hank Callahan, the retired air force officer, the senate candidate. They'd all gathered in front of the fire here in Ty's kitchen and eaten chili and drunk beer, talking late into the night—she remembered Ty insisting on walking her back to her cabin as if it wasn't something she'd done on her own a thousand times when his mother was alive. It was cold and so still they could hear their footsteps on the dirt driveway, and when they got to her door, he kissed her good-night.

That was when she should have fled to Boston, not six months later after the damage was done.

He walked into the kitchen and pulled out a chair, turning it so that he could face the fire. He sat down, sighing heavily, collecting his thoughts. "Manny figured going into business for himself would be good for Val and Eric, that it'd give him more freedom to make his own schedule. But he hates it. He doesn't like the work, he doesn't like the people he has to work with. He'd have given it up if the Rancourts hadn't hired him."

"Funny how these things work out sometimes," Carine said, still on her feet.

"He was in Cold Ridge in September to visit Eric. I wasn't here. Neither were you. Gus was on a hiking trip. While Eric was in class one morning, Manny drove up to the Rancourt house to see if anyone might be up there, get the lay of the land so he could make recommendations. It was just something to do, really." He paused, glanced up at Carine. "Guess who was there?"

"Jodie? She's come up here on her own a number of times."

Ty nodded. "Yep. She was here. With Louis Sanborn."

"In *September?* But the Rancourts only hired him two weeks ago. I didn't realize they already knew each other. Louis acted as if they didn't—"

"Sterling Rancourt didn't know Louis. Only Jodie."

"Oh." Carine sank onto a chair, wincing at the implications. "Ouch."

"Somehow or another, the rescue last fall made Sterling feel vulnerable, so he started paying more attention to his personal and corporate security. He hired Gary Turner, then Louis Sanborn. He got Manny in to consult."

"If Jodie and Louis were already having an affair, you'd think she would have tried to stop her husband from hiring Manny."

"For all we know, she tried. Manny met with Sterling Rancourt, Gary Turner and Louis Sanborn in Boston a

few days after Sanborn was hired. He realized right off the
bat that Sanborn was the same guy he met in September."

"Did Sanborn say anything?"

Ty shook his head. "And Manny was pretty sure Jodie
Rancourt introduced Sanborn under a different name.
Tony something. Italian."

"Jesus—so she knew he was using an alias? Then why
hire Manny? If he'd already met Louis under a different
name why take the chance? Unless there's an innocent explanation for the alias and no one was worried about it."

"Manny couldn't swear to what Jodie told him in September, at least according to the log." Ty sighed, leaning
back in his chair. "You should see this thing. He's not a
talker on a good day, but there are places he's downright
cryptic. A lot of it's in military lingo. No wonder Val
couldn't make much sense of it."

"He must have told the police all this."

"I'm not making any assumptions at this point. He decided something wasn't on the level and started digging
into Sanborn's background. Nothing added up. He already
knew the guy sure as hell wasn't southern—"

"That was an act?"

"According to Manny. He's a Texan. He thinks he can
smell a Yankee at a thousand yards."

Carine smiled. "Why isn't the reverse true?"

"Because we Yankees don't give a rat's ass." But Ty's
humor was strained, and he leaned over and, without getting up, grabbed a log and pitched it one-handed onto the
fire. It landed hard, the sparks just missing Carine's toes.
He went on, settling back in his chair. "Manny thought
Sanborn might have a Cold Ridge connection."

She shook her head. "I'd have recognized him if he did,
wouldn't you think? The way he acted, I'd be surprised if

it had occurred to him I might recognize him—I'm sure it didn't. He played the southern guy who thinks fifty degrees is cold. How far did Manny get in his background research before he went up to Boston?"

"Not far enough."

Ty was silent, and the fire hissed, one of Carine's logs breaking up into red-hot chunks. She watched it, trying to piece together different conversations she'd had with the Rancourts in the weeks since she'd started working for them, with Louis—or whoever he was—before he was killed. But there was nothing. She'd had no idea anything was going on beneath the surface until she walked into the library on Wednesday afternoon and found Louis dead. And even then...

But she realized Ty had drifted into silence. "What else?" she asked quietly, knowing there was more.

"Speculation."

"What kind of speculation?"

"Carine—it could all be nonsense. We don't know."

"Okay, with that caveat, what kind of speculation?"

"If Manny's right..." Ty sank back in his chair and rubbed a hand over his head, then sighed, plunging on. "He made a note in his log about the weapons the Rancourts have up here. Expensive rifles. Bolt action and semiautomatic. Scoped. Jodie Rancourt had them out, showing them to Louis the day Manny met them up here. Sterling told him about the guns when he discussed what training he wanted Manny to do."

"A lot of people up here have guns, but I had no idea the Rancourts did."

Ty rose, his back to the fire as he started unloading the day pack. "Manny intended to get to the bottom of whatever was going on with these people. Nothing was going to stop him."

"It makes sense if it was his job—"

"Not because of his job. He has a kid up here. And there's you."

She took her wilderness medical kit off the table where Ty had laid it and slipped it into her coat pocket. "Because I worked for the Rancourts?"

But she knew that wasn't the whole answer, even before Ty spoke. "And because you're from Cold Ridge, and because of last November."

The shooting. The burned-down shack, the missing smugglers. "Manny can't think the Rancourts had anything to do with that smuggling operation. Louis? Could he have been—" She stopped herself, not wanting to phrase the question. Could Louis have been involved? Was that why he came up with an alias? "The police don't have any suspects."

"Not that we know of."

"Nate—he'd know."

Ty shook his head. "He won't tell you even if he does know. Neither would you in his place." He lifted a water bottle out of the pack and set it on the table. "I won't be going to Boston. I see now why Manny put me on Carine Winter duty. You're not on the sidelines, babe. Whatever's going on, you're right in the thick of it."

North split wood until he'd worked up a blister on one hand. He thought about letting Carine treat it. But he was sweating, irritable, ready to jump out of his damn skin. He'd decided to give Val ninety minutes before calling her back. It seemed like enough time for the cops to execute their search warrant and clear out of the Carreras' apartment.

He'd debated heading back up the notch road to ask the Rancourts to explain their relationship with Louis Sanborn, *aka* whoever, but he'd had a good dose of the Rancourts yesterday. And there was Carine.

There was always Carine.

She sat on the back steps, bundled up in a moth-eaten wool blanket she'd dug out of a hall closet, so old it might have been left behind by one of her ancestors.

"Doesn't the wool scratch?" he asked her.

"Not that much. It reminds me of being a kid."

"I think that's the same blanket Nate and I used when we rolled you and Antonia up and sent you down the hill over by the road."

"I remember that. We almost got run over."

He sat next to her, smelling the damn blanket. Mothballs, dust, that musty wool smell. "You didn't almost get run over. Gus just said that when he yelled at us, and it stuck in your mind. You were, what, six or seven? You didn't know enough not to believe everything your uncle said."

Even then, there'd been an unspoken rule in his life. *Never get involved with the little sister.* Nate was his friend. The Winters, in many ways, were his family. Ty had violated the bond between them by falling for Carine—never mind that she hadn't exactly been dragged kicking and screaming into bed with him. He'd still made the first move. It was his doing more than hers.

And there was no undoing it. He'd learned that in the last few days. Even now, it wouldn't take much for him to carry her and her moth-eaten blanket upstairs for the rest of the afternoon.

Maybe Gus was right, and he needed to sell the house. If not for the damn trust fund, he would have had to by now, anyway.

He could sell the house, quit the air force, buy a boat and sail away.

Or go find other mountains to live in.

Carine had placed his cell phone on the steps. He grabbed it and clicked onto his phone book, found Val's number and hit the button for an automatic dial. She answered almost before it rang, static making her hard to understand. "Ty? They're gone. They took the computer, a bunch of folders he had—he doesn't have an office yet, so he's been working out of here."

"You okay?"

"I just wolfed down cold pepperoni pizza, right out of the refrigerator. You'd have thought I was starving. It was disgusting. All that coagulated grease."

Ty smiled. "Val, you're a trip and a half. Anything out of Manny?"

"Are you kidding? He's lucky I don't drive up to Boston and shoot him myself."

She was handy with a gun. Ty wouldn't put it past her, except he'd never seen a couple more committed to each other than Manny and Val Carrera. "He must be cooperating with the police. He has nothing to hide. If it turns out Louis Sanborn traces back to the shooting here last year, we'll know it. Law enforcement will put the pieces together."

She sighed, deflating. "This past year—it hasn't been easy. He did good work as a PJ, you know? He loved it. Then Eric got sick, and I went kerplooey on him—"

"Kerplooey?"

"Yeah." He could almost feel her smile. "It sums up

what happened to me rather nicely, a very nasty mix of clinical depression, burn-out, stupidity and guilt."

"Manny says you just need a job."

"He does better with other kinds of head injuries than the kind I had. He got sucked into this Rancourt mess, Ty. He's not going to let go until he's got it sorted out. That's the way he is."

North nodded. "I know."

"This business thing wasn't a great idea. I saw that crap in the file about doing it for me. Bullshit. I think—" She swallowed, no hint of any good humor coming through from her end now. "I'm not sure he likes the idea of being alone with me for the rest of his days. With Eric away at school—"

"Val, don't do this to yourself, okay? You two are going to the home together. You know that."

"I keep thinking—" Her voice quavered. "I don't know, if I could just do something to bring order back to the universe."

Ty tried to smile. "It's not your job to bring order to the universe, Val. Jesus. Some days it's enough just to get in three meals and eight hours of sleep."

But she didn't relent. "Haven't there been times in your life when you've felt as if you're under siege and nothing's ever going to go right again?"

"You bet, Val," Ty said gently. "We've all had those times."

When he hung up, Carine eyed him, obviously curious about what Val had said, but he put her off and dialed Hank's cell phone, remembering the Pave Hawk pilot he'd flown combat missions with just a few years ago was a senator now. But his voice-mail message was unchanged—*"Hi, it's Hank. Leave a message..."*

"Check on Val Carrera if you can," Ty said. "She's had a bad day. The cops searched—ah, hell, Hank. You're a senator. You can't get mixed up in this mess. Forget it. Val will be fine. So will Manny." He clicked off and tossed the phone onto the steps. "Gus and I agree on one thing. Cell phones should be banned."

Carine slipped her hand out of her blanket and placed it on his thigh. "Val knows she has to hang in there. She will."

He covered her hand with his, noticed that even without the blanket, his was warmer. "You do realize your brother-in-law is a senator?"

"It's sinking in. I'm not registered to vote in Massachusetts—isn't that awful? I didn't even vote for him." She lifted Ty's hand and examined his blister. "I've still got my first-aid kit. I can treat it."

"It hardly even counts as a blister. Share a corner of your blanket with me?"

She tossed a section of it over his shoulder, and he scooted in closer to her. But the thing didn't make him feel nostalgic at all. It stunk, and it scratched. He put a finger through one of the holes. She smiled. "Waste not, want not. Saskia got that part of living up here. I tried to explain to Louis that we Yankees are frugal, not cheap. There's a difference." She took a breath, her voice cracking almost imperceptibly. "Except he wasn't southern after all."

"We don't know that for a fact. We just have Manny's notes."

She shook her head. "Ty, I never would have guessed he wasn't on the level. Never. He was funny, irreverent, *nice*. Jodie—she lied, too. I never would have guessed they were having an affair. I must not be a very good judge of character."

"Louis could have been funny, irreverent and nice and still not be on the level."

"Not nice. That's what Manny said to me on Wednesday before the police got there. *Louis Sanborn wasn't a nice man.* I guess he was trying to warn me."

Ty said nothing, just leaned back against the step, taking Carine with him in the blanket. She laid her head against his shoulder, the smell and the roughness of the old blanket apparently not fazing her. He kissed her hair, which was soft and smelled of some citrusy shampoo, not mothballs, and if he smelled like sweat and sawdust, she didn't seem to mind.

Nineteen

❧◦❧◦❧

Carine tried to go for her run on her own, but Ty put on running shorts and a ragged shirt and joined her, saying he could provide motivation for her to get her speed up.

Just what she needed.

At some point, he'd mapped out the same mile-and-a-half route she had. He also had the same three-mile, five-mile and ten-mile routes. Ten miles was as far as she'd ever run. Any farther, she was in hiking boots and packing food and a tent.

But her morning hike and the tension of the past few days affected the muscles in her legs, her stamina, her breathing. She couldn't get a rhythm going in her stride. She had on close-fitting leggings, a moisture-repelling running shirt, special running socks and her expensive running shoes, but they weren't doing her any good.

"I'm dying here," she said after they'd made the turn and were on their way back. "I feel like I'm sprinting."

Ty trotted alongside her with little apparent effort. "Push harder. You can make it."

"You should see me do five miles. It's this damn speed—"

"Carine, you're not running that fast."

"Easy for you to say." They turned into her driveway, and she glowered at him when she saw that he wasn't even breathing hard. "North—I hate you. I've always hated you."

"The refrain." He grinned at her, the run obviously not fazing him. "No, you have not always hated me. That's what kills you."

Her knees were wobbling, and she was sweating and gasping for air, her chest aching, when just a week ago she'd have been fine—not breaking any records, but not ready to drop, either. Ty looked as if he'd just done a warm-up. Plus, he'd chopped wood. *And* he'd gone on the hike with her.

"Couldn't you at least cough and spit?" she asked him. "Get a stitch in your side?"

"Can't stand the heat, get out of the kitchen."

She scowled at him. "My body must have been possessed by aliens when we were engaged."

"Well, maybe your mind was. I know your body wasn't." He swatted her on the rear end. "Now, come on. Hoof it the last few yards. Sprint. Go all out."

She tried to kick him, but he was ready for her and bobbed out of her reach. The hell with it. She dove for his midsection. Headfirst, the way she always had. But he grabbed her by the hips, flipped her over, and before she knew what was happening, she was upside down, looking at the ground. "Hey!" she yelled. "You're going to step on my hair."

Her running shirt dropped down to her chin, and she felt the cool air on her overheated skin—and his hands. "Christ, you have been doing your ab work."

She did her level best to kick him in the jaw.

He laughed and swooped her back over and onto her feet. The blood that had rushed to her face while she was upside down rushed back out again, and she felt herself get dizzy and almost tripped. He caught her by both shoulders, steadying her. "You okay?"

She blinked at him. "I should have thrown up on your shoes."

"Yeah, probably."

"The idea was for me to think twice before I attack you again?"

"No, the idea was for me to feel your abs."

"You felt my abs the other day."

"I wasn't paying attention. I was more interested in other parts of your body."

"Ty." She put her hands on her hips, breathing hard. "Damn, you're not cutting me any slack, are you?"

He shrugged. "Who just plowed into who?"

"I'm standing here having this wonderful fantasy of hanging *you* upside down by your toes. But it'll probably never happen, will it?"

"Not literally. Figuratively—" Something changed in his eyes. "One way or another, babe, you've got me hanging by my toes every damn day."

His comment, his delivery, unsettled her enough to give her the spurt of energy she needed to sprint the rest of the way to her back deck.

"I'll have to remember that," he said, walking to the deck. "Nice way to get you moving. You showering here?"

"Damn straight," she muttered, scooting inside before he could get to her even more.

She skipped her post-run stretches and climbed up the ladder to her loft, and when she opened a dresser drawer, she heard a distinctive squeaking inside the slanted ceiling. Damn. More bats. And mice droppings in her underwear drawer.

She had visions of scurrying rodents and bats swooping up in the rafters while she slept. Her loft—her bed-room—was in the rafters.

Not a good development.

Ty wandered into the great room below her, and she leaned over the rail. "I'm going to have to sleep up here with a baseball bat."

"Hey—"

"Not because of you. I've got bats and mice. Your house has been empty even longer than mine. Why don't you have rodents?"

"I pay people to take care of the place. You've got Gus." He smiled up at her. "I also have ultrasonic pest-chasers. I think I have a few extra if you'd like me to fetch them."

"Sure. Run there and back so you can work up a sweat. By the way," she said, rising up off the rail, "your abs aren't so bad, either. I could feel them when you had me upside down."

"Watch it, toots. If you think I can run fast, you should see how fast I can climb a ladder."

It felt good to laugh, but after she got out fresh clothes and slipped back down the ladder to shower and change, she found herself making a detour into her studio. She wiped her palm over her dusty filing cabinet and opened the bottom drawer, squatting down to flip through the files, until she came to one labeled simply Hunting Shack, because she needed no further prompting to remember what was inside.

She laid the photos one by one on the floor, on the rug Saskia North had designed and hooked for her one winter.

The police had the memory disk. She'd printed out copies of the photos before it had occurred to anyone to ask her for it. She hadn't touched them in a year. In hindsight now, as she looked at the pictures, she realized the photo of the shack never would have worked as a Christmas card or anything else. The lighting was off, the building itself more an eyesore than a quaint relic of rural New England. There were no vehicles, no people, no snow or footprints—yet minutes after taking the pictures, someone shot at her. Then blew up the shack and let it burn to the ground before the police could get there.

One of the best shots was of the front porch. She'd had to get down low for it. A pair of antique cross-country skis was tacked above the door, and she'd captured about a dozen old-fashioned signs mounted on the outside wall. She took the photograph to her worktable and turned her lamp on it, then got out her magnifying glass for a closer look.

Was someone in the window?

No. And surely the police would have noticed if there were.

She smiled at the moose-crossing sign. There were also cow-crossing signs, but most of the signs were of stores and dairies long out of business—including the Sanborn Dairy. It had gone out of business in the early 1960s. Its old glass bottles were a collectors' item. Carine thought she had a couple in the cellar. They had black lettering, with a line drawing of the heads of two happy-looking cows. The last of the Sanborns had sold off their acreage to the local paper mill that owned the land on which the shack was located. But they owned hundreds of acres, and Sanborn wasn't an uncommon name.

When Ty returned with the pest-chasers, Carine brought him back to her studio and showed him what she'd been up to. "Kind of an odd coincidence, huh?" She handed him her magnifying glass, noticing he'd showered and changed into jeans and a sweater, the ends of his hair still damp. "You've heard of the Sanborn Dairy."

FREE Merchandise is 'in the Cards' for you!

Dear Reader,

We're giving away FREE MERCHANDISE!

Seriously, we'd like to reward you for reading this novel by giving you **FREE MERCHANDISE** worth over **$20** retail. And no purchase is necessary!

You see the Jack of Hearts sticker above? Paste that sticker in the box on the Free Merchandise Voucher inside. Return the Voucher promptly...and we'll send you valuable Free Merchandise!

Thanks again for reading one of our novels—and enjoy your Free Merchandise with our compliments!

Pam Powers

Pam Powers

P.S. Look inside to see what Free Merchandise is **"in the cards"** for you!

We'd like to send you two free books like the one you are enjoying now. Your two books have a combined price of over $10 retail, but they are yours to keep absolutely FREE! We'll even send you 2 wonderful surprise gifts. You can't lose!

REMEMBER: Your Free Merchandise, consisting of **2 Free Books** and **2 Free Gifts**, is worth over $20 retail! No purchase is necessary, so please send for your Free Merchandise today.

Get TWO FREE GIFTS!
We'll also send you 2 wonderful FREE GIFTS (worth about $10 retail), in addition to your 2 Free books!

Visit us at:
www.ReaderService.com

Books received may not be as shown.

YOUR FREE MERCHANDISE INCLUDES...

2 FREE Books **AND** 2 FREE Mystery Gifts

FREE MERCHANDISE VOUCHER

2 FREE BOOKS and 2 FREE GIFTS

Please send my Free Merchandise, consisting of
2 Free Books and **2 Free Mystery Gifts**.
I understand that I am under no obligation to buy
anything, as explained on the back of this card.

194/394 MDL GKCM

Please Print

FIRST NAME

LAST NAME

ADDRESS

APT.#   CITY

STATE/PROV.   ZIP/POSTAL CODE

NO PURCHASE NECESSARY!

SUS-516-FMH16

READER SERVICE—Here's how it works:

▼ If offer card is missing write to: Reader Service, P.O. Box 1867, Buffalo, NY 14240-1867 or visit www.ReaderService.com ▼

BUSINESS REPLY MAIL

FIRST-CLASS MAIL   PERMIT NO. 717   BUFFALO, NY

POSTAGE WILL BE PAID BY ADDRESSEE

READER SERVICE
PO BOX 1867
BUFFALO NY 14240-9952

NO POSTAGE
NECESSARY
IF MAILED
IN THE
UNITED STATES

"They delivered pint bottles of milk to school when Gus was a kid."

"Suppose that's where Louis got his alias? He could have grown up in the valley and picked Sanborn because it was convenient, or maybe he's a distant Sanborn cousin or something."

"That doesn't make him one of the smugglers."

She shrugged. "It doesn't *not* make him one of the smugglers."

Ty peered through the magnifying glass. "Did you ever steal a deer-crossing sign?"

"That's not a deer, that's a cow and a moose—"

He glanced at her. "I know it's a cow and a moose. Jesus."

"*You* stole a deer-crossing sign? Ty, that's low."

"Nate helped."

"How come I never knew?"

"You and Antonia would've ratted us out."

"We were not tattletales!"

He rolled his eyes and handed her back her magnifying glass. "I think I used a Sanborn Dairy bottle for target practice once. How's that for a coincidence?"

"All right, so it's a weak theory, but it's something, anyway. A nibble. Maybe Louis was one of the smugglers and saw the sign, and when it came to pick an alias, he chose Sanborn, not realizing where he got it. Manny was looking for a connection between the smugglers and Louis."

"Good. You can tell him it's a defunct dairy."

"If Louis and Jodie met up here—" She sighed, knowing she wasn't going to get anywhere with him. "Oh, never mind. We're just chasing our tails. The police are probably way ahead of us."

"We? Us?"

She smiled. "Go install your pest-chasers. How many did you scare up?"

"Three. They should help."

Carine quickly put the pictures away and headed for the shower, not wasting any time rinsing off, toweling herself dry and jumping into fresh clothes. Ty had her on edge, no question about it. Val Carrera's call and Manny's computer log didn't help, but they weren't the main cause. The teasing, the sexy comments and looks, the easy manner he had with her all reminded her of their first days together last fall, before they'd tried to commit to something deeper. Marriage. A life together.

Don't think.

Yes. Much better that way. She'd learned her lesson. She wasn't going to get ahead of herself with him again.

She combed her damp hair, not bothering to pull it back, and returned to the kitchen. Gus had called before her run to say he was bringing dinner. She slipped out onto the back deck, shivering, the air chilly against her shower-warmed skin. She noticed Gary Turner's midnight blue car in her driveway. He waved to her over its roof and joined her on the deck, his all-black attire and the fading light emphasizing the whiteness of his hair, the blandness of his eyes and skin.

"Sorry to bother you," he said.

"You're not bothering me. I'm just getting a breath of air."

"Your hair's wet—don't catch cold." He cocked his head, smiling at her. "Have I ever seen you with your hair down?" But he didn't wait for an answer, straightening, his manner becoming more formal. "I assume you've heard the latest."

"That Louis Sanborn is an alias?" Carine nodded. "I heard yesterday. After my last visit with the Rancourts,

I didn't think it appropriate to go up there and chat with them about it."

"Understandable. They're furious with me now, too."

"Because you didn't know?"

He shrugged, not really answering.

She was aware she hadn't invited him inside and wondered where Ty was with his pest-chasers. "Did you hire him?" she asked.

Turner narrowed his colorless eyes on her. "He came well recommended—"

"By Jodie Rancourt?"

He sighed. "Then you know."

"I don't know anything, but they were having an affair."

"She told her husband it was just that one time in the library. It's none of my business. I've tried not to interfere in their relationship. Of course, if anyone believed her affair with Louis had anything to do with his murder, I'd speak up."

"Have you told the police—no, never mind. That's not fair of me to ask. You must be in an incredibly difficult situation."

He paused a moment, his expression unreadable. "Regardless of the circumstances of how Louis came to me, I should have gone deeper into his background. I liked him, and I figured I'd keep an eye on him, see how he worked out."

She decided not to tell him about Manny's log, how sure he was that it was Louis he'd run into with Jodie Rancourt in Cold Ridge in September—under a different name. Maybe Turner knew, maybe he didn't. It wasn't for her to discuss the contents of a computer file that the police, after all, also had.

"I think we were all taken in," she said. "Gary—do

you know who took the pictures in the library? It couldn't have been Jodie or Louis, but I suppose one or the other could have persuaded someone—"

"The pictures are irrelevant. I'm history with the Rancourts. I guess I don't blame them." He seemed genuinely unconcerned. "After this week, they're skittish about the whole idea of hiring their own security experts. They'll probably contract out with an established firm."

"What will you do?"

"I have options." He tilted his head back, the fading light darkening his eyes just a notch. "What about you? Does the big city still beckon?"

"I like my apartment. No one else seems to."

He smiled gently. "That's because they've seen this place."

"I have great neighbors in the city. I don't have any neighbors here—"

"Tyler North."

She swallowed. "He's active-duty military. He's not around much. It just so happens that he's here this week." Up in her loft, as a matter of fact, she thought, installing pest-chasers. "I had a lot of projects in the works before the Rancourts lured me with easy money and a kind of sexy job, taking pictures of a historic mansion."

"But you don't have that anymore."

"There's a shop on Newbury Street that's after me to do a brochure for them. I did some work for another shop a couple of months ago—haven't done much commercial work, but it could be fun."

He seemed amused, but not in a patronizing way. "Keeping your overhead low preserves your options, so you can pick and choose what jobs you take."

"It hasn't been easy keeping this place here and renting an apartment in the city, but I've managed. Louis—

whoever he was—teased me about being a tight-fisted Yankee."

Turner laughed, but his heart obviously wasn't in it, the stress of the past few days taking their toll on him, too. "I wonder if the southern act was real. I wonder if anything we knew about him was real."

"He's dead. There's no question of that."

"No, there isn't, and murdering him—that was a terrible thing, no matter who he was. I imagine the police will sort out whatever history exists between Louis and Manny Carrera. I've been ordered not to get involved. 'Let the police handle it' is the mantra."

"I suppose it makes sense."

"Carine—" Turner shifted, intense but quiet, even self-conscious, making no excess movements. "Please be careful until this situation gets resolved. I told you—something's happening under the radar."

She wondered what he might know that Manny didn't—that she and Ty didn't. "Gary, if there's anything I should know—"

"I'm operating more on instinct and experience than on fact. I'm sorry you found Louis on Wednesday." He paused, taking a breath, and she thought she noticed his hands shaking. "I've enjoyed getting to know you, although I don't claim to know you well. If I can swing it and you plan to stay on there yourself, I'd like to get another job in Boston. I'd appreciate seeing you from time to time. Maybe—" He took another breath, swallowing visibly. "Maybe we could have dinner."

She crossed her arms on her chest, not wanting to hurt his feelings or to encourage him. "Gus is bringing over a lasagna out of the freezer." Her hair felt like ice in the cold breeze, and she smiled, the friend, the woman who

liked him but wasn't attracted to him. "We can have dinner right now."

"I meant in Boston, with you." He glanced around, the
bare trees clicking in a strong gust of wind, then sighed,
calmer, his hands no longer shaking. "I doubt you'll be
going back to Boston, at least not for any length of time.
You belong here, Carine. But you do know that, don't
you?"

"I love it here. I don't know about belonging—I like
to think I belong with the people I care about. But I don't
know anymore." She dropped her arms, the wind penetrating her lightweight sweater. "It hasn't been an easy year."

"No, I suppose not. Well, I'll see you around. The Rancourts won't give me the boot until they're assured they
don't need me to keep them safe. Don't let Mrs. Rancourt's
affair with Louis fool you, Carine. She and her husband
are two of a kind. Whatever works, I suppose."

"Not me. I value fidelity."

He smiled, a rare warmth coming into his eyes. "And
that's a surprise? You're good, Carine, and you expect
other people to be good."

"I'm not that good."

He kissed her on the cheek. "Take care of yourself."

"Gary—"

"It's all right."

"I hope things turn out well for you."

He blew her a kiss as he jumped down from the deck.
"They will."

When she returned to the kitchen, North was there,
chair pushed back, his boots on her small table. She noticed his thick thighs, his flat stomach, the soft color of
his eyes as he watched her pull out a chair. "Turner's had
a hell of a week, too," he said. "Don't feel bad for him
because he took a liking to you."

"I'm not. I just—what just happened isn't a typical experience for me."

"What, guys wanting to take you to dinner? That's because you don't see that many guys. You're always hanging off a cliff somewhere. You might not run fast, babe, but I'd hate to have to chase you up a mountain."

"I haven't hung off a cliff, as you put it, in months. It was good getting out in the woods today. Ty—"

But he caught her by the wrist, throwing her off balance just enough that she landed on his lap, and his arms came around her. "I'm sorry," he whispered. "I should never… Carine, I've loved you for a long time. I love you now. I can't help it, but the thought of another man—"

"Ty, don't."

"I didn't pull out of the wedding because I didn't love you."

"I know. That just makes it worse."

But he didn't let her go, didn't stop. "I hoped you didn't love me as much as I loved you and I'd hurt more than you did, or at least that I'd spare you more pain in the end."

She felt tears coming and turned away so he wouldn't see, then slipped her arms around him and lay her head on his shoulder. "It's easy to love you, Ty. It's the rest that isn't so easy. There's too much going on right now for either of us to think straight." She sat up, and he touched a thumb to a tear that had escaped, but she slid to her feet, then nodded toward the back window and managed a smile. "Gus is here with the lasagna."

He pounded on the back door and walked in, grunting at them knowingly. "Thought I might catch you two up to monkey business."

Carine groaned. "Gus, don't you think we're old enough—"

"Old enough, just not smart enough. Age's got nothing to do with it. People do crazy things in their eighties when it comes to romance. Turns you stupid." He set the foil-covered lasagna pan on the stove. "I'm telling you two right now, I'm not going through again what you did back in February. Get your heads screwed on straight before you drag your family and friends through another drama like that."

"You *two?*" Carine gaped at him. "I didn't do anything!"

"You did plenty."

Ty rolled to his feet. "Relax, Carine, he's just irritable because he's sweet on the local egg lady, and he knows it's stupid."

"Stupid—hell, it's insane. She's got hanging beads for doors." He sighed, switching on the oven to Preheat. "Do you know how many different kinds of chickens there are? Ask her. She'll tell you."

Carine went over to him, slipped her arm around his lean waist and hugged him. "I love you, Uncle Gus."

"Yeah, kid, I know. It won't stop me from chopping your head off if you and North here—"

She changed the subject. "Bats and mice moved in while I was out of town. Ty's been installing pest-chasers."

"They're not working. He's still here."

Ty rolled his eyes without comment.

Gus put the lasagna in the oven, then went to the back door and yelled for Stump. "Come on, boy. Come inside."

"Gus!" Carine charged to the door, hoping to head off Stump before he got into her kitchen. "There's not enough room in here for Stump—"

But the big dog burst into the kitchen, excited from his romp outside, and he slid on the wood floor all the way into the great room, then crashed into the unlit woodstove. Once he regained his balance, he jumped on the couch and panted.

"I'll get a bottle of wine," Ty said into Carine's ear. "You negotiate house rules with Gus and Stump."

"Stump hasn't been here in a while. He's forgotten," Gus said, then snapped his fingers. "Stump! Off the couch, boy!"

Stump ignored him, and he ignored Carine when she ordered him off the furniture. She finally had to get him by the collar and drag him down to the floor. Abruptly calmer, he slunk under the kitchen table and collapsed.

"He likes to push the limits," Gus said as he returned to the kitchen. "Antonia and Nate both called. Antonia said to tell you Hank would check on Val Carrera tonight. Nate was making sure I knew he'd told you to go mountain-climbing today. He's flying up here tomorrow. I think he knows something."

Carine sank against the counter. "Gus, how did we end up with a doctor and a U.S. marshal in the family? Why not three nature photographers?"

He smiled. "Because you all three were pains in the ass and each had to be the best at something. Come on. Relax. You look like the weight of the world's on your shoulders. It'll be good to have your brother up for a visit. It's been a while. Hey, here's North with the wine."

"I grabbed a merlot." Ty gave a mock shudder. "I won't tell you what I found down in the cellar, but bats and mice—they're nothing."

Twenty

~~~~~~~~~~

Sterling picked up the phone several times to call Carine Winter and Tyler North and try to make up for his abysmal behavior yesterday. He was embarrassed. Whatever had possessed him? But he didn't make the call, and now Jodie was crying nonstop, ripping his heart out because he could, again, after all, feel sympathy for her. He was shocked by how quickly he'd switched from blaming himself for her infidelity to blaming her. Now he didn't know who—what—to blame.

She staggered into the living room, trembling, visibly weak and overwrought. Her face was red and raw from tears, her eyes puffy, her nose running. She joined him in front of the bank of windows that looked out to the mountains. They could see for miles, but it was dark now, the glass reflecting their own images back at them.

Sterling hit the remote control that shut the shades, their hum the only sound in the sprawling, empty house.

Jodie sank onto the sectional couch. She looked ugly to him, pitiful. He turned away, wondering what in God's name had happened to them. How had he come to this state of affairs? A murdered employee—a man who'd tricked them, lied to them, betrayed them. Sterling won-

dered, now that he was calmer, if Louis Sanborn or whoever he was had played on Jodie's weaknesses, used her
in one of the worst ways possible.

And Turner. That stupid bastard. Asleep at the switch
at best.

Manny Carrera wasn't technically an employee, but
there was no doubt the police suspected him of murder.
Sterling had read that in the faces of the Boston detectives last night when they interviewed him and Jodie about
the pictures. Separately, of course.

Pictures of his wife with another man were now in the
hands of the police. They'd promised to be discreet, but he
and Jodie were a wealthy, prominent couple—the media
would eat up the pictures.

"Dear God," he whispered.

Carine and Tyler…two people he admired. They had
to hate him now. Hank, Antonia. They'd have nothing to
do with him after his behavior, after this horrible scandal.

Once again, Sterling thought miserably, he'd failed to
rise to the occasion.

"Manny Carrera did it." Jodie spoke quietly, stoically,
as if she didn't have the strength for any more emotion;
but her voice was hoarse from crying. "He killed Louis.
All these people—Tyler North, Hank Callahan, Carine
Winter. They'll ruin our lives in an attempt to prove Carrera's innocence."

Sterling stared at the blind-covered windows. "They
want the truth to come out, Jodie. That's all."

She shook her head, adamant. "No, no, Sterling, you're
being naive as usual. The truth, maybe, but how much of
it? How much of our privacy will be sacrificed in their
effort to deny the reality that their friend killed a man in
cold blood?"

"Jodie—Jodie, please don't do this. I'm too tired."

"They'll rip our lives open, just because they can't deal with the fact that Manny Carrera murdered a man."

"That's why we have an attorney."

"It won't matter." She cleared her throat, but her voice remained hoarse. "Manny's a pararescueman. A war hero. He doesn't commit murder. If he kills, it's justified."

Sterling shifted to look at her and wondered if it would be cathartic to cry and scream, fall down on the floor and thrash as she had. Then maybe he could come to this place of calm and certainty. "For all we know at this point, it *was* justified. We don't have enough information."

"Don't we?"

She tucked her feet under her, her robe falling open and revealing the swell of her breasts. Were the police, even now, examining his wife's naked breasts under a magnifying glass? How much of her could they see in the pictures?

"Sterling?"

With an effort that was almost physical, he shook off the image of gloating, drooling detectives. Of Louis Sanborn banging his wife. It was a beautiful, old house with a long history. Were they the first to have illicit sex in the library? Louis was the first murder to occur there. That much Sterling knew for certain. It was a blot—a permanent stain that he knew he and Jodie would never overcome even before he'd learned about her affair.

"Sterling!"

With her voice as hoarse as it was, she hadn't managed much more than an annoyed croak. He sighed. "I'm sorry. What were you saying?"

"I'm saying that Manny was at the house on Wednesday. He was in Boston to get you to fire Louis. What if that wasn't good enough? What if he saw—" She hesitated, placing her hand on a polished toe peeking out from her robe, staring at it as if it had her total attention. She took in a breath, then went on. "He could have decided to capitalize on the situation and grabbed Carine's camera, took those pictures, called me—"

"How could he have called you? He was under police surveillance."

Her brow furrowed, but she didn't let go of her theory. "He'd make it look like an innocent call. The guy's not stupid, Sterling. He'd figure out a way."

He sat on a chair at a diagonal from her. "You're jumping way ahead of yourself."

"No, I'm not. What more do the police need? Why don't they arrest him?" She fought back a fresh, sudden wave of tears, sobbing hoarsely at the ceiling. "I can't stand it! I can't!"

"Jodie...dear God..." What if she were losing it, having a nervous breakdown? Sterling couldn't make himself move toward her. "Jodie—please. Pull yourself together. You're not doing either of us any good."

"Louis used me, and now Manny Carrera and his friends are using both of us." Her voice was angry, bitter, belying the tears that spilled down her cheeks. "We're fair game because we have money. Nobody cares what happens to us. We don't mean anything to them."

"Don't say things like that," he said softly.

"Why not? It's true. You know it is. They resent us." She dropped her feet to the floor and jumped up, fire in her eyes as she sniffled and brushed the sleeve of her robe across her tears. "That idiot Turner—how could he not know about Louis? He'll try to shift the blame. Don't let him."

"Jodie, listen to me. It'll take time. It'll take patience and perseverance." He got to his feet and held her by the elbows, feeling how bony she was under her silky robe.

"But I promise you, I'll get to the bottom of what's happened. Who failed us. Why. All of it."

All the heat and anger went out of her. She looked scared, he thought. Old and scared. "Sterling? What are you saying?"

"I think you're right, Jodie. I think we've been used. By everyone."

He saw her in thirty years, a whining old woman, and couldn't stand it anymore. He had to get away from her. He ran downstairs, out through the front door, not bothering with a coat or hat. The night air was cold, clouds blocking the stars, and even in the darkness, he could see fog swirling in valley pockets.

He'd loved this place. If someone had asked him a month ago if he had to give up one, this house or the one on Commonwealth Avenue, which would it be, he wouldn't have hesitated. The Boston house. No question.

But now he wished he'd never stepped foot in Cold Ridge.

He'd never felt so damn inadequate in his life as the night he and Jodie were rescued by Tyler North, Manny Carrera and Hank Callahan, something he'd never acknowledge to anyone. It wasn't their fault. He admired them.

He was fascinated by their training, their incredible range of skills, everything from emergency trauma medicine to combat maneuvers, scuba diving, parachuting, high-altitude mountain climbing—and he couldn't even do a challenging but popular ridge trail in the White Mountains without getting into trouble.

The cold air drove him back inside.

He and Jodie would pack up and leave Cold Ridge in the morning. Once the police made an arrest for Louis Sanborn's murder, he'd put this place on the market. Then, after a decent interval that gave people time to forget the horror and scandal of what happened in the library, he'd sell the house on Commonwealth Avenue. He and Jodie might even leave Boston altogether. People moved all the time. So did companies.

In the meantime, he'd soak in the Jacuzzi for twenty minutes and go to bed early. Without Jodie. Until he decided otherwise, she was sleeping in the guest room.

Twenty-One

◦━━⟨⟩━━◦

When the phone rang, Val pounced, hoping it was Manny, or Tyler, someone—anyone—with news. It'd been a long damn day, and she could feel herself creeping past the point of rationality, past her capability to resist her impulses to get off her butt and do something. Act. Waiting. Damn, she'd never been good at it.

"Do you want to help your husband?"

She sat up straight on the couch. The voice on the other end was toneless, dispassionate, not one she recognized. "Of course I do. Who is this?"

"The police are about to arrest your husband."

The voice didn't change—there was no emotion, no way, even, of telling for sure whether it was male or female. Male, Val thought. "How do you know?"

"I know. Trust me. The evidence against him is stacking up. The police can't continue to ignore it. He'll be convicted of murder—"

"No, he won't, because he's innocent."

There was a wry laugh. "Ah. True love. I know he is innocent, Mrs. Carrera—Val. But I also know what will happen if you don't act. I can help him."

"How?"

"I can't do it without your help. You must do exactly as I say. Remember, I know more than you do, and I'm on your side. It won't be easy, but you must follow my instructions."

"This is nuts."

"Don't hang up." The intonation didn't change. "I understand your skepticism. You've seen it all, haven't you, Mrs. Carrera? The wife of a career military man, the mother of a sick son—"

"What do you know about my son? You leave him out of it!"

Again, there was no obvious change in the voice of the other end of the phone. "Listen to me. I'm a friend. I can help."

"The police were here today with a search warrant. Maybe they bugged my phone while they were at it. I hope they're out on the street in some van, listening to you, tracing this stupid-ass call—"

"Quit the tough-girl act, Val. Or is it always Valerie?" This time, she thought she sensed a smile, a touch of kindness. "Here is what you need to do. It's simple, but it's not easy. I need you to bring Hank Callahan to Cold Ridge. Tonight."

"What? Are you out of your goddamn mind? He's a senator. I can't just—"

"You can. You have to. Senator Callahan is the key to proving your husband's innocence. He likes you, Val. He believes in your husband. He'll want to help you. Talk him into driving to Cold Ridge with you tonight."

"Then what?"

"Everything will be fine. Trust me."

She licked her lips, squeezing her eyes shut as if that might help her figure out what to do. "I don't even know where he is. I can't—"

"You have one chance to help your family. Don't squander it. It's time to trust someone. Trust me, Val."

"But who are you?"

"I told you. A friend."

She shook her head. "No way. I know all of Manny's friends."

"No, you don't."

She took a breath, unable to speak. Was it possible this call was legitimate? At this point, was *anything* possible?

"Hank and your husband performed dangerous combat search-and-rescue missions when they were in the military together. Play on Senator Callahan's sympathies, his sense of loyalty."

"Nothing will happen to him? You won't hurt him?"

"Val, I'm a friend. I'm not going to hurt anyone. I just have to be very careful. The forces against your husband are—let's just say the deck is stacked in their favor."

"The Rancourts, you mean?"

Silence.

"The *police?* Do they have the police in their pockets?"

"I'll call back when you're on the road and give you further instructions. You can do it."

"If I don't?"

"Then I can't help you."

Click.

Shaking, sobbing, Val dialed 911, then slammed down the phone. What if the caller wasn't screwing around? What if powerful people wanted Manny to take the fall for murder?

And how could she just call 911? She needed to call the FBI or something.

She tried Manny's cell phone, but didn't let it connect. Then Nate Winter's number and Tyler North's number, neither time letting the call connect.

She dialed Eric on his cell phone. He answered on the third ring, sounding sleepy. "Eric—it's Mom. Did I wake you?"

"Yes."

"Everything all right?"

He coughed. "Yes, ma'am."

"You're sure?"

"I'm sure."

It was a conversation they'd had dozens of times. She'd tiptoe onto his room at night and stand over his bed, check to see that he was breathing. Sometimes he'd wake up, and she'd scare the hell out of him, standing there like some ghoul.

To him, this was probably the same. Reassure his crazy mom, then go back to sleep.

"I'll call you in the morning when you're more awake, okay?"

"Yes, ma'am. Good night."

She hung up and burst into tears, because there was no way—no way—Eric could bear to lose his father.

Fifteen minutes later, a car pulled up in front of her apartment, and Hank Callahan, the junior senator-elect from Massachusetts, got out and walked up to the front of her building.

"Jesus," Val breathed, as if Hank's presence was a gift from God.

Twenty-Two

Carine wrapped herself up in a quilt she'd made one summer and sat on the floor in front of her woodstove. By unspoken agreement, she and Ty had decided to spend the night at her cabin. Gus had left, after a long discussion about defunct dairy farms and how, between farming and logging, much of New Hampshire had been denuded of its forests in the nineteenth and early twentieth century, before so much of it turned into national forest. He'd searched his memory for Sanborns he'd known over the years. But Carine could tell he wasn't that taken with her discovery.

In any case, what did it prove? The man who'd called himself Louis Sanborn was dead. Whether or not he was one of the shooters from last fall, it didn't say who his murderer was.

Ty checked the cabin for various critters—bats, mice, chipmunks, squirrels, God knew what else—and emerged from the cellar, picking cobwebs off his shirt. She had a feeling he'd found a snakeskin down there, but he wouldn't tell her.

"Don't protect me," she said. "Just give it to me straight."

"It was a grizzly bear with cubs."

She laughed, but only for a moment. The fire popped behind the screen, startling her, reminding her of how on edge she still was. "When I think back to Wednesday, finding Louis, it's like my senses were heightened," she said. "I can see myself standing in the hall when I realized something was wrong. I can see the blood oozing toward me—his hand was in it. I can hear myself yelling for help, feel the sun on my neck when I ran outside and Manny was there. I can see the pigeons on the mall. Every detail is etched in my mind in a way it wouldn't have been if I'd just gone back and taken pictures, and it was a normal afternoon."

Ty sat on the floor next to her, not taking any of her quilt. He put one knee up, his other leg stretched out, his toes almost against the stove. He'd pulled off his boots, and she noticed he had on the kind of expensive socks Gus sold. "That can happen when you're under a high level of stress."

"Is it that way for you when you're on a mission?"

"I focus on the job I'm there to do."

"But afterward—"

"Afterward there's another job."

"I didn't have a job to do in the library. I wasn't sent in to rescue Louis or treat him, investigate his murder—I'm a photographer. I'm not a doctor like Antonia, a U.S. marshal like Nate, a military guy like you. I didn't have any protocol or orders to follow. I had no professional responsibility."

"If any of us came unexpectedly upon the murder of someone we knew, I doubt we'd react all that differently than you did."

"Me? I screamed my head off and got the hell out of there."

He smiled. "You see?"

"I remember the shooting last fall in excruciating detail, too. I never thought of my job as having inherent dangers, especially compared to what you do for a living. Dangling out of a helicopter—"

"I don't dangle. I'd be in a shitload of trouble if I dangled."

She looked over at him, picturing him decked out in a flight suit and all his gear, fast-roping out of a helicopter. "The idea would be for you to get people out of trouble, not get in any yourself."

"That would be the idea, yes. But things can go wrong."

"Well, I thought I'd be safe in the woods taking a picture of an owl. And you and Manny and Hank—you weren't on a mission. You were just there to steal my food."

"Share, not steal."

"My point is that anything can happen, anytime. I can't live my life worried about it. I do my job, I take sensible precautions."

He gave her a skeptical look. "You were out in the woods alone."

"I can't take someone with me every time I go out— that's part of *my* job. I suppose that's one of its inherent risks." She frowned at him and lifted a corner of her quilt. "You cold?"

"No, but I like the idea of being under a blanket with you."

She shook her head. "Only if you tell me what's in the cellar. Snake?"

"Dragon."

She let him under her quilt with her, anyway, and scooted next to him, her leg pressed up against his. "Do you suppose Louis Sanborn really was one of the shooters? He was always so nice to me in Boston." She didn't wait for Ty to answer. "I don't get what's going on. Maybe we're off base totally and Manny was on a secret military mission."

Ty kissed the top of her head. "Maybe you're so tired you're getting screwy."

"I can make us tea—"

But she stopped abruptly, seeing his expression. He didn't want tea.

"Suppose instead of tea," he said, "I carry you up to bed."

"You can't. There's just a ladder."

"Bet?"

She had no time even to scramble to her feet before she was over his shoulder, sack-of-grain style. She didn't ask him to put her down. She didn't kick or thrash. Without even the hint of a misstep, he had her up the ladder and into her loft, then flopped her onto her back on her bed.

She laughed and whacked him on the shoulder. "You're insane!"

He wasn't particularly out of breath. "Tell me this isn't better than tea."

She smiled, rising up off the bed to hook her hands around his neck and kiss him, bringing him back down with her. "Much better," she said against his mouth. "What if you'd tripped?"

"I didn't trip."

He settled on top of her, the weight of him firing her senses, burning up her ability to talk. She let her hands drift down his back to his hips, pulling him against her, knowing they wanted the same thing. They'd been dancing around it for two days, trying to be sensible and not repeat their body-clawing, mind-numbing madness at her apartment.

But he resisted her attempt to get on with it before she

could think too much. He eased back, slipping one knee between her legs. "Not so fast."

There'd be no crazed lovemaking that she could attribute to stress and the moment in the morning—it would be slow and deliberate, and she might as well give herself up to it.

It was, and she did. At least for a time.

"We should have been making love like this for months now." His voice was a whisper as he lifted her sweater over her head, tugging it off, casting it onto the floor. "Maybe years."

He touched her breasts through her bra, a kind of erotic torture, then unclasped it, not fumbling even the slightest. Because his movements were unhurried, she had time to think, react, even feel a spurt of self-consciousness when she was exposed to him. In so many ways, they weren't the same people they'd been last winter, before he'd knocked on her door. He'd gone back to fight. She'd fled to Boston. The falling in love, the cutting and running, the pain and anger and embarrassment—they'd all had their effect, not just on her. On him, too. She could feel it in his tenderness, in his determination to give her the chance to make sure this was really what she wanted.

She could have dumped him back down the ladder, but she didn't, and she knew he didn't want her to.

It was warm in the loft, the heat of the woodstove rising, and it was dark in the loft, the only light from the fire's glow through the rail. She could see him outlined above her, feel him as his mouth lowered to her, taking first one nipple, then the other. She moaned, but he didn't pick up his pace. Her jeans came next, an even slower torture of hands, tongue and teeth, as if he was oblivious to her mounting urgency. She fought back, tearing at his clothes, and finally got her chance.

But he was ready for whatever tortures she had in mind.

When at last she straddled him and he lifted her hips, lowering her onto him, his hands smoothing up over her stomach and breasts, she gasped as if it was the first time.

Everything changed. She couldn't hold back and saw that he couldn't, either, not any longer. She wanted speed and heat and ferocity, and he responded in kind, his strokes hard, fast, relentless. She ended up on her back, taking all of him she could get, and when she was filled up, spilling over, he came at her all the harder, again and again. Her release washed over her, endless, and her cries seemed to echo across the isolated meadow. She knew she was spinning out of control and didn't care.

But he didn't stop. He was slick with sweat, his heart beating rapidly against her, and when he came, she thought she would die.

Her vision blurred, and a treacherous mix of love and raw need ripped through her.

She'd promised herself never again. And here she was.

Later, Ty slipped down the ladder and tossed another log on the fire. He debated sleeping on the couch, but Carine would take it the wrong way. Or so went his rationalization as he climbed back up the ladder and into bed with her. She had a mountain of quilts and blankets. He thought he'd suffocate. He peeled one off and threw it on the floor with their clothes.

"Gus says we never returned the snowshoes he gave us for a wedding present," she said sleepily.

"Only Gus would give someone snowshoes for a wedding present, and we did return them. He tried to send them back to the manufacturer. He said they were tainted."

She rolled onto her side, pulling the covers up over her

breasts. "I don't have to marry you, Ty, but I can't—I can't just be there whenever you decide you want me there."

"I know."

"And you—it's not right for you to be there whenever I want you."

"Right."

"Ty?"

He smothered her urge to talk with a kiss. It seemed like the right thing to do, and in a minute, she was the one kicking off blankets.

Twenty-Three

Val talked Hank into going out for coffee. They took her car, but she asked him to drive, because she was too damn nervous and barely knew her way around Washington, D.C., on a good day. For all she knew, her caller was around the corner with night-vision goggles, watching her every move. Maybe he was a law enforcement officer. The CIA. Military intelligence. Maybe she was out of her mind.

Plus, she had an unloaded Glock in her glove compartment, and she couldn't reach it if she was the one driving. And she'd seen in the movies—when you kidnap someone, you make them drive.

Except she wasn't kidnapping Hank. Really, she thought, sitting next to him. She was just going to ask him to drive her to Cold Ridge. Or not? Should she pretend she'd never gotten that bizarre call?

He had on a sweater and a lightweight suede coat. It'd be colder in New Hampshire, but he'd be fine. She'd resisted the impulse to drag out her winter coat and instead pulled on a denim jacket. Jeans, turtleneck, sneakers, denim jacket—she looked perfectly normal, even if she felt as if she should be locked up somewhere.

"Where to?" Hank asked, mercifully oblivious to her wild thoughts.

She chewed on her lower lip. Should she tell him about the call? Or just make up some story about why she wanted him to drive her to Cold Ridge?

"Val? What's wrong?"

He was frowning at her, absolutely one of the best-looking men she'd ever met. And kind. So kind. It was dark on her street, not busy. A beautiful Saturday night in Washington. She and Manny should be at the movies. Eric—even if her life was normal, Eric would be in Cold Ridge. *But that's what he wanted.*

Hank pulled out into the street and headed to the main intersection and onto a four-lane highway of strip malls and chain restaurants. He seemed to sense something was up. He was so quiet, just glancing at her occasionally out of the corner of his eye. Val almost started crying. She couldn't believe what she was about to do. "Hank, I can't stand it," she said. "I—I need to see Eric. He didn't sound that great the last time I talked to him. If I leave now, I can be there by morning. But I can't—I'm too out of it to drive."

"Do you want to take the shuttle? I can drive you to the airport."

"No." She shook her head, not knowing what the hell she was doing. Why not just tell Hank everything and let him help her figure it out? He was a retired air force major. He'd performed combat missions. He was a damn *senator.* A Massachusetts Callahan. He knew everyone. He had connections. "Never mind. There's a place where we can have coffee down the street."

"Val, I know this has been hard on you—"

Her cell phone rang, and she jumped, gasping in an exaggerated startled reaction. She answered it, her hands

Cold Ridge 245

shaking violently. She could feel Hank's narrowed eyes on her.

"You have him?"

Again it was that toneless voice. Her heart thumped painfully in her chest. "What am I supposed to do now?"

"Do you have him?" the caller repeated calmly.

Hank slowed to a crawl on the busy Arlington street. "Val, who are you talking to?"

"I hear him." But there was no note of satisfaction in the caller's tone. "Good work. Bring him to Cold Ridge. It's your only chance, Val. Do you understand me? Your only chance. *Manny's* only chance. Do what you have to do. Just get Senator Callahan to Cold Ridge."

Her hands were like ice, her fingers gripping the phone as if it might suddenly fly itself out the window. She moaned in despair and frustration. "Don't you get it? I can't drive all the way to New England with a senator!"

Hank slammed on the brake and snatched the phone out of her hand. "Who the hell is this?" He listened a moment, then handed the phone back to her. "Get rid of him. Understood?"

She nodded, although she was past understanding anything.

"Cute trick," the caller said. "I told him I'd only talk to you. Val, be strong. I'm trying to help. The only way I can help is if you bring Hank Callahan to Cold Ridge tonight."

"But—"

"I know it sounds scary and strange." This time, she thought she sensed an undercurrent of friendliness, caring, in the otherwise unchanged voice. "But once I can reveal what I know, once you have the whole picture— both you and the senator will thank me. In the meantime, you *must* follow my instructions to the letter."

"If I don't?"

"Then you'll bear the responsibility for whatever happens. Good or bad. I'm being honest with you. I have the means to help your husband, but only if you're willing to do your part." A pause, calculated, she thought, to further unnerve her. "Mrs. Carrera, please don't mistake me. Some very bad people are after your husband."

"It's something like ten hours to Cold Ridge." She avoided looking at Hank next to her, felt her stomach muscles twist, aching, acid rising up in her throat. "We can take the shuttle and be there in a couple of hours."

But the caller didn't even hesitate. "You know that won't work. Too many air marshals. Drive all night. It'll be okay. Just do as I say. I'll call back when you're farther north and tell you where to bring the senator."

"What if I call the police the second I hang up? What if Hank does?"

"If either of you contacts the police—if you tell anyone—all bets are off, and you'll have to live with the consequences."

He hung up, and Val gulped for air, not thinking as she yanked open the glove compartment and fumbled for her Glock. She pulled it out and pointed it at Hank, who just stared at her, his jaw set, his teeth clenched. He wouldn't know it was unloaded. "Val, for Christ's sake."

"Please." She didn't know what the hell she was doing. "We can't call the police. Something bad'll happen, and I couldn't live with myself—just drive to Cold Ridge. It's a long way. I'll—I'll figure out something in the meantime."

Hank was steely-eyed, outwardly calm. "Your hand's shaking. Mind not pointing that thing at me?"

She didn't lower the gun. She'd meant to check out Washington D.C. gun laws but hadn't gotten around to it. She was fairly certain that handguns, concealed or otherwise, were illegal in the nation's capital. But, kidnapping a U.S. senator was illegal everywhere.

"Hank—please, just do as I ask and let me *think*. I need you to drive us to New Hampshire tonight. You and me."

"I can't do that, Val. I have a wife. I have a job to do."

She pretended not to hear him. "Take I-95. It's an awful road, but it'll be the fastest."

"Why should I do as you say? What was that call all about? Val—"

"Goddamn it, Hank, my head's spinning. Give me a minute, okay? And get back on the road. Don't fuck with me right now. You know I can shoot."

"You won't shoot me."

"Not dead, but I can make you bleed."

He glanced at her. "And I can feed you that damn gun."

"You won't." She managed a faltering smile, even as she fought back tears. "You know I'm desperate. I'm— I'm trying to buy us some time. I don't know if this guy's on the level. If he is, great, at least he's on our side. If he's not—well, then we're screwed, anyway."

"Val, trust me. Talk to me." His voice was earnest, serious, and she remembered Manny telling her Hank Callahan was one of the coolest pilots under fire he'd ever seen. "Tell me what's going on. I can help."

"Just drive."

"Let me call the police."

"No. I can't risk it." Her head was throbbing, as if she had cobwebs growing in her skull, multiplying, squeezing her brain, so that she couldn't think. "Manny's incommunicado. Tyler's already in Cold Ridge. Eric—I talked to him a little while ago. He's in his dorm, asleep. I'm out of the loop. If I do something wrong—I couldn't live with myself."

"You're doing something wrong now."

"He—at least I think it's a he. Maybe not. Anyway, I'll get another call with more instructions when we're closer to Cold Ridge. Jesus, that's a long time."

"You're goddamn right it is."

"But you'll do it, won't you?"

Hank nodded tightly, turning onto the interstate. Traffic was heavy, endless rows of headlights and brake lights, the whoosh of passing cars and trucks, all of it adding to her confusion and anxiety. He had a thousand options, but Val suspected he wanted to buy himself some time to think, too. And he'd want to find out what was going on in Cold Ridge as much as she did.

He sighed at her with his first hint of real irritation. "Just put the fucking Glock away, will you?"

"The f-word, Hank?" She smiled faintly, not letting go of her gun. "If your constituents could hear you now."

Twenty-Four

Ty reached for the phone when it rang and answered it before he thought about where he was—in Carine's loft bed. But it was Antonia, as collected as ever despite the obvious note of concern in her voice. "Did I wake you?" she asked. "I called your place first. I thought you and Carine were staying there—never mind. Hank got your message and went over to Val's over two hours ago."

"What time is it now?"

"Almost midnight. He's not back, and I haven't heard from him."

Carine stirred, and Ty sat up. He had the inside of the bed, next to the slanted ceiling. "Did you call over there?"

"No answer. I'm trying not to overreact. Hank's cell isn't on, and I don't have Val's number." She sighed, her calm faltering. "Tyler, what the hell's going on? I know Val must be scared to death about Manny's situation. Have you talked to her?"

"Not tonight. Earlier today. The police were at her door—"

"We heard about that. They had a search warrant. Well, that's enough to frighten anyone. I've got the media here—they showed up not long after Hank left for Val's.

They've made the connection between him and Manny.
I think they're gone now."

Carine touched Ty's arm, and he gave her a reassuring nod, although he felt a twinge of uneasiness. Val Carrera was volatile on a good day—funny as hell when she wasn't depressed, but impulsive. And no one who knew her wanted to piss her off. "Antonia, is there anything I can do?"

"I don't know. I don't give a damn about the media, but—Hank—" She gulped in a breath, revealing some of the stress she was accustomed to keeping so carefully hidden. "He's sympathetic to Val's situation."

"We're all sympathetic, but it's late."

"I could go down to her apartment."

"Not alone."

Carine, impatient, motioned for the phone, and North handed it to her. "Antonia? What's up?" She listened a moment, then shook her head. "No, you listen to me for a change. Give Hank thirty minutes. If he doesn't get in touch with you, you don't go down to Val's. You sound the damn alarm."

Antonia called back twenty minutes later. Carine was in the kitchen making tea, debating whether or not to call Gus and get him up. Ty talked her out of it. He simply had to suggest she put on more water for tea—it put the same image in her head that he had, Gus and Stump in her cabin at one o'clock in the morning.

He could hear the relief in Antonia's voice. "Hank called. He and Val are on their way to Cold Ridge."

"They're driving up here tonight?"

"Val wants to see Eric. Hank says she's very stressed out and hanging by threads, and you know how he is. He's loyal, and he's a good guy. He also said Val's worried about Eric—you know that's all it'd take. Hank's got a soft spot where children are concerned."

Ty knew. Ten years ago, Hank had lost his first wife and three-year-old daughter in a car accident while he was serving overseas. He'd dedicated himself to his work and public service, but it had taken Antonia Winter to get him to let himself take the risk of falling in love again.

"How'd he sound?" Ty asked.

"I don't know—he's very good at concealing what he's really feeling. It's such a stressful situation." She sighed, breaking off. "I'm coming up there. I'll take the first plane I can out of here in the morning."

The kettle whistled, and Carine, frowning at him, grabbed a pot holder and filled her chipped teapot with the hot water. But she didn't snatch the phone out of his hand, and he said, "Nate's coming tomorrow, too. Maybe you two can meet up at the airport."

"That'd be good. I don't want to be a worrywart, but it's just—" Antonia faltered, a rarity for her. "Never mind. You have enough on your plate without fretting about me. Carine? You're keeping your promise?"

He smiled. "I don't know about that."

"Liar. You know damned well what you've been up to. So do I. I *am* a doctor—and I know you two."

"Goodbye, Antonia. Safe flight tomorrow."

He hung up. Carine unwrapped tea bags and dropped them in the hot water, their tags hanging over the sides of the teapot. Normal tea bags. But Ty could see the tension in the way she held herself. They'd pulled on their clothes, but there was no pretending what happened in the loft hadn't happened. She knew it had, and she wasn't sure she approved.

Well, who would?

But he pushed the thought out of his mind and dialed

Manny's cell phone, and when he got his friend's voice mail—again—he left a pointed message. "You have Val's cell phone number? Call her. She's up to something."

Twenty-Five

With as much adrenaline as she had pumping through her, Val didn't get sleepy on the long drive north. Hank wasn't dropping off, either. He sat rigidly as he drove, as if he were on some secret military mission. She'd let him call Antonia and reassure her, although it didn't sound like she was thrilled when he told her he was on his way to Cold Ridge.

After he'd hung up with his new wife, he glared at her. "Get this straight, Val. I'm not driving you to Cold Ridge because you've got your goddamn gun. I'm driving you because I know you're frightened and feel you're out of options. So, let's just get there."

The hours ticked by. It was a dark, cloudy night, but there was no rain. Traffic eased, and when they crossed the border into New Hampshire and the sun came up, she wondered if she'd imagined the calls. Wouldn't that be nice? She'd rather be delusional than have to face the caller again.

The yellow and orange leaves had vanished, in their place, bare limbs and patches of oaks with brown-and-burgundy leaves. The air was colder. She could feel it even with the heat on in the car. The sun and the blue sky were deceptive. She looked up at the looming mountains, stark against the clear sky, and saw that some of the highest peaks had snow.

They were off the interstate now, almost to Cold Ridge.

She sighed at Hank, trying to distract herself. "Do you ever wish you'd stayed in for thirty instead of retiring?"

He glanced over at her. "Right now I do."

She ignored his tight undertone. "Manny had no business getting out. Don't you think he'd make a great PJ instructor? He's like this old warhorse. He's done all these different kinds of missions. He's seen it all. I don't want him back in combat, but he could be an instructor."

"Val," Hank interrupted softly, "let me help you."

She stared down at the Glock in her lap. "I don't know what to do."

"Talk to me."

Her fatigue was eating away at her reserves. They'd had no food, no water since hitting the road. They'd had to stop for gas, but Val had done the pumping, her unloaded Glock tucked in the waistband of her jeans. They'd managed a bathroom run, and that was really when she'd realized Hank wasn't going to try to escape—he was playing along with her, because he was her friend, he knew her, he knew she was scared and desperate and stupid.

He was so damned caring. Nobody could ever fault Hank Callahan for not caring.

She sank her forehead into her hands and started to sob.

"Val...what would Manny want you to do?" Hank's voice was gentle, breaking through her fog of desperation, her sobs. "He loves you. I've never seen a man love a woman as much as he does you. Twenty years from now, if Antonia and I have what you two have—"

"Don't—Hank, please don't."

"He'd want you to trust me."

She lifted her head, sniffling. "He'd want me to jump out of this car so you could run me over."

She could feel Hank's smile. "Well, that, too."

"Oh, shit." She threw back her head and swore at the top of her lungs, then looked over at him. "I could have been an astronaut, you know."

"Val…"

She told him everything. What was in Manny's computer files, about the police search warrant—and about her caller. Hank listened without interruption. That was another of his virtues. He listened to people. Not Manny, she thought. Mostly, Manny liked to be listened to.

"I'm sorry," she said. "I'm so sorry."

Hank stayed focused on the narrow, winding road. "We're in Cold Ridge now. It's where we both need to be, don't you think?"

She nodded. "When you say it, it sounds sensible."

He reached over and wiped a tear off the end of her nose. "Wait'll Manny sees you. What a mess."

"He didn't kill that guy."

"I know."

Her phone rang, and she managed to answer it without dropping the gun. "Yes?"

"Where are you?" the toneless voice asked.

"I'm not saying until you tell me who you are."

The caller paused, then gave a sad, long-suffering sigh. "You've told Senator Callahan, haven't you? He's calling the shots. I thought it might come to this. Well, allow me to persuade you in another way."

"Look, if you really are a friend—"

"You called your son last night."

"What?" She couldn't grasp what he was saying, couldn't make the leap. "What about my son? How did you know I called him?"

"I was with him. You called him on his cell phone. You assumed he was in his dorm room—"

"No!"

"I made him take the phone with him, Mrs. Carrera. I have your son."

Hank didn't say a word or try to take the phone from her; he just pulled over to the side of the road and waited.

A numbness crept up her neck and into her cheeks. "What—what do you want me to do?"

"Mom?" It was Eric, coughing, scared. "Mom, he made me pretend I was asleep—"

"Where are you?"

But the caller had grabbed the phone away. "Feisty little kid, for an asthmatic." There was no friendliness in the toneless voice now. "He has his rescue inhaler and his EpiPen, but it's November in the mountains. Open the window. Feel the air. He won't last long."

"Don't hurt my son. *Please.*"

"If you cooperate, he'll have a chance. If anything happens to me, I promise you, Mrs. Carrera—Val—no one will find your son in time."

She gulped in a breath. "We're on the main road into the village. What do you want me to do?"

"Turn onto the notch road. Hank knows it. There are two scenic pullovers. The first one is at a lake. Don't take that one. The second one—the one you want—is at a picnic area. A couple of picnic tables, a lot of rocks. Pull in and wait for me. I'll find you."

"Eric—"

"Any cops, any curveball at all, your kid is dead. It's cold, he's sick. But I don't want him. Do you understand?"

"No, I—"

"I want the senator in exchange for your son."

That was all. He was gone. The phone was dead in her hand.

She kept gulping in air, not exhaling.

"Val." It was Hank, his voice gentle, trying to penetrate her shock. "Val, breathe out, sweetheart."

"He's got Eric." She clawed at Hank's arm. "Oh, my God!"

"What does he want?"

She didn't want to tell him. Kids were Hank's weakness. Everyone knew it. If he could exchange himself for Eric, even die in his place, Hank Callahan, senator-elect from Massachusetts, would do it without hesitation.

"Val?"

She clenched his arm, and she could see it in his eyes. He knew.

Twenty-Six

~⊰⊱⊰⊱~

Carine had dozed on the couch in front of the fire, but she doubted Ty had slept at all. They kept expecting Hank or Val to call or roll in the driveway. It'd been hours since they'd set off—they had to be getting close to Cold Ridge. But their cell phones and phone lines remained quiet.

And not a word from Manny Carrera.

They walked back to his house, where Ty made coffee and they tried to eat a couple of pieces of toast. But Carine could see the waiting was getting to him as much as it was to her. She stared out the window at the bleak morning, fog and mist settling on everything. "If Val wants to see Eric, she'll probably go straight to the school—"

"Grab your coat."

The campus of the Mount Chester School for Boys was quiet so early on a Sunday morning, just a couple of intrepid boys out on the track. Ty parked in front of Eric's dorm, another ivy-covered brick building. He and Carine were greeted at the front door by the young couple who served as house parents. Brendan and Penny O'Neill—Carine had met them before.

Brendan, a bearded man in his late twenties, led them down a carpeted hall to Eric's first-floor room, his door covered in posters. "We saw him last night," Brendan said. "He seemed preoccupied but otherwise all right. Is there any news about his father?"

Ty shook his head and rapped on Eric's door, but he spotted a note folded and tacked to a *Lord of the Rings* poster. He pulled it off, opening it as Carine and Brendan O'Neill read over his shoulder.

> To whom it may concern:
> I have gone on a hike in the mountains. Don't worry about me. I have everything I need. My dad taught me to climb. I have to do this on my own.
> Sincerely,
> Eric Carrera

Brendan swore under his breath, but Ty was tight-lipped, rigid in his control. The note oozed all the angst of an unappreciated fourteen-year-old boy with too much on his mind, but it was short on specifics, which, given Eric's reaction to the seniors who'd had to be rescued the other day, surprised Carine. He'd printed the note, obviously hastily, but had signed his name in cursive.

Using his pass key, Brendan unlocked Eric's door and pushed it open. It was a typical dorm room, with a neatly made bed, a chest of drawers, a desk, a chair and a closet—and more posters, the emphasis on *Lord of the Rings*. The room wasn't tidy, but it wasn't a pigsty, either.

"We didn't see him leave," Brendan said, his distress evident. "I can't even imagine where he's gone, what he did for transportation. Damn it! At least it's good weather today, but it's windy up high, and the temperature must be below freezing. If he's not prepared…" He didn't finish.

Ty quickly checked Eric's desk, stacked with binders and textbooks. "Does he keep his meds here?" he asked.

O'Neill shook his head. "The infirmary dispenses all medications. Eric only carries his EpiPen and rescue inhaler. He *must* have those with him—he wouldn't go anywhere without them. He knows that."

"Where's the infirmary?" Ty asked. "Eric takes four different medications on a daily basis. We need to know when he had his last doses."

"It's down the hall, but I can call." Brendan went back out into the hall and grabbed a wall phone, dialing numbers, his hand visibly shaking. He spoke to someone on the other end—obviously a nurse—then hung up. "He was in after dinner yesterday for his second dose of Serevent, a long-acting inhaler, and his dose of Singulair—it's an anti-inflammatory. He's supposed to take an allergy medication and a nasal steroid spray in the morning, but he hasn't been in. I don't—honestly I don't know what he could be thinking."

Ty opened Eric's closet, squatting down. "His hiking boots are here. I don't know if he had a second pair, but I doubt it." He looked up as he stood up straight. "We need to find this boy."

"I'm calling the headmaster," Brendan said shakily, dialing more numbers.

Carine touched Ty's arm as he joined her out in the hall. "We should call Gus and get the ball rolling on a rescue, start checking trails, get the word out—notify the park ranger, the shelters. If Eric shows up in the meantime, great."

"You see what it's like out there. It'll take all his strength to manage the climb in this cold and wind. If he gets above three thousand feet without hiking boots, good clothing, food, he could be in real trouble, fast. Cold and anxiety aren't a good mix for anyone, never mind an asthmatic kid hiking solo."

"Maybe he went with a friend. He must be more upset about his father than any one of us realized." Carine sighed. "Let's hope the wind and cold are to his advantage and they at least deter him from hiking alone."

Penny O'Neill drifted down the hall, obviously sensing there was a problem, but she maintained her composure while Carine quickly explained what was going on. Penny shook her head, firm in her conviction. "I can't believe—it's just not like Eric to go off on his own this way."

"Call the police," Ty said, handing the stricken couple the boy's note. "I don't think Eric did go off on his own."

They found Gus in his backyard hollering for Stump. "I heard," he said. "The school's not wasting any time. The New Hampshire Department of Fish and Game and the National Park Service are coordinating with the police on an organized search. I'll check the local trails."

But as he opened the passenger door on his truck and Stump roared in, Carine noticed something different in her uncle's manner. "Gus? What is it?"

"I shouldn't tell you—" He slammed the door shut and raked a hand through his brittle hair. He had on his hiking clothes, thoroughly ratty but with years of wear left in them. "I was going to wait and tell Nate when he gets here. It's just a crazy theory. Like you and the Sanborn Dairy."

Ty settled back against the hood of his own truck, but nothing in his manner was easy or calm. "Spit it out, Gus."

"You know that old bastard, Bobby Poulet?"

"Yeah." Ty nodded. "Bobby Chicken, we used to call him."

"Christ, no wonder he's a crank. He's a survivalist these days. He has a place up past the woods where Carine got shot at last fall. I warned her to stay away from him when she went up there."

"I remember," she said. "The police interviewed him."

"Within a day or two after the shooting, right. He's got guns out the yin-yang, but he's harmless. He heard the shots—he said he figured it was some guy exercising his God-given right to bear arms." Gus spoke without inflection, just saying what he had to say. "He didn't see anything. That was the end of it, as far as the police were concerned. But this past spring, he showed up at the shop on his annual trip to town. Gave me shit about the merchandise."

Ty shifted, restless. "Gus, come on—"

"I'm getting to the point. While he was bitching and moaning, Bobby told me about a guy he'd helped out back in late January, early February. He was lost in the woods. He was frostbitten, and he had this skin infection, like it was rotting off. Bobby gave him first aid supplies and something hot to drink and offered to take him to a doctor, which tells you how bad a shape this guy was in. Bobby doesn't offer anybody anything. The guy's lucky he wasn't run off with a shotgun."

Carine grabbed her uncle's arm in shock. "Did Bobby think this man was going to lose a couple of fingers?"

"He was sure of it. He said they practically fell off in his soup bowl."

"Jesus Christ," Ty breathed.

"I tried to get him to talk to the police," Gus went on, "but he didn't want to. He doesn't trust the police. He's pretty much a paranoid old fart."

"Did you tell the police yourself?" Carine asked.

He nodded. "By then, there wasn't much to be done. The guy was long gone. I hadn't thought about the story in ages, until I saw that guy at your cabin last night. I didn't get a good look at him—" He shook off whatever he planned to say next. "Oh, screw it. A lot of people have missing fingers."

Carine turned up the collar of her coat, the cold wind penetrating her light layers of clothing. "You never mentioned Bobby's story to me."

His eyes held hers for a moment. "It was March. You'd just had your heart broken. I didn't want to remind you of the shooting. That's when you went haywire and fell for North." Gus looked tired all of a sudden, as if he'd missed something important and now everyone was paying the consequences. "I talked to the police this morning and reminded them about Bobby's guy, told them about Turner. They went up to the Rancourts. I guess they're leaving for Boston—they're probably gone by now. Turner'd already left. The cop I talked to figured they'd get in touch with the Boston police. I don't know. It could all be bullshit."

Ty ripped open his truck door. "I'm going back to the house. I'll check the ridge trail for any signs of Eric and try Manny again. Carine—maybe you should go with Gus."

"Sure," she said quietly. "But, Gus, if I'm going with you, the dog stays. There's just not enough room."

"All right, all right." He seemed relieved to be back in action, not talking about a crazy survivalist with a tale of a freezing man with rotting fingers. He opened up his truck door. "Come on, Stump. Back inside."

Carine stood next to Ty, could almost feel his concentration. She realized she was an unnecessary distraction for him, and that was why he was sending her off with her uncle. "We can check the trail up by the Rancourt house," she told him. "The Rancourts used it when they got into trouble last year and you and Manny rescued them—Eric'll know that."

"And Hank," Ty said, climbing in behind the wheel.

"He was here that weekend. Now he's missing in action, too. So's Val Carrera."

"Everyone in the whole goddamn state'll be on it before too long," Gus said, taking Stump back up the walk to the house. But he sighed, giving North an encouraging look. "We'll find them."

Carine glanced up at the blue, cloudless sky and could almost feel the high winds and cold of past hikes. "We don't have a lot of time."

Twenty-Seven

Sterling stood in the doorway of the warming hut and let his eyes adjust to the poor light inside, in case he was wrong. The tension and stress of the past few days could have affected his vision—or his mind, making him see what wasn't there. A fire in the potbellied stove. A boy tied up in the far corner by the back door. Gary Turner standing in the middle of the hut, his white hair stark against the dark wood walls.

"The local police were just here," Sterling said, his voice sounding almost disembodied. "I told them you'd left."

Turner shrugged, matter-of-fact. "I parked my car out of sight."

Sterling squinted at the back of the hut. The boy wasn't gagged, but he was pale, his breathing labored—the Carrera boy? *Dear God.* "What's going on here? Turner? Who are you?"

"Have you ever wanted something so much you'd do anything?" He withdrew his nine-millimeter pistol from his belt holster, without any obvious change in his calm manner. "Kidnap an innocent boy? Kill your best friend? Risk everything?"

The bite of fear Sterling felt was unlike anything he'd ever experienced. It made him cold. It made him pretend he couldn't see the boy suffering, terrified, in the corner. "Jodie and I are leaving as soon as we get the car packed. I told the police we were on our way. They—" He hesitated, but didn't stop himself from finishing his thought. "They have no reason to come back up here."

But Turner didn't seem to hear him. He fingered the tip of his gun, but his attention was squarely on Sterling. "You were born with a silver spoon in your mouth. What would you know? You've had money and good health all your life. A beautiful wife, even if she does fuck around."

"I should get back to the house—"

"You've never wanted or needed anything, except to prove yourself to a few air force guys who don't think twice about you."

Sterling backed up a step. "I'm sorry things didn't work out."

Turner lifted his colorless eyes. "You pretend it's your wife who doesn't connect with other people, but it's you, Rancourt. It's all about you. Always. What if someone killed her? What would you do?" He continued to speak in that rational, detached manner. "Would you hunt whoever did it to the ends of the earth? Would you make them pay?"

"Revenge—" Sterling coughed, his throat was so tight that his voice sounded strangled. "Revenge is a complicated thing."

"No, it's not. It's simple. You put it all on the table. You go against the odds. You accept that you'll probably have to die. You accept that you might even have to sacrifice your own moral code."

"I'm not—Gary, I'm not a part of this."

Turner jumped forward, his nine-millimeter pistol at

Sterling's throat before he could draw his next breath. "One word and the kid dies for sure. Do you understand? One fucking word to anyone."

"Yes. Yes, I understand."

"Right now it's not my intention to hurt him. He's just a kid. But I will if you talk. Just so you'll have to live with what you caused."

"Nothing. Not a word. Promise."

"Go back to the house. Get your slut wife. It wasn't just the one time in the library with Louis. Ask her. Ask her on the way out of here who he really was." He tucked the gun back into his holster and smiled cockily. "She knows."

Sterling wasn't breathing. Through the dim light, he could see the boy, obviously weak and in pain, staggering to his feet. He was stooped over, but he managed to run for the back door. If he could just incapacitate Turner, Sterling thought—but how? The man had a pistol.

He did nothing, and Turner swooped across the small hut and grabbed the boy around the middle, dumping him onto the blanket on the floor. "You little fuck. I told you to stay put."

The boy erupted into a spasm of coughing, a wet, sloppy sound that turned Sterling's stomach. He'd watched the scene unfold in horror. But there was nothing he could do to help the boy—he had to keep his mouth shut and get himself and Jodie out of there.

Sterling ran down the dirt track to the house, the wind swooping up the hills and blowing hard. Jodie had the back of the SUV open, loading in one of her endless bags. Sterling pushed her aside and shut the tailgate. "Whatever you have packed will have to do. We're leaving. Now."

"What's going on? Who were you talking to up—"

"Don't speak to me. Not now."

He grabbed her by one shoulder and opened the passenger door, pushing her. She stumbled, then quickly got the message and climbed up into the seat. Her lower lip trembled in fear.

Sterling got into the driver's seat, surprising himself that he wasn't shaking. "Be glad I'm even taking you with me," he said. "Just keep your lying mouth shut and come with me."

A car—not Turner's car but an old Audi they kept in New Hampshire—lurched down from the hut. Sterling didn't look to see if the boy was in there with him. How would he know, anyway? Turner could have him stuffed in the trunk.

It was so clear and perfect, it was as if they were in the middle of a postcard, the mountains cascading all around them, a darker blue against the sky.

The Audi quickly disappeared.

"Gary," Jodie said hoarsely. "He's a part of it, isn't he?"

Sterling glared at her. "A part of *what,* Jodie? Hmm? What?"

"Nothing." She was ashen, her voice small. "I don't know what I'm saying. You're right—let's get out of here."

Twenty-Eight

It wasn't much of a picnic area. Val edged forward in her seat, peering out at the rocks, the birch trees and evergreens, the two unpainted picnic tables in a small clearing. A sign said there were no facilities, meaning, she assumed, no rest rooms. No trash cans, either. She didn't know why she noticed such details, except it gave her something to do, something to focus on. She didn't want to think.

The mountains, every inch of them visible on such a clear day, rose up on both sides of the road—a notch, Hank had told her, was basically a pass in the mountains. Yet even with the perfect visibility, she felt claustrophobic, enveloped by the mountains, hemmed in. Probably, she thought, she wouldn't have made a good astronaut, after all.

She was done. Spent. *I'm in over my head... Eric...*

She handed Hank the phone. "Call the police." Even to herself, she sounded exhausted, past the point of coherency, never mind logic. "I'm just playing into this bastard's hands."

He glanced at the readout. "There's no service here. I

remember last fall we had trouble getting through—Carine and Ty stopped at a lake down the road."

"That's why the bastard picked this spot. In case I changed my mind, I wouldn't be able to call for help." She shoved the Glock at him. "Here, take it. You make the decisions. It's not loaded, but I think there's a clip in the glove compartment."

He shook his head. "You hang on to it." He pushed her hand back with the gun, then thrust the phone at her. "I'll wait here. You get to a house or a place where you can call."

"No! Hank, he wants *you.*"

"Exactly. Val—"

"You can't, Hank. This guy's not going to keep his word."

But Hank was determined—and very clear about his intentions. "I have to try to make the exchange. If there's a chance he'll let Eric go and take me in his place, I have to at least give it a shot. If nothing else, perhaps I can buy the authorities more time."

Val noticed how quiet it was around her. "I wish he wanted me. I can't—Hank, I can't let you do this."

"If you'd go, then let me go."

"He's not your son."

"Does it matter? He's an innocent fourteen-year-old boy who's caught up in something not of his own making." He brushed her cheek gently with the back of his hand. "Trust me, Val."

It was as if she was on a treetop, looking down at herself, a small, dark-eyed, stupid-assed woman who'd made too many mistakes in the past twenty-four hours. The past year.

She pushed open her door and climbed out, composed, as if she'd disassociated herself from her fear. "I'll call the police as soon as I can," she said. "Just stall for time, okay? Oh, listen to me, like I'm the combat veteran."

But something had diverted Hank's attention, and he leaned forward, looking out the windshield, then lunged across the seat at her. "Val—behind you! Get down!"

She dove onto the front seat, but she felt a burning pain in her left side even as she heard the shot. Hank reached for the Glock, but a white-haired man had his door open, a gun to Hank's head. "On your feet, Senator. My car's parked on the other side of the rocks. If you want the boy to live, you will do as I say."

Val could hear Hank's voice. "Understood."

"I won't have to kill him. Time and the elements will. He's a very sick kid."

"Eric…" Val tried to yell but nothing came out. She tried again. "Don't hurt—"

But she didn't know if she'd made a sound. She held her side, remembering that Manny had told her to apply pressure to a wound—and it hurt. God, it hurt. She could feel her own blood warm on her hands. She was collapsed face first on the car seat, could hear Hank getting out of the car. She couldn't think, couldn't really see.

"Val—"

Hank's voice. She held her side, unable to move but knowing she couldn't just pass out and die out here in the cold. Not yet.

The man with the white hair snorted. "Val Carrera is dead."

Twenty-Nine

A fourteen-year-old boy hiking alone would draw the attention of any alert hiker, North knew, but when he checked the main trailhead above the meadow, he didn't see signs of *any* hikers, never mind Eric Carrera. It was the off season, and conditions weren't great on the ridge. There weren't going to be many hikers out today.

North, however, had his doubts about Eric's note and didn't believe the boy was on an illicit hike to prove himself, to his father or anyone else.

He headed back to his place. First on tap was to try to reach Manny again, then call Antonia for any word from Hank and Val. And the police. Ty wanted to touch base with the local police *and* the Boston police.

But pulling into the driveway ahead of him was Carine's ancient Subaru sedan, which he'd last seen parked on her street in Cambridge. Ty rolled to a stop behind it and got out.

Manny Carrera unfolded himself from within the small car's confines and climbed out. "What a rattletrap. Doesn't she know cars don't run forever?" He rolled his big shoulders, stretching, but his eyes were serious when he focused on North. "I got your message about Val and slipped out of town. I'm not under arrest. I can go where I want."

"Manny, this isn't a good idea."

"If it was your wife, what would you do? I talked to Antonia about an hour ago. She said Val and Hank are on their way up here. I figured we could head them off at the pass, so to speak. I tried reaching you but didn't get through up here in the boonies."

"I was at the school."

Manny frowned. "The school?"

Ty's head pounded. "You don't—shit, you don't know. Manny, Eric's missing."

His friend had no visible reaction as he absorbed the news. "Talk to me, North."

"He left a note on his door. It sounds like bullshit to me—he says he's gone hiking. But he didn't stop at the school infirmary to take his morning meds. He could have forgotten—"

"He didn't forget."

"Or not bothered. He's upset. It's possible he just wants to prove himself."

"He's got nothing to prove."

"I know that. The police and forest rangers are on it. Conditions are tough up on the ridge—if his note's legit, he could have changed his mind about a hike and stopped at a coffee shop and had breakfast. Or maybe he went with Val, and she made him write the note for reasons we don't understand."

Manny thought a moment. He had on a black wool jacket, a lightweight wool sweater, jeans and cowboy boots. "Where are the Rancourts?"

"On their way to Boston. And Gary Turner's left, too. Supposedly. I don't know what's relevant anymore, but Gus—ah, hell, this sounds screwy." Ty looked up toward the ridge, which looked innocuous from his elevation. But he knew the winds would be bad above fifteen hundred feet, and fierce above the treeline. "Remember the survivalist from last fall? The police questioned him."

One corner of Manny's mouth twitched. "The chicken guy."

"Bobby Poulet. A few months after Carine got shot at, a man surfaced at Bobby's place with frostbite and a skin infection—Bobby said it looked like he was going to lose a couple fingers. Gary Turner's missing a couple of fingers."

"Christ. You people up here." Manny motioned for North, obviously ready to take action. "Come on. In the car. Let's go see what the story is at the Rancourts'. Shit's hitting the fan at the school because they lost my kid?"

"Major league."

"Good. He's got his EpiPen, his rescue inhaler?"

Ty nodded. "Looks like it."

"One bright spot. All right. If the Rancourts are there, I torture them for information. They've been holding back. If they're not there, I break in and see what's what."

"Manny. The police—"

"You can stay here."

North didn't hesitate. "We'll take my truck."

"Now you're talking." He gave Carine's rusting car a disparaging look. "I feel like Fred Flinstone driving this goddamn thing."

Manny's wry humor in a tight situation was legendary, but Ty knew not to underestimate his friend's focus. At this moment, his sole mission was getting to his wife and son. Nothing else mattered—and that, North thought, was where he came in. He couldn't let Manny cross the line. It'd never happened before, but the stakes had never been this personal.

"Did you slip out from under police surveillance?"

"They know I'm not their man."

Which didn't really answer Ty's question. He got in behind the wheel. Manny didn't argue. "You know the terrain." He gave a mock shiver. "Hell, it's cold up here. I always forget."

"Winds above the treeline—"

"Yeah. I know. Close to hurricane force. I listened to the weather station on my way up."

Ty pulled out onto the main road. "Your turn, Carrera. Talk to me."

It seemed to give Manny something to do while they drove. "Louis Sanborn's real name is Tony Louis Apolonario. Apparently his great-grandfather—"

"Was named Sanborn and owned a local dairy?"

"You figured it out?"

"Carine."

Manny smiled slightly. "She's got bird-dog potential, don't you think? I didn't find out until it was too late. The police have everything I do, by the way. Looks like Louis/Tony was involved in that smuggling ring we ran into last fall. The Canadian authorities were on to them, and the feds were closing in—then came the incident with us and Carine. They burned down the shack, their base of operations, and disappeared. Not nice guys. They were into smuggling guns, people, drugs. Whatever paid."

"You think Gary Turner's one of them? Makes sense. He started work for the Rancourts months ago, but after the shooting. Louis only started a couple of weeks ago— something there, you think?" But Manny didn't answer right away, and North sighed. "This wasn't in your log."

"My computer log? Val was on it?"

"Apparently she tried every password possibility she

could think of before she called me. *I-l-u-v-a-l.* Christ, Manny."

He grinned in spite of his obvious tension. "I knew it'd stump her, keep her nose out of my business. I figured if things went south, you'd at least have enough to go on. I pumped a source for information."

"Nate Winter?"

Manny scoffed. "Are you kidding? A Winter as a snitch? I've never seen a more tight-lipped, closemouthed, stubborn bunch. No, another guy I know in Boston. It started really coming together Tuesday night, Wednesday morning. Then Louis calls me to meet him at the Rancourt house—fool that I am, I went. By the time I got there, he was tits up. Dead as a doornail."

"You didn't see Jodie Rancourt or whoever took those pictures?"

"Not a thing. I went outside to call the police on my cell. I should have seen Carine going inside and stopped her—"

"She's handling it."

"Then the cops were all over us. I knew I wasn't the killer. I was pretty sure Louis Sanborn tied back to the shooters last fall. I didn't know about Gary Turner—I thought he could be legit. I was more interested in the Rancourts."

"Because they'd hired Louis?"

"And me. That didn't make any sense, either."

"Did you know Louis and Jodie Rancourt were having an affair?"

"Suspected." He stared out the side window as Ty turned onto the notch road. "I thought the police'd sort it out. I cooperated with them. I put you on Carine. I shut Val out. I figured Eric was safe at school." He was silent a moment. "I guess my plan didn't work out that well."

But North's focus was up the road, where an elderly man had jumped out in front of them, waving them down, a Ford Taurus with Maine plates was parked crookedly in back of him. There was a second car—it had veered off into a dry ditch, its front end smashed against a granite ledge.

Ty pulled over, but Manny was already kicking open his door. "That's Val's car."

He was out of the truck before they'd come to a full stop and charged down into the ditch. When Ty climbed out, the old man, decked out in a winter parka, hat and gloves, was on him. "She was coming from the other direction and crossed right in front of me—I knew something was wrong. I think she must have had a heart attack or something. I didn't know whether to leave her and go call an ambulance."

Manny ripped open the driver's side door. Val fell out into his arms. Ty shoved his cell phone at the old guy. "Call 911. When you connect, give the phone back to me." He grabbed his medical kit out of the back of his truck and ran down to Manny and Val. He could see the blood on her front, mostly on her left side. He opened up his med kit, setting it on the ground. "What's her condition?"

"She's been fucking shot."

"Manny—"

"Airway, breathing, circulation are okay." The ABCs, the basics. "Skin's clammy, she's shivering—she could go into shock."

Ty grabbed gauze and moistened it with IV fluid, then thrust it at Manny, who immediately applied pressure to the wound. It was his wife—he didn't bother with protective gloves. "Abs?" Ty asked.

"Guarding."

They both knew that was a positive sign. Manny

checked for bowel sounds in all four quadrants, then nodded, satisfied. They needed to get Val to definitive care,
the sooner the better. The "golden hour" rule. Every minute care was delayed, the patient's chances of recovery
dimmed.

Ty handed Manny an Ace wrap to hold the dressing in
place. "You okay?"

He nodded, concentrating on a task he'd performed
hundreds of times in simulations and missions. The training took over, and if he was going to panic in a crisis,
Manny Carrera wouldn't have lasted as a PJ for twenty
years. Ty helped him put in a saline IV and let it run wide
open—Val had suffered enough blood loss that she needed
fluid or she might not make it to the hospital.

Ty leaped back up from the ditch and got a blanket out
of his truck, and he and Manny laid Val on it and wrapped
her up as best they could to keep her warm. Then they el-
evated her feet, to keep blood flowing to her vital organs.

"Val," Manny said, "what happened, sweetheart?"

"White hair, missing fingers." She tried to sit up,
clawed at her husband's arm. "He has Eric and Hank."

"How long have you been out here?"

"A few minutes. Not long."

The old man handed the phone down to Ty. "I've got
the dispatcher. There's a lot of static."

Ty nodded and spoke to the dispatcher, explaining that
he was a paramedic and knew local procedures—they
needed to get an ambulance to pick up Val and take her
to the soccer field at Mount Chester, and they needed to
get a medevac helicopter there to fly her to the regional
trauma center.

Val rose up and hit Manny in the chest. "Goddamn it,
leave me out here! Go find Eric and Hank! He'll leave
Eric to the elements. Manny, he'll die—"

"Val—Jesus, how can I leave you?"

Ty got to his feet. "Carine and Gus headed up to check the east ridge trail near the Rancourt place. I'm going up there. Ambulance will be here in a few minutes. Val, you hang in there. You're going to be okay."

But her eyes were locked on her husband, her teeth chattering as she shivered, even with the blanket over her. "Go, Manny, for God's sake. There's nothing more you can do for me here. I'll be fine."

She sank back, her breathing rapid, her color not good. Manny looked up at the old man. "You'll stay with her? Apply pressure to the wound. She's not going to die on you."

Despite his obvious confusion, he didn't hesitate. "Of course. I'll do my best."

Manny kissed Val on the forehead. "You hang in there, okay? I love you."

She didn't answer, and Ty could see how hard it was for Manny to leave her. He didn't look back as he climbed up the steep wall of the ditch and got into Ty's truck. "This fuck Turner wants us. It's payback for last fall. He and Louis must have been in cahoots. We put an end to their nice little smuggling operation. He doesn't want Eric. He can have me. He used my wife—my boy—"

"Don't go there." North thought about Turner on the back deck with Carine, talking to her about the pictures, asking about having dinner with him sometime in Boston. "Hell, he wants Carine, too."

"She's up by the Rancourts? We need to warn her. That fuck's out here somewhere."

Ty pulled out onto the road. "Knowing Hank, he'll have this all sorted out by the time the police get there."

"Yeah. Damn pilots."

"It's going to work, Manny. I gave the dispatcher the

lowdown. The cavalry's on its way. If we find Turner first, we isolate the situation until a tac team can get in there. Right?"

Manny didn't seem to be paying attention. "Don't you have a gun?"

"No."

"Val did." He pulled a bloodied Glock out of his waistband, then shook his head. "It's unloaded. No ammo. That woman."

Ty manufactured a smile. "This is why she works in a bookstore."

Manny looked down at his wife's bloody gun, his wife's blood on his clothes and hands. He glanced out the window when they turned up the access road to the Rancourt house and the east ridge trailhead. "So, what happens if Callahan's elected president—he gets a mountain named for him up here?"

And Ty relaxed slightly. Manny was with him.

Thirty

Gus narrowly missed a head-on collision with the Rancourts' SUV as it careered out of their driveway onto the access road. He veered off to the side, almost plowing into a hemlock. "Jesus Christ! What the hell do they think they're doing?"

"Obviously they didn't expect anyone else to be on the road," Carine said, jumping out of the truck.

Sterling rolled down his window and gave her a cool, unfriendly look. "The sun was in my eyes. Is Gus all right? Is his truck hung up on the rocks?"

"He's fine. I thought you'd gone already." She shivered in a stiff gust of wind. "Have you seen Eric Carrera?"

"Up here, you mean? No, why? Is something wrong?"

"He left a note saying he was on a hike, but it doesn't all add up. The police and forest rangers are on the case, but we were hoping to catch up with him before he'd gone too far."

"I'm sorry. We just don't know anything."

Carine knew she'd been dismissed, but she didn't give up. "What about Gary Turner? Is he here?"

"I assume he's left, but I don't keep track of him. Goodbye—"

"How did you end up hiring him? Did he come to you, or did you go to him?"

"Carine, this isn't the time or the place for this discussion. I'm glad we didn't collide. Give your uncle our best—"

Carine straightened. "The Sanborn Dairy was before your time up here."

"I beg your pardon?"

Gus circled around the back of his truck and took her by the arm. "Come on, honey. We'll go back to North's, figure out what's next."

Jodie Rancourt jumped out of the passenger side of the SUV and came around the front, Sterling banging the steering wheel in frustration. Jodie ignored him. "My God, I wish we'd never met those bastards. Gary and Louis, Tony, whatever his name was. Louis was so charming and sexy. They came to me, separately. First Gary, months ago. Then Louis. I manipulated Sterling into hiring them, playing on his anxieties following our ordeal last fall." Her voice was hoarse, but her words were distinct. She shrugged, and said without sympathy or apology, without so much as a glance at her husband. "I was bored."

Sterling banged the steering wheel again with the palm of his hand and made an angry hissing sound.

"Did you know they were the smugglers?" Carine asked.

"I was aware Louis had a past he wanted to hide. My God, don't we all? I wasn't sure he and Turner knew each other. I suspected it, but I wasn't positive. And I didn't ask. I—frankly, I wasn't interested."

"The pictures?"

For the first time, she showed a hint of embarrassment. "I've wanted to believe it was Manny Carrera. It was more convenient to think that whatever they were involved in, Gary and Louis wouldn't hurt anyone—me included. I don't know who took the pictures. I never saw, never heard, never suspected a thing. I left, and Louis said he was leaving. Then—he was killed. And the next day I got the call about the pictures. It had to be Gary."

"Why would he want Louis dead?"

"I think Gary wants everyone dead. But specifically Louis—I don't know. I wouldn't be surprised if Louis had his own game, if Gary found he couldn't control him." She averted her eyes, staring down at the valley. "I doubt Gary liked the idea of us having a...whatever it was."

Carine shoved her hands into her pockets. "Right now, all I want to do is find Eric. Hank Callahan and Val Carrera are on their way up here, too. If you see them—"

"We're leaving," Sterling said, his voice strangled, hoarse.

Jodie Rancourt raised her eyes to Carine. "The boy is in the warming hut. Turner has him tied up. He threatened to kill us if we said anything, but I can't—he's a child."

"Eric's *here?*" Carine was stunned. "And you haven't called the police?"

Sterling glared at her. "I don't have to explain myself to you."

Gus swore. "I'm going up there—I won't do anything stupid. Carine, take the truck and get where you can make a call."

"Where's Turner now?" she asked the Rancourts.

Sterling ignored her. "Jodie, get back in the car," he said coldly. "We're leaving. We have to save ourselves from this madman. He'll hunt us down, just the way he has Hank Callahan, Manny Carrera—Carine, you and North are next. I don't know why. Some kind of revenge.

Frankly, you're risking making the situation worse by interfering."

"What about Val Carrera and Hank?"

"I have no idea where they are." He winced, the color draining out of his face as he looked down the road. "Christ. We're out of time. Jodie!"

She jumped back into her seat. The SUV screeched forward, narrowly missing an old Audi careering up the road, turning onto the driveway.

Gary Turner was driving, Hank Callahan in the seat next to him.

Carine dove into Gus's truck, hitting the floor, hoping Turner hadn't spotted her. She got onto her knees and peered over the dashboard, and she saw Gus pause and look back, the car charging for him.

She kicked the door open, screaming, "Gus!"

He dove, but too late. Turner was gunning for him and caught him on the right front bumper of the Audi. Gus went sprawling, facedown, onto the damp grass along the side of the driveway.

The Audi sped on up the driveway.

Carine ran to Gus and knelt beside him, pushing back a rush of panic. "Gus—Gus, are you okay? Talk to me!"

He was writhing in agony, every few words a swear. "Fuck… I'm okay. Goddamn it! I think I broke a leg— my ribs…"

"Don't move. Come on, Gus, be still. If you've got a back or a neck injury—"

"I don't. *Shit!*"

Swearing seemed to help his pain. Carine took a breath. "Turner—he's got Hank. I didn't see Val. I have to do something. I can sneak behind the house and try to get a view of the hut and see what's going on. Don't worry,

I won't do anything nuts. But if Turner starts hurting anyone—I don't know, maybe I can create a diversion."

"You're a sitting duck out here. Take cover, will you?"

She picked up a softball-size rock off the side of the driveway. "I used to be pretty good with a rock."

"Christ, kid."

She blinked back tears. "Eric…he's just fourteen…."

"Something starts going down, look to Hank for guidance. Understood? He's got combat experience. You don't—well, you didn't used to." Her uncle winced, holding his right side with one arm, in obvious agony. He was pale, pearls of sweat on his upper lip. "I'll see if I can get into my truck and get a call out to the police."

"You shouldn't move—"

"Just fucking stay out of the line of fire, will you?"

She nodded. "I plan to."

Jodie was white-faced as they drove down the hill, but Sterling kept his eyes on the twisting road. His jaw was clenched, and he had to fight with himself to concentrate on his driving. This was no time to two-wheel a sharp curve or lose control and go airborne off the damn mountain.

"We have to call the police," Jodie said quietly, wringing her hands in her lap.

He glanced at her coldly. "You lied to me about everything, didn't you? Your affair with Louis. When you met. What you knew, what you suspected. What else?"

She turned away, staring out at the scenery. "I met Louis up here over the summer. We didn't—" She broke off awkwardly, and he could see her fighting for the right choice of words. Or perhaps just another lie. "I put him off until he moved to Boston."

"Put him off?"

"He'd made it clear he was…interested."

"I see."

"No, I don't think you do." Her voice was surprisingly flat, as if she didn't care anymore. "I didn't want to tell you that we knew each other. I knew you'd be suspicious—"

"Rightly so." Nothing in his tone or demeanor let her off the hook—he didn't want it to. "He asked you to recommend him to Gary Turner?"

"He pressured me to get Gary to hire him. He never said there was a connection between the two of them. Neither did Gary."

"You had nothing to do with their smuggling operation?"

"No! Of course not. I was just—a pawn."

Sterling gave her a cold look, feeling in control again. He'd lost it up on the hill, when he'd almost plowed into Gus Winter's truck, and then Carine had stood there, so damn self-righteous. "You were more than a pawn, Jodie." His hands relaxed slightly on the wheel. "You were a willing participant. Did you tell the police everything?"

She stared down at her hands and gave a small shake of the head. "No. I didn't tell them I knew Louis from up here. Manny Carrera—he saw us together in September. I'd hoped he wouldn't remember."

"For Christ's sake, Jodie, with his training and experience—"

"He's not a law enforcement officer, he's an air force pararescueman. He wouldn't even be involved in our lives if you hadn't called for help when we were on the ridge. We could have made it on our own."

"We'd have died."

"You've been trying to prove yourself and protect yourself ever since. You hate feeling vulnerable, inadequate. It's made you impossible this entire year."

"Don't blame me for your own failings."

"Sterling—" Her voice cracked, all her remoteness and reserve suddenly gone. "Let me at least try to get through to the police. Eric Carrera could be dying on *our* property. If you don't get the human component, at least, for God's sake, think about how it'll look. Carine and Gus know we left that boy up there."

He said nothing. Big chunks of the puzzle were still missing, but he had a fair idea of what had happened. They'd drawn attention to themselves last fall when they were rescued off the ridge, and Turner and Sanborn had seized the opportunity to take advantage of them, exploit them, use them. Louis had preyed on his wife. They'd both preyed on him.

"Jesus…" Jodie's voice was barely more than a croak now. "You hope Turner kills them, don't you? Then they can't report what a goddamn coward you were."

"What? Jodie, for the love of God, *no,* I'm not hoping he kills anyone. But don't you get it? Turner *is* a killer. We're caught in the middle. He won't harm us unless we give him reason to. If he gets away—what do you think he'll do? He got away last fall, but did he slink off and disappear? No. He used us to get access to the people who ruined him. He wants them dead. What do you think he'll do to us if we ruin his revenge?"

"Nothing if he's in prison!"

He shook his head. "I'm not taking that chance."

Her eyes shone with tears. "What happened to us? We used to be better than this."

"I'm being smart, Jodie, not a coward."

"Sterling…"

He bit off a sigh. "All right. We'll call the police the

first chance we have. We'll tell the police we were scared and didn't want to cause more problems. Remember your crisis training classes—your first job is to escape a dangerous situation. The police don't need two more hostages on their hands."

"If we'd helped Eric while Turner was out—"

"I didn't know where Turner was, how fast he'd be back. What if he'd caught us and killed all of us? Killed the boy in front of us? Then how holier than thou would you feel?"

She was crying now. "I just… I just don't know what to do."

"Then shut up and let me think."

When he reached the bottom of the hill, he turned left instead of right toward the village of Cold Ridge. He didn't want to run into the police or any search parties already out looking for Eric Carrera. Jodie stared at her cell phone, but Sterling knew there wouldn't be service—or a house where they could call—for at least several more miles. Any delay wasn't his fault. Then he'd let Jodie notify the police, and he'd call their attorney to meet them when they arrived back at their house on the South Shore.

Thirty-One

Ty pulled in behind Gus's truck, parked off the road just before the Rancourt driveway. Manny, his hands wiped off and disinfected, jumped out and checked the truck, but shook his head. Ty joined him, feeling the drop in temperature even at this elevation.

"No sign of anyone," Manny said, squinting up toward the Rancourt house. "Think they spotted Eric and went after him?"

"The trailhead's just up the road. It's possible—"

But he saw a movement up on the left side of the driveway, someone waving to them from behind a low stone wall, then collapsing back out of sight. Manny saw it, too. "That's Gus. Looks like he's down."

Manny was already on his way. North grabbed his medical kit from the back of the truck and ran, forcing back any intrusive thoughts—Carine? Where the hell was she? What had happened to Gus? But he knew not to get ahead of himself.

Manny leaped over the stone wall and squatted down next to Gus, who was conscious but in obvious pain. "Where are you hurt?" Manny asked. "What happened?"

"Turner bounced me off the bumper of his fucking car. I think I broke a leg, maybe a couple ribs—"

"Christ, Gus," Ty said. "You need to stay still, take it easy."

"Relax, I'm fine." His breathing was rapid, his eyes on Manny. "He's got your son and Hank up in the shed."

Manny had no visible reaction. "You saw them?"

Gus shook his head, wincing. "Just Turner and Hank. The Rancourts said he's got Eric up there, too. They knew and did nothing."

"Where's Carine?" North asked.

Gus winced. "Sneaking around back with a rock."

Ty pictured her last year, zigzagging up the hill from her cover behind the boulder. She was a scrapper. She'd do anything, but she wasn't stupid. He shook his head at Gus. "Jesus. I shouldn't have let you and Carine come up here on your own."

Manny fished a cervical collar out of North's med kit. "Too late, North. We're all here now."

Gus tried to sit up on an elbow. "You're not putting that fucking collar on me. Go find Carine. Turner must have hit me five, ten minutes ago at most. You didn't pass the Rancourts on the road? They said they'd call the police."

"Police are on their way," Ty said, but deliberately didn't tell him about Val. Gus had enough on his mind, and his pulse was rapid, his skin getting clammy. He needed an ambulance. "You warm enough?"

"Yeah. Toasty. Will you quit?" He licked a little blood off the corner of his mouth. "Bit my fucking lip. That hurt."

North quit arguing. "Just stay still."

"Carine won't do anything crazy."

Manny crouched behind the low stone wall and looked up the hill at the remaining length of driveway, the dirt track, the warming hut with its surrounding trees and natural landscaping. There was a lot of rock. "Think he's seen us?"

"I don't know," Ty said. "I'm guessing yes."

"North!"

The shout came from the warming hut. Turner.

Manny gave North a quick sideways look. "Well, he's seen you."

"Do you think I care if you bring in helicopters and every cop in the state?" Turner yelled. "Kill me. It doesn't matter. So long as I kill you and your friends on my way out."

"Shit," Manny said, "one of these suicide types. And he's got my kid."

North gave him a warning look. "You with me?"

Manny exhaled, nodded. "I'm going up there."

"Let's talk money." Turner, although he was shouting down the hill, sounded calm, even conversational. "How much for your senator? For your friend's son? For your woman, Sergeant North? How much for her?"

"No way he has Carine," Manny said. "She'd never go quietly. Gus would have heard something."

Her uncle grunted. "This is bullshit. Turner doesn't want money. He had the Rancourts, for Christ's sake. They've got more money than all of us put together."

Ty took a breath. "Let's talk," he called. "Face-to-face. You send out the boy, I'll come up there and talk money with you."

"I tried that trade once. I was almost double-crossed by Mrs. Bitch Carrera."

"I'm killing him," Manny said. "Understood?"

Ty ignored his friend. "Then let's get it right this time. Let the boy go, Turner. You don't want to hurt a kid."

"I've investigated you, Sergeant North." This time,

Turner's voice held a note of sarcasm and superiority. "Suppose you give me some of that trust fund you've got tucked away?"

Manny looked at North. "Trust fund?"

"My father left my mother some money," he said. "When she died, she left it to me."

Gus frowned. "I wondered how she managed to live off making collages and painting waterfalls. Christ, you have a father after all, huh? How much money he leave you?"

"I'm comfortable."

"How comfortable?" Manny asked.

North ignored both of them. They were all, he knew, focused on the job at hand. "I don't think Turner saw you," he told Manny. "I'll keep him talking. You want to get up there?"

Manny nodded. "I'll see what Carine's up to. A rock. I hope it's a big one." He glanced at North. "The Rancourts have rifles. I'll see what I can grab. But if things go south up there, I'm going in."

"Valerie Carrera's dead." Turner's voice seemed louder, almost echoing across the valleys and ravines. "Someone should have found her body by now. Did you pass her on your way up here?"

"Tyler! *Mom!*"

Eric Carrera. His voice wasn't as strong as Turner's, but it was distinct. Manny couldn't stand it and jumped up. "Your mom's alive, son."

North grabbed him and jerked him back down behind the stone wall, but Manny was already diving. A shot sounded, hitting a rock two feet to their left, just above their heads, sending a chunk flying. It struck Manny on the right side of his head, tearing out a two-inch strip of flesh above his ear. "Negotiate, my ass. He's fucking out to kill us. Damn boonies, or we'd have a tac team here by now."

"There's only the one road up. They're not going to come in here with guns blazing. They'll plan it out first." North reached for a bandage in his med kit and handed it to Manny. "At least we know where Turner is."

Manny patched his bleeding head. The flying rock probably would have knocked anyone else unconscious. "Yeah. He's up in the fucking shed with my kid, shooting at us."

"At least Eric can talk," Ty said. "That's a positive."

Gus tried to move but moaned in pain, gritting his teeth. "Hank's up there—I'm betting Turner hasn't hurt him yet. He'll want to keep all his bargaining chips as long as he can."

Blood had dripped down the side of Manny's face onto his neck, but he didn't seem to notice. "He wants us dead, but on his terms."

North nodded. "We contain the situation. We keep Hank and Eric alive until we get help up here."

"Easiest way is to kill this fuck," Manny said, crouching down low, then moving quickly, making his way from cover to cover up the hill.

Thirty-Two

❧❧❧

The shot had been close enough that Carine had felt its concussion, as if the air around her was compressed, the oxygen sucked out of it by the velocity of the gun burst. It was so unexpected, so startling, she'd almost screamed, and ended up biting the inside corner of her mouth.

Turner didn't have her. In fact, he'd slipped out of the warming hut and was moving around back, near her position in the trees. She was cold—no hat, no gloves, just her barn coat. At least she was basically out of the wind.

"Carine," Turner said softly, dried leaves crunching under him, "I know you're here. I have a soft spot for you. Join me. You didn't know about North's trust fund, did you? We can get away from here. I won't hurt anyone if you come with me."

Maybe North had a trust fund, maybe he didn't, but she didn't believe Turner planned to do anything but shoot her the first chance he got. Either he really was losing his grip on reality or he was just pretending to, toying with her, manipulating her. She sank low behind a low-branching white pine. If she moved, he'd hear her—she couldn't see him, but she knew he was close.

"I'm sick. I have cancer. It's all through me. No one's fault."

If true.

"It gives me perspective." His voice was eerily calm, almost toneless. "I know what I want before I die. Who I want to see die first. But I'd give that up if I could spend my last days with you."

She stiffened to keep herself from shivering with fear, the cold. She didn't dare look around the tree, make even the slightest sound.

"Tony—Louis—and I had a good thing going. I planned to live out my last months in style. I had a wife." His voice cracked. "The smuggling was to help set her and her idiot brother up for the future."

Carine had no choice but to let him talk. If he was talking—hunting her—he wasn't shooting anyone else. But had he seen her, heard her? Was he just playing with her before he pounced?

"Jodie Rancourt took up with Louis a year ago, before you took the pictures of our base of operations. She knew he was up to something, but she liked the sense of danger, the risk. She let us try out her and her husband's expensive guns."

Good God, Carine thought, wishing she had a tape recorder.

"He had them for show," Turner said as he crept around in the woods to her right, nearer the Rancourt house. "Louis wanted to kill you. I stopped him. I wanted to get the camera, make sure there were no incriminating pictures and make sure you were too scared to talk. Then the PJs and Hank Callahan showed up on the scene. I had to cut my losses."

She spotted him in the trees, up on the hill above her, still to her left, but if she stayed where she was, he'd see her. She picked up her rock and eased around the other side of her pine, making relatively little noise in the bed of red-brown pine needles. She hit grass, then quickly slipped into the back door of the hut.

Maybe it was what he'd planned all along. Corner her. Shoo her into the hut with Eric and Hank.

Eric was in the corner, sobbing and choking for air. Carine knelt down, setting the rock on the floor next to her, and quickly undid the bungee cords around the boy's wrists and ankles. "You heard your dad out there, right?"

The boy nodded. "He—he only tied me up this morning." But talking was clearly difficult for him, and once free, he immediately grabbed his inhaler, then sagged and threw it down. "None left."

"Look—sit tight," Carine said. "I'm going to untie Hank. Turner's outside looking for me. Maybe your dad and Tyler will intercept him."

She quickly ran to the front of the hut, where Hank was bound and gagged next to the small potbellied woodstove. Carine pulled the gag.

"Eric—he's going out the back. If Turner sees him—" Hank sat up straighter. "Go after him, Carine. I'll be okay."

He was bound with thin rope, the knots pulled tight. She tugged at them, trying to stretch the rope. "I can't get them without a knife."

"Go!"

She could hear Turner out front, stepping onto the ground-level porch. "What the fuck's going on in there?"

"We're out of time," Hank hissed.

She ducked down and ran toward the back of the hut, diving outside and down behind a woodbox next to the door. Eric was up by her pine tree, but he didn't stay put.

He made a mad dash up the hill, into the woods, thrashing through the dried leaves.

Carine took a breath, pretending she was the one making the noise. "Gary," she said. "I told everyone you weren't trying to kill me that day last fall. The shack—you set it on fire?"

He was inside, moving toward her position. "I had to burn down the evidence. Manny Carrera was almost there—"

"He would have waited for the police. He was unarmed."

"I couldn't take that chance."

"What happened?"

"My wife was there. She tried to talk me out of burning everything down. She didn't want to give up. She and Tony Louis—they thought we could kill all of you." He kicked at something on the floor just inside the door, probably Eric's bungee cords. "They were right. I should have listened. The explosion and fire killed her. I watched the woman I love burn to death."

"I'm sorry, but why didn't anyone find her body?"

"I buried her in the woods, before the ground froze. She didn't die right away, but I couldn't take her to the hospital. Louis ran—Jodie Rancourt helped him. I don't know if she guessed who he was then, knew it all along. I hid in the woods for weeks. I got a skin infection. Frostbite. I lost my fingers, a couple of toes."

"I'm sorry." She held her rock, wondering if he'd come outside and she could bonk him on the head before he shot her. "But hurting people because you're hurting—that's not your way. I can tell."

"I don't expect you to understand. It'll feel good to see those bastards go before I do. They think they can do anything."

He was out the back door, two feet from her. She didn't dare breathe.

"Are you armed, Carine?" he asked in a conversational tone. "The boy won't last. There was peanut oil in the energy bar I made him eat a little while ago. He doesn't know. He's deathly allergic to peanuts.

"North! Carrera!" It was Hank, yelling from inside the hut. "Eric's free. Turner's going after Carine. I'm setting this place on fire. I'm his only hostage."

Turner spun around. "What? Goddamn it—"

The sound of crashing metal—the potbellied stove—came from the hut, Hank still yelling information, instructions. Carine shot out from her woodbox cover and beaned Turner with her rock and ran, darting up the hill into the woods. He swore viciously, and she glanced back, seeing him down on one knee, grabbing his head where she'd hit him. He hadn't dropped his rifle.

She knew she'd only bought herself a few seconds.

But she could smell smoke. Hank had set the hut on fire, presumably creating a diversion—confusion, chaos—for Manny and Ty to act.

Carine zigzagged up the hill from tree to tree, trying to pick up Eric's trail and stay out of Turner's sight. Had he gone back into the hut to grab Hank? He wouldn't want to lose his only hostage.

But if he had, it wasn't for long.

She could hear him down the hill, behind her in the woods.

Thirty-Three

❧❧

North and Manny had made it to the trees just below the hut when Hank decided to set the goddamn place on fire.

"Carrera, North—go after Turner!"

But the fire would spread rapidly—smoke was already pouring out of the front door. No way would they leave Hank in there to burn to death.

Without discussion, North ran, Manny with him. Automatically, Manny ducked to one side of the front door, Ty covering his mouth as best he could and bursting inside, crouched down as he grabbed Hank and dragged him out. Manny took over, throwing Hank over his shoulder and running a few yards back down the hill, dumping him behind a boulder.

Ty coughed, but he hadn't inhaled that much smoke. He dove behind the boulder and glanced back. Flames were eating up the wall where the woodstove had been. Hank wouldn't have stood a chance.

Manny got a knife from North's med kit and quickly cut the ropes on Hank's feet and hands. He was coughing up soot, his lips and cheeks swelling.

"Looks like you singed most of the hair off your face,"

Ty said. "Eyebrows, eyelashes. That's going to look good on TV."

"I'll be okay." Hank winced in pain, pushed North's hand away when he started to dig in his med kit. "Go after Turner. Intercept him before he gets to Carine and Eric."

Ty had already thrust a tube of burn ointment at him. "This hut's going to keep burning. Stay clear of it."

Hank hissed irritably. "Jesus Christ, I know. I hope I bought Carine enough time. He's gone after her. He knew you'd storm the place once the fire started, and he wouldn't have a chance against all three of us."

"Eric?" Manny asked.

"He's not in good shape. He used the last of his inhaler. He tried—"

North checked a lump on Hank's forehead. "What'd you do, jump the woodstove?"

"Turner hit me on the way up here. He wants Carine dead as much as he does us. Maybe more. She took the pictures last fall, she turned him down on his offer of the good life together—and Eric. Turner'll use him if he has to. He wants revenge. We ruined his life. He'll ruin ours."

North got to his feet. "No one knows these mountains better than Carine."

"Cold, fear, an uphill climb—Eric's going to collapse." Manny's head was bleeding through the bandage and had to be pounding, but Ty knew he wasn't going to stop. "Go, North. Pick up his trail. Don't let me slow you down. If I can't keep up, don't count on me."

Hank coughed and spat black soot. "I'll meet the police when they get here and get a rescue team in place. Gus?"

"Banged up pretty good. He's down by the stone wall."

"I'll hook up with him. If you see this guy—he's done playing games. He wants to kill someone. Don't take any chances."

* * *

Carine thought she'd gone too far and must have bypassed Eric somewhere down on the trail. She made the last, steep burst onto the main ridge trail, but kept going, not daring to call him.

Although she was still below the treeline, the wind was blowing hard, the temperatures dropping, the cold penetrating her barn coat and freezing her ears. She couldn't imagine Eric in his sweatshirt. What if he'd fallen? What if he'd collapsed? But she couldn't think about that—she had to keep moving, find him, stay ahead of Turner, hide from him.

She ducked on and off the trail, trying to stay within cover of trees or boulders, intensely aware she was unprepared for the conditions. But Eric had spent the night in the cold hut, kidnapped, terrified, conserving his inhaler as best he could. She could keep moving.

The trail meandered along a section of rock, marked with splashes of blue paint and rock cairns.

And then she saw Eric, collapsed in a patch of grass a few feet off the trail. Carine shot over to him. Fear and determination had gotten him moving fast, but now he was prone, barely breathing as he lay on the cold ground. She glanced around her for Turner, then grabbed the boy and half carried, half dragged him to the base of a fifteen-foot ledge, several stunted fir trees concealing them.

Eric was wheezing, raising his shoulders and lifting his head as he struggled to get air. She noticed he was blue around the mouth and knew that had to be a dire sign. Carine stemmed her panic and tried to talk to him, but he just mumbled incoherently, ripping her heart out. She thought she remembered that it was easier for an asthmatic patient to breathe sitting up, but her first aid skills were limited. She didn't know if he was suffering more from asthma or an allergic reaction. It seemed to make common sense, however, and she put her arms around his thin shoulders. "Come on," she said, "let's sit you up.

She searched his pockets and found his EpiPen, which she knew was intended to combat a severe allergic reaction, but she wasn't sure how to use it. She slipped off her barn coat and wrapped it around him, hoping that if she could get him warm, maybe he could tell her what to do. Self-management had been key for him. He couldn't have gone to Mount Chester without knowing how to deal with his illness.

But nothing Carine did seemed to help. Eric was laboring to breathe, not even mumbling now. She held him close to her in an attempt to transfer some of her body heat to him—at least they were out of the worst of the wind. She could hear it whistling and howling.

She heard Turner—someone—on the trail nearby.

"You're not armed, Carine."

Turner. Calm. Superior.

"You can't hold out against me. You can't hide."

His voice seemed to be coming from the ledge above where she and Eric were tucked amid the stunted firs. She pulled Eric against the rock wall, in its shadow, where they were less likely to be seen from above. The shallow soil was moist under her. She tried to cover Eric as best she could with her own body and protect him from the elements. But she was cold herself, shivering in her cotton shirt.

Eric gave a rattling, frightening wheeze.

"I hear the kid."

Heartless bastard.

If Turner spotted them, they didn't stand a chance, but Carine knew the area where she and Eric were hiding well. The footing was tricky, deceptive on the ledge. Turner undoubtedly would attempt to track Eric's wheezing—maybe it was something she could use to their advantage.

"Be careful, Gary." She tried to match his tone. "There are places you can get hurt up here. And maybe you've gone up, but you still have to go down. The police, Manny, Tyler and Hank will all be waiting for you. And Gus. Don't count him out."

"But you'll be dead. You killed my wife."

"You killed your own wife."

"And Louis—"

"You killed him, too. Why? He had you take the pictures of him and Jodie Rancourt so the two of you could blackmail her? You realized what a loose cannon he was?"

"He wanted money. He didn't understand that I had other priorities to see to first."

"But you want money—you did try to blackmail her."

"I wanted it all, Carine. I still do. Money, justice. You."

She could hear him moving on the ledge, trying to find her. As she'd hoped, he was well off the trail, onto one of the most treacherous sections of the ledge. It was one of her favorite spots for taking pictures, but a deceptive growth of stunted balsam made it look like there was proper footing where there was none—she'd almost fallen there herself.

"What if I cooperate with you?" She kept her voice low in an effort to lure him, but not to give away their position completely. "What if I help you get Manny, North and Hank? Three for one. That's not a bad deal."

"What about the boy?"

"He's not doing well. I wouldn't worry about him."

"Tell me where you are."

She debated her next answer, but knew she had to take the chance. "We're down here. At the base of the ledge." Then she spotted him above her, slightly down from her, his rifle raised, but she hoped he still couldn't see her and Eric concealed within the rock and trees. She took a shallow breath. "I can see you, but you can't see me. Be very careful. The footing's tricky up there. You don't want to fall. Do what I say and you'll be okay."

"Fine." He sounded shaky, dubious. "Where to from here?"

Carine knew he didn't believe her. He was doing to her what he'd done to Louis with the pictures—pretend to cooperate, then he'd pounce. She held Eric more closely, feeling how cold he was. He was shivering uncontrollably. He kept raising his shoulders and his head, fighting for air. The sand had run out of the hourglass. She had to get him out of here.

She concentrated on what she had to do. "See the small evergreens? They're balsam firs. Stay out of them. You'll fall. Instead, go backward a few steps and up to your right."

They were the proper instructions, but, just as she'd hoped, he did the opposite and went for the fir trees, losing his footing almost immediately. He swore dropping his rifle as he grabbed onto weak branches that couldn't support his weight. It was a precipitous twenty-foot drop, and he yelled all the way down.

Manny appeared up on the ledge, and Ty bounded out of nowhere, getting to Turner just as he landed five feet from where Carine was hidden with Eric. She heard his head hit rock, then saw him sprawl forward onto his left wrist, which snapped under the impact of his fall. But he was conscious, moving—going for his nine-millimeter in his belt.

Ty kicked him in the head, then swooped in, snatched the handgun and pointed it at Turner. "Hands where I can see them. Don't move."

Turner sneered at him. "Fuck you." But his voice was weak, his head bleeding from where he'd struck the granite, never mind where Ty had kicked him and Carine had earlier pelted him with her rock.

Manny dropped silently onto the rocks next to Carine and collected Turner's rifle, handing it to Ty, then dropping down next to Eric. Carine, shivering herself now, was still holding the boy. "I tried to keep him warm. I didn't know what else to do. Turner told me there was peanut oil in an energy bar he made him eat. I don't know if it's true."

Manny quickly examined his son and injected the epinephrine, then shook his head. "Christ. This isn't just asthma. His epiglottis is inflamed from the peanut oil. His airway's getting obstructed—North, I've got to do a crike."

Ty tossed over his med kit. "Want me to do it?"

Manny shook his head. "I've got it."

He got out what he needed—a small scalpel, gauze, first aid tape, a breathing tube. Carine moved out of the way, but she could see Manny was in trouble. He blinked blood out of his eyes from his own head wound. "Manny…"

Ty, keeping the nine-millimeter leveled on Turner, eased in next to his friend. "Manny. Come on. Your head's a mess. I'll do it."

Manny gave a curt, reluctant nod, not speaking as he stood up and took the guns from Ty, letting him get to work on Eric.

Turner was unconscious, not that Manny took any chances—he kept the gun pointed at him, the rifle cradled in one arm. Carine offered to take the rifle, but he shook his head. "You're shivering. You'll end up shooting someone."

"He wanted us all in the hut. He was going to set fire to it and let us burn to death, set right what he did to his wife last fall. She was badly burned when he blew up the shack and ended up dying. It was an accident. He didn't mean to kill her. He didn't listen to her. She wanted him to shoot us all that day and disappear. That's what he planned to do this time. Kill us all and disappear."

"Better late than never, I guess. Bastard. He tell you all this?"

"Most of it. Some—not in as many words."

By unspoken agreement, she knew, they were trying to focus on something besides Eric's condition, but Manny glanced back as Ty made a small incision in the boy's neck—it bled like crazy, but he quickly stanched the blood with gauze.

"What's a crike?" Carine asked, hoping that talking helped.

"Cricothyroidotomy. It's like a tracheotomy, except you use the cricothyroid space. It opens up the airway. It's a—" Manny paused, swallowing, obviously struggling to control his fear for his son. "It's a simple procedure."

"What happened to your head?"

"Flying rock. Mine got me worse than yours got you last fall." He glanced at her, and she thought he might have tried to smile. "Lucky for you."

Ty inserted a breathing tube into the airway, secured it with tape and packed it with more gauze. "He's got mild hypothermia. We need to get him out of here."

Manny peeled off his coat and covered his son with it, cradling his son against his big body. North took over guard duty, handing his cell phone to Carine. She managed to get hold of Gus, but she was shivering uncontrollably. Her head was fuzzy. She managed to get out the basics of their situation.

"They're stuffing me into an ambulance," Gus said. "A rescue team's on its way on foot."

"Eric's in bad shape. There's no time."

Ty looked at her, his concern for his patient evident. "Tell him we need to get a helicopter up here. Winds are tough, but it'll be okay. They can ask Hank. He'll tell them."

Carine repeated his words to Gus, who grunted at her. "You freezing?"

"More or less."

She clicked off, and Ty eased his leather jacket over her shoulders. "I'm sweating from hoofing it up this goddamn mountain," he said. "You did say you liked a sweaty guy—"

"Covered in wood chips. A key ingredient."

"What if Turner had believed you and did what you said?"

"I had another rock picked out."

"That's the spirit."

She nodded at Turner. "What about him?"

"Broken wrist, concussion. When Manny gets done with Eric, he can hold a gun on Turner and I'll treat him. There's not much I can do."

"Is he—"

Ty read her thoughts. "Nah. He'll live."

She could feel the warmth of his jacket, her shivering slowly subsiding. "He would have killed you, me. Hank. Manny. Eric. Gus. All of us. He waited to get us together, at the right moment—it was like he got satisfaction from manipulating us, playing us."

But Ty didn't answer, edging closer to her. He tucked the nine-millimeter into his waistband and held on to the rifle with one arm, slipping the other around her shoulders. "You need to stay warm. Gus'll have a fit when he sees you up here in cotton. He'll recommend to Fish and Game that you pay for your rescue."

"I did the rescuing. Some of it."

North smiled at her. "Damn, babe. You do have the prettiest eyes."

Thirty-Four

Nobody could get Manny into a litter. He carried one end of his son's litter and climbed into the National Guard rescue helicopter with him. They took Gary Turner, too. He'd regained consciousness, but was incoherent.

A Cold Ridge police officer, part of the rescue team that arrived on foot after the helo took off, relieved North of Turner's rifle and handgun. He was freed to argue with Carine about getting her ass in a litter and letting the rescue team carry her off the ridge.

He didn't win that one, either.

She was determined to walk. North went with her. The rescue party provided them with warm clothes and warm fluids, but Carine had had a hell of a few hours—so had he. By the time they got back down to the Rancourt house, Gus and Hank had already been transported by ambulance to the hospital. All hell was breaking loose over a United States senator turning up in a hut on a New Hampshire mountain with a madman.

Except Gary Turner was stone-cold sane. North had no doubt about that.

Antonia Winter Callahan, M.D., met them at the hospital. She was in trauma-doctor mode, checking on her husband, her uncle, her sister, the entire Carrera family. Val was in surgery. Eric was responding rapidly to treatment for a severe allergic reaction, asthma attack and mild hypothermia. He'd helped save himself. There was no question about it. He'd conserved his Albuterol as best he could and consciously tried to lower the level of his anxiety. If he hadn't responded the way he had, he'd have been dead before Carine found him on the ridge.

Manny, no surprise to North, wasn't the most cooperative patient, but he finally, reluctantly, agreed to let someone do a CT-scan of his head—just so they'd all leave him alone. He said his head was fine. He was right. The CT-scan was negative.

Antonia shoved a cardboard cup of gray-looking coffee at North in the ER waiting room. "The doctor orders you to drink. You've had a hell of a day, but I see you're as indestructible as ever."

"That piece of rock could have hit me instead of Manny."

She smiled faintly. "The key here is that it didn't."

He sipped the awful coffee. "I can tell you, you wouldn't have seen me kicking over a damn woodstove with my hands and feet tied together—what'd Hank plan to do, slither out of there like a snake?"

"No, he planned for you and Manny to rescue him. He says that's what you guys live for."

But her face was pale, and she looked strained and tired. "I'll bet right now Hank knows exactly why he married an ER doc."

"He won't even be admitted. He'll just need to grow new eyebrows." She teetered suddenly, and North grabbed her. "I think—oh, hell, Tyler, I'm going to be sick."

And she was, right there on the waiting room floor, damn near getting his shoes.

"I know you hate barf," she said, embarrassed.

He got her onto a chair, and a nurse came running, but Antonia waved her off. "I'm all right. I'm—" She smiled through her wooziness. "I'm pregnant."

"Antonia!" It was Carine, coming around the corner into the waiting room, eavesdropping as usual. "That's wonderful. Are you okay? Can I get you anything?"

"Have you told Hank?" Ty asked.

Antonia lifted her head. "It took the cocky pilot right out of him."

North figured the voters of Massachusetts would either get used to their new senator's way of doing things or they'd give him the boot in six years. Kids came first with him. Period. He was the kind of guy who'd kick over a woodstove while he was tied up if it meant giving an asthmatic kid an extra few minutes' lead, to escape his captor.

Nate Winter finally wandered in, pissed off and pacing, in full U.S. marshal mode. He was tall and rangy like his uncle, with about as much patience. He glared at the younger of his two sisters and then at North. "I told you two to go mountain climbing."

Carine ignored him. "How bad a bad guy was Gary Turner?"

"Considering he kidnapped a fourteen-year-old boy and a U.S. senator and planned to kill them and you, Manny Carrera and your ex-fiancé here, I guess he was pretty goddamn bad."

"Yeah, but before that?"

His mouth twitched. "Before that he wasn't so hot, either. He likely committed two murders in Canada. Tony—Louis was a trip, too. Extortion, smuggling, forgery. He was very good at forgery. Smuggle people into a country, they need papers."

"The wife?"

"Turner was devoted to her. They had some weird relationship—looks like he went to pieces when he accidentally killed her. The doctors treating him say it's a wonder he made it out of the mountains last winter. It doesn't look as if he ever sought medical help for his fingers and toes."

"He's talking?" Carine asked.

"Some. He wants credit. Hell—" Nate bit off a sigh. "If he goes downhill or shuts up, investigators can just talk to my baby sister and wrap this one up."

Carine didn't wither under her brother's impatient scrutiny. "Will I get a medal?"

"Pain in the ass," he said.

The Rancourts were talking to the police, but only through their lawyer. They'd stopped ten miles up the notch road to call the police and, according to Nate, acted like victims.

She sipped some of Ty's coffee, made a face and dug money out of one of her endless barn coat pockets for the soda machine. "Antonia, I'll share a Coke with you, provided I don't catch what you've got."

Her sister tried to smile, but she was done in. North winked at her. "Long goddamn night and day for a pregnant lady."

"Long night and day for all of us."

They all went up to Gus's room. He bitched about having his leg in a cast and the prospect of missing even a minute of snowshoeing and cross-country skiing season, but he hadn't incurred any permanent damage. He'd be back on the ridge before the winter was out. He had no sympathy for Carine's brush with hypothermia. Apparently he'd offered to stop at her cabin for her to put on more appropriate clothing, and she'd refused.

"The doctor lectured me on wearing cotton," she told

him. "It was an *accident*. I never wear cotton hiking, not even in the summer."

North smiled. Winters, even when they were being treated for their injuries, never liked being told something they already knew. They were a loving but contentious lot, and as he looked from green-at-the-gills Antonia to rangy Nate to brittle-haired Gus to Carine, blue-eyed and auburn-haired and not nearly as fragile as everyone thought, North knew he could never leave Cold Ridge. Not forever, anyway.

Val figured she was dreaming or maybe dead. She didn't care which, just so long as it didn't end. Manny was there beside her hospital bed, holding her hand and telling her he loved her, that Eric was okay, they were all okay.

He was crying. That part she could do without.

She touched his stubble of beard. She had all kinds of tubes and crap in her, but a doctor had told her she'd be fine, she was lucky. She liked that. Lucky.

Manny kissed her fingertips, and she felt his tears warm on her hand.

"I just didn't know what else to do," she said.

"I know. Neither did I."

Thirty-Five

❧❦❧

Carine rented her apartment to a special education teacher who "loved" her bright colors, which was a good thing, because her landlord hadn't had citrus green and mango and lavender in mind when he'd agreed to let her paint the place. She moved back to her cabin on the edge of the meadow and cleaned it from top to bottom. Satisfied there were no more bats, mice, snakes or any of their droppings, bones and skins, she let herself relax.

It was a cold, bright winter morning, with six inches of fresh snow on the ground. She had her winter hiking books out, new crampons, her serious backpack, her subzero sleeping bag, her Nikon with her longest lens—she'd taken a Gus-approved workshop on winter camping, and it was definitely more complicated business than summer camping.

She was good on her own, she thought, filling up a water bottle at her kitchen sink. She didn't need anyone to complete her and never had. But Tyler North was her soul mate. There was no way around it.

He'd gone back to Hurlburt. She wasn't sure exactly what the team leader of a special tactics team did, but she figured she'd find out—she had tickets to Florida. She'd never been on an air force base. She'd go and see how far she got before someone threw her out or pointed her in Ty's direction. She suspected that the incident in November had reinforced his notion that he was dangerous—that he was bad luck and could die on her and she deserved someone "safer." She wanted to disabuse him of that notion. As far as she was concerned, it was just an excuse. He wasn't used to letting anyone in. His mother had been like that—it wasn't just the way he was raised. It was the way he was. Independent, solitary, good on his own.

Well, so was she. She'd redone her Web site and got back to work on her series of guidebooks, beginning with one on the White Mountains. She'd dug out her pictures, started jotting down descriptions of her favorite trails and listing people she needed to contact and places she needed to go.

She could work on the guidebook from Florida if she ended up staying. Air force guys moved around a lot. Ty might not stay in Florida. It didn't matter. Cold Ridge was her home—she belonged there in a way she never would anywhere else. But Ty was definitely her soul mate, and she wanted him to know what that meant to her. She hadn't really known what it meant last February when he'd canceled their wedding. She'd needed this past year to figure it out. In the past weeks, she'd thought of him— she'd thought of herself—on Cold Ridge in November with Gus run over, Eric Carrera near death, Hank Callahan tied up—all of them at the mercy of a determined murderer. What if she'd been killed chasing up the ridge after Eric? What if Ty had been killed rescuing Hank from the burning hut? Anything could have happened. But they'd done what they'd had to do.

She thought she heard a dog barking. A small dog—it was more a little yelp than a proper bark. At least it wasn't

Stump. A stray? She didn't have any neighbors, except for Ty, and he wasn't around.

But he was. He knocked on her back door and pushed it open before she could even adjust to his presence. He wasn't wearing a hat or gloves, just a fleece pullover and jeans, his boots, and he gave a mock shiver. "Damn, it's cold out there. I've been in Florida too long." He gave a loud whistle out the back door. "Come on, now, be a good girl."

Carine took in his broad shoulders, his green eyes— everything about him—but couldn't believe she hadn't conjured him up. "Ty—what—"

He winked at her. "Thrown you right off balance, haven't I? Wait just a sec." He patted his thigh several times and whistled again. "Don't make me come and get you."

And next thing, a black-and-brown ball of fur charged into her kitchen and banged against the stove, then bounced up and skidded into the great room on Carine's newly polished wood floors.

A puppy, all of eight weeks old.

"She's excited," Ty said.

"What are you doing with a puppy?"

"She was free. Nobody'd pay money for Stump's off-spring. She's his granddaughter. She was born the day Gus got out of the hospital. You can tell she and Stump are related, because she just peed in my truck."

Carine got down low and called the puppy, who came running, lapping her hands, jumping all over her. She laughed. "What's her name?"

"I don't know. I thought you could help me think one up." He stood at her table and fingered her snowshoes, her backpack. "Going somewhere?"

"Winter camping."

"Alone?"

She rose, the puppy flopping on her feet. She had on cross-country ski pants and a winter hiking top she'd picked up at Gus's at full price. "I told you, solitary hiking is one of the hazards of my profession."

His green eyes settled on her. "Does it have to be?"

She shrugged. "I don't need a lot of distractions."

He picked up her crampons and examined them, as if he wasn't sure they met his standards. "I heard you tried to access my trust fund."

"Nate, that big mouth. I thought since he was a U.S. marshal—" She paused, realizing she wasn't the least embarrassed. "I didn't try to 'access' it. I just wanted information. I can't stand watching your house go to ruin. I figured it was my heritage, too, since my family built it and owned it for almost a hundred years—"

"Less than seventy-five. Mine's gaining on you."

"Well, Nate was no help whatsoever. Gus said the trust fund was from your father?"

"He was an old guy on the Mount Chester board of trustees. He was in his seventies when he and my mother had their fling—supposedly he planned to marry her, but he had a heart attack and died first. But he left her a little money."

"She was a wonderful woman, Ty. You're not her, you won't ever be her—but she was something. Gus is digging in his attic and cellar for any old artwork of hers, now that it's worth something."

"How's he been on crutches?"

"Miserable. He's drawing up plans for redesigning his kitchen."

"Uh-oh."

"I only know it involves chickens. It has something to do with the egg lady."

"Back to Nate," Ty said. "He proved trustworthy?"

"He proved close-mouthed and stubborn. I couldn't even get him to check and see how much money you have."

"Less now. You heard Manny's back in?"

She nodded, trying to follow his ping-ponging changes in subject. "He's a PJ instructor at Kirtland. I told him I passed the PAST, except I did it over a whole day instead of three hours seeing how I am over thirty. I think he should overlook that 'guy only' thing and let me in, don't you?"

"He's at the end of the pipeline. You'd have a shitload to get through before you got to him, and there'd probably not be much time to take pictures of birds."

She resisted a smile. "Okay, so what's he got to do with your dwindling trust fund?"

"I invested in a bookstore with Val. She's something else—she'll probably double my money in a year, never mind independent bookstores falling on hard times. Eric's handling the Tolkein section. The dry western air agrees with him, but he loves New Mexico."

"No more Mount Chester?"

"He went through a hell of an ordeal. He needs to be with his family."

"Val would have made a good assistant for Hawk, but I never saw her and Manny in Washington."

Ty scooped up the puppy and held her in his arms, letting her lick his face. "They're happy. It's good to see. Manny says it's just his luck to end up with a couple of bookworms."

"Ty—you're a big softie at heart, aren't you?"

He smiled. "What have I been saying?" He set the puppy back on the floor, and she charged around the small house. "I told Eric I was getting a puppy. He says we should name her Strider."

"Strider's a male character—"

"It's got a nice ring to it, though, doesn't it? Here, let me see if it works." He whistled again, snapping his fingers and calling "Strider!"

She came running, ears back, tongue wagging.

"You could have called her anything like that and it'd work," Carine said.

He ignored her. "Hey, Strider, good girl."

The puppy licked his hand and charged off into Carine's studio.

Ty surveyed her stack of camping food on the counter. "Well, we could scramble up something here and sit by the fire and pet our puppy, or we could have freeze-dried stroganoff on the ridge, after we've set up our tent in below-zero temperatures and hurricane-force winds—"

"Not hurricane-force winds. The wind's relatively calm today."

"I like how you say 'relatively.'"

Carine hesitated, hearing the fire crackle in her wood-stove, remembering how quiet it had been in her cabin just a few minutes ago. "I have tickets to Florida for when I get back from camping."

"Thought you'd sneak onto base, did you? I wondered how long you'd last without seeing me."

"I can do my job from anywhere. You can't. I mean, there are no air force bases in Cold Ridge." She breathed out. "Not that I'm getting ahead of myself. But I have options. I'm not sure I saw that a year ago."

"We both have options. The military's been my life since I was eighteen, but I'm not going to be doing this job forever. I can become a weekend warrior and go into the reserves, keep my hand in that way and figure out something to do around here. I still have to make a living. The trust fund's helped me hang on to the house, but it's not like I'm a Rockefeller or something. I want to train our puppy. Raise our kids. The rest we can figure out together. Carine—" His eyes were serious now. "I was wrong in February. Scared, stupid. Crazy.

"I knew you had a tough year ahead of you. You didn't want to put yourself through worrying about me—put me through worrying about you.

"I'm used to doing things on my own. But I love you, Carine. I always have."

She could barely speak. "I know."

He brushed a hand over her hair and touched a finger to the side of her mouth. "Let me try again." His voice was low, sincere. "Let me get it right. I want to marry you more than anything else in the world."

"I said yes once."

"I understand. You trusted me with your heart once—"

"No, no!" She shook her head, smiling. "You don't understand. What I'm saying is that my yes is still good. I just—wait a minute, okay?"

She ran into the great room and pulled out the ash bucket she kept beside the woodstove, digging down with her hands until she found her ring. She held it up, blowing off the soot and ashes. "I let Stump tear up my wedding dress and bury it in the backyard, but the ring—I guess I couldn't get rid of it."

"No, but you could bury it in the ashes. What if you'd accidentally used those ashes for compost?"

"Accidentally? That was the plan, but I didn't get to do a garden this summer. Look. It'll clean up nicely." She got to her feet and handed him the sooty ring. "Do you want to put it on my finger?"

"You've got soot all over you. There's a black spot on the end of your nose."

She knew he didn't give a damn about the soot. "I love you," she said. "I've always loved you."

He smiled. "I knew that's what you meant when you'd say you hated me."

"It wasn't, but that's another story."

He slipped the ring on her finger, and kissed her softly, soot and all, their puppy pulling at his boot laces. "It's good to be home."

* * * * *

SHELTER ISLAND

One

"*Antonia...*"

Antonia Winter stopped abruptly in the middle of the mostly empty hospital parking garage, certain she'd heard someone whisper her name. She glanced at the parked cars and the exits, but saw no one else. She took a cautious step forward, her dress shoes echoing on the concrete. She'd changed from the more casual clothes she wore in the E.R.—she had a dinner date in Back Bay.

It was tension, she decided. Simple tension had her turning ordinary garage sounds into someone whispering her name.

"*Antonia Winter... Dr. Winter...*"

She gasped and ran the last five steps to her car, clicking the button on her key that automatically unlocked the door. Her hands shaking, she ripped open the door and threw herself in behind the wheel. She hit the button that locked all four doors.

This couldn't be happening to her. She *had* to be imagining it.

This wasn't the first incident.

Wasting no time, Antonia stuck the key into the ignition and started the engine. It was just after seven o'clock on Saturday evening. She'd been on duty a full twelve hours. She was a trauma physician in the busy emergency room of a downtown Boston hospital. None of her cases today had been easy ones. But that was her job, and she was good at it—she was accustomed to dealing with its demands. She wasn't one to go off the deep end and imagine things that hadn't happened, draw the most dramatic conclusion to innocent events.

At least she'd never been that sort. Maybe the demands of the rest of her life had finally gotten to her. Demands like Hank Callahan, she thought. He was her dinner date that night. She'd been half in love with him for months, but their relationship had complications. Her work, his work. Her family. His past. Her past.

Hank…

No. She couldn't blame him—she wouldn't.

She wasn't hearing things or making up things that hadn't happened. That was the problem. They were *real*.

Someone had just whispered her name in the parking garage.

She edged out of her space, glancing in the rearview mirror and side mirror every few yards as she made her way to the exit. She almost asked the parking attendant if he'd heard anything, but she knew he wouldn't have. Once out on the street, she forced herself to take several deep breaths.

Yesterday, it had been an anonymous instant message. The third in a row. *Your patients trust you, Dr. Winter. What if you betrayed their trust?*

All were on the same theme. A doctor's trust. A doctor's betrayal of that trust. Without going into detail, she'd asked a friend more familiar with computers than she was about instant messages, and he'd said that tracking down an instant messenger who wanted to remain anonymous was very difficult, if not impossible.

There was nothing overtly threatening in the messages. And certainly no mention of Hank Callahan, a candidate for an open U.S. Senate seat from the Commonwealth of Massachusetts. The election was the first Tuesday in November, less than two months away. If the messages had mentioned him, Antonia would have to report them, tell Hank. She didn't want to cause an unnecessary stir—she wanted a sensible explanation for what was going on. If something *was* going on. She still didn't want to believe someone was trying to get under her skin. Creep her out.

But who would want to?

Why?

Was someone stalking her?

No. It couldn't be. Tension, fatigue and her imagination must have turned the whir of a car engine or an exhaust fan into someone whispering her name. Maybe the instant messages were from someone whose screen name she just didn't remember. A friend or colleague working on a paper or struggling with an ethical question, idly instant messaging her. Maybe they weren't meant to be anonymous or creepy.

But when she reached the restaurant, Antonia paid extra to have her car valet parked and avoided another parking garage. She stood in the warm evening air and took several deep breaths to calm herself. *There. It'll be all right. I can do this.*

She had on a simple black dress, black stockings, black heels. Gold earrings. Her dark auburn hair, chin-length and straight, was tucked neatly behind her ears. No lipstick—she didn't have time for it now.

As promised, Hank was waiting for her at their table.

He was, she thought as she smiled at him and waved, the most drop-dead-handsome man she'd ever met. Forty-one and tall, with graying dark hair, a square jaw and eyes so blue they took her breath away. She'd met him last November in Cold Ridge, her small hometown in the White Mountains of New Hampshire. Almost a year ago, she realized. He'd just thrown his hat into the senate campaign in bordering Massachusetts. His weekend in New Hampshire was to have been a break. Hiking with his air force pals, Tyler North and Manny Carrera. Instead they'd come upon Antonia's younger sister, Carine, a nature photographer, being shot at in the woods. Later that same weekend, Hank, Ty and Manny had rescued a wealthy Boston couple stranded on the ridge for which her hometown was named.

Complications, Antonia thought. So many complications.

Hank smiled, getting to his feet. Other diners watched. He was a man in the spotlight. There didn't seem to be any reporters around, but she couldn't know for certain, another reminder that it wasn't just her reputation as a respected physician that would suffer if she rushed to judgment or cried wolf about a possible stalker. His would, too, as a man who was asking Massachusetts voters to trust him. With just weeks left in the campaign, she had to be sure before she said anything, although she had to admit, her own nature made her reluctant to speak up. She was thirty-five and accustomed to handling her own problems.

But it wasn't just Hank's campaign or her own reserve that made her cautious—it was Hank himself. He was a Massachusetts Callahan, the current most visible member of a visible family of dedicated men and women who were expected to do their share in the military, in public service and in business. Hank had left the air force two years ago as a major, a helicopter pilot who'd flown countless search-and-rescue missions: on his last mission, he and a team of pararescuers had performed the dangerous high seas recovery of five fishermen whose boat had capsized. It had put his picture on the front pages of newspapers across the country. While emergency operations conducted in conjunction with civilian agencies sometimes hit the press, his many combat search-and-rescues hadn't received such coverage—Antonia had learned that the military didn't necessarily publicize when and how it went after aircrews downed behind enemy lines.

Hank would come to her rescue in a heartbeat.

And not just because he was trained to rescue people.

He lost his family ten years ago when his wife and young daughter were killed in a car accident while he was serving overseas. It still haunted him—everyone knew it, could see it. He wasn't even on the continent when the accident happened, a head-on collision with a car driving on the wrong side of the interstate. The other driver was a woman in her mid-fifties who'd had a stroke. Brittany Callahan, three, was killed instantly. Her mother, Lisa, thirty, never regained consciousness and died in the hospital three hours later. Hank wasn't with them—it wasn't possible for him to have been with them. But he didn't look at it that way, at least not emotionally, and probably never would, no matter how much he'd come to accept that his wife and daughter were gone.

No, Antonia thought, making her way to their table. She couldn't just *think* she might have a stalker or some weirdo trying to get under her skin. She had to be certain before she breathed a word of her fears to anyone—even Hank. Maybe even especially Hank.

* * *

Robert Prancer peered through the restaurant window. The bitch doctor was sitting across a small, candlelit table, drinking wine and having dinner with the wannabe senator.

Didn't she know?

Robert had to struggle to keep from screaming into the window and drawing attention to himself. Damn it, didn't she *know* what she was doing to him? Seeing her with another man. Knowing she didn't care about him. That all his fantasies were just that. Fantasies. Delusions.

He didn't know what to do. He'd been lashing out, acting on impulse for the past couple of days. But there was no satisfaction in instant messages—he couldn't see her getting them, could only imagine the look on her face. Her curiosity about who it was, whether the messages meant anything. Was she in danger? Was someone trying to scare her? She wouldn't know for sure. He'd designed the messages so she wouldn't.

And she wouldn't overreact. Not Antonia Winter, M.D. Robert had watched her work for almost three years. She wasn't one to panic. Her coolness under stress was just all the more reason to build to a crescendo and see her quivering with fear, incoherent with it, begging for her life.

He thought a moment, watching the two in the restaurant laughing with the waiter. Was that really what he wanted? Dr. Bitch begging for her life? Was he willing to go that far?

Farther?

Tonight in the parking garage—brilliant. He'd heard her stop and gasp. But, still, he couldn't see her.

And he wanted to, he realized. He really, really wanted to.

He'd taken the subway from the hospital. He could still

smell oil from where he'd sat on the concrete floor in the parking garage. How had he missed a damn oil slick the size of the Exxon Valdez spill? Fucking thing was huge. But he hadn't dared to move. He'd spotted Antonia Winter, M.D., Dr. Winter, the bitch doctor—he'd spotted her walking to her car, her heels *click-clicking* on the concrete. She was in a rush to see the wannabe senator. She didn't rush with her patients. Then she was all calm and empathetic and dedicated.

What crap.

Robert thought back to a few weeks ago when he had shot himself in the foot and had gotten a good dose of her idea of dedication to her patients. She'd turned him in. He'd had to explain the gun to the cops and the shooting himself in the foot to them and the shrinks. Took him days and days to get *that* all straightened out. His damn foot still hurt. He'd meant only to get her attention, try to bridge the gap between them. Her a doctor, him a fucking floor-mopper in the same hospital. He figured he needed to do something dramatic to test her, as a doctor, as a woman. As *the* woman. He had never loved anyone else. Never. He'd been completely true to her.

He should have shot someone else. Another of the floor-moppers, maybe. Get her attention that way. He could have delivered the victim to her. She liked heroes, right? Look at the hero wannabe senator, saving pilots and fishermen.

Live and learn.

After his foot healed, it was back to pushing his broom and wringing out his mop in the E.R. Putting up with the assholes and losers who thought it was a good job, patronizing doctors and nurses and administrators who told him what a contribution the cleaning crews made. Listening to them all talk about a hard day's work for a hard day's pay

and how the hospital couldn't run without it being clean.
His co-workers bought lottery tickets and followed the
Red Sox and took their kids to school, exchanged recipes
and fifty-cents-off coupons and thought they had a life.

Robert had a goddamn 156 IQ. He knew he should be
running the place. His nitwit co-workers didn't see that.
They teased him about his name. *Dancer and Prancer,
Comet and Vixen...*

He didn't tell them his zero of a mother had made it up.
He'd never known his father. She probably hadn't, either.
But leave it to her to name her one and only son after a
reindeer. She'd died when he was eleven. Good riddance.
Stupid people annoyed him.

He'd thought Antonia Winter had recognized his bril-
liance, his potential. He'd seen in her a kindred soul. A
soul mate. A woman who understood him.

Fat chance.

He walked up the street, trying to control his breathing. No! He couldn't talk like that. Maybe he still did
have a chance.

"Maybe."

She was so damn beautiful, with her auburn hair and
blue eyes, that straight nose and small, slim body. Brainy-
looking but also physical.

His type.

"No." He shook his head, aware of people passing him
on the street, looking at him like he was some loser who
talked to himself. But he had important issues on his
mind. "No, she's not my type."

His type wouldn't have betrayed him.

The bitch doctor had. As a physician, as the woman
he loved. On every level. Broke his damn heart. He was
smart—he wasn't bad looking. Sandy-haired. Fit. He'd
taken up running on her account, before the foot thing.

The balmy late summer temperatures had brought out the crowds. Robert figured the bitch doctor and the wannabe senator would be at dinner for a couple hours, anyway.

Well, what the hell. He knew where she lived.

And he had a key.

Two

Hank Callahan had exactly one hour between the lunch at the Cambridge homeless shelter he'd just left and his upcoming three o'clock meeting with local small business owners—enough time, surely, to drag information out of Antonia Winter's little sister.

If not, he'd just have to come back.

Antonia had gone missing on him, and he intended to find out what was going on.

He parked in front of the tenement building off Inman Square where Carine Winter had rented an apartment in late spring, a move that had caught her family and friends by surprise. She didn't belong in Cambridge. She belonged up in Cold Ridge, New Hampshire. She should be taking pictures of birds and mountain scenes, living in her little log cabin in the shadows of the ridge that gave her hometown its name. She was a nature photographer, a good one. But she'd had her life turned upside down in February when her fiancé walked out on her, and she'd made up her mind that she needed to live in the city.

Once a Winter made up her mind, that was usually it.

Tyler North—her ex-fiancé and one of Hank's closest friends—had tried to warn him about the Winter siblings, not that Ty had heeded his own advice. He'd fallen for Carine after some smugglers had shot at her last November, and then he'd asked her to marry him. They'd known each other all their lives, but the prospect of Tyler North and Carine Winter actually marrying had taken everyone by surprise.

No one need to have worried. Ty pulled the plug a week before the wedding. He still insisted it wasn't cold feet—he said he'd come to his senses in the nick of time. He couldn't marry Carine. She'd lost her parents when she was three and wanted to lead a peaceful life, and Tyler North wasn't a peaceful man.

But now Hank had to suffer for his friend's bad behavior, too. It had put Antonia at arm's length from him for months. Only recently had Hank managed to get her not to think about her broken-hearted sister when she looked at him. It didn't matter that Antonia had known Tyler even longer than he had—they'd shared a military career. They'd performed missions together.

"The Winters are thick as thieves," Ty had once tried to explain. "Don't let their bickering fool you. Hurt one, you've hurt them all. They're about as hard-bitten and stubborn as anyone you'll ever meet."

It was true. When it came to being hard-bitten and stubborn, the only one who rivaled the Winter sisters, their brother, Nate, and Gus, the uncle who'd raised them, was Tyler North. He'd grown up in Cold Ridge and still called it home, although he was a master sergeant in the air force, a nearly twenty-year pararescue veteran. Ty had seen it all, and he'd done it all.

Except marry Carine Winter.

Which complicated Hank's life, but he wasn't just going to stop being Ty's friend. The mutual respect they'd developed for each other in the military had solidified into

friendship now that Hank was out of the military and frat-
ernization rules were no longer an issue. Ty was the one
who'd invited him to Cold Ridge in the first place. Otherwise, Hank thought, he wouldn't have been there last
November to meet the Winter sisters.

But he knew he had to be patient. Although Antonia
didn't say so in as many words—she didn't have to—she
felt she was being disloyal to her sister by falling for one
of Carine's ex-fiancé's military pals.

Hank gritted his teeth. He'd trust Tyler North with his
life, but there were days he wouldn't mind tracking his
friend down wherever he was—on a training mission,
deployed to some remote battlefield—and knocking the
shit out of him. Had he *ever* intended to marry Carine?

Five minutes, Hank thought. Five minutes he'd wasted
dithering over his situation. He couldn't change reality.
Carine Winter was living in Cambridge. She insisted she
hated Tyler North. And Antonia was on her sister's side.
Unconditionally.

And Hank now had less than fifty-five minutes to get
her younger sister to give him the information he wanted.

He kicked open his car door and climbed out onto the
busy, narrow street of multifamily houses. He'd been in
combat. He'd ditched helicopters. He'd endured the media
onslaught that came with being a candidate for the senate.
Damn it, he could handle the Winter sisters.

Carine almost didn't let him in.

Hank frowned at her through the grimy front door window. "Carine—I'm worried about Antonia. I just want to
talk to you."

It wasn't true—he wanted to pump her for information.
But with obvious misgiving, Carine pulled the door open
about a foot. She was two inches taller than her sister, her

auburn hair a couple of tones darker, but she and Antonia had the same blue eyes. "She's not here."

"I know that. May I come in?"

"I'm kind of busy—"

"Carine. Please."

She sighed, and he could see that her heart wasn't into being rude to him. It wouldn't be nearly as satisfying as pitching Tyler off a cliff, which, last Hank had heard, was what she'd threatened to do the next time she saw him. But Ty hadn't surfaced in Cold Ridge in months, and Carine, too, had stayed away. Hank could see it worried Antonia, but Carine's state of mind was, by unspoken agreement, a forbidden topic.

She opened the door the rest of the way and pretended to peer out onto the street. "What, no entourage?"

"I came alone."

"Really? They let you do that?" She didn't bother to curb her sarcasm, as if she lumped him in with Ty and he deserved for her to give him a hard time was the best she could get. "Do you have a limo waiting? I'll bet your people keep a tight leash on you—"

Hank unclenched his jaw and tried to smile. "I'm just a guy doing his best."

"Yeah, right. That's what all the ex-rescue pilots turned senate candidates say." But her sarcasm let up, her tone lightening slightly as she sighed, then motioned at him. "Okay, okay. You might as well come in."

He followed her down a poorly lit hall to her first-floor apartment. The place was the polar opposite of her little log cabin in New Hampshire, just down the road from the sprawling center-chimney house Tyler North had inherited from his wacky mother.

"I see you've been painting," Hank said, noting the bright colors of all the walls and furnishings in the apartment's adjoining three rooms. He couldn't see the bathroom, but expected it, too, was bright. The kitchen cabinets were a citrus-green, the walls mango-colored.

"My landlord said I could."

"You don't think he meant white?"

She gave him a quick, unexpected smile and sat at her kitchen table, painted a cheerful lavender-blue. Somehow, all the colors worked together. "I didn't ask."

A photograph of a red-tailed hawk hung above the flea-market table. It gave Hank a start, as most of Carine's photographs did. She had a gift, one she couldn't be using to its fullest in Boston. He'd avoided asking Antonia too many questions about her younger sister, but the last he'd heard, Carine had taken a commercial assignment with a Newbury Street shop.

But he stayed focused on his mission. "I'm wondering if you've talked to Antonia recently."

"Why?"

Hank didn't respond to her reflexive suspicion. "We had dinner together on Saturday." That was three days ago, he thought. Three days and not a word from her. "She'd just come off shift and was tired, maybe a little on edge. She seemed to have a lot on her mind. She said she planned to go out of town for a few days to work on a journal article she'd been putting off. I assume that's where she is?"

Carine was the youngest of the three Winter siblings, orphaned when they were three, five and seven, and she wasn't one to easily give up what she knew—even on a good day. "She didn't tell you?"

He shook his head. "I might not have been clear on the dates, or just missed it when she said where she was going. I left several messages on her cell phone. She hasn't returned my calls."

Carine lifted her blue eyes to him. "Maybe you should take the hint."

"Carine, for God's sake—"

She kicked out her legs and folded her hands on her lap in a gesture of pure unrepentance. "How's the campaign going?"

"Fine. It has nothing to do with why I'm here."

She ignored him. "A retired air force major. A hero. A Massachusetts Callahan. A candidate for the United States Senate. I guess you wouldn't be used to people giving you the brush-off, huh?"

"Antonia wouldn't sneak off if she wanted to get rid of me." He knew he couldn't back down, show even a hint of weakness—otherwise he wouldn't get a thing out of Carine. "She'd tell me. She's a straightforward woman—"

"A clean, quick death instead of a slow one," Carine said, her tone suddenly quiet. "Either way, in the end, it still hurts, and you're still dead."

"I'm not Ty North, Carine."

Her moment of melancholy vanished as quickly as it had appeared. "That's true. If you were, I'd have stink-bombed you out on the porch." She dropped her hands to her sides and sat up straight. "Hank, honestly, I can't help you. I'm sorry."

She wasn't sorry. He saw it now. She was stonewalling him—on purpose. It wasn't just her close-mouthed nature at work, or the tight bond between the two sisters. Carine knew something, and she didn't want to tell him. Or wasn't supposed to tell him. Or both.

"Carine, normally I wouldn't be here." Hank tried to keep his tone reasonable. "I'd wait for Antonia to get back and talk with her then. But she wasn't herself the other night at dinner. She blamed her work, but I'm worried it might be something else."

"You, maybe?"

Ty had warned him that Carine could worm her way right down to a person's last, raw nerve. Hank controlled himself, refusing to react defensively and let her see she was getting to him. "Maybe. I'm serious about her, Carine. If my campaign's made her nervous—"

"That's not what you think," Carine said confidently. "Am I right?"

"You're right. It's not the campaign."

"On the other hand, maybe whatever's going on with Antonia is her problem, not yours, and what you should do is mind your own business."

Her tone was matter of fact, as if he should have thought of this point on his own. Independent, Hank remembered, was another word Ty had used to describe the Winters, right after hard-bitten and stubborn. Hank figured his only defense was to stay the course—get Carine on his side, get her to trust him. But her emotions were still raw after what Ty had done, and she had good reason not to trust anyone, especially one of her ex-fiancé's friends, so easily again.

"What if it's something she can't or shouldn't handle on her own?" Hank asked, trying to appeal to her common sense. "What if she's in over her head?"

Carine averted her eyes, and Hank knew he had her— she was on the defensive. He wasn't crazy. Something was up with Antonia. But he made sure he didn't let any victory, any smugness, show. Too much was at stake. Every instinct he had said so.

But ten seconds stretched into thirty, thirty into a minute, and she didn't say a word.

Hank let a hiss of impatience escape. "If you don't want to tell me what's going on, Carine, okay, I can't make you." He paused, debating, then said, "I'll just call Gus."

She didn't like that. Gus Winter had raised them since he'd carted the bodies of his brother and sister-in-law off Cold Ridge thirty years ago, when he was just twenty years old himself and in no position to take on three little kids.

Carine jumped to her feet, her long hair whipping around as she flounced across the small, dingy linoleum floor to the scarred stainless steel sink. "What do you mean, you'll call Gus? Like Antonia and I are twelve years old or something?"

Hank leaned back against the ancient counter cabinets. This was working. He couldn't back off—he had to go for the jugular. "All right. Forget Gus. I'll get Tyler here. He can hang you out your window by your toes until you talk."

She stopped dead, one hand on the sink faucet, color rising high in her cheeks. "Go ahead. See if I care."

"I just want you to understand that I'm serious. Something's going on with Antonia. I think you know it, or at least sense it, but you want to make this hard because you promised her you'd keep your mouth shut." Hank let his tone soften slightly and attempted a smile. "I figure Antonia will forgive you for talking if you tell her I stooped low enough to threaten to sic Ty North on you."

"Meaning you're bluffing?"

"Meaning I wouldn't underestimate my determination."

She let out an exasperated sigh but said nothing.

"Is Antonia in some kind of trouble, Carine?" Hank asked. "Are you?"

"Not me." Her eyes spit fire at him. "I'm in good shape now that I have all you military types out of my life."

"I'm just a senate candidate these days."

She scowled. "Don't think I'll vote for you."

He grinned at her. "You will, and you know it. You liked me before Ty bailed on you. You have a soft spot for us military types." He took a step toward her. Tyler North was one of the bravest men Hank had ever known—except when it came to Carine Winter. She was without a doubt the one woman Ty would ever love, and the dope had skipped out on her. Hank knew it still hurt. "Give Ty a little time—"

"I'm not giving him anything. He's out of my life. I don't even think about him anymore, unless people like you insist on bringing up his name."

She was such a liar, but Hank decided not to tell her so.

"Anyway," she said, "he's got nothing to do with what's going on with Antonia."

That was his confirmation. He was right. There was something.

Carine turned on the faucet and filled a mason jar with water. Her cheeks were red, but her underlying color was pale, the strain of the last months evident. Despite the bright colors she'd used on the walls and furnishings, the place was still old and run-down, a testament to her hand-to-mouth existence. Hank didn't know if she lived the way she did because of the temporary nature of her life here or because she didn't have any money—or because she was just too tight-fisted to part with it. She could always sell her log cabin in New Hampshire, but Hank knew she hadn't even rented it out.

And she thought of herself as an artistic type, a sensitive soul, not a typical risk-taking Winter. Something about her tended to bring out people's protective urges. But as Hank watched her gulp down her water, he knew he had to keep up the pressure. "Tell me what you know, Carine."

She turned on the tiny television on a shelf above the

table. Hank had no idea what she was up to. The TV was tuned to the Weather Channel, which was giving the latest coordinates on Hurricane Hope, a menacing Category 3 storm working its way up the east coast. Its maximum sustained winds were 120 mph, with even higher gusts. No watches or warnings had yet gone up in New England—Hope was expected to turn out to sea before it got that far north.

Carine glanced back at him with a studied nonchalance. "What do you think of naming a hurricane Hope?"

"I hadn't thought about it at all."

"We Winters are mountain types ourselves. We've been in the White Mountains since Madison was president. One of the high peaks is named after him, did you know that? Mount Madison."

"Carine—"

He might not have spoken. "Put me on top of a five-thousand-foot peak in the White Mountains when the weather gets bad, and I'd know what to do." She shifted back to the weather report. "I can't say I'd know what to do in a hurricane."

Hank wasn't following her, but checked his impatience. "Are you worried about Hope?"

"Not for my sake. I'm not as exposed here as you all are on the Cape and the islands. Your family's on the Cape, right?"

"Brewster. We've done lots of storms." His family owned a popular marina on Cape Cod Bay. He spoke warily, uncertain of the ground he was on now—he didn't want to miss any signals, veer off in the wrong direction and lose her completely. "People have learned to pay attention to watches and warnings. They heed evacuation orders. They don't fool around."

"That's because they know their coastal storms, and

they have access to the warnings, weather reports, evacuation orders. If someone didn't—" Carine licked her lips, staring up at the small screen. "Let's say you don't know storms, plus you've got other things on your mind. You're alone on an isolated island, and Hurricane Hope doesn't turn out to sea—you could be in a mess real fast, couldn't you?"

"You could. But that's theoretical. I don't know how you could be alone on an island off the Cape—"

"It could happen. Even these days."

Hank narrowed his eyes on her, aware of her intensity of emotion—her ambivalence about what she was doing. "Carine, are you saying Antonia is alone on an island, without access to storm reports and evacuation orders?"

"I'm not saying anything."

But her breathing was more shallow and rapid as she shifted back to him, as if she was waiting for him to figure out what she was saying and do what she already knew he would do.

He fished out his cell phone and dialed Tyler North's cell number. Ty was stationed at Hurlburt Field Air Force Base in the Florida panhandle, where he was assigned to the 16th Special Operations Wing as the Team Leader of a Special Tactics Team. God only knew where he'd be. Hank expected to have to leave a message, but Ty picked up on the second ring. "North."

"Where are you?"

"Florida. Drinking a beer. You?"

"Cambridge. I'm with Carine."

Ty was silent.

"Something's up with Antonia. She must have sworn Carine to secrecy, so I can't get any straight answers."

"Good luck, pal. She's not talking unless she wants to talk."

"She's given me a hint. Apparently Antonia is on an island somewhere off Cape Cod, and Carine's worried she'll be stuck there if Hurricane Hope doesn't turn out to sea—or she'll ride it out, because she doesn't have access to weather reports or doesn't know any better."

Ty grunted. "She'd know better, but she'd ride out the fires of hell if she thought she had to. Both of them would."

"Yeah. Carine did almost marry you."

"We're not going there, Major."

Tyler only called him major nowadays when he wanted to distance himself. Hank had put him on the spot. "She knew I'd call you."

"Carine did?" His tone changed, becoming more serious. "Then you damn well know there's something wrong. I'm the last person Carine would let you turn to for help. Hank? What the hell's going on?"

"That's why I'm here—to find out."

"Carine's okay? She's safe?"

Hank's pulse pounded in his temple. He couldn't figure out what had happened to Ty. One day, Hank was making plans to attend his friend's wedding in Cold Ridge. The next day, the wedding was off, and Tyler had taken off into the White Mountains with not much more than a jackknife and a pair of crampons.

"She's fine," Hank said. "She's standing here watching the Weather Channel and pretending she doesn't realize I'm talking to you. I'm guessing she thinks you know where Antonia is."

Tyler sighed. He'd known these women all his life—in many ways, they were the only family he'd ever had. "Shelter Island. You're a Cape Codder. You must know it."

Hank was confused. "Of course I know it—it's a tiny barrier island off Chatham. But it's a national wildlife refuge. I thought there weren't any cottages on it anymore, and it's illegal to camp there."

"You wouldn't get Antonia in a tent, anyway," Ty said. "There's one cottage left on the island. Antonia has this friend in Boston—she's like a hundred or something. She has a life-lease to the last cottage on Shelter Island. When she dies, it goes to the birds, literally. Antonia used to go there to study for exams when she was in med school."

She had never mentioned her friend or her cottage, another reminder, Hank thought, of just how much he still had to learn about her.

"You're going down there?" Tyler asked.

"Yes. As soon as possible. I have a feeling there's more going on than just a hurricane that might or might not hit. Antonia was on edge when I saw her last on Saturday."

"Carine knows more?"

"Almost certainly."

"Want me to drag it out of her?"

He'd do it, too, Hank thought. "I'm not having you go AWOL on my account. I'll handle it. If Carine knows anything that would help me help her sister," he added pointedly, for Carine's benefit, "she'd tell me."

Carine didn't respond, still pretending not to be listening.

"The Winters don't think like normal people," Ty said. "How many women do you know who would stay by themselves in the only cottage on a barrier island with a hurricane churning up the coast? If Antonia doesn't think she needs to leave, she's not going to."

"Any advice?"

"Bring her a toe tag. Then the rescue workers can identify her body."

"North, for God's sake—"

"It'll get her attention. She's an E.R. doctor. She knows

what happens to people who don't heed safety warnings made in their best interest."

He hung up.

Hank stared a moment at his dead phone. The surprise wasn't that Tyler North had canceled his wedding to Carine Winter at the last minute. The surprise was that it had ever been on in the first place.

He sighed at her. "You were really going to marry him?"

She managed a halfhearted smile. "It seems crazy now, doesn't it? Are you—Hank, Antonia specifically asked me not to tell you—"

"I suspected as much. And yes, I'm going."

"She's very independent. She's not used to—" Carine broke off, then resumed. "She won't like the idea of anyone thinking she might need to be rescued. Me, you. It doesn't matter. It means we think she's in a situation she can't handle on her own."

"It's not a fun place to be. But if you're there, you're there."

Carine nodded, saying nothing.

"Carine, is it just the hurricane?"

"No." Her voice was barely audible, but she cleared her throat and went on in a normal tone. "There's something else. But she wouldn't tell me."

She left it at that, and for the first time, Hank saw the sadness that still clung to her. Usually it was buried under anger and stubbornness—the resolve not to let Tyler North be the ruin of her. But not this time. "Do you know anything?" Hank asked softly. "Do you have any ideas?"

"I think she's scared. That's not like her." She pushed a hand through her hair and seemed to force her mood to shift from its palpable uneasiness. "Are you taking a posse with you or going alone?"

By posse, Hank knew she meant not just the people who surrounded him as a candidate, but his air force buddies, led by pararescuers Tyler North. But he shook his head. "I'm going alone."

She forced a smile. "I guess there are some things you can still do alone."

Three

Follow the wannabe senator.

Robert didn't know how he'd manage it without being caught, but he figured with the 156 IQ, he'd find a way.

How had he let the bitch doctor slip through his fingers?

Actually he knew. It was the sister's fault. She'd loaned Dr. Bitch her car so she could sneak out of town.

Carine Winter, the jilted nature photographer. Robert had slipped into her apartment one afternoon a week ago and borrowed the set of keys she had to Antonia's apartment, had them copied and returned them. Then he'd checked out her laptop and read some of her sent e-mails. Pitiful. Really pitiful. Except she had a tough streak— man, he wouldn't want to be the guy who'd given her the boot.

He'd sent the bitch sister one of the instant messages from the laptop. A stroke of genius, he'd thought.

He'd debated fire-bombing Miss Carine's dump of an apartment, but he had to keep his eyes on the prize.

Antonia Winter, M.D.

Scared. Sweating. At his mercy, the way he'd been at her mercy with his foot.

Begging for her life.

It was the image he came back to over and over as he considered his next move. He knew he should probably have a master plan, but he loved the spontaneity—hell, he didn't know what he'd do next, never mind Dr. Bitch Winter.

He honestly didn't know if he'd kill her. He might, he might not.

Probably he would.

He sat cross-legged on Dr. Winter's soft, pretty bed in her Back Bay apartment. It was kind of a girly room. Elegant, expensive, but Robert hadn't expected the framed photographs of flowers—the little sister's work—and the scented candles, the lace-edged sheets. He'd gone through her lingerie drawer. Nice stuff. Silky. But he got to thinking about how she'd treated him in the E.R., how she was so sweet and caring at first, making him think he might have a real chance with her. That he was right about her, and she just needed him to injure himself to give her an excuse to make a move on him, put out the vibes for him to make a move on her.

Then she turned him in to the cops. She said it was the law, that she had to report any suspected gunshot wound. Bullshit! It wasn't like he'd committed a crime. He'd shot *himself* in the foot! Big deal! She could have let it go. It wasn't as if he'd shot someone *else* in the foot.

They'd left him alone for about a half-second in the X-ray room, and he'd pulled out his IV and made a run for it, shot-up foot and everything. The cops caught him in the parking lot. Chased him down like he was a runaway dog. If he hadn't had the limp, he'd have made it to safety. He knew the hospital terrain better than the damn cops did.

Yeah, thinking about his little trip to the E.R. had pissed him off.

He'd found scissors and shredded the bitch doctor's underwear. Bras, panties, slips, camisoles. All of it. In pieces.

That'd scare the shit out of her if he didn't catch up with her first and she made it back here. If he decided not to kill her after all.

It was only his second time in her apartment. He resisted overdoing it. Miss Carine, another loser, didn't realize the keys had even been missing, never mind that he'd scared the crap out of her sister using her very own laptop.

Robert grinned to himself. See? That high IQ at work.

His granny, who'd raised him after his loser of a mother croaked from a drug overdose, said he could do anything he put his mind to, he was just that smart. She'd dropped dead of a stroke when he was sixteen. He'd found her facedown in her rice plate. Poor old thing.

But Robert didn't want to think about his grandmother. He stood in the middle of Antonia's soft, thick rug. Somehow he had to pick up Superman Hank's trail again. How hard could it be? Figure out where he was making his appearance and follow him from there—Robert had done it before. As a strategy, it made sense. If the major knew where the bitch doctor was, he'd go to her. If he didn't know, he'd find her.

Robert snatched up her telephone and hit the redial button. See who the good doctor had talked to last. Why not?

"Good afternoon, Winslow residence."

What was this? Robert cleared his throat and adopted his most polite, kiss-ass voice. "Sorry to bother you. Mrs. Winslow, right?"

"Yes."

He loved old people. Who told shit to strangers over the phone anymore? He kept up with the polite voice. "I was wondering if Dr. Winter is there."

"Dr. Winter? No, no." It was a woman's voice, but she sounded like she was a million years old. "She was here several days ago. She's spending a few days at my cottage on Shelter Island. Excuse me, I didn't catch your name?"

"I'm a friend from the hospital. It's okay, Mrs. Winslow, I understand my mistake now. Thanks for your help. Have a good day."

He hung up before the old lady could say anything else.

Shelter Island.

Robert had never heard of it, but he was a goddamn genius. He could find it.

Four

Antonia stood on a mound of sand, beach grass and bearberry down a narrow path from her borrowed cottage and, once again, concentrated on trying to relax. A white-crested wave pushed onto shore. The tide was up. The air was warm, decidedly not hot, the wind nearly constant. A lone bird—some kind of raptor, she thought—rode the breeze overhead.

She exhaled, feeling the tension release in her muscles. She was safe. It'd been a good idea to come down here. She'd bought herself a few days to work, think, rest.

"It'll be okay," she said aloud. "It really will."

How could it be otherwise on such an incredibly beautiful day? It was late afternoon, but she'd removed her watch once she'd arrived at the cottage and didn't know the exact time. Still, there was no mistaking that it was September—the sun was setting earlier and earlier. She'd never been out here in winter.

She was alone on a beautiful, peaceful island refuge, exactly, she thought, where she needed to be right now.

Shelter Island was a stopover for migrating birds, and home to shore birds, seabirds, waterfowl. Dozens of different species rested, fed and nested on the small island.

Sandpipers, plovers, terns, ducks, gulls, owls, falcons, eagles. Antonia had learned to recognize some of their calls and signs, but she was still a beginner at birdwatching—she didn't have her sister's skill or patience when it came to birds. But she recognized that she was the intruder here, and she did what she could to keep her impact at a minimum.

Only Carine knew where she was. Antonia had sworn her sister to secrecy, probably a bit of unnecessary drama on her part, but it had seemed to make sense at the time. She'd wanted someone to know where to find her in case of emergency, but she didn't want Carine involved in whatever was—or, more likely, wasn't—going on with her possible stalker.

She hadn't given Hank any specifics. The less he knew, the better. He couldn't worry about, act on or say anything about something he didn't know. A few days off on her own—it was all the specifics he needed.

The wind hinted of the tropics, tasted of higher humidity. It was a reminder that Hurricane Hope remained a danger. Antonia's crackly National Weather Service radio indicated a hurricane watch could go up for Cape Cod and the islands by morning—meaning hurricane conditions were *possible* within thirty-six hours. Evacuation orders would no doubt follow for exposed areas like Shelter Island.

Antonia wasn't sure she wanted to leave. The storm still could turn out to sea before it reached New England. It was tempting to take her chances, bet on Hope instead of her stalker.

Three days at her laptop, she thought. Three days going through patient records and thinking, thinking, thinking, and she still didn't have any answers. Who would want to get under her skin? Who would be so sneaky and relentless about it? She wasn't even sure herself that anything was going on, never mind had enough to convince anyone else. Strange instant messages. Whispers in a parking garage. What did that prove? Did she really want the police involved at this point, digging into her life on every level? What could they do? There was *nothing* to go on.

And that didn't even take Hank into consideration.

After dinner on Saturday, they'd almost ended up at her apartment together, but she was aware of how distracted she was, still preoccupied with the whispers she thought she'd heard in the garage. She knew Hank didn't understand. But she'd rationalized to herself that she was doing him a favor by not telling him. Figure out what, if anything, was going on. Then talk to him.

She'd trudged upstairs to her Back Bay apartment and fought back tears as she'd walked into her bedroom.

There, to her immediate disbelief, she found her bedroom curtains billowing in the evening breeze.

She was positive she hadn't left the window open—but there was no sign of a break-in, nothing in her apartment missing, nothing disturbed. Her window was cracked, and she knew she hadn't touched it. She *never* left her windows open when she wasn't home.

She'd grabbed her phone and dialed the 9 for 9-1-1, but stopped. She was on her way out of town. She could add billowing curtains to the instant messages and whispers in the garage and try to figure out who, if anyone, might be obsessed with her. Do her own investigation from the safety and isolation of Shelter Island. Away from her possible stalker. Away from her sister. Away from her work. And, perhaps most of all, away from Hank.

If given half a chance, the media would dig their teeth into her stalker story and not let go.

With any luck, while she was away, whoever was trying to scare her would pull himself together and give up his campaign against her.

But breaking into her apartment—if it was her stalker, it was crossing the line. It couldn't be explained away. It was black and white. A crime.

She referred to her stalker as "he" to herself and believed it was a man, but she supposed it could be a woman.

Or no one.

When she got back to Boston, she'd change her locks.

The wind was at her back as she followed the sandy path back among the pitch pine and juniper to the cottage. She had on a lightweight sweatshirt, shorts and water sandals, her leg muscles getting a good workout in the soft, shifting sand. The cottage was tiny and rustic, classic Cape Cod with its weathered cedar shingles, white trim and blue-painted doors. It sat on what passed for high ground on Shelter Island, its front porch overlooking Nantucket Sound.

Antonia had met Babs Winslow when she was in medical school and Babs was volunteering at the hospital. Despite their age difference, they became friends. Babs was a true blueblood eccentric. Wealthy, but not one for anything flashy. She hadn't made improvements to her cottage in years—she hadn't even been down here in years—but Antonia liked its simplicity and lack of modern amenities. A small generator provided limited power for the pump, a pint-sized refrigerator and a lightbulb that hung from a beam in the middle of the cottage's single room and was turned on with a string. Two ancient kerosene lamps provided supplemental lighting. There was no hot water—she had to heat water in a lobster pot for dishes and her sponge baths.

At least Babs had gotten rid of the outhouse. Antonia didn't think the cottage would be nearly as romantic without its modest bathroom facilities. Carine wouldn't have minded an outhouse, she thought. Tyler, either.

When she reached her front porch, Antonia checked to see if the beach towel she'd hung over the rail was dry, then went still.

She'd heard something. Not a bird, she thought. Not the wind, not the ocean.

She didn't breathe, forcing herself not to panic as she concentrated and tried to block out the sounds of the ocean and birds and listen.

Whistling.

Someone was whistling!

"It must be a bird," she said aloud, hearing her own tension.

But there it was again—and no way was it a bird.

She recognized the tune. It was "Heigh Ho," the dwarves' working song from Disney's *Snow White and the Seven Dwarves*.

Her first impulse was to smile at such a cheerful tune, but then she thought—*no. You don't know who it is.*

She couldn't let herself be lulled into a false sense of security.

She slipped into the cottage, careful not to let the door slam, and automatically, without thinking, grabbed a carving knife from the utensils drawer in the kitchen area. Just in case. Most likey, a passing boat had spotted her brightly colored beach towel hanging on the porch and reported the possibility of an inhabitant, and a local official was checking on her, making sure she knew a hurricane was approaching and she had a way off the island.

Surely a stalker wouldn't announce his presence by whistling a Disney tune.

But she wasn't taking any chances. Taking her knife with her, she darted out the back door, making no noise as she tiptoed quickly down the rickety steps, thinking only that she needed to get to a place where she could see but not be seen.

She ducked behind a sprawling beach rosebush that grew close to the back steps and, mindful of its thorns, crouched down. She held her knife as if it was a surgical instrument, not something she might use to defend herself against attack.

The whistling had stopped.

Maybe it was Gus. If Carine had even hinted about Cape Cod and a hurricane, Antonia obviously unnerved, their uncle would get in his truck and head south, without stopping to consider that she was thirty-five, an experienced physician capable of making her own decisions.

And who's hiding behind a rosebush with a carving knife?

She groaned to herself. Sometimes Gus did have a point.

It wasn't Carine, that was for sure. Carine couldn't whistle worth a damn.

Heavy footsteps sounded on the front porch on the other side of the cottage. "Antonia? It's me, Hank. Hank Callahan."

As if there were other Hanks in her life. She almost collapsed to her knees in relief. How had he found her? Carine? It had to be, but not voluntarily—Hank must have tripped her up. Charmed her. Used Ty North to throw her off balance. He and Hank were unyielding when they thought they were in the right and someone was trying to thwart them, keep them from getting done what they meant to get done.

What did Hank mean to do?

Belatedly, Antonia realized that her own behavior must have aroused his suspicions. She supposed she hadn't done a good job of concealing how upset she was at dinner, and then she'd taken off without telling him where she was going. Even if he hadn't seen her agitation, Hank would wonder what was going on with her. She'd hoped he'd be too busy to act on it. Then there was Carine—she'd recognized Antonia's jumpiness for what it was and had asked what was wrong. Antonia hadn't told her, which probably only fueled her sister's concern.

And now, for whatever reason, Hank had tracked her down.

He wouldn't regard crouching behind a rosebush with a knife as the ordinary precaution of a woman alone on an island. Innocent. Unsuspicious. If he wasn't already on alert, finding her right now would do it.

She stabbed the knife into the sand and stood up, easing out from behind the bush. Her sleeve caught on a thorny sprig. As she freed herself, she pricked her index finger, drawing blood.

"I'm out back," she called, thinking she sounded reasonably composed. "How on earth did you find me?"

She heard him inside the cottage. He hadn't bothered knocking or waiting for her to let him in, which made her wonder just what Carine had told him. But, Hank wasn't one to stand on ceremony when he set out to do something.

The screen door creaked open, and he walked down the back steps to the small yard that was mostly overgrown with bearberry and beach roses, with a few patches of juniper, foot-tall doomed pine and oak saplings. Lilacs, long out of bloom, grew along one side of the cottage. An invasive, nasty patch of poison ivy swarmed up a stand of pitch pine that marked the yard's far border.

Antonia noticed she'd pushed through a cobweb on her

way out from behind the rosebush. She brushed it off her arm and picked it out of her hair. "Hank, what a surprise."

His blue eyes raked over her, and he didn't smile. "You're looking a little pale there, Doc."

"Am I?"

"Did I startle you?"

"A little." It wasn't an outright lie. "I'm supposed to be alone out here. Don't you have campaign appearances?"

"I canceled them."

His tone was difficult to read. Was he angry? Worried? She'd piqued his curiosity—that much she could see. "I haven't heard the latest report on the hurricane. Anything new?"

"It's not looking good." He sounded calmer, his tone less abrupt. The sun hit his eyes, which seemed as blue as the sky and sea. "It's picking up speed. It could hit the Cape after all before it makes its turn east. That would put you in the bull's-eye."

The bull's-eye. She'd hoped being out here would take her *out* of the bull's-eye, at least her stalker's bull's-eye.

What was the saying? Out of the frying pan, into the fire. Out of the way of a stalker who might not be real, into the path of a hurricane that was very much real.

"I've got plenty of time to evacuate if a watch goes up," she said.

"How did you get out here?"

"Kayak—a new one. I bought it just for this trip. I know I shouldn't kayak alone, but there were enough boats out in the inlet when I paddled over here that I wasn't worried. I had a water taxi bring my supplies."

"Quite the adventure."

She ignored the bite—the hurt—in his tone. She hadn't told him she was coming down here. It was that simple.

She shrugged, giving up on any attempt to smile. "It's been fun."

His eyes stayed on her. "Seas could get rough fast for a kayak."

"It's not that far to the mainland, and I'm a pretty good kayaker. I'd wave down help if I needed it."

"Would you?"

He didn't seem to expect her to answer. He stepped down onto the grass, browned from the long summer, and it struck her that he looked taller than she remembered. He had on khakis, a dark polo shirt and running shoes, but there was nothing casual about him. He had that straight spine of a military man and the power demeanor of a U.S. senator, even if he wasn't one yet. He wasn't a man who took a lot of b.s. From anyone. Ever. And he had to know, she thought, that that was exactly what he was getting from her. She was skirting the truth, hedging, dodging, lying. And she didn't much like herself for it, no matter her excuses and rationalizations.

His vivid blue eyes could be so kind and tender—she'd seen them that way. But they weren't that way now. They were calculating, questioning, alert, making her wonder again what all Carine had told him.

"My sister said I was here?"

"Not in as many words. I had to get Ty to fill in the gaps."

Antonia almost choked. "He's not in Cambridge with her—"

"He's in Florida. He says Gus'll kill him the minute he sets foot back in New England."

It was only a slight exaggeration. Antonia sighed. "I don't get it. Gus wanted to kill him for asking Carine to marry him—now he wants to kill him for *not* marrying her."

Hank managed a half smile, without letting up on his intensity. "Don't try to make sense of it."

She waved a hand and picked the last of the cobweb off her arm. "I stopped trying to make sense of anything to do with Tyler North a long time ago. Why were you whistling 'Heigh Ho'?"

"I didn't want to sneak up on a woman alone on an island."

"Good thinking." She resisted an urge to glance back at her knife stabbed into the sand behind the rosebush. "I suppose a bad guy could whistle a cheerful tune to put me off guard—"

"I'm not a bad guy."

His words were so direct, so unexpected, Antonia had to catch her breath. Despite her efforts not to, she thought of the instant messages, the whispers in the garage, the curtains billowing in the breeze. Maybe no one was stalking her. Maybe she was overreacting to a few odd coincidences because of Hank. Because she was falling for a retired air force officer, a national hero, a Massachusetts Callahan, a likely United States senator—a man who'd lost a wife and a child, who'd lived a lifetime before she'd even met him. Hank Callahan could easily overwhelm the life she'd carefully built for herself day by day, year by year.

And none of that even took into account his longstanding friendship with the man who'd broken her sister's heart.

How could she let herself fall in love with him? It made no sense, and Antonia prided herself on being sensible when it came to matters of her own heart.

Maybe there was no "let" about it. She remembered the moment she'd walked into Carine's cabin last November and saw him standing there, felt the instant attraction, the sparks flying—all of it, every cliché there was.

Hank moved closer to her, until they were almost touching. He'd grown up on Cape Cod and had been around the ocean all his life—yet he'd chosen to become a pilot. A rescue helicopter pilot.

He eyed her again, studying her. She'd always suspected he had a keen ability to read people. He touched a finger to her hair and caught the last of the cobweb. "Tyler said I should bring you a toe tag in case you refuse to leave."

"He thinks he's funny, doesn't he?"

"He was serious. He said if you dug in your heels—"

"Why would he think I'd dig in my heels?"

"I wonder."

She didn't pursue that one. "Well, I don't intend to stay out here if a hurricane watch goes up, never mind a warning."

"But you're tempted, aren't you?" His expression lost all its humor and gentleness. "What's in Boston that would tempt you to ride out a hurricane on a barrier island instead of going back?"

It was a close call, she realized. Crazy, because a barrier island was no place to be during a hurricane. "We're not under a watch yet. I still have time."

As if to disprove her point, a strong gust of wind rolled over the top of the cottage and rattled the windows. "You don't do brinksmanship with a hurricane," he said.

"Hank, I trust myself to make good decisions. You should trust me, too." But Antonia curbed her sudden feeling of defensiveness. "Did Carine tell you I don't know anything about hurricanes?"

"More or less."

"More than less, I'll bet. Look, Hank, I can see you're

concerned about me, but don't be. I've been a little pre-occupied lately—I just wanted to come down and clear some things off my deck."

"You don't have a phone, do you?"

He wasn't backing off. She could see now that she'd miscalculated when she hadn't told him what she was up to. She shook her head. "No phone. There's no cellular service, either." She smiled suddenly. "I have emergency flares."

"Flares." He smiled back at her, his grim mood easing somewhat. "You're something, Dr. Winter. Most people would stay at an inn to clear their decks, not sit in an old cottage out here all alone."

"I love it out here." But she didn't belabor the point, because if he'd dragged her whereabouts out of Carine, she didn't stand a chance herself if he decided to press her about what all she wasn't telling him. "Did you come alone?"

"Yes, ma'am. All by myself."

His comment struck Antonia as deliberately intimate, and she felt a rush of heat and awareness so fierce she had to turn away. "At least you didn't come by helicopter. You're not getting me up in one of those things."

But he was good with both helicopters and boats—and she was good with neither. In many respects, she had more in common with Tyler North than she did with Hank Callahan. She and Tyler had grown up together in northern New Hampshire, and as a pararescueman, he was a highly skilled paramedic. But he was impossible. If Gus didn't skewer him for what he'd done to Carine, Antonia thought, she might.

But if she wasn't careful herself with the air force type she had in her own life, she'd end up like her younger sister, nursing a broken heart. Maybe there'd been something in the air that night in Carine's cabin, and they'd both been gripped by forces beyond their control, doomed to fall in love with the wrong men.

Antonia gave herself a mental shake. She was getting *way* ahead of herself. She and Hank had been out to dinner together, the theater, a couple of movies, a pathetic baseball game—and they'd landed up in bed once, memorably, a few weeks ago.

But no one was tinkling wedding bells in the background. Hank had lost a family once. Antonia could see it wasn't easy for him to get beyond just having a nice time with a woman, moving to something deeper.

Which was just as well, because "deeper" meant "more complicated," and right now, Antonia thought, her life was complicated enough. Was that why she'd lied to him, withheld from him? To put him at arm's length?

"I have a boat anchored on the other side of the island." His tone was matter of fact, but he wasn't relaxed. "It's out of the worst of the wind. We can leave in the morning."

The morning. It was, she thought, a very small cottage. One bed, a lumpy couch. Antonia pushed a flood of unbidden images to the back of her mind. "It'll get into the papers," she said. *"Senate candidate Hank Callahan rescues doctor from island ahead of hurricane."*

"Hate being rescued, don't you?"

"I hate having put myself in the position of needing to be rescued. I don't mind that you're here. It's nice you came after me."

But his eyes narrowed on her, his hard gaze lingering on her face until she had to turn away. "You're on edge, Antonia." His tone was soft, but there was no mistaking his intensity. "Why?"

"A Category 3 hurricane bearing down on me, maybe?"

"That's not it," he said with certainty.

She stepped past him, her arm brushing against his arm, adding to her sense of agitation. How could she think? A stalker, a hurricane, Hank Callahan. She glanced back at him as she headed up the steps to the back door, a warm gust of wind rolling over the top of the small cottage. "What would you do if I change my mind and refuse to leave in the morning, even if a watch goes up?"

He mounted the step behind her and smiled. "Do likewise."

"You mean you'd stay?"

He grinned at her, with no warning. "Gives you a little shiver of excitement, doesn't it? You, me, a storm, a one-room cottage—"

"Don't you have staff and security people who'd worry?"

"So? You have people who worry. It hasn't stopped you."

"I'm not going to win this argument, am I? Luckily I don't have to." She returned his grin and faked a half-swoon. "I'm willing to be rescued."

Five

~⦁⦁⦁~

Robert set up camp behind the tallest dune on the Nantucket Sound side of Shelter Island. He felt intrepid. He dropped his pack in the sand and tufts of grass—he didn't know his beach vegetation—and crouched down, pulling up his pants leg.

"Shit!"

Ticks. A million of them on his legs and ankles.

The bitch doctor's fault.

He was maybe fifty yards from her cottage, but she had no idea he was there. He was sure of it. He'd arrived about an hour before Superman Hank showed up on the island. Pissed Robert off, totally. He'd known Callahan would find her but thought, given his good fortune with Babs, that he'd get a better jump on him. Maybe work it out so the wannabe senator could find his new girlfriend dead.

Breathing hard, Robert used his fingernails to pick tiny deer ticks off his lower legs. He didn't have tweezers. Dr. Bitch probably had a medical kit in the cottage with her, but she wouldn't help him. She was such a phony.

One of the ticks had a good hold on him. He drew blood digging it out.

These weren't the big wood ticks, he thought—dog

ticks some people called them. These were the tiny deer ticks that carried Lyme disease. It could be treated with antibiotics, but damned if he wanted to get it. Some of the little bastards were barely the size of ground pepper. He'd picked them up tramping through the poison ivy and brush, chasing the wannabe senator across the island. Being brighter than most people, Robert knew if he'd stuck to the path, Callahan would nail him. No point in that. A left hook from Mr. Air Force, and he'd be toast.

He had to think. Be proactive. He could put up with a few ticks, take his chances with Lyme disease.

"Keep your eyes on the prize," he said aloud, still panting and wheezing from exertion.

He supposed he could have shot Callahan and been done with him. Robert wasn't surprised the would-be senator had found his way to his bitch's island refuge. It was getting there so fast that bugged the hell out of him. Now he had to scramble, deal with two people instead of one.

He sniffled, digging at another tick. "You're making adjustments, asshole. You're not scrambling."

Right.

The guy, Callahan, was a stud. Robert had followed him once, seen him in the papers and on TV a lot, plus with the bitch doctor. The two of them. What a pair. The handsome hero senate candidate, the beautiful blue-eyed doctor. Robert was nothing to them. Like one of these ticks that had to be removed, squeezed dead and tossed. But not ignored—nobody ignored deer ticks anymore now that they carried Lyme disease.

A light rain that seemed to come out of nowhere washed some of the sand and blood off his legs, but when he moved, more sand stuck. He was covered in it. He felt like one of those little hermit crabs digging its way out of the wet sand at low tide. He didn't know whether it was low tide or high tide now, just that the ocean was out there, rolling, getting scary on the other side of his dune. He wondered if Hurricane Hope was kicking up the surf or if this was normal.

If Hope hit, he'd be swept away out here behind his dune. Drown in the storm surge. Get hit by flying debris.

Callahan's boat was anchored in shallow water on the other side of the island. Robert had come over by water taxi, telling the guy this big lie about meeting a friend and kayaking out before the hurricane had a chance to move in. It hadn't occurred to him until the taxi boat bounced back over the waves that now he was stranded out here, too. The only way off the fucking island was Callahan's boat and the bitch doctor's kayak, which Robert had spotted in the brush. Something to consider in his future planning.

He'd swiped the kayak paddle. That was thinking ahead. Antonia Winter wasn't going anywhere unless Robert wanted her to.

Granny used to tell him that even as smart as he was, she was afraid he didn't think like regular people. He used to think she was just a sweet old stick in the mud with no imagination, no sense of adventure, but nowadays, sometimes, he wondered if she'd been on to something after all. Here he was, stranded, on an island—a goddamn wildlife refuge—a hurricane on the way, deticking himself, risking his life—and for what? *A little payback. A little justice in this world. That's what.*

It made him sick, thinking about himself in pain, with the bloody foot, hoping Antonia—Sweet Antonia, he used to call her—would give him some kind of hint that she was interested in him. He'd fantasized that she'd seize the opportunity he'd provided for her and let down her guard, open up to him, show her feelings. Instead, she'd made him feel like a goddamn loser. A twelve-year-old with a crush. Some jerk-off who didn't have a clue, thinking he had a chance with a woman like her.

After she'd called the cops on him, she'd probably gone out with Hank Callahan.

Robert sank back against the dune, getting more sand on him. Justice. Revenge. She couldn't get away with what she'd done to him. It wasn't right. She'd betrayed him, humiliated him, and she had to suffer. She wasn't the woman he'd thought she was. He'd believed in her, and where had it gotten him? Out here behind a goddamn dune.

Whatever he ended up doing to her, he wanted her to know it was him. No more anonymity. He wanted to hear her beg, see her fear, and know he'd caused it.

"Amen." He opened his eyes against the rain, letting it wash onto his upturned face. "Amen!"

He smelled like salt and sweat and dead fish. He dug his camouflage rain poncho out of his wet pack and wrestled himself into it. It had one of those floppy hoods that wasn't worth a damn. It blew right off his head. He tried tying it on, but the stretchy tie snapped and the end hit him on the finger—it hurt like hell, made him want to kill someone.

It wasn't much of a campsite. No tent. No little stove or firewood. He hadn't even packed a sleeping bag. He'd brought food, but not that much. Some crackers, apples, cheese, all bagged up in plastic. A twelve-pack of water.

He wasn't riding out a hurricane behind a goddamn dune, not with a cottage just up the path. It must have survived dozens of similar storms, decades of crappy weather. If Hurricane Hope chugged north and reached Shelter Island before Robert could take care of business, he'd be in the last structure on this little island. No question about it. He did, after all, have a gun.

A spider crawled up his leg, as if the bitch doctor herself had sent it out to torment him. He yanked it off and tossed it into a puddle forming in the sand behind his dune. He crawled to his feet and looked over the dune, out at the churning water. He'd never understood the appeal of the beach, the ocean, Cape Cod. It was just sand and water to him. This place was supposed to be a bird refuge, but he hadn't seen that many birds. Maybe they were all clearing out for the hurricane. Maybe they knew it would hit. Never mind the meteorologists and the storm-tracking planes—just follow the birds.

He checked his gun. It was a .38 Smith & Wesson. Basic. But he wondered if he could get by without it. If he played his cards right, Hope would keep Mr. Callahan and Dr. Winter on the island with him, and he could blame their deaths on the storm.

Kill two birds with one stone.

Have his cake and eat it, too.

Robert smiled. "Yeah. I like it."

Six

He and Carine were right, Hank thought. Something was up with Antonia. And whatever it was, it wasn't good. He checked out her cottage, similar to countless old-fashioned cottages he'd been in since he was a kid. It was tiny, cozy, with inexpensive furnishings that were functional and at least as old as he was. A lumpy old couch. A heap of musty-smelling quilts, mismatched chairs and dishes, mason jars filled with matchbooks, tacks and rubber bands, soggy decks of cards and the ubiquitous Scrabble game. The bathroom was prosaic, to say the least. He noticed the stack of threadbare towels.

The bed was behind a curtain, the sheets clean and white.

Hank didn't let himself linger gazing at the damn bed.

Antonia said that Babs Winslow was ninety-seven, and when she was gone, this place would be, too. That was the deal. She had a life-lease on the cottage, but the land under it was a National Wildlife Refuge. As, they all believed, it should be. Shelter Island and nearby Monomoy Island were uniquely located as stopovers for migrating birds, their spits of sand at the elbow of Cape Cod well-suited as home to dozens of species of rare and endangered birds.

And time and time again, storms had rearranged what passed for land along this exposed stretch of the Cape—they would again. It wasn't the best spot for the trophy houses that surely would have doomed Babs Winslow's cottage long before now. Development pressures, the sky-rocketing prices of beachfront land, were tough to resist.

But he could see why Antonia liked to come here to think, relax. It was about the perfect escape from a busy urban emergency room, not that getting away from work, hiding out to write this journal article she was supposedly writing, explained why she was here now. They certainly didn't explain her mood. She was a dedicated physician and hadn't taken a break in months, but she'd been on the island for several days—why still the drawn look? Why still the edginess that he'd noticed at dinner in Boston?

He motioned to the laptop computer on the rickety table. "How's the article coming?"

"What?"

She seemed to focus on him, then went pale and suddenly swooped in front of him and hit the power button, not bothering to shut the computer down properly. But this way, Hank thought, he couldn't see what was on the screen. Which made him wonder what was on the screen. He doubted she'd have jumped like that if it'd been medical jibberish about some aspect of trauma medicine.

"The article's coming along, but it's slow work." She snatched up a spiral notebook, closing it before Hank could read her scribblings there, too. She shoved it into a backpack on the floor and smiled unconvincingly at him. "I think I brought my laptop more so I could play FreeCell than anything else. Nights here can be pretty lonely."

"Tonight won't be."

Her cheeks turned a healthier pink, but even that didn't

last as she grabbed the laptop and it followed the notebook into her backpack. "The battery's about run out."

"Antonia—Antonia, what's wrong?"

"Nothing."

Hank didn't respond this time, hoping to let the silence work for him. He heard birds outside—common seagulls—and the rhythm of the ocean, the whoosh of the wind, and all at once his own life seemed very far away. The pace of the campaign, the constant questions and careful consideration of every word he said, the burning desire to commit himself to doing what he could as a legislator. It wasn't that he could be himself here—he was himself on the campaign trail, too. He saw no point in pretending to be someone he wasn't. But out here, with Antonia, the "doing" part of his life didn't seem to matter so much. He remembered walking the long stretches of Cape Cod beaches as a kid, unaware of the hours ticking by.

But Antonia was obviously caught up in his intrusion into her escape here, into making sure he didn't stumble on whatever it was she was hiding from him. She zipped up her backpack and shoved it under the table, as if she'd marked her territory.

She sat on a chair that looked as if it'd been smuggled out of a sixth-grade classroom from the 1940s and twisted her hands together. "You meant it, didn't you? If I refuse to leave, you'd stay here with me."

"I make it a point to mean most things I say." He shrugged, trying to take any pompous note out of his words. "It's just easier that way. I never was any good at bluffing."

"It's what you leave unsaid—never mind. I'm in a profession where I have to watch my tongue, too. Mean what you say, say what you mean. But you never know what the other person's hearing, do you?"

"Do you have a problem with someone, Antonia?"

But she seemed preoccupied, staring at her hands as if he hadn't spoken, then jumped to her feet and walked out onto the small front porch. Hank didn't follow her. He remained standing in the middle of a thin rug and watched her through the window as she whipped her beach towel off the rail, tossed it over one shoulder and came back inside. "It's raining. I wonder if it's because of the hurricane."

Hank had seen enough fear in his military career to recognize it in someone else, especially someone as unaccustomed to experiencing fear as Antonia was. She was used to being the calm one in the room, the physician who had to concentrate on treating the patient in front of her—who saw fear in others but who couldn't let it affect her. She had a job to do, and her patients counted on her to do it.

Now she was the one who was frightened and fighting for control. He could feel it, see it in her stiff movements, in the way her dark auburn hair hung in her face and her eyes tried to avoid focusing on him for too long. But he'd had years of training and experience, too, that had taught him to push back his own fears and focus on the job at hand, to stay calm when it was necessary. Then later, when he was alone and safe and the job was done, he could fall apart.

He wondered if that was why Antonia hadn't told him about Shelter Island. She'd held herself together because she knew she had these days here coming up, and she could be alone and safe and let herself fall apart now that the job was done.

Had she screwed up with a patient?

No—she was *afraid*. It wasn't regret he was sensing, or self-doubt, or second-guessing. It was fear.

She nodded curtly at him, her tension palpable. "You'll want to check yourself for ticks. You don't want to get Lyme disease."

"Thanks, Doc. I'm from the Cape. I know about ticks and Lyme disease."

"And mosquitoes. Did you get bit on the way over here? West Nile virus can be a nasty business."

He pointed at her and smiled, trying to break through her tension. "A good role model would be in long pants, not a little pair of shorts. At least you're wearing a long-sleeved sweatshirt."

"I know the symptoms of Lyme disease. And West Nile." She seemed to try to go lofty on him, just to tweak him, but couldn't quite pull it off. "Most people who get bit by a mosquito don't get West Nile, and most people who get West Nile don't get its severest form—"

"I'm not worried about getting bit while I'm here," he said. "By a tick or a mosquito."

She gave him a halfhearted scowl. "Do you know how many times I hear something just like that every day? *I didn't think I'd get hit, bit, knifed, shot*—"

"And you didn't think I'd come after you." He stepped toward her, not in any kind of menacing way, just to be closer to her—to get into her space, maybe, and get her to relax with him. "Did you, Antonia?"

Her eyes lifted to him. "Why did you?"

"Because something's wrong, and I want to help."

She nodded. "Fair enough. Thanks for coming." All at once her tone was formal, even awkward, as if he were a fellow doctor on a consultation. She added, in a near mumble, "It really is good to see you."

Bullshit, he thought. But she seemed to sense he was about to pounce and shot over to the cottage's ancient sink, tossing her beach towel over the back of a chair.

Hank sat on the old couch, watching her, decided he'd give her a chance to dig a deeper hole for herself.

Then he'd pounce.

He wasn't sure of much when it came to the lovely Dr. Winter, but he knew whatever was wrong, it wasn't just him, it wasn't just his friendship with the man who'd pulled the rug out from under her sister. They were a part of why she hadn't confided in him, perhaps, but he doubted they were much more than that. Still, he knew he had to proceed cautiously. Antonia was a woman used to dealing with her problems on her own. He was aware of the baggage he carried. There had been days, many days, when he'd thought he'd break under the weight of it, but he hadn't. And he wouldn't.

He'd been attracted to Antonia the minute he'd met her in Cold Ridge last fall, but Tyler's subsequent behavior toward Carine had put a damper on their own budding romance. When they started seeing each other again a few months ago, he'd never meant to go beyond having a drink and raking Ty over the coals with her—he'd had a family once. A wife, a daughter. He'd loved them with all his soul and didn't think he wanted to make that kind of commitment again. Have fun with Antonia. Enjoy her company. Keep his emotions on the surface. Don't go deep, he'd told himself a thousand times.

But here he was, with her because she was in trouble— because, he thought, he was already in deep with her.

"You've left out a few details of this island vacation of yours, haven't you?" he asked.

"I'm working on a difficult article. I needed solitude."

"Medical journal articles make you jumpy and pale? It's not me, is it?"

She shook her head, rinsing off a plate. "No."

He knew it wasn't but thought it was a way to get her

talking. But she didn't go any further, and after a moment, Hank gave up. "Carine thinks you're more like Gus and Nate." Their uncle was an outfitter and guide in the White Mountains, their brother a U.S. Marshal in New York. "You like the thrill of adventure."

"My life's much more ordinary than Carine thinks it is."

"Everyone's life is more ordinary than Carine thinks."

Antonia wiped her hands on a ragged dish towel. "That's because she only has a theoretical idea of what an ordinary life is, never having lived one herself. She'll survive Tyler North—she *is* surviving him. She was so in love with him, though."

"She'll never admit it. She thinks she was possessed by demons."

"Maybe she was." Antonia walked over to the couch and, without warning, sat on his lap, draping her arms over his shoulders. "She doesn't like you."

"She'll get over it. And she used to like me just fine, before Ty drop-kicked her into oblivion. Gus likes me."

"That's saying something. He doesn't like many flatlanders."

Hank laughed. "I impressed him with my mountain-climbing skills last fall."

"It's that you know how to fly a helicopter—he hates them as much as I do. But a rescue helicopter saved his life in Vietnam. He doesn't talk about it. I think it was a marine helicopter." She let her fingers ease up his neck, into his hair. "Which is the real Hank Callahan? The Pave Hawk pilot or the man who would be senator?"

"Different chapters in the same life."

"I like having you here with me. I feel safer with you here. But if you hadn't figured out where I was, I'd have managed on my own. If I didn't—if I capsized kayaking or fell off the porch—it wouldn't be your fault."

He could feel his eyes darkening, but she kept hers on him and didn't turn away. "Antonia—"

"You're not responsible for what happens to me."

"Guilt isn't always rational."

She nodded. "For years, I thought I bore some responsibility for my parents' deaths. If I'd been better, they might not have gone mountain climbing that day. If I'd asked them not to go—if I'd realized the weather was getting colder and they'd be caught up there—"

"You were five years old."

"I know."

"It's not the same—"

"No, it's not the same. You were an air force pilot doing his duty overseas when your wife and daughter were killed. But there was nothing you could do to save them, and there was nothing I could do at five to save my parents." He could see her swallow. "I'm sorry. I have no right—"

"You have every right."

His mouth found hers, and she smiled into the kiss, pulling him down onto the lumpy, quilt-covered couch. He'd thought of this moment for hours. During the drive from Boston to the Cape, during the short boat ride from the mainland. He'd even imagined the pitterpat of raindrops on the roof. But her urgency took him by surprise. Not, he thought, that he was complaining. She slipped her hands under his shirt and smoothed her palms up his sides, even as their kiss deepened.

"I hoped you'd come," she whispered into his mouth. "Not consciously, but—" He eased his hand up her thigh, over her hip, and she inhaled. "Hank..."

He smiled. "We can talk later." Her skin was warm

under his hands, but she had on one of those sports bra things that would take a war plan to get into. "Antonia… hell…"

"Allow me."

She stretched out under him on the couch and lifted off her shirt and the armored sports bra in a couple of swift, efficient moves. Hank caught his breath at the sight of her. "You're the most beautiful—"

"What was it you just said? We can talk later."

A gust of wind rattled the windows and doors. The old cottage creaked and seemed almost to move with the wind, not fighting it. Hank felt the isolation of the place. It was as if he and Antonia were the only two people on the planet. He couldn't even hear the birds over the sounds of the wind and ocean.

He tasted salt on her skin, savored the taste of her, the small moans of pleasure she gave as he took her nipple into his mouth. He didn't rush. It was late afternoon and raining, and they had no other distractions. He pulled her shorts down over her hips and heard her sharp intake of breath when her silky underpants came with them. In a moment, she was naked under him.

She managed to clear her throat. "No—no fair."

But when she touched him, he pulled back, knowing that he'd lose all patience the second he felt her hand on him. "Let's take our time."

She didn't protest, just took a small breath when he slipped one hand between her legs. She was warm, moist, and he doubted either of them would last much longer. When he touched her, there was none of the tentativeness of the first time they'd made love. Her natural reserve fell away, which only emboldened him. He wanted to touch, lick, nibble on every inch of her—and she urged him on, until he couldn't stand it anymore and finally ripped off his own clothes. He had to feel her hand on him. Her mouth. Her tongue. Feel himself inside her.

When he entered her, she stopped breathing. He wondered if he'd hurt her, if he'd thrust too hard, too deep. "I'm okay," she whispered, moving under him. "Don't stop...don't stop."

She matched his rhythm, lost herself in it. He could see it, feel it happen. They rolled onto the floor, where they had more room, and she tried to pause, tried to keep herself from coming first—but it didn't work. He felt her quaking under him. She grabbed his hips and pulled him harder into her, again and again. There was nothing he could do. She filled up all his senses, and he exploded with her, crying out with his release.

A long time later, he managed to pull a thick quilt onto the floor and lay with her on it. He kissed her forehead, realized she was still sweating from him. She looked at him, her blue eyes serious, but not, he thought, because of what they'd just done.

Her voice was a hoarse whisper.

"I think I have a stalker."

Seven

Before she explained, Antonia felt the need to get dressed. She slipped behind the curtain that separated the sleeping alcove from the rest of the cottage and pulled on fresh clothes. Lightweight sweatpants, sweatshirt, athletic socks and sneakers. It was cool in the cottage now that the sun had gone down. She'd never gotten spooked out here by herself—until she'd heard Hank whistling his Disney tune.

She sat on the bed and tried to collect her wits, staring at the pillows and blankets. She'd never spent an entire night with Hank. But he wasn't going anywhere tonight, especially now that she'd told him she might have a stalker.

He'd want to know everything.

Well, she thought, there wasn't all that much to tell.

She rejoined him in the outer room. He was fully dressed and making tea, pouring boiling water from a dented pan into two mismatched mugs. The wind and rain had died down, and Antonia wondered if they were a leading edge of the hurricane or an entirely separate weather system. Hank had the National Weather Service radio on. A static-filled report indicated that Hope had picked up speed but lost a bit of its strength as it hit colder northern waters. It probably would be downgraded to a Category 2 storm by morning, but was still a powerful, dangerous hurricane. A tropical storm watch was up for the Cape and the islands—it would undoubtedly be upgraded to a hurricane watch before morning.

So much for her island refuge, Antonia thought as she sank onto a rickety chair at the table. Hank glanced at her expectantly, and she took in a breath and began. "I've tried hard not to jump to conclusions."

And she told him, as if she were reciting a patient's vital signs to a colleague, about the instant messages, the whispers in the garage, the billowing curtains. Hank didn't interrupt. He just went on making tea.

Finally, she sat back in her chair and sighed. "It's probably just a series of unrelated coincidences."

Hank glanced at her. "Have you ever had strange instant messages?"

"No. I normally don't have instant messages at all. I don't even know how I ended up with that feature on my computer."

He brought her a mug of tea, the tea bag still dangling over the rim. "Have you ever had someone whisper your name in a parking garage?"

She shook her head. "But I could have imagined it—"

"Did whoever it was whisper Antonia or Dr. Winter?"

"*Antonia... Antonia Winter... Dr. Winter.* At least, that's what I heard." She winced, touching the end of the tea bag with one finger—it was one of her tea bags, not one of the ones left in the cottage. "Or think I heard."

"And the curtains—you don't have a cleaning service?"

"No."

He smiled. "Gus's influence. You Winters are all too damned cheap."

"Frugal," she corrected, "not cheap."

"Hair-splitting."

She laughed in spite of her tension and lifted the tea bag out of the mug, setting it on the folded up paper towel Hank had also brought. "I'm not home often enough to make a big mess. And I don't mind cleaning. It makes me feel as if I've accomplished something."

"Unlike sewing an accident victim back together?"

"It's different."

He sat at the end of the table with his own mug of tea. "Did you clean that morning?"

"No."

"The window didn't open itself, Antonia."

"Carine has a key. She might have done it."

"Did you ask her?"

"No." She sipped some of the tea. It was stronger than she normally would make it. "She'd have worried."

"She worried, anyway."

Antonia felt a pang of guilt. "I know. I wish I'd never involved her."

"But you haven't mentioned any of these events to anyone?" Before she could answer, he added seriously, "Not that I'm your stalker, Antonia, and trying to see if you've said anything—"

"Hank! Of course I know you're not this guy, if there even *is* a guy. Anyone. It never occurred to me you could be the one—" She groaned in amazement at the thought of Hank Callahan hiding in a parking garage, whispering her name. "I didn't tell you what was going on because I thought you were responsible, but because—"

"You didn't want to worry me. You were trying to protect me." He leaned toward her, his eyes piercing even in the dimming light. "I don't need protecting, not that kind. I don't care if I'm in a tight campaign race for the senate.

I don't care if I become a senator. If something's going on with you, I want to know about it. Period."

"It's not that simple."

"It *is* that simple."

Most people, she thought, would back down under that kind of certainty and conviction, but Antonia stood her ground. "What if our positions were reversed, and I had a lot of important commitments at work and didn't need any distractions, if you thought you might hurt my reputation—"

He shook his head. "I'm not buying it. You're just not used to telling people anything. You play it close to the vest, Antonia. It's not just me and my reputation, my guilt over what happened to my family—it's you. The way you are."

She paused. "You're probably right," she admitted finally.

His eyes flashed with sudden humor. "Probably?"

She waved a hand at him. "You cocky military types. Honestly. Okay, I didn't know what to do. I'm not sure I realized how rattled I was until you got here and I—"

"Ran for your life?"

"Damn close. Maybe I've been in denial, I don't know. I had this time on the island planned—I hoped it'd all go away by the time I got back to Boston. It still might, you know."

"Or it might not." His outward calm deteriorated, and she could see his jaw tighten. "Damn it, Antonia, what if someone attacked you because you didn't go to the police to save me the embarrassment in case you'd imagined the whole thing? Tell me that."

She drank more of her tea, which was still very hot, and looked at him over the rim of her mug. "You're not responsible for the choices I make."

"That's not what I'm saying, and you know it."

"Frankly, I think I've behaved very sensibly." But her bravado didn't last, and she set her mug down. "I've been so immersed in my education and career for years—I never thought—" She broke off, at a loss for the right words. "Carine wears her heart on her sleeve, but I don't."

"I'm not Gus. I'm not your brother. I'm not Carine. God knows I'm not Tyler North. I don't fit into your life that way. I'm not family, I'm not a friend you've known all your life—"

"Tyler's not a friend anymore."

"He is. You all can't help it. First sign of trouble with one of you, and who did I think to call?"

"Big help he was. *Toe tag.*"

"He gave me the name of the island." Hank drank more of his tea, then leaned back in his chair, eyeing her with a seriousness she found unnerving. "All right. You know what I'm saying. I won't belabor the point. You have any ideas who this stalker might be?"

"If he's real—"

"He's real."

She fought a shiver of fear, uneasiness. "I brought a disk with recent patient records on it. I get my fair share of difficult cases. Crime victims, crime perpetrators, psychiatric patients—I thought something might jog my memory, make sense to me."

"No luck?"

"Not yet. I don't think whoever it is wants to hurt me. If he did, he's had plenty of opportunities."

Hank shook his head. "Just because he hasn't hurt you yet doesn't mean he won't. He could be toying with you—"

"The cat with the mouse."

Hank didn't answer, and she got to her feet, feeling

the darkness all around her, just the one naked 80-watt bulb penetrating the pitch black. Antonia debated lighting the kerosene lamps. She didn't even know what time it was. Past dinnertime, for sure. She was faintly hungry but knew she couldn't eat.

"I thought coming here would at least help me clarify my options." She didn't look at Hank as she tried to put words to the conflicting thoughts and emotions she'd experienced the past week. "Call hospital security, don't call hospital security. Call the police, don't call the police."

"Tell me, don't tell me."

There was no hurt in his voice—he was under tight control. She didn't flinch, made herself turn and look at him. "That's right."

He was on his feet, and before she knew what was happening, he had her in his arms. He held her shoulders. "Antonia, listen to me. When you look at me, I don't want you to see a senator or an air force officer, or a man who's lost his family and can't bear to be hurt again—I want you to see me. Just me. Do you understand that?"

"I do, Hank, but you're all of those things. You can't separate—"

"What I can't do is let someone I care about put herself in danger because of me. I can't have a woman I'm in love with hold back on me because she's trying to protect me."

She was too stricken to speak.

"I *am* in love with you. I know it's awkward as hell. My timing couldn't be worse with your sister's botched wedding, my campaign, this mess you're in, but—" He stopped, letting his hands slide down her back, his mouth find hers in a kiss that was brief, fierce and impossibly tender, leaving her breathless, even more out of control. When he pulled away, he smacked her on the butt and smiled. "Talk to me next time, okay?"

"I was trying to do the right thing. You know that, don't you?"

"You're a Winter, Antonia. You're a natural risk-taker. Take a risk with me. *Talk* to me."

"I will, but tell me something first, Hank. You say you're in love with me. I don't mind, because I've been in love with you since I saw you in front of Carine's wood-stove. But are you fighting it?"

He stared at her a moment, then didn't answer. "What do you have in here for supper?"

"Hank—"

"The only thing I'm fighting is whether I'd rather eat dinner now or make love to you now."

He'd wormed his way under her defenses, until she could only laugh. "First things first. Always."

Eight

∽⟋◠◡◠⟍∾

A hurricane watch went up overnight for Cape Cod and the islands. Mandatory and voluntary evacuation orders had been posted for vulnerable areas. Hope remained a Category 2 hurricane and looked as if it would hit the Cape before it made its expected turn east.

No one, Hank thought, would be concerned about the one cottage left on Shelter Island, even if they thought of it. The spits of sand along the elbow of Cape Cod had been rearranging themselves for millennia and would again with this storm. Shelter Island could take an entirely different shape by the time Hope blew over. North Monomoy and South Monomoy Island were formed in the notorious blizzard of 1978, when the single main island split into two islands. Both were part of the Eastern Massachusetts National Wildlife Refuge Complex, eight ecologically diverse refuges that provided habitat, resting and feeding grounds for a wide variety of plants and animals, in addition to birds.

Hank hoisted his backpack onto one shoulder, Antonia's onto the other as they set off across the narrow island. If the powerful winds and surf and torrential rains of Hurricane Hope rearranged these stretches of sand again, at least he and Antonia wouldn't be around while it happened.

They took a twisting path through stunted pitch pine and patches of juniper, low-growing wild blueberry bushes, the ever-present bearberry and beach grasses. It was just spitting rain, but the wind had kicked up, and he could hear the waves pounding the shoreline. Antonia would never have made it across the narrow inlet to the mainland in her kayak. The inlet wasn't as choppy as the Sound, but, as they walked out onto the beach, which was just down from a fertile salt marsh, he noticed the white-caps. Even with the stiff, steady wind at her back, she'd be lucky to keep herself afloat, never mind on course.

She'd put on jeans, a polo shirt and a windbreaker for their ride back to the mainland and seemed less strained and preoccupied. Hank liked to think it was his pres-ence. She'd finally told someone about her unsettling in-cidents—he thought their lovemaking might have helped a little, too. He smiled to himself, but noticed her frown as she paused at the water's edge. "Where's your boat?" she asked.

Hank hadn't even thought about his boat, just assumed it'd be where he left it. But it wasn't. He squinted out at the water, seeing only whitecaps and seagulls against the graying sky. Where the island's myriad of birds were, he didn't know—it was as if they'd all vanished ahead of the hurricane. "It should be right here," he said. "I dropped anchor just off shore."

"Maybe it pulled loose."

"It should have held, even in this weather. Damn it, I grew up in a marina. I know how to secure a boat."

"But you spent all those years in the air force tinker-ing with helicopters."

"Tinkering?"

"It's not like you were in the Navy or the Coast Guard." But Antonia's halfhearted attempt at humor didn't seem to work even with her, and she abandoned it. "I don't know what to say. Now what? I still have my flares. We can always try to alert a passing boat."

Hank continued to gaze out at the water, not liking this development, then glanced at her. "Where's your kayak?"

"We can't both take it. It's just a one-person kayak—"

"Antonia, I didn't make a mistake. My boat should be here, and it's not." He studied her, her skin quickly going pale again, ghostly, her eyes taking on the strain he'd seen in her yesterday when he'd first arrived. Her muscles were visibly tight, and he guessed she was thinking along the same lines as he was—that his boat wasn't missing by accident. "You know I didn't screw up, don't you?"

"My kayak's over here off the beach."

She hoisted her backpack high onto her shoulder and, with a nod of pure determination, set off across the wet sand, back along a sloping dune. Hank followed her with the two other packs, and she led him into a stand of pitch pine.

"Mind the poison ivy," she said, pointing to a vine of it streaming up one of the pines.

Her kayak was tucked among the trees. It was a sleek red touring kayak, obviously expensive, obviously new. Fat drops of rain splattered on its unscratched finish. Hank noticed rain shining on Antonia's hair, felt it splatting on his shoulder, the top of his head. Except for the occasional lull as the storm moved north, the weather conditions would get worse—far worse—before they got better.

"The paddle." She almost couldn't get the words out and had to pause to clear her throat. "Hank, the paddle's not here."

"You left it with the boat?"

She nodded.

"When?"

"When I arrived. I haven't been back here."

He turned over the long, narrow kayak, but the paddle wasn't under it. Antonia checked the brush and the surrounding area without success. Hank absorbed what had transpired so far—his boat gone, her kayak paddle gone.

"Maybe the wind blew the paddle away," she said lamely, then sighed, some of her physician's calm and decisiveness restoring itself. "If someone finds your boat adrift, there might be enough time for them to launch a search before the hurricane gets here."

"It won't be that easy to put the pieces together. The boat belongs to friends of mine in Chatham. They said I could borrow it anytime, and I did. They're in Prague right now. It'll take a while for authorities to sort all that out."

Antonia digested his explanation without any evidence of increased anxiety. "Given the conditions, it wouldn't be unreasonable for them to think the boat pulled loose prematurely and no one was in it. I hope that's the case. Better you messed up than—"

"I didn't mess up. Someone scuttled my boat and took your paddle."

She swallowed, nodding. "I know."

"It means we're not alone."

Robert swore viciously. He was in agony. His skin was burning, itching, covered in lumps and bumps and oozing crusts. Now thorns were pricking his arms and back from the rosebush behind the bitch doctor's cottage.

Just what he needed, more shit gnawing on him.

He was covered in bites and red welts. The humidity was building in ahead of the storm, and he couldn't stand it in his poncho—it was like a damn steam bath, and sweating made him itch and burn even more. He couldn't think. He couldn't plan. But he didn't see what choice he had, and he put his poncho back on, just for protection from the thorns and the bugs. He'd given up on the deer ticks. One ankle was damn near black with them. He'd just have to get some antibiotics when he returned to the mainland. Maybe he could get Dr. Antonia to write him a prescription before he killed her.

Meanwhile, bring on the Lyme disease.

At least he was well-armed against the bitch doctor and the stud boyfriend. It had nearly killed him last night, knowing the two of them were in the cottage. But now he had no illusions whatsoever. He had no doubts. He didn't have to second-guess himself. He'd done the right thing, stalking her, sneaking out here with his Smith & Wesson. Deep down, he knew it would come to killing her. And killing the wannabe senator, too. It was why he'd kept picturing her begging for her life. Because it was the right thing to do. It was necessary.

The bitch doctor would never let him into her orbit.

He was a nonentity to her. He didn't have the nuisance value of even one of the ticks stuck to his leg, sucking his blood, spreading disease. He was just the floor-mopper who showed up for work every day and once, for reasons that she must have thought didn't concern her, had arrived in the E.R. for treatment.

Well, the instant messages, the spooky way he'd whispered to her in the garage and left her bedroom window open, cutting up her underwear—that all had more than deer-tick-level nuisance value. But she didn't know it was him. She didn't even know he'd slashed up her silky underthings. She didn't know he was the one who'd set Superman Callahan's boat adrift, who'd stolen her paddle, who was out here now, plotting his next move.

That was paramount, he thought. She *had* to know it was him. He couldn't just sneak up on her and gun her down. There was no satisfaction in that, no real justice. Damn it, he wanted credit.

"What's this?"

It looked like a knife handle. He pulled on it, and realized it was a five-inch carving knife. A signal from God! The green light!

Here's another weapon, Mr. Prancer. Do what must be done.

Amen!

Robert wiped the blade clean on his wet pants. Another length of thorn-studded rosebush backhanded him in the face and ripped a trail of scratches across his cheek. It was all he could do not to start hacking at the goddamn bush with his new knife.

Patience, he reminded himself. He had to remember what he was here to do—it wasn't getting all pissed off at a rosebush.

Crouching down, he undid the paddle so that it was in two parts. Too easy to end up smacking himself in the head when it was one long paddle, but one of the halves he could maneuver easily. He pictured himself jumping up out of nowhere and whacking Callahan on the side of the head with it—Robert didn't mind if the wannabe senator never knew what hit him.

A paddle, a gun, a knife. Not bad.

It was his own damn fault he was under the rosebush and not in the cottage. He'd decided to follow his two hostages—even if they didn't know it yet, they were his hostages as far as he was concerned. He wanted to see the looks on their faces when they discovered they were stuck on the island for the duration—when they realized they weren't alone.

Keeping them from hearing him wasn't a problem with the wind, the rain, the ocean. It was keeping them from seeing him that almost tripped him up. Not a lot of tall trees to hide behind out here. Once, he'd had to burrow down in the bird shit.

He sank the boat last night just after dark. It wasn't easy, either. He'd had to wade out into the water and beat a hole in the bottom with the anchor. He'd cut his hand. He'd been tempted to shoot the damn thing, but he didn't dare risk alerting his hostages to his presence prematurely. Mr. Military Man would recognize gunfire when he heard it.

And Robert didn't just want to set the boat adrift—for all he knew, it could float back to shore. He wanted it at the bottom of the ocean.

Even when the damn thing filled up with water, it didn't go down fast. He'd sat out there in the dark, mosquitoes chewing on him as he watched the boat float out into the inlet and slowly sink.

By the time he reached his campsite, he was covered with at least a hundred mosquito bites. He wondered if Dr. Antonia would treat him if he broke out in a fever or got West Nile or malaria or something. She *had* to. It would be unethical not to. Illegal, even. She was the one who'd told him she had to report his gunshot wound to the police.

The looks on their faces when they discovered the boat was gone—it had been worth it. They were back in the cottage by the time he'd slipped back across the island, but that was okay. He still had time, and he liked the idea that they had a few minutes to fret, try to put the pieces together, come to terms with the gravity of their situation.

It did suck. He wondered if they had any idea just how much it did, in fact, suck.

The cottage broke some of the wind coming off the Sound, but it was raining again, not a soft, gentle rain, either. Robert was already tired of it, but knew it'd only get worse.

He had to get his final plan together, but he couldn't think with all the distractions of his pain, his itching, his delight in imagining the two of them scared shitless just a few yards away.

The back door creaked open.

Robert sank low, not breathing, as Hank Callahan walked out onto the back steps.

Superman Hank. He didn't look as if he'd been fretting. He looked like some kind of sniper on the lookout. He had an alert, military feel about him that Robert didn't like at all.

Bastard. The arrogant *bastard*.

He should be quivering! Scared out of his mind!

Robert felt his nostrils flare, like he was a pissed off bull in a rodeo or something. "Screw it." He didn't know if he spoke out loud, didn't care. He wasn't taking any more chances with this puke—time to put the major out of commission. "Yeah. Screw it."

Without further angsting, Robert raised one half of the kayak paddle in one hand and the knife in the other and leaped out from the sprawling rosebush, thorns ripping harmlessly across his poncho. He slipped in the wet grass, but didn't fully lose his footing as he lunged for the back steps.

Callahan was looking in the opposite direction. The wind and the ocean were making so much noise, Robert was able to get a split second jump on him.

Flawlessly, in one effective motion, he hit the major in the kidneys with the paddle.

It was like hitting a tree trunk.

Robert was stunned. "Fuck!"

He'd planned to follow up with a knife in the heart, but

Superman Callahan didn't even go down on his knees. He absorbed the blow and swung around fast and hard, his entire body poised for the fight. Major Stud knew how to handle himself in battle. That was clear. Robert did not. He was a floor-mopper—he used to get the shit kicked out of him at school. He could feel the old panic welling up in his throat.

He slashed the knife wildly, catching Callahan in the upper arm.

Next thing, the major had the kayak paddle. Robert had no idea how the bastard had gotten it. He could feel himself breaking out in a sweat under his flapping poncho. Now what?

His gun—damn, it wasn't in his waistband under his poncho. He must have dropped it behind the goddamn rosebush!

He pointed the knife at the major. Stand off. Robert knew if he went after Callahan, he'd get the kayak paddle up the side of his head. On the other hand, if the wannabe senator went after him, he'd get the knife up whatever Robert could reach first.

"You don't want me to kill you now," Robert said, like he had the definite upper hand and didn't realize it was a standoff. "Then the bitch doctor will be at my mercy."

They were both drenched, fighting the wind. Puddles formed at their feet. The grass was so slippery, it made it almost impossible to get any decent traction. If he fell, Robert figured he'd end up stabbing himself. Then he'd bleed to death. The doctor wouldn't help him now that he'd stabbed her stud boyfriend and nailed him in the kidneys. Forget the Hippocratic Oath. Forget the law. She'd let him bleed to death in the sand. Pretend Hope had done the damage.

That would be it for him. The end of the story. There'd be no revenge, no justice, no satisfaction.

"The storm's hitting," Callahan said, ignoring his bleeding arm as he kept a tight, menacing grip on the paddle. "You don't want to be out here. Put down the knife—"

"So you can kill me and tell the police it was self-defense? Hell, no."

The major didn't react. It was amazing. Talk about control. "What's your name?" he asked, all tight-lipped.

"Fuck you."

"Come on. Put down the knife. You haven't hurt anyone yet."

"You."

"Not that much. I'll let it go if you put down the knife and come inside with me. The hurricane—"

"I'm not worried about the hurricane."

But Robert glanced up at the cottage. The bitch doctor was there in the screen door. *So beautiful.* Damn, it wasn't easy to be strong and go through with what he knew he had to do.

He wasn't going to beat Callahan in a fair fight.

That left him two choices, Robert thought. Surrender, or get the hell out of there.

He wasn't surrendering.

He turned abruptly and ran away from the cottage, leaping through the brush and sand and bird shit, hoping he didn't slip and stab himself in the heart. Another bad ending to the story. No ending at all, accidentally stabbing himself to death.

But he didn't slip, and he hung on to the knife, so at least he could defend himself if Callahan followed him.

He didn't look upon himself as retreating. In a way, he'd accomplished his original mission. Callahan wasn't dead, maybe not even entirely out of commission, but he was hurting. He knew Robert meant business.

They'd both be scared now.

Robert pushed through pine trees and junipers and splashed through ankle-deep puddles, then rolled down his big dune on the other side of his campsite.

Christ Almighty. The ocean was there.

A monstrous wave caught him and knocked him backward on his ass. He choked on saltwater and rain, the wind tearing at his clothes, kicking up sand that ate away his skin. He screamed in agony and frustration, letting it all out, knowing no one could hear him, and scrambled up the dune, back down to his campsite on the other side. He didn't have long before the water would reach it.

The red welts on his hands and forearms were on fire. He thought he'd go out of his mind.

Fuck. They weren't bug bites. He had poison ivy. It bubbled and oozed and burned and itched and swelled. No wonder he hadn't managed to give Callahan a knockdown blow! He was a goddamn mess!

Robert managed to stand upright, but he could see that the sky and the sea and the landscape were all a greenish-gray now, the wind gusting hard enough to lift him off his feet. He could taste the tropics in the air, feel the cloying humidity sucking at him.

And this wasn't even the full brunt of the hurricane.

Jesus.

He had to get back to the rosebush and find his gun. He dug in his pack and checked his ammo. Twelve bullets. That was it. He wished he had a machine gun, but his .38 and a dozen bullets would have to do. He still hoped he wouldn't need to shoot them, not with a perfectly good hurricane on its way.

Snorting, trying not to scratch, or scream again, he

made his way back to the cottage and took up position in the scrub pine, never mind the water dripping off the tangle of poison ivy. Why worry about poison ivy now?

The good doctor would be tending the major's wounds.

Robert knew he had to act now, while they were distracted.

He gulped in a breath and dove for the rosebush.

His gun was still there, in the sopping grass. Leave it to the two losers inside not to know he'd left it behind. He cocked it, so that all he had to do was pull the trigger and a bullet would zip out. He knew just enough about guns and shooting to be dangerous, he decided. Not that he'd ever had any instruction in firearms. He figured any idiot could handle a gun, and since he was smarter than most people, he wouldn't have any trouble. He had no patience with learning things, practicing—he liked just to know them.

He retreated back to his position in the pines. He was drenched. Mad with itching. He used his thumbs to get the rain out of his eyes, figured he was spreading poison ivy into his eyes and pretty soon they'd be swollen and itching, too. But he could see okay now and peered at the cottage. It had two windows on this side, a bunch of lilac bushes—he could see the front porch and the back steps from his vantage point. He didn't worry about the one side he couldn't see, because it had no windows.

But if he could see them make a move, they could see him. It wasn't another standoff since he was the only one with a gun.

Presumably, he thought. He wasn't about to stick his head up and get it blown off. Not the best way to find out for sure they were unarmed. But a doctor? A guy running for the senate, out here after the doctor, no idea she was in trouble? Nah. They didn't have a gun.

"I've got you covered." Even to himself, he sounded like a maniacal John Wayne. "You have no way out. Stick your foot out a door or a window, I'll blow it off. Your head? Same thing."

No response. He wondered if they'd heard him. If they were in there, cowering. He could do it, he thought. He could shoot Antonia's foot off. He was a good enough shot—why wouldn't he be?—and he'd waited long enough to see her bleeding and in pain.

"Scared?" He waited, but still no answer. "Good. I hope you are. I was scared when I came to the bitch doctor for help. How about it, Dr. Winter? Suppose I give you the same treatment you gave me? How'd you like that?"

He remembered her slender hands on him as she'd examined him. Her soft, kind words. He'd trusted her, believed in her. He thought she'd finally open up to him. He assumed she'd recognized him.

But she didn't. She'd asked him his name, as if she'd never seen him before, and even before she turned him in to the cops, he knew he'd misplaced his trust and affection.

He was a nobody to her. A zero.

Then he thought—hell, she and the boyfriend didn't know he had a gun. They didn't know they had to take him seriously.

"In case you doubt me, here's a little taste of your future!"

Robert fired a bullet into the side window, the gun kicking back the way it had when he'd shot himself in the foot. The loud bang startled him. The wind was howling so much, he didn't hear the old glass in the window shatter. But he saw it, and smiled.

He didn't know what he'd do next, but right now, he had the big important doctor and her hero boyfriend under his total control.

Nine

The wind blew water and bits of leaves and twigs in through the shot-out window above the sink. The bullet had lodged in the bathroom door. It hadn't hit anyone, no thanks, Hank thought, to the son of a bitch outside. Why the hell take a potshot at them? Just to scare them? Why not burst into the cottage and shoot them both, before they realized he had a gun?

Whoever the guy was outside, he had his own agenda, his own way of thinking—but now that they knew he had a gun, Hank realized, they had a chance. Staying low, out of the bastard's line of sight, his arm bleeding from the knife wound, his back aching from the hit with the kayak paddle, he and Antonia had quickly barricaded the front door with an overstuffed chair and the back door with a couple of extra folding chairs. Their handiwork wouldn't stop an intruder with a gun, but it'd give them warning, trip him up so Hank could act. He had a knife of his own now, as well as the kayak paddle and the determination not to be taken by surprise a second time.

But he didn't think Antonia was up to any kind of combat, and he hoped it wouldn't come to going after the man outside—killing him—in front of her.

Despite her obvious fear, she stayed calm and, once they'd secured themselves as best they could inside the cottage, insisted on bandaging his arm. "Fine," Hank said, "provided I can keep an eye out for our friend."

She nodded. "If I were him, I'd hide in the trees along the edge of the side yard. That way I could see both entrances and the windows. Since he shot the window above the sink—"

"It makes sense."

They moved the table down along the wall so that Hank could sit at one end and still have a view of most of the side yard, without exposing himself in the window.

Antonia set an ancient first-aid kit she'd pulled out from under the bed on the table and rummaged in it. He could see her tension, but knew she had the training and experience to focus on what she was doing. "You should have stitches."

Hank grunted. His arm throbbed, but he'd endured worse injuries. "I should have fed the bastard that goddamn knife."

"Ty would have."

"North's trained to feed people knives." Hank smiled, because he knew she'd deliberately made that comment to get him to smile. The doctor easing her patient's mind. "I'm just a mild-mannered helicopter pilot."

"Ah." She found a tube of antibiotic ointment and squeezed a bit onto a supposedly sterile gauze pad—the stuff had to be long past its "use by" date. "That's *just* what I thought when I saw you take the kayak paddle from our friend outside. Mild-mannered helicopter pilot."

"Scared the hell out of you, didn't he?"

"Yes. He has a gun—"

"I know, but first he has to get to us."

She glanced at him. "You're not saying we have the upper hand, are you?"

"I'm saying right now we're okay. First things first, Antonia. We're doing everything we can."

If possible, she was even more pale, but she wasn't one to panic. "Let's see this arm of yours."

She helped him get his shirt off, and he'd been touched when she blanched at his injury—not because she didn't see worse every day, Hank assumed, but because this time it was him. She worked quickly and efficiently. He watched her, noticed that her hands were steady as she swabbed and dabbed and bandaged.

"You won't have to amputate if I don't get stitches, will you?" he asked lightly.

"Only if you get a nasty infection and we can't get to proper help."

"Thanks, Doc. I appreciate a straight answer. You're supposed to say no, you'll be fine."

She managed a smile. "No, you'll be fine."

He moved his arm the wrong way and caused himself a stab of pain. "Now I feel a lot better," he said with good-natured sarcasm. He wasn't worried about his arm. He'd done worse working on boats as a kid. What he worried about was the bastard outside with the gun. He peered through the rain and wind, but saw no sign of their guy. "I can't believe I let that SOB nail me."

Antonia taped a gauze bandage over the ointment-covered wound with a few deft moves. "You're lucky. The cut's not deep, which is a good thing. I'm not set up here for major wounds and fractures."

It didn't look to Hank as if she was set up for three-inch superficial knife wounds, either, but he liked the feel of her fingers on his skin. "I should at least have followed him," he said. "I don't think he had his gun on him when he came after me. I could have kept him from getting it—"

"What if you were wrong and he did have the gun? What if you'd passed out?"

"I wouldn't have passed out."

She added one last piece of tape, then waited, appraising her handiwork, he assumed. "Ty not only could take on this guy outside, but he could bandage your wound. He jumps out of helicopters with a fifty-pound med ruck strapped to him—"

"I know. He jumped out of my helicopter enough times."

She nodded absently, and he could tell her mind wasn't on Tyler North or helicopters, or even Hank's wound now that it was bandaged. She wasn't trying to distract him anymore. She was trying to distract herself. She peeked out the window. "Tell me what he looked like to you," she said quietly.

"You saw him—"

"I didn't get a close look—I was more worried about you. And you're objective. I'm not. Not if it's who I think it is."

Hank didn't push her for more information. "White male in his mid-twenties. Five-eight. Blond. Clean-shaven. His hair was medium-blond, curly, long enough to put in a ponytail if he wanted to. He was quick—quicker than you'd expect at first glance."

"Physically, you mean?"

"Yes. Mentally, I'd say he's a survivor. He wanted me to think about what would happen if I went after him and didn't succeed—I fell for it. It distracted me long enough for him to clear out."

"If not for the hurricane—"

"I'd have his ass."

Antonia smiled faintly, but was still clearly distracted.

She nodded at his bandaged arm. "I can't vouch for the ointment, but the bandage is just about perfect. How's the pain?"

"I hurt more where he smacked me with your kayak paddle."

She didn't smile. "There's not much I can do about that with anything Babs has left behind. Just let me know if you pee blood."

"Sure, Doc, I'll do that." He rolled his eyes, but he couldn't make her smile again. "I can take on bad guys if I have to?"

"I have plenty of bandages."

He winked at her. "That's the spirit."

"Hank—"

"We'll get out of this mess, Antonia." He got to his feet, avoiding standing near a window, and slipped his shirt back on. It was damp and bloody, but he was running out of dry clothes. "You recognize this guy, don't you?"

She sighed, nodding reluctantly. "It's Robert Prancer."

Hank had never heard her mention the name before. He was sure he'd have remembered if she had. "Is it a guess, or are you positive?"

"I'm positive. The knife—" She lifted her eyes to him. They were doctor-serious. "I should tell you that it was my knife. I grabbed it when I heard you whistling. It made sense at the time."

"You thought I might be this Prancer character."

"I didn't have him in mind as a suspect at the time. He's one of perhaps a dozen names that I jotted down to look into—patients I'd treated in the past few weeks."

"Who is he?"

But he doubted she'd even heard him. "I thought I'd covered my tracks, so that no one could follow me from

Boston. I didn't tell anyone where I was going. I even borrowed Carine's car."

"That all makes sense now that I know—"

"But I—I had no idea. I hid behind the rosebush out back. It seems ridiculous now."

"Imagine if it'd been Prancer instead of me," Hank said. "Not so ridiculous after all."

"You're probably right, but when I look at your arm—" She didn't finish the thought. "I didn't want to look silly when I realized it was you whistling, so I stuck the knife in the sand and forgot about it."

Hank shrugged. "Prancer could just have easily got it out of the sink while we were on the other side of the island. Hell, we're lucky we didn't find him hiding under the bed when we got back. He's probably kicking himself for not thinking of it now that he's outside and we're in here."

Her eyes settled on him. "I'm sorry."

He stood to one side of the back door and looked outside, but saw no sign of Prancer. "If he hadn't had the knife and the kayak paddle, he might have used his gun on me instead of the window. Maybe the knife's what saved my life. Antonia—this guy—"

"I treated him for a gunshot wound to his left foot. I had to report him to the police."

Hank nodded. "It's the law."

"I don't think he realized that. It's surprising how many people don't. He wouldn't tell me what happened—the wound was almost certainly self-inflicted. I sent him for X-rays, and he took off from the X-ray room. I don't know how he managed it. He was in a johnny, he was on an IV, he had a bullet wound in his foot—he must have pulled out the IV himself."

Hank pictured the lunatic who'd come after him and

could see him pulling out his own IV, running off with a bullet wound in his foot. "How long ago was this?"

"Three weeks? Maybe less. The police caught up with him out in the parking garage. I don't know what made him think he'd get away, not with that injured foot." Antonia groaned, tense, frustrated. And scared, Hank thought. More scared than she wanted to admit, possibly because she knew the guy outside. "He works at the hospital. He's on the cleaning crew. Hank, I have the greatest respect for the people who clean—"

"That's not what this is about, Antonia. It's about some sick ideas he has about you, not any ideas you have about him."

"I understand he's very intelligent, but he can't get along with people. I didn't recognize him at first when I was treating him—I was focused on what I was doing. Then I played it cool. I wasn't sure what was going on. I didn't want to embarrass him or make his situation worse. It was an awkward moment, to say the least."

"Think he has a crush on you?"

Color rose in her cheeks, which Hank took as a good sign. "It's possible. I'm usually oblivious to that sort of thing."

"Then not only did you betray him by turning him in to the police, you betrayed him by going out with me. And now if he can't have you—"

She shuddered. "I know. That's what I've been thinking. I just wish it didn't have to involve you. You're getting swept up in something that has nothing to do with you."

"If it involves you, it has everything to do with me."

She said nothing.

He grinned at her. "At a loss for words, Dr. Winter?"

"You amaze me," she said. "I have a feeling you always will."

Hank buttoned his shirt, feeling the throb in his upper arm where Prancer had nicked him. It could have been worse. He didn't want to think about what would have happened if Prancer had managed to incapacitate him. If he'd done the sensible thing and shot him on the back steps. "It doesn't help to try to figure this guy out at this point, does it? He's operating according to his own logic. Did you save his life?"

"I cleaned his wound, which probably kept him from getting a nasty infection, but that's unpredictable. Otherwise—no, I can't say I saved his life."

"He came in on his own?"

"He called for an ambulance himself."

"He wanted you to treat him. It could have been a ploy for attention and sympathy."

A strong gust of wind shook the cottage and rattled the windows, and more debris and water blew in through the shot-up window. They'd have to do something about it or they'd end up with the whole Sound in on them. The National Weather Service radio was just static now, but Hank thought it was a fair bet the Cape and the islands were under a hurricane warning at this point—Hope was moving fast.

"We should concentrate on getting through this hurricane," Antonia said. "At least Prancer won't have a chance to surprise us again."

Hank grabbed her beach towel and, staying low, stuffed it in the blow-out window above the sink. "Damn straight."

"If we can't get off this island, neither can Robert." Her voice was less strained, and he knew she was focused on what they had to do now—not what she'd done, or should have done, weeks ago. "He's not going to want to stay outside in a hurricane, not when he's the one with the gun."

"Then we have to get to him first."

Ten

Robert was up to his ankles in water. High tide, torrential rains, storm surge. Fierce wind that never stopped. He didn't know if it was Hope or the leading edge of Hope or what, but he had no intention of staying outside one minute longer than was necessary. Babs Winslow's little cottage awaited him, he thought, wrapping himself in his camouflage-style poncho. He'd also managed to grab a bright blue tarp that'd blown off the cottage porch and wrapped up in it, too.

He felt like he was in a body bag, but a part of him also savored his misery. His suffering would make killing the two in the cottage that much more satisfying.

Killing someone should have its costs. Granny had told him that the best things came with sacrifice and commitment, even suffering.

The rain and humidity were intolerable. He was clammy, sweating inside the poncho and tarp. He might as well have been breathing water. He coughed, tasting salt, and looked around for any dry ground where he could think straight and put together his plan of attack.

"Robert! Robert Prancer!"

He went still, crouching down low under the tree. It

was Antonia Winter, calling his name as if in a dream. He stopped breathing and listened over the sounds of the rain and wind. She knew him now. She realized he was the one out here with the gun. The one who'd attacked her stud boyfriend.

Yes, Robert thought, he was in her thoughts now. He wasn't just some mindless, nameless attacker on the loose. He was Robert Prancer. She could picture him, even if it was with his goddamn mop.

Perfect.

He couldn't see her through the blinding rain. Was she calling him from the back door? A window? He doubted she was at the front door, not with the porch in the way—he'd never hear her over the howling wind, the crashing surf, the lashing rain. What a mess.

"Robert, you can't stay out there."

Although she had to yell to be heard over the oncoming hurricane, she managed to sound concerned, reasonable. But she was an E.R. doctor. She was good at faking concern and reason.

He didn't answer her. The hell with her. This wasn't a dream. This was a ploy on her part. She was trying to play to his weakness for her.

"Hurricane Hope is hitting us," she continued. "It'll only get worse. Robert, you'll be killed if you don't take cover."

"What do you care?" he yelled, despite his resolve to keep his mouth shut.

He knew he was giving away his position. Didn't matter. She and Callahan weren't going to do anything. He was the one out in the goddamn hurricane, and he was the one with the gun. They weren't going to seize the lead from him. What happened next was *his* choice.

"I'm a doctor, but I'm also your colleague at the hospital. I know how hard you work—"

"Fuck you! You don't know anything about me! You'll celebrate if I'm dead!"

He sounded like a head case. He winced, pulling the tarp more tightly around him, the rain pelting on it, bouncing off. He had to *think*. If he stormed the cottage—gun or no gun—they'd see him coming and set up a defense. Ambush him some way. He needed to create a distraction, then move in when they weren't looking. A Molotov cocktail. Homemade napalm. Something like that. Firebomb the cottage. His hostages would have to deal with the fire, and he could move in with the gun.

He'd just have to be careful not to burn down the place. Talk about cutting off your nose to spite your face.

Where could he get the fixings for a Molotov cocktail? A bottle. Some gasoline. Dry fabric for a wick.

But the bitch doctor hadn't given up. "Robert, please. Let's talk before we get in any deeper. I know you're here because of me." He thought he could hear her hesitation. Her regret. "Because of a mistake I made. Come inside. We'll ride out the hurricane together."

Was she serious? Had his actions helped her to see the light? Robert edged out of his cover of pines, the blue tarp trailing after him like a bridal train or a king's robe. The poncho hood wouldn't stay on his head. He was soaked, rain pouring down his face and neck, and the poison ivy and bug bites were driving him insane. He could feel his .38 tucked in his waistband and realized he didn't much like toting a gun.

Visibility sucked with all the rain and wind. Dr. Winter and Superman Callahan couldn't possibly see him.

"If I come in," Robert yelled, "you and Callahan are my hostages!"

"We are, anyway. Robert, you can't stay out there. You can't!"

That last sounded like she was desperate to save him. Like she didn't want his death on her conscience.

Did she care, now that she knew it was him out here, drowning, in danger of being swept into the ocean? Maybe Callahan didn't look so good to her, now that Robert had taken him on, drawn a little of his blood.

But he fought back any sympathy for her. Who did she think she was, inviting him to join her inside? Offering up herself and her boyfriend as hostages? Like she had the upper hand. *He* had the fucking upper hand.

He paused, fighting the poncho and the tarp so he could get to his gun, get it and his hand out in the open where he could start shooting. Did she really think he was so stupid he wouldn't use the advantage he had? Stay out here when he could shoot them both dead and make himself a nice cup of tea and ride out the hurricane in the cottage?

He could kill her and Superman Callahan without reloading. Just do it. Get it over with.

No more fooling around.

Robert had no intention of waiting out a hurricane with two hostages who'd be looking for any advantage, any opening to slit his throat. No way. Forget letting the storm kill them. Forget prolonging the pleasure of their misery. They had to die now. *He* had to do it.

Then he'd have the cottage to himself. After Hope, he'd find a way out of there before anyone found the two bodies he left behind.

He used the lack of visibility to his advantage and headed toward the cottage, gun drawn, ready to fire.

The wind grabbed the front door and almost ripped it off its hinges, but Hank was prepared and managed to latch it before it gave him away. He stayed low, out of Robert Prancer's line of fire. He seemed to be in the line of trees off to the side of the cottage. A good position, one that he could hold indefinitely if not for the oncoming hurricane.

Inside the cottage, Antonia knew what to do. Hank didn't like it, but they'd agreed that Prancer would go on the attack—he wouldn't remain outside in the hurricane. He'd risk everything, and he'd kill them this time. His little cat-and-mouse game was over. All he needed was the right opening.

Hank had the half a kayak paddle he'd appropriated in one hand and a kitchen knife, not as good as the one Prancer still had, in the other. If he got close enough to Prancer, it'd be a fight, at least.

He heard a shot out back.

It didn't startle him or concern him, because he was confident Antonia had done her part and poked open the back door with a broom handle. Prancer, as they'd predicted, had responded to the provocation by firing, instead of waiting until he saw an actual person. If nothing else, it meant he wasn't worried about running out of ammunition.

As backup, Antonia also had a pan of water boiling on the tiny cottage stove. If Hank failed in doing his part and Prancer got into the cottage, she'd throw it on him. She was a doctor. She'd know how and where she could do the most damage, should she be required to act in self-defense. But she wouldn't unless she had no other choice. She treated the results of violence. She didn't cause violence.

Pushing aside his misgivings, Hank focused on the task at hand, letting his years of training and combat missions kick in, take over. He stepped into the swirling water and sand at the bottom of the porch steps. Rain lashed at him, and the roar of the ocean and wind surrounded him—he meant to use all of it to his advantage. The noise, the lack of visibility, the sense of urgency. Robert Prancer couldn't be in a good place right now, mentally or physically.

Hank edged around to the back of the cottage, using the lilacs and the weather for concealment.

"Antonia! Bitch doctor!" Prancer had definitely moved down from the trees toward the cottage, but Hank couldn't see him. "Come outside. I want my gun at your head. I want the wannabe senator to see you cower and hear you beg for your life."

Hank gritted his teeth and kept a tight hold on the kayak paddle and the knife.

"I'm afraid," Antonia said. "Not of you—of the storm."

That's it, keep him talking. Hank peered through the dripping lilac leaves and the gray rain and spotted a bright blue tarp about five yards behind the cottage. It moved, and he realized it was Prancer, the tarp half off him, more hindrance than help.

"Come out where I can see you," he screamed. "Now. I have lots of bullets. You can't win."

"All right—"

"Wait." The blue tarp stopped moving. "Where's Callahan? Your stud ex-major. Have him talk to me."

Antonia ignored him. "Robert, I'm coming out—"

"I said wait! Shit. He's not in there, is he? You fucking bitch."

He dropped the tarp, kicked his way out of it as he ran toward the cottage, splashing through the water-soaked grass and sand. Hank could clearly make out the gun in Prancer's right hand.

Moving fast, Hank jumped out from the lilacs. Prancer spotted him and fired—but not at Hank. At the back door.

Antonia was supposed to be inside with her pan of boiling water.

Hank dove for Prancer, hitting him in the solar plexus with the paddle. Prancer staggered backward, and Hank followed up with another hit, dislodging the gun. But the SOB was still on his feet. And he had his knife.

Antonia swooped down from the back steps and, without the slightest hesitation, stomped on Prancer's left foot—the same one she'd treated a few weeks ago. He screamed out in agony, dropping the knife as he fell onto his hands and knees.

Hank grabbed the gun out of a puddle and pointed it at Prancer. "Up on your feet. Hands in the air where I can see them."

His hands went up, but he sneered as he got to his feet. He was white-faced but seemed oblivious to any pain he was in. "You won't kill me. It'd do in your chances to be elected."

Hank paid no attention to him. "Antonia?"

"I'm okay. He didn't hurt me."

She was lying. There was blood on her upper right arm. Hank could see it out of the corner of his eye. "Can you make it back inside on your own?"

"Of course."

He almost smiled. His lovely Dr. Winter was nothing if not independent. "We'll need something to use to tie him up."

"Gus says duct tape works best."

Leave it to Gus to explain such things to his doctor niece. Hank waited until she was back in the cottage, then compelled Prancer inside at gunpoint. He'd lost some of his cockiness, moaning in pain, limping. His shirt was torn, his skin ravaged, his long hair matted down from rain. Blood trickled down one side of his mouth—he'd probably bit his lip. Hank knew he hadn't hit him hard enough to cause internal bleeding. He hadn't got good footing in the wet grass.

Hank ordered him to sit on a chair at the kitchen table.

"Go to hell," Prancer said.

But he sat down, and Antonia rummaged around under the sink and produced the roll of duct tape. Hank saw the blood on her arm but didn't say anything until they finished tying up their prisoner. She had a surgical approach to the duct tape, and he saw her examining Prancer for injuries. She would treat the patient in front of her, even if it was someone who had just tried to kill her.

Finally, she sank shakily onto a chair at the end of the table. "A bullet grazed my arm. I think—" She made a face, obviously not relishing what she had to say. "I might need your help patching it up."

Hank smiled at her. "Don't pass out, Doc. You'll need to tell me what to do."

Eleven

❧❦❧

Hank didn't need as much help treating her wound as Antonia had anticipated. He'd flown scores of search-and-rescue missions in his military career and knew medical basics, never mind that he was a pilot, not a pararescue-man like Tyler North. But none of them could prescribe medications, she thought, feeling a little woozy and defensive—she was a doctor, so she could write prescriptions. She wished she had something for the pain.

The bullet hadn't lodged, but it was a nastier gash than what Prancer had done to Hank with the knife.

"Why were you in the doorway?"

"I wasn't. The bullet—I don't know how it hit me."

"The police can figure it out."

The police. It had come to that, after all.

Robert, tied securely to his chair with duct tape, looked on silently. He was wide-eyed, fuming, soaked and in pain himself, although there wasn't a lot Antonia could do for him. She sat on the couch and focused on what Hank was doing as he cleaned and bandaged her wound.

"You're going to watch?" he asked.

"Of course."

He worked quickly, efficiently, no visible tremble to

his hands. She admired his ability to concentrate. "You need stitches," he pronounced, applying the last bit of the ancient first-aid tape to hold her bandage in place.

It was true. The bullet had torn a gash in her upper arm, but at least it had gone right out again—she hadn't relished the idea of walking Hank through digging a bullet out of her. But her wound did need stitches, if not surgery. She sighed. "I don't think we'll be off the island in time. But it'll be okay. You've done a nice job."

He looked troubled. "Antonia—"

"There's nothing more we can do. How's our prisoner?"

There was a lull in the weather, but the storm was still approaching, relentlessly, from the south. Antonia had no idea how long before it arrived. But Robert Prancer was no longer a threat. He was obviously in some discomfort from his bites and poison ivy and the kayak paddle to the solar plexus. His foot was bruised but Antonia hadn't done any serious damage—she'd checked.

Her arm bandaged and throbbing, she applied ointment to his bites and offered him Benadryl, but he refused. She wasn't surprised. As they'd tied him up, he'd spat out his lengthy list of grievances. He was convinced she'd betrayed him as a patient, as a co-worker at the hospital, as a man who had fallen in love with her from afar. He'd adored her, fantasized about her—or at least an idealized version of her. Supposedly not remembering his name, telling the police about his gunshot wound, taking up with Hank Callahan. It was one betrayal after another. Antonia was responsible for everything he'd done since that day she'd treated him in the E.R.

Hank discouraged her from trying to talk to him. At this point, Robert Prancer was a problem for the authorities.

But first, she thought, they all had to deal with Hurricane Hope.

Babs Winslow's cottage had endured countless storms, but there were no guarantees it would survive this one. Antonia and Hank collected towels to tuck under the doors and windows in case water started seeping in, and they filled every jug, pitcher and bowl available with fresh water. She tried not to envision the roof blowing off, the cottage splintering with them inside.

"You betrayed me." Robert's voice was calm, almost matter of fact. "You're a traitor to your profession. Bitch doctor. That's what everyone's going to call you. I'll say it loud and clear at my trial. I won't be convicted. You know that, don't you?"

Hank picked up the roll of duct tape. "One more word, and you're getting gagged."

"Fuck you. Fuck the bitch doctor."

That was all Hank needed. He ripped off a six-inch length of duct tape, but Prancer promised to keep quiet. Hank winked at Antonia. "He'll be convicted." But he went still, then grinned suddenly. "I hear a helicopter."

"What? I don't hear anything." But she stopped, because now she heard it, a steady whir that she'd thought was the wind or the surf. "Do you think—I should get my flares."

But she didn't need them. When they ran out onto the front porch, the helicopter was already low over the island. Hank grinned. "Feels weird to be on this end of a rescue."

"Carine. She must have sounded the alarm."

"Tyler, too. He'd raise hell."

"He's in Florida—"

"Not if he found a way up here." Hank opened the front door and shouted back to Prancer. "I'm looking forward to introducing you to my friend Master Sergeant Tyler North."

Antonia felt a tightness in her chest. Her arm ached,

but she didn't mind that so much. "Hank, I've put you in a terrible position."

"I put myself here. You didn't. I did what I had to do. No regrets. No second-guessing." He slung an arm over her shoulder, careful to avoid her injury. "Well, Doc, looks as if you're going to have to ride in a helicopter after all."

She managed a laugh. "For once, I don't mind. It beats staying out here in a hurricane." But that was bravado— she didn't like helicopters. "The police aren't going to like it that a senate candidate was knifed."

"Hell, I don't like it. They won't like having an E.R. doctor shot, either."

The helicopter landed on a relatively dry spot near the cottage, and within minutes, Hank was proved right. Compact, green-eyed, tawny-haired Tyler North, a lion of a man, jumped out. He had somehow wormed his way onto the rescue flight. Now he was their link between disaster and the helicopter.

Hank swore under his breath. "Damn. I'm never going to hear the end of this, am I?"

Tyler grinned at him. "Never. Dr. Winter? You need a litter?"

"I can walk."

But, actually, she couldn't. He saw that before she did. So did Hank. They strapped her into a litter and got her on board the helicopter, another crewman waiting with Robert Prancer. Then they got him on board.

Mercifully, Antonia, who didn't like helicopters, passed out for the short ride back to the mainland.

Tyler disappeared before Hope hit.

"Marry Antonia, will you?" he told Hank. "It'll take Gus's mind off killing me."

"Carine—"

"She'll be fine. She won't want to get in the way of her sister's happiness. Trust her."

"Is she here?"

"She's here. Gus, too."

Hank had known his friend wouldn't stick around. He knew, too, that Ty hadn't found his way to Cape Cod to earn Hank's undying gratitude—he'd done it because that was what he did, because it was Antonia, and it was Carine. Ty was gone before she made her way to Antonia. Gus was at her side, fifty years old, rangy, totally pissed off.

Antonia ignored all of them and got access to a proper medical bag so she could sew up her own arm, informing everyone who tried to dissuade her that she did this sort of thing for a living.

Stubborn. Hard-bitten. Independent. Hank grinned. For all his faults, Tyler North did know the Winter family of Cold Ridge, New Hampshire.

There were police to talk to. Antonia muttered something about pulling another faint to get out of it, but she handled all the questions with a calm and directness Hank had come to expect of her, and knew he would always admire.

Carine, it turned out, had let herself into her sister's apartment in Boston and found shredded lingerie hanging out of Antonia's dresser drawer, and that was it. She called the police. The evidence led them to Robert Prancer. They got a warrant to search his apartment and found it wallpapered with pictures of Antonia. There were some of Hank, too. Most were smeared with red paint.

A missing E.R. doctor. A missing senate candidate.

"That's when the shit really hit the fan," Carine said with a faltering smile as they finally gathered in a local tavern to ride out the storm. It was too late to make it over the bridge to Boston, or farther inland to higher ground.

"Gus was already on his way?" Antonia asked.

"He was already *there*. Ty called him. The bastard."

Hank suspected no one had told her that Ty had participated in the rescue—the media hadn't got hold of that one.

Gus shifted in his chair. He was drinking hot chocolate—no alcohol, he said, until the storm was over. No one else paid any attention. He glowered at the older of his two nieces. "You should have come to the mountains. What do you know about the ocean? We could have pitched this Prancer asshole right off a cliff."

She smiled. "I love you, Gus. And Hank and I handled him."

"Yeah. You and Hank."

Carine raised her pink drink—a cosmopolitan. "I think you and Hank make a great couple. An E.R. doctor and a U.S. senator. Has a nice ring to it, doesn't it?" She sipped some of her drink, of which she'd already had too much. "To an autumn wedding for a Winter!"

"Carine!" Antonia blanched, sinking low in her chair. She'd popped a pill—pain medication, Hank suspected—and was avoiding alcohol. "We've all had too much excitement, I think."

The wind howled and whistled outside, but the inn they'd picked had been around since the late eighteenth century. It was filled with various rescue and work crews ready to go out after the storm had passed, and they all were making no pretenses about listening in.

Carine was unapologetic. "Oh, come on, Antonia. No time to be repressed. Hank's so in love with you. What's the word I'm looking for, Gus? Besotted?"

"Sloshed," her uncle said. "Time to keep your mouth shut, Carine."

Hank, sitting next to Antonia, leaned in close to her. "Your sister's right. I am in love with you. Besotted."

"I'm feeling light-headed." Antonia sipped her water. "I think it must be the medication. I forget what I took—"

"You didn't forget," Hank said.

She smiled. "No, I didn't." She couldn't seem to stop herself from giggling, something Hank doubted Antonia Winter, M.D., did often enough. "Oh, God. I love you so much. I have from the second I laid eyes on you. You remember? You were standing in front of the woodstove in Carine's cabin."

"I remember. I knew you were stricken." He grinned at her. "I could tell."

Carine sniffled. "I love happy endings."

The two auburn-haired, blue-eyed sisters started giggling, and Gus rolled his eyes and motioned to the bartender. "No more of those pink drinks." He looked darkly over at Hank. "You set the date, you're sticking to it. You got that? I'm not mending another broken heart."

Hank nodded but said nothing. Antonia touched his thigh under the table. "We'll make it a simple wedding."

"Not account of me, you won't," Carine said, shaking her head adamantly. "Hank, if you want Tyler to be in your wedding—"

"Carine!" Antonia sat up straight, more alert now. "We wouldn't do that to you! You're going to be my maid of honor."

"Do what to me?" She set her jaw in that stubborn Winter way that Hank had come to know. "I've known Ty since we were tots. I have the scars to prove it. It's no big deal. He can be in your wedding."

"He'll be out of the country," Hank said quietly.

Carine scoffed. "What, on a secret mission?"

"Maybe."

But someone at the bar pointed to the television, and a meteorologist was saying what they could all feel— hurricane-force winds were hitting Cape Cod.

Hope weakened rapidly and didn't do its worst to Cape Cod. Damage would be limited mostly to flooding, torn shingles, trees down, flying debris, lost boats. Everyone in the tavern agreed they were lucky. They'd dodged disaster.

A Coast Guard helicopter flew over Shelter Island after Hope had moved on out to sea, and the pilot reported that Babs Winslow's cottage had survived with just a few shingles torn off and a window blown out.

Antonia felt a pain in her gut, remembering that Robert Prancer had shot out the window. The damage wasn't from Hope.

Her quiet refuge was now a crime scene.

The rescue and work crews had dispersed, but she and her sister and uncle—and Hank—remained in the tavern. The bartender passed out free sandwiches and reported media swarming in the lobby.

Gus grinned. "Must be because of me."

Carine, who'd fallen asleep on their uncle's shoulder as if she were a little girl again, elbowed him in the stomach. "Gus, you're not that funny."

Antonia realized they were just trying to distract her. They'd rehashed the events on the island all through the storm, tried to make sense of Robert Prancer and his motives, his reasoning, but he clearly operated according to his own logic, reacting to events according to whatever he was feeling at the time. He'd never had a clear, specific, calculated plan, which, in a way, made him even more frightening. There was no way to predict what he'd do. Taunt her. Scare her. Hurt her. Kill her.

But she and Gus and Carine, and Nate, were a family

who'd seen their share of crises, and they knew how to deal with them.

Hank tucked stray locks of her hair behind her ear. "Looks like I need to conduct an impromptu press conference."

She nodded. "They'll want to know everything."

"I plan to tell them everything. I'm a man who was worried about the woman I love, and I went to her." He kissed her on the forehead. "Do you want to be there?"

"At your side?" She smiled, kissing him softly. "Always."

* * * * *

REQUEST YOUR FREE BOOKS!

2 FREE NOVELS
FROM THE SUSPENSE COLLECTION,
PLUS 2 FREE GIFTS!

YES! Please send me 2 FREE novels from the Suspense Collection and my 2 FREE gifts (gifts are worth about $10). After receiving them, if I don't wish to receive any more books, I can return the shipping statement marked "cancel." If I don't cancel, I will receive 4 brand-new novels every month and be billed just $6.49 per book in the U.S. or $6.99 per book in Canada. That's a savings of at least 18% off the cover price. It's quite a bargain! Shipping and handling is just 50¢ per book in the U.S. and 75¢ per book in Canada.* I understand that accepting the 2 free books and gifts places me under no obligation to buy anything. I can always return a shipment and cancel at any time. Even if I never buy another book, the two free books and gifts are mine to keep forever.

191/391 MDN GH4Z

Name _____ (PLEASE PRINT) _____

Address _____ Apt. # _____

City _____ State/Prov. _____ Zip/Postal Code _____

Signature (if under 18, a parent or guardian must sign)

Mail to the **Reader Service:**
IN U.S.A.: P.O. Box 1867, Buffalo, NY 14240-1867
IN CANADA: P.O. Box 609, Fort Erie, Ontario L2A 5X3

Want to try 2 free books from another line?
Call 1-800-873-8635 or visit www.ReaderService.com.

* Terms and prices subject to change without notice. Prices do not include applicable taxes. Sales tax applicable in NY. Canadian residents will be charged applicable taxes. Offer not valid in Quebec. This offer is limited to one order per household. Not valid for current subscribers to the Suspense Collection or the Romance/Suspense Collection. All orders subject to credit approval. Credit or debit balances in a customer's account(s) may be offset by any other outstanding balance owed by or to the customer. Please allow 4 to 6 weeks for delivery. Offer available while quantities last.

Your Privacy—The Reader Service is committed to protecting your privacy. Our Privacy Policy is available online at www.ReaderService.com or upon request from the Reader Service.

We make a portion of our mailing list available to reputable third parties that offer products we believe may interest you. If you prefer that we not exchange your name with third parties, or if you wish to clarify or modify your communication preferences, please visit us at www.ReaderService.com/consumerschoice or write to us at Reader Service Preference Service, P.O. Box 9062, Buffalo, NY 14240-9062. Include your complete name and address.

SUS15R

CARLA NEGGERS

32990 THE WHISPER	___ $7.99 U.S.	___ $9.99 CAN.
32926 KISS THE MOON	___ $7.99 U.S.	___ $9.99 CAN.
32824 COLD DAWN	___ $7.99 U.S.	___ $9.99 CAN.
32773 THE MIST	___ $7.99 U.S.	___ $9.99 CAN.
32608 THE ANGEL	___ $7.99 U.S.	___ $8.99 CAN.
32586 TEMPTING FATE	___ $7.99 U.S.	___ $7.99 CAN.
32419 CUT AND RUN	___ $7.99 U.S.	___ $9.50 CAN.
31779 HARBOR ISLAND	___ $7.99 U.S.	___ $8.99 CAN.
31743 ECHO LAKE	___ $7.99 U.S.	___ $8.99 CAN.
31669 THE CABIN	___ $7.99 U.S.	___ $8.99 CAN.
31615 STONEBROOK COTTAGE	___ $7.99 U.S.	___ $8.99 CAN.
31603 DECLAN'S CROSS	___ $7.99 U.S.	___ $8.99 CAN.
31588 CIDER BROOK	___ $7.99 U.S.	___ $8.99 CAN.
31453 HERON'S COVE	___ $7.99 U.S.	___ $8.99 CAN.
31420 THAT NIGHT ON THISTLE LANE	___ $7.99 U.S.	___ $9.99 CAN.
31393 THE WATERFALL	___ $7.99 U.S.	___ $9.99 CAN.
31368 SAINT'S GATE	___ $7.99 U.S.	___ $9.99 CAN.

(limited quantities available)

TOTAL AMOUNT	$ _____
POSTAGE & HANDLING	$ _____
($1.00 for 1 book, 50¢ for each additional)	
APPLICABLE TAXES*	$ _____
TOTAL PAYABLE	$ _____

(check or money order—please do not send cash)

To order, complete this form and send it, along with a check or money order for the total above, payable to MIRA Books, to: **In the U.S.:** 3010 Walden Avenue, P.O. Box 9077, Buffalo, NY 14269-9077; **In Canada:** P.O. Box 636, Fort Erie, Ontario, L2A 5X3.

Name: _____
Address: _____ City: _____
State/Prov.: _____ Zip/Postal Code: _____
Account Number (if applicable): _____

075 CSAS

*New York residents remit applicable sales taxes.
*Canadian residents remit applicable GST and provincial taxes.

MIRA®

www.MIRABooks.com

MCN0216BL